Nato Kipiani

THE FOREST OF MEMORIES

The book is published with the support
of the Writers' House of Georgia.

Published by BookLand Press Inc.
15 Allstate Parkway
Suite 600
Markham, Ontario L3R 5B4
Canada
www.booklandpress.com

Printed in Canada

Library and Archives Canada Cataloguing in Publication

Title: The forest of memories / Nato Kipiani.
Names: Kipiani, Nato, author.
Identifiers: Canadiana (print) 20240412990 | Canadiana (ebook) 20240414160 | ISBN 9781772312423 | ISBN 9781772312430 (EPUB)
Subjects: LCGFT: Novels.
Classification: LCC PS8621.I655 F67 2024 | DDC C813/.6—dc23

Edited by Phillip Price

Cover design by Cindy Williams

THE FOREST OF MEMORIES

I

"Genji!" A penetrating, high-pitched voice blasts through Dylan's ears, jolting him awake.

His eyes flicker open and in an instant he is overwhelmed by wrathful rays of sunlight shining through the cloudless sky, lancing deep into his naked eyes. He rubs his eyes, slowly adjusting his vision as he scans his environs. Everything looks bleached and frail in the hazy sunshine, but Dylan would recognize this place under any circumstances. Tall sunflowers, yellow and radiant, hover over him as if trying to shelter him from the sharp beams of sunlight. Warm grass pokes his sides, sticking uncomfortably to his sweaty, glistening limbs.

He feels at home, enchanted by feelings of familiarity, safety, and comfort. It is truly a blissful moment, and a feeling of giddiness fills his entire being. Beaming from ear to ear he rests his eyes once more, sighing in satisfaction as the light breeze rustles through the tall grass, teasing his hair and kissing him across his face, cooling his hot, rosy skin.

"Genji, where are you?" He hears the kid yell once again, the tone different this time, sounding more urgent, more desperate.

And Dylan knows.

Dylan knows better than anyone who the voice belongs to. To a person who once brought so much joy, so much excitement to his life but left him with a bittersweet aftertaste.

Dylan sits up swiftly and his eyes roam around in panic. There is no one there, the field is empty and abandoned, only the tall, green grass keeps him company.

"Genji? It's not funny, I'm scared." The child whispers in a trembling voice, sounding on the verge of tears. "Genji?! Help me!" Without warning Dylan is startled by a head-splitting wail, blasting through the field, blowing the sunflowers and spinning their petals as it travels through the befogged sky.

He jumps up from the comforting ground and, jerking his head from side to side, he agitatedly tries to locate where the voice is coming from, but the cries echo, ringing from different sides, leading him only to confusion. With his mind clouded, he runs deeper into the maze-like field, his feet taking off in search of the owner of the sobs. The heart-wrenching longing to find him, hold him in safe arms, promise to the moon that he's right next to him and he will protect him from any evildoer—this is the only thought keeping him going, giving him the energy to run faster.

And just like that, the peaceful scenery morphs into something altogether more ominous.

The vibrant, blue sky bleeds into a bloody red and is wrapped in black clouds that shadow everything beneath, striking all colour from nature and turning the surroundings a dull grey. The sky seems to get closer and closer to the land with each step he takes, swallowing everything into a dead abyss, and if he didn't know any better he would think that the world was ending, crumbling apart.

But Dylan knows.

He knows the reality behind this direful world. He knows what awaits him at the end of his goal.

The story always ends in one of two opposite ways, but it's the aftermath that stays the same. In one epilogue, the happier one, he successfully finds the kid, a little boy, but Dylan never gets a chance to talk to him, to apologize before being consumed by white light.

The second ending is more brutal. He ends up running in circles whilst listening to woeful cries before he's sucked into the darkness within.

He continues to run, even as the ground swallows him whole, while cries continue to flood his ears. The boy keeps on calling his name, Dylan's name falling from his lips like a prayer. He hears the silent cries of "Genji" choked down by sobs, he hears weak, broken pleas, "Save me", repeating over and over again, driving him crazy as he shuffles around the field, the voices leading him further astray with each step.

This world is an enormous maze which, no matter how hard he tries, he can never find a way to beat.

As he parts the tall grass, a dark forest appears in front of him. The old woods induce the same terror in him as they did that star-crossed night. The oracle trees, mighty with the deepest secrets of mankind, reach desperately towards the crooked moon that shines down on him with its twisted smile.

Stopping in his tracks, he sees a petite silhouette hunched down on the ground, its face buried in its knees. He exhales a long, relieved sigh, and as he regains his composure he clutches his chest, feeling each erratic beat of his heart. He feels like crying, tears are already welling up in his sinful eyes as he walks closer to the boy, who unexpectedly stops crying when he hears the grass rustle behind him. He turns his head sharply up towards Dylan and…

Right…

As always, his face is blurred, as if any facial features had been erased.

Dylan can't remember what he looks like—after all, it was he himself who tried so hard to erase this face from his mind, leaving his brain with no other option but to generate images of a faceless boy. He can tell from the eager movements of the boy's chin that he's speaking directly to him, but as usual he can't hear him, he can't hear anything, everything is eerily silent as if the life has perished from the sonorous night.

His vision grows gauzy as the world lightens and pales, and as the white light begins its conquest, the urge to sleep washes over him. His eyes close and he loses sight of the kid once more. Before drifting away he hears him whisper, "You've found me"

Only he didn't.

Dylan rises from bed with a heavy gasp as if his whole soul is being drawn out of him. His eyes, wide in terror, stare into space, and while holding his breath he slumps back down into a sitting position, head hung low. His low panting is the only thing disturbing the seemingly peaceful night as he tries in vain to steady his uneven, sharp intakes of oxygen, hands clenching his chest as each breath stabs his lungs, making it harder and harder for him to catch his breath.

When he is finally able to fill his lungs with air once more, he stays in the sitting position for a moment. Burying his face in his clammy hands, he listens to his roving heartbeat throbbing in his ears, pumping out blood through his veins, making black dots appear in his vision. He huffs one last time and follows it up with a quiet grunt, the noise coming out muffled through his clasped hands, then he counts to ten, trying to compose himself as he becomes uncomfortably aware of the cold sweat dripping from his forehead, mixing with fresh tears.

Feeling grossly wet and sticky, he finally forces himself to look up. It's still dark outside, he notes, the only source of light is the silver moonlight peeking through the window, illuminating his whereabouts. He's in his room, safe and unharmed, no danger pronounced, no reason to panic, but as the images of his dream float in the back of his mind, his lip, caught between his teeth, starts to wobble and he lets out a pathetic sound, somewhere between a choke and a dry sob.

Eguchi Ayumu.

His name is the only thing Dylan remembers for certain about the boy; everything else has become blurred between the lines of his brain, a result of him trying to erase every memory associated with the boy but remembering every small detail nonetheless, as if the boy were trying to taunt him.

Dylan slowly sits up from his bed, rubbing his heavy eyes, and glances at the wall. The clock reads 6 AM, meaning he has more time to get ready for his daily routine, yet another day alive.

The moment he steps out from the piles of warm blankets he feels a coldness embracing him in an unpleasant hug, raising goosebumps all over his sickly pale body.

You see Dylan, previously known as Genji, had been a rather shy but polite kid, living in a small village on an island located in Japan. Even if his memories about the place are vague, he can tell you confidently that he loved living there. He recalls riding his bike around the shore, carefree, a breeze kissing him across the face and a feeling of warmth, and the salty aroma of the sea is forever inked on his skin like a tattoo.

He quickly shuffles into the bathroom, not even bothering to eat breakfast, repulsed by the sticky layers of sweat and tears. With trembling hands, he strips down as fast as he can, yet still careful not to slip on the ice-cold floor. He sprints inside the shower in search of any source of warmth to heat up his corpse-like cold body. As the hot stream pours down on his tensed muscles he lets himself rest and, shutting his eyes, he lightly bumps his head on the wall and lets out a sigh in both satisfaction and irritation.

The memories of his next-door neighbours, Mr. and Mrs. Eguchi, Kuragari and Mizuki, and their son Ayumu reappear in his vision, continuing to live on in his brain.

Dylan doesn't know wherever to feel blessed or cursed by that.

He still can feel in his heart the love and fondness he held towards this family. Which is reasonable as his mother, Moriko, had lived her whole life in the same place and had been friends with Eguchis even way before Dylan's birth. They'd been around him from the moment he was brought to life, being the ones who had taken his mom to the hospital, supporting her as much as they could, making her labour pains a bit more tolerable, and Mizuki had been the first person his eyes ever landed on as she took care of him while his mother was recovering.

So it was understandable that Dylan would think of them as his own family, and he quickly became accustomed to calling them his uncle and aunt. He remembers being particularly fond of Mizuki, seeing her as his second mom as she stayed with him the most, sometimes more than his own mother, babysitting him when Dylan's mom had to leave for her numerous part-time jobs.

Dylan doesn't know why or when his legs gave way, causing him to slide down onto the floor as the shower continues to rain down on him, burning his skin. He buries his face in his knees as memories fly back to him like a hurricane carrying him away. He doesn't want to remember but is too afraid to forget.

Two years after Dylan was born, their son Ayumu was introduced to the world. Barely two years old, Dylan couldn't really comprehend what was happening when he was taken to Eguchis' to celebrate the birth of their son, and as his mom recalls, that night they were so loud that another neighbour threatened to call the police.

But the loudest was Ayumu; his cries overpowered their screams of joy when he started to wail in terror, frightened by the overexcited adults.

At the end of the story Dylan's mom always finishes with a sad smile, tears each time dangerously close to spilling, recalling how baby Dylan had watched with much interest and even a little judgment at the adults' desperate attempts to calm down the crying new-born and how, after observing for a while with his round curious eyes, he had wobbled unsteadily over to Ms. Eguchi, who took him into her lap.

And this is how Dylan found himself snuggling against Ayumu, instantly cutting his cries short.

It was only after that fateful night, when their souls finally found each other, that it seemed their lives had truly begun. Two halves became one as an invisible red thread bonded them, interlacing them to levels outsiders of their little realm couldn't decode, and after that it was always Genji and Ayumu, Ayumu and Genji, walking hand in hand across the shore.

Years went by, and as they grew older together, their bond only strengthened with each passing day.

Genji naturally took the role of the older, protective brother, stopping hot-blooded Ayumu from putting himself into dangerous situations, sometimes going a bit overboard with the scolding and making the kid cry hot tears, but at the end of the day, they always made up because just the thought of being separated from each other was enough to give the little kids nightmares.

Ayumu was irreplaceable for Genji, he was his first ever friend, he was there when Genji took his first footsteps out into the wider world, and he had been following behind ever since. When Genji said his first sentence, Ayumu was lying next to him, blubbering through drool, trying to mimic the older. When Genji first learned to read, it became second nature for him to read fairy tales to the baby. Ayumu was around for all of his early stages, experiencing his firsts with him along the way, always next to him. The kid had been around him for so long that it was hard to imagine growing up without him.

It was the same for Ayumu, even more so—Genji was his whole world, his day started and finished with him, he was completely dependent on him. Genji was the only person who could calm Ayumu down when he had a tantrum. Genji was the one he searched for when he was hurt and when he was happy, and Genji always was waiting with open arms, ready to console him or share his excitement with him.

Sometimes Ayumu's mom even asked herself if Ayumu loved Genji more than his own mother, cackling as she retold the infamous story of Ayumu's first word.

According to her, when she heard little Ayumu burbling over and over again, she got all excited thinking that his first word obviously would be "Mom" but oh, imagine her surprise when Ayumu babbled something that sounded very much like Genji. His speech was slurred and sounded more like gibberish than an actual word, but she swore that her son's first word was Genji.

They went through all their ups and downs together, shed their first tears of sadness and joy together, covered their tiny bodies with scratches and bruises during their never-ending adventures, learned how to give and receive love and about the responsibilities that came with caring for your loved ones and countless other sweet moments Dylan wishes little Genji hadn't just taken for granted. Because Genji assumed that there would be thousands of more moments like these.

He thought they had forever ahead of them, he thought he had a long journey to go with Ayumu.

But the universe had other plans.

How could Genji know that time was ticking, counting down their days? And it was already too late to react when the last grain of sand ran out.

Dylan doesn't know how long he has stayed in the shower, sitting in a foetal position as each drop burns his flushed skin. The humidity in the small space is high enough to make it hard to breathe, to suffocate him, but he can't bring himself to stand up, to fight back the tears, to stop himself going back to vulnerable little Genji once more. Overwhelming feelings of grief and guilt dig their claws deep into his heart, leaving more scars behind to remind him of his past mistakes, the regret he has had to carry throughout his whole life.

It all started and ended on May 5th, 2000, on Ayumu's sixth birthday, fifteen years ago, when Dylan had just turned eight and Ayumu was six.

At that time Dylan remembers thinking he was all grown up and taking his older brother role more seriously, and Ayumu accepted this without complaint, letting the older one take care of him, guide him, and teach him.

That night nothing seemed out of the ordinary, the whole neighbourhood gathered together to play hide and seek and the parents were unaware that they had any reason to be concerned. There were different age groups mixed together and they thought that the older kids would keep an eye on youngsters.

Genji and Ayumu were there as well. Genji kept hold of the younger boy's hand the whole time. Even during the games Ayumu attached himself to Genji, following him wherever he went. Genji tried many times to explain that he couldn't do that during hide and seek, but when Ayumu started crying he gave up. Even the other kids realised that Genji and Ayumu were inseparable so they always let them play together.

Among Dylan's many regrets, the choices he made that night were the most sorrowful, the most unforgivable.

The first mistake he had made was to wander deeper into the virulent forest whilst taking little Ayumu with him, only because he wanted to win after losing two rounds in a row. It was only because of his childish antics that he put himself and Ayumu in unnecessary danger.

The second mistake was that he was being selfish and irresponsible.

When Ayumu croaked a tired "Genji" while rubbing his sleepy little eyes, Genji knew he wanted to go back home, it was way past his bedtime, but he decided to put the kid's needs below his own. When Ayumu mumbled through a yawn, "I'm sleepy.", Genji pretended not to hear him. And it was only when Ayumu puffed out his round cheeks and stomped his legs on the ground, whining "I want to go home!" that Genji looked at him, feeling unreasonable irritation filling him as he gently put Ayumu's face into his palms, looking straight into his hooded eyes.

"Let's play this last round and Genji will take you back home, I promise."

He promised.

But still he took the kid deeper into the woods.

The third mistake, and probably his most foolish decision, was when he let Ayumu fall asleep on his lap, his pink cheeks squashed against his shoulders as he himself proudly sat down in his perfect hiding place, not caring that they'd found themselves in the middle of nowhere.

This led to the fourth mistake, then the fifth… Which eventually led to the catastrophe awaiting them.

Dylan can't hold back the sob trapped in his throat anymore so he lets his emotions flow, crash against his rib cage like surge waves during a storm, releasing and setting themselves free from the locked hollow of Dylan's soul. He cries and cries, body shaking uncontrollably as he continues to weep into his hands. The pain he feels, the rue weighing him down, crushing his bones while the guilt eats him alive, is too much for Dylan to bear.

It's as if for a moment Ayumu is with him and the next moment he is gone, leaving behind only images of Ayumu crying, him screaming at the kid, chasing him in the darkness, the terror in his doe eyes. Then everything goes dark and only the sound of the brook is there to accompany him, pulling him into an ocean of regrets, where some days his head stays up in the air, allowing him to breathe, and other days he drowns.

Today is one of the other days.

Dylan is torn apart by his brain trying to block out the disquieting deed while also reminding him of his inexcusable mistakes.

His memories are hazy; he can only remember parts of what happened after the disaster. He can recall a flashlight blinding his vision, the heart-wrenching sound of his mother cries, icy tears dripping onto his face, mixing with his blood, but it is the image of Ayumu's mom, her crazy, shaky eyes, and her pleas to tell him where her son is, that will haunt him till death.

Ayumu's body was never found...

At first, Dylan couldn't understand the severity of the consequences of his actions; he just wanted to find his friend, bumping into the policemen's legs and blocking their way, trying to help as much as he could, but slowly the realization sank in, bringing nothing but torment into his life ever since.

The first few months were probably the hardest for Dylan—no matter where he looked Ayumu was watching his every move through the piece of paper. Even when he was still in hospital there were posters of a missing child, Ayumu, smiling brightly in the photo, a photo Dylan's own mom had taken. He remembers waking up every night in a cold sweat on the hospital bed and the poster of Ayumu watching him from afar, his lifeless eyes burning him with shame, blaming him.

And Dylan steadily realized that he indeed was the only one to take all the blame, everything was his and only his fault, all the pain had been caused by his reckless actions. The divorce of the Eguchis was his fault, Kuragari moving away was his fault, his mom losing any contract with Mizuki was his fault, and Ayumu's mom looking bone skinny, her eyes always red and bloodshot from crying, was his fault.

And most importantly, it was his fault that Ayumu went missing.

The book of regrets is once again opened, a constant reminder of what might and what might not have happened if he had made different decisions that night, if only they had gone back home when Ayumu asked to, if only Dylan hadn't fallen asleep, if only he hadn't yelled at him...

Dylan is stuck in this never-ending loop, a wicked loss of control, a permanent heartache that will forever linger in his soul.

After he was released from hospital is when the true horrors started.

Every night Ayumu would appear in his dreams, every night he relived the past like a broken record, each night he was so close to catching him but in the end, he always slipped away from his reach, and every night he would wake up drenched in sweat, feeling a sense of dread big enough to consume him whole.

This is when the lines between reality and delusion became blurred in poor little Dylan's mind. More than once his mom caught him talking aloud to himself, calling out Ayumu's name and bursting into tears each time she tried to convince her son that Ayumu wasn't there, that Ayumu was gone.

Because of him.

She never added the latter but Dylan knew she blamed him. He knew Ayumu's parents blamed him—he could see the resentment in Mizuki's eyes. He knew the whole village blamed him, despised him. But no one could ever despise him more than he did himself, and as he listened each night to his mom's soft cries, mourning the kid she'd thought of as her own, his hatred for himself only grew bigger.

And slowly his imaginary friend Ayumu became his only friend, living in the illusive world he himself built, where Ayumu was safe and unharmed. No matter where he looked Ayumu was there, always lurking in the corners of his room, watching him with a smile. He could hear him call out for him but as he turned, he was always met with nothing. Like an uttered curse, he could feel Ayumu's presence everywhere he went.

Dylan could sense that he was losing his touch with reality as the days went by, that he slowly was going insane—but it was what he deserved, he had to be punished for his sins.

No amount of therapy, no amount of counselling, no amount of "happy" pills the doctors shoved down his throat could loosen the wires wrapped around his heart, tightening each time he tried to forget, to move on, and he became a prisoner of his own mind, his past caged him, holding him hostage.

And Dylan had to live with it, live with the fact that he had taken someone as precious as Ayumu from everyone's lives and Ayumu himself became a thief of his joy, taking Dylan's soul with him, leaving him only with incurable open wounds.

Dylan continued to wake up each morning, continued to breathe, continued to pretend that he was doing better, if only for his mom's sake, but his mother knew, mothers always know, so she made a selfless decision and sent him to live with his father in Canada.

And this is how Dylan's story turned the page to the next chapter of the book of regrets.

At first, it was hard, awfully so, he had a hard time adjusting to his new environment; he was too afraid to meet the world, everything seemed bigger and scarier, and he didn't leave his room for months.

But slowly and surely he learned everything all over again, he learned how to speak without stuttering after each word, learned how to stop shaking each time someone gave him a mere glance, how to smile, how to laugh, how to trust his peers.

In elementary school he befriended his cousin Sophia. She went through every up and down with him, held out a helping hand without asking for anything in return, she comforted Dylan day and night, calming him down during his everlasting tantrums and panic attacks, which still happened often but less frequently than before.

As the years went by, the ambulance was called less and less, and Dylan learned how to control his emotions better, hiding them deeper in the corners of his poisoned mind.

Eventually Dylan faced the fact that even if he was at fault, he could do nothing to change the past, he had to move on. He didn't check the news every day anymore, didn't read the news with the dreadful feeling of waiting for the worst. He learned how to continue to live on with the guilt and shame heavy on his shoulders. He tried his best to think less about his childhood friend, to blame himself less as the string of hope he still held tightly onto weakened with each passing day.

He felt terrible about the thought, but he knew that Ayumu probably wasn't coming back, and he could only wish that wherever he was, he was happy. Little Dylan would have called this place heaven, but his faith was one of many other things Dylan lost after he had prayed every night away through hot tears, begging God to bring his friend back, but God had decided to turn a blind eye on him and ignored his pleas.

He cried less, and his imaginary friend Ayumu slowly faded away from reality. Along with his imaginary friend, the image of Ayumu also became more uncertain, eventually becoming completely unrecognizable.

As a teen Dylan couldn't even remember his face, memories of the kid slowly vanished from his mind, leaving him with only a reminiscence of his voice, his high-pitched, nasal voice calling out his name every night, calling him Genji, a name he also didn't go by anymore.

Dylan tried his best to leave everything back in the past so that what happened in Japan on May 5, 2000 stayed in Japan, but you just don't forget about your childhood friend, your first ever friend, the first ever person who taught you how to love, how to trust, laugh and so much more.

He didn't completely discard Ayumu from his mind, he could never, he was too much of a coward to do so. Somewhere in the depths of his subconscious he still exists, safe and happy.

So this is how Dylan currently lives, and now he is trying with all his might to enjoy his life for once because he knows better than anyone that life can turn upside down in mere seconds, not giving you any time for second-guessing.

Dylan will be okay, someday he will, when he finally gets closure he will be able to close this book and start a new one with clean, unstained pages, but until then, he can do nothing but wait.

Without putting much thought into his mess of an appearance, Dylan lumbers through the halls of the campus. He should probably feel embarrassed, his hair looks like it's been struck by a thunderbolt—more like a demolished nest than an actual head of hair. He counts his steps as he marches through the gathered crowd of students, some chatting with friends, others alone, bound up in their own little world.

It's all too overwhelming to be caged in a room full of life when you feel dead inside, and so, in a desperate attempt to flee from his erratic heart, Dylan throws his gaze outside the window.

He watches the autumn stir, with the slender trees and their red hues and fallen leaves scattered around the streets, giving everything a sense of warmth, but a harsh shove of his shoulders forces his eyes away from the beautiful scenery outside the cell-like room.

"Hey, Dylan!" The feminine voice reaches his side and with a quick glance he recognizes the familiar blonde hair. The young woman smiling not so authentically is Emma Wilson, who shares a few classes with him.

Not trustworthy.

Her beautiful face distorts into pitch black, and as she stands there faceless in front of his eyes, the dread deep inside his heart awakes and his heartbeat accelerates, raging inside his ears. He squeezes his eyes shut, feeling the heavy sensation of angst settle inside him, and quickens his pace as he tries to shield himself from the mass. One by one everyone turns into shapeless figures, hovering over him as they watch him go, obsessing over his every move. Almost running, he frantically squeezes himself out from the crowd only to be shoved behind yet again with a stronger bump than before.

With a grimace creeping over his face, he looks up at the causer of his disturbance and is met with those familiar cat-like caramel eyes that always seem to flame with distrust. Felix Scott shares almost every class with him—he's also a psychology major. What's more, he works at the same clinic as Dylan and is his next-door neighbour.

Dylan waits patiently for Felix's face to fade away from his mind, to disappear from his brain because Felix is ruthless, rude, mean even, ready to drag anyone foolish enough to disrespect him through the firepits of hell.

Felix is unapologetic, he doesn't care who you are, who your parents are, about your social status, he's ready to throw you into the mud, ready to hurl what's left of your dignity to the ground, he will destroy each and every person alive who happens to be stupidly brave enough to challenge him, he has no mercy when it comes to his peers or even the authoritarian professors.

But Dylan has also seen him be kind.

Felix loves to feed the birds, he is soft-spoken with the kids, and if you treat him right he will have nothing but respect for you. He is also smart, unbelievably so, he always gets the best grades and he's the one who always gets praised by the authorities in the university. Not only that, he's also an amazing intern, he is the one you call when a kid is acting up, he is the one who can coax down any child in mere moments, even the most disobedient ones. Everyone has his number on an emergency call and every parent goes to him for help. But Felix still stays humble, everyone would probably disagree with Dylan wholeheartedly, but they don't observe the boy as much as he does. Felix knows his place, he never puts himself above or below anyone. He's independent, brave and unbiased.

Felix is everything Dylan isn't.

Normally they would have become good friends because their paths cross so often, but that wasn't the case when it came to Felix for he seemed to take a dislike to everyone around, only focusing on being the best at everything he does. Dylan reckons the boy will probably be a hunchback at a young age because every time he catches a glimpse of him, Felix is always hunched over his laptop in positions that can't possibly be comfortable. Even though Felix and Dylan take the majority of classes together and work at the same workplace, he barely ever sees him. He is always moving from one class to another, rushing out from lectures to take mysterious calls, and at work, he gives all of his attention and time to the kids.

So it's all too confusing for Dylan, he can't see either pure evil or pure good in him, but before he can dwell on these thoughts Felix is already disappearing into the mass.

With a sigh he adjusts his bag and wanders into the classroom.

The professor dims the light and switches on the projector for the slide show. Then he claps his hands and clears his throat to gain the audience's attention.

"What is *arche*?" he asks. "It is a Greek word and it translates to origin. My question is, how do things start?"

"What exactly do you mean?" The familiar voice of Felix rings inside Dylan's ears and he takes a peek at the boy as subtly as he can, careful not to be caught staring.

"Anything, how does anything start?"

"Like, how did the world start?" Another student flows into the conversation but yet again the professor just shakes his head, still smiling, pleased to see students more active with their answers.

"No, by anything I mean *anything*." Everyone falls mute, most of the students visibly deep in thought, Felix included, he looks up at the ceiling, trying to come up with a possible answer.

"With… the Big Bang?" A girl musters shyly, clearly uncertain, but the assuring smile on the professor's lips just widens.

"And what did the Big Bang do?"

"Made the universe? It was the start of everything."

"So the Big Bang caused the world to start," the professor muses while gently leaning against the desk with his chin in his palms, watching the students sanguinely. "But what caused the Big Bang then?"

"Every speck of energy fixed into a very tiny point and it made a huge explosion, a Big Bang." Dylan's voice echoes through the room as he finally gains the courage to speak.

"Okay, that's right but there must be something that caused these energies to come together."

Felix quickly joins the debate. "So, if I'm guessing right, what you're trying to say is that the start of everything is more than one event leading to another, right?" Felix feels the familiar raven eyes burn into his flesh but he doesn't dare to look back.

The professor glances at Felix, his expression showing that he has been waiting for him to speak up as his face breaks into a beam. "You're close Felix, thank you. But let me explain better."

Felix looks delighted as he smiles shyly to himself, but when the stinging sensation of being watched doesn't vanish he twirls his face behind him to find Dylan gazing at him with his usual fond smile.

Felix scowls, unable to read the expression on Dylan's face. He narrows his eyes, searching for any slip in Dylan's round eyes, any sign of dishonesty, something to prove Felix right in his suspicion that Dylan, just like everybody else in this room, is untrustworthy.

Felix thinks Dylan Yamaguchi is strange. But what's even stranger is the dislike he feels towards him. Dylan Yamaguchi is a good student, with great grades, and he's always been nothing but nice to Felix. He even tried to start a conversation with him once or twice, only to give up after Felix blatantly pushed him away. In anyone else's eyes Dylan Yamaguchi would be perfect, but Felix can't help but feel an overwhelming irritation towards the boy. Dylan does nothing in particular to annoy Felix, he just…

Felix slowly turns his head back again only to be met with the same raven eyes once more.

He just watches.

No matter where he looks he finds these dark eyes following him. Anywhere he goes he feels those eyes burning into his skull without shame. During lectures, at the library, in the clinic, no matter how far Felix runs, he is always lurking somewhere nearby. And there is something in the way he looks at him, although Felix can't pinpoint what. He can't find either pity or dislike inside those black eyes. The emotion his gaze holds is something Felix can't put a name to and it irks every nerve inside him.

Dylan catches himself staring and quickly looks away. He always does that, averting his gaze like the coward he is.

Dylan Yamaguchi may not be two-faced like most of the students out here but he is a coward, Felix concludes.

Felix has never seen him argue nor any trace of irritation show up on his face; he just goes with the flow, ready to please everyone. He's a coward, that's what he is, and that's why Felix finds himself disliking the boy. Still, there's no point beating a dead horse, and he soon averts his gaze back to the professor.

"Let's say that one event causes the creation of another event. We call it an effect. This means the cause is partly accountable for the effect, and the effect is partly reliant on the cause. In general, causes all exist in its past, but an effect can turn into a producer of many other effects, which all exist in its future." When he takes in the puzzled demeanor of his students, who look utterly lost, he exhales heavily and with a loud, distressing groan he sits up from the chair and walks towards the blackboard, and for a moment the only sound that can be heard in the room is chalk scraping against the surface.

"To explain it more simply, since event Y followed event X, event Y must have been produced by event X. And avoiding event X will halt event Y. Do you understand now?" When he finishes writing all of this, he puts the chalk back in its place and, shaking the white dust off his palms, he walks towards his seat once more.

"So if you'll think about it carefully, we fall into a kind of loop—we call it a causal loop, which means a chain of events, and people produce other events which are also among the products of the first event. We see stuff like this a lot in the media, especially in shows about time travel." The professor exhales heavily after finally finishing the sentence and grabs a bottle of water.

"So, something like the butterfly effect?" The girl from before speaks again, more confident this time.

"Certainly. Call it the butterfly effect, a chain reaction, a domino effect, or a snowball effect, the idea remains the same." Finally, some understanding lights up on the students' faces and the professor can only sigh in relief, but then he clears his throat to continue speaking.

"But we have also seen it have a negative outcome, right?" The students nod. "How about a cascading failure, for example? This may happen when one part of the system fails, and when it happens, other particles must then compensate for the failed part. This in turn overloads these nodes, causing them to fail as well, prompting additional nodes to fail one after another. And again we fall into the loop. So what do you think, is there any way to break this loop and avoid a catastrophe?"

"We again go back to the same topic, we need to find the cause of the loop." Felix declares, gaining a few annoyed groans from around him, which he promptly ignores.

"Not the cause, but the reason for the loop." Felix frowns but the professor just smiles thankfully before sitting more comfortably in his seat. "Every event, every cause happens for a reason. And in Greek, it's called etiology, which translates as "giving a reason for." He switches to the next slide. "Psychologist Carl Jung thought that events are "meaningful coincidences" if they happen with no relevant relation yet seem to be meaningfully related. Jung believed that, just as events may be related by cause and effect, they may also be related by meaning. And events related by meaning need not have an explanation, so what do we do then? How can we prevent a loop from forming that will lead to the failure of the system?"

"How can we be sure that coincidences really happen?" asks Dylan, leaning against his desk and sounding more agitated this time. "As you said, everything happens for a reason."

"Like Aristotle has described, we can never be sure. A thing that exists potentially does not exist, but the potential does exist." But before he can answer the questions better, the bell rings. "Okay guys, the class is over, thanks for coming," he says and turns the lights back on. The room fills with the chaotic sounds of students chatting and gathering their stuff, but then a loud ringing interrupts the hectic life of the students and Dylan sees Felix take one of his many mysterious calls as he rushes outside, leaving Dylan gawking at his back.

Dylan steps haltingly through the halls of the clinic, his head slumped down and his hands fidgeting in his pockets as the bright, white walls sting his eyes, making the faces in the crowd blend into one another. He exhales heavily—the journey towards the changing room seems to be taking longer than usual, and the more he walks the longer the hall seems, or maybe it's just the illusion caused by these damned white walls, or maybe Dylan is just sleep-deprived. On his way, he meets a few of the regular kids, held tightly by their parents, and this time Dylan smiles more genuinely, greeting them cheerfully and fist-bumping by way of goodbye.

Dylan loves his job. He loves working with kids, adores each and every one of them, loves listening to them ramble whilst digging deeper into their minds, connecting the invisible dots and trying to find solutions for their problems. Working with kids is obviously hard as they can be pretty unpredictable, lacking logic when it comes to their distress, but it only took Dylan a month or two to get used to their sudden outbursts.

At his workplace, Dylan has met numerous kids with complex personalities. There are the shy, unsocial, introverted ones, but most of the time they are easiest to handle thanks to their quiet, passive personalities. On the other hand, there are also the disobedient, restless and violent ones who put so much stress on their doctors and everyone around them. But they are only kids, and it's their job to help them with whatever is bothering them, so Dylan has no right to complain.

Dylan hears shrieking ringing through the hallway and quickly realizes that today is one of those days when a kid is refusing to compromise with anyone around. With hurried steps he follows the sound of the cries, and when he bolts inside the playroom it doesn't take him long to recognize the kid glued to the corner, whipping a metallic toy from side to side as a weapon each time the doctors try to get closer to him.

His name is Nathan, the worst case of all. At first glance the kid looks harmless, frail to the touch, and like everyone else, Dylan was initially fooled by his appearance, but he quickly learned that Nathan's personality is completely different from the way he looks.

Nathan is dealing with a lot of behavioural problems, making him the hardest kid to handle. None of the tricks ever work on him, and every time he goes into an episode of rage. His mood swings are always unmanageable, always out of the blue. One moment he can be playing with the other kids and the next thing you know he's already latched onto someone, hitting and biting them. As of now, the doctors still can't unravel the child's triggers. Even if his adoptive parents are nothing but loving, as supportive as they can be with a misbehaved child, there is still a lot they don't know about their son, about his past household or his biological parents, and observing his behaviour, it seems very unlikely that the child came from a healthy family.

Even now Dylan's heart aches at the sight of the tear-stained face of the kid; the fear in his doe eyes makes him wonder what kind of monsters lurk behind closed doors, monsters that are ready to hurt vulnerable, innocent little kids.

His thoughts are cut short when something that looks like a book flies dangerously close to his face, almost hitting him, and only then does he notice the huge crowd gathered around the scene. From the corner of his eyes, he sees Felix tightly holding one of the regulars close to his chest and murmuring something, after which he sits his charge gently on the floor, tenderly takes her face into his palms, and whispers something that is impossible for Dylan to hear, but he sees the girl nod, still gazing at Felix who then hurries away, disappearing into the crowd.

Dylan turns his head towards the unfolding chaos again. Nathan is still hiding in the corner and his cries get louder each time someone steps closer to him. He watches as the doctor tiptoes behind the raging kid, probably trying to take him into his arms, but Nathan is quick to sense him, jumping away from his reach and latching onto the nurse's arm. They go back and forth for a while, the doctor desperately trying to catch the kid and Nathan pacing around, hiding behind the nurse and forcefully swinging her body from side to side, and then everything becomes a blur. Dylan doesn't know when or how Nathan ends up pushed down onto the floor but after a minute of pure silence, as the kid watches everyone with a bewildered expression, Dylan sees the fear, the real terror wash over the child's eyes, which is followed by loud, throaty sobs.

"What is wrong with you?" Felix's roar startles Dylan and everyone else in the room. Dylan looks at him, finding him glaring directly at the nurse in both disbelief and rage, shaken to see the boy so alarmed.

Dylan can only watch shell-shocked as one expression replaces another on Felix's face. Over the three years of knowing him, Dylan has never seen Felix so unnerved, never seen his emotions get the better of him, he's always so calm and collected but today is different. He looks as frightened as Nathan does and Dylan can' really comprehend why.

Felix's outburst was enough to cut the kid's cries short for a while. He gazes at Felix, who is still standing in the centre, and his chest heaves with each short, unsteady breath he takes. With a huff he steps towards the child but the kid shrieks, taking one of the toys into his hands again, aiming, and ready to throw it at Felix.

"Please calm down," Felix pleads weakly and makes yet another step but the kid stumbles further into the wall, hugging himself. "I won't hurt you." He eyes the boy worriedly, lovingly, caringly, and understandingly. He quickly scans the kid for possible injuries while still keeping a distance between them. He sighs in relief when he sees none but Nathan is yet to calm down, he's still screaming from the top of his lungs and punching the air as his wails become so loud that his voice breaks, causing him to go into a choking fit and gasp for air. Felix takes his chance and jumps towards the kid, a decision which he quickly learns wasn't the brightest as Nathan kicks him painfully in his shin, making him kneel with a yelp.

As Felix falls to the ground, the kid throws everything his fingers can reach at him and the doctors are ready to interlude when suddenly Felix gently holds the boy's tensed arms and gazes straight into his frightened eyes. "I know you don't want to hurt me, Nathan, so please calm down," he says while making a fist with his hand and then slowly opening up his palm, an action which the kid unconsciously follows. "See, it's not hard. I know you're angry but I want you to try to calm down, okay? Can you do that?" And Felix speaks so calmly it's clear he knows what he's doing.

Nathan's face is still boiling red, but as Felix starts demonstrating breathing exercises, the kid slowly but surely follows along, inhaling deep breaths and exhaling even more heavily. "You feeling okay now?" Felix asks with a soft tone, still squatting on the floor and gazing at the child on the same eye level, and it takes a moment or two before Nathan nods hesitantly, guilt crawling over his tear-stained face, but Felix just smiles. "You did great," he says, ruffling the messy blonde locks of the child who just stands there for a minute, rocking back and forth, his lips pursed as he chews down on his bottom lip, and then to everyone's surprise the kid sprints towards Felix, caging him in a suffocating embrace that evidently takes even Felix by surprise, judging from how he stumbles back, almost losing his balance, but then he just sighs though a tired smile and takes the boy protectively into his arms.

He stands up carefully and with hesitant steps walks away as Nathan nuzzles his face further into his nape, hiding from judging eyes. He slowly moves towards the crowd but doesn't forget to throw a piercing glare towards the nurse, who visibly flinches.

And with that Felix disappears from the mass.

Dylan just stands there for a while, lost in his trance-like state. He remains frozen in place like a statue even after the crowd splits apart, leaving him standing alone in the room.

Felix always has been great with kids, sure. But never during these past few months has he lost his cool. There was something different in Felix's gaze today. As if he knew something that others didn't, something Nathan must have felt as well, judging from his reaction.

Dylan sighs. No matter how much he looks, Felix is a mystery he can't crack.

"Are you crazy?!" The shout makes Ayumu flick his eyes open only to be blinded by the brightness of the room, so he squeezes his eyes shut, darkening his vision darkens once again. "We can't take him! You've seen the posters! His family is searching for him!" The booming voice roars once more, making Ayumu's limp body jolt from the bed.

"He calls me mom!" The female's head-splitting wail makes Ayumu regain full consciousness as he opens his eyes wide in panic, only then to soften as he scans his surroundings, relieved to find himself lying on the familiar hospital bed. "We'll never have a chance like that again! We had a connection! It was fate, can't you understand?!" Ayumu doesn't understand a single word they're saying and he's curious to know what the nurse is talking about so agitatedly, but after another angry groan a silence falls inside the room and for a moment Ayumu thinks that it was all a dream, but then his vision becomes clear and he recognizes two familiar figures standing in front of his bed.

"But everyone knows he's here," the man sighs. "The police will find him anyway." The male doctor whose name Ayumu can't remember sits down on the chair beside Ayumu's bed and buries his face in his palms.

"Don't worry, I took care of everything, we just need to take him to Tokyo first and then..." The nurse catches Ayumu's eyes and smiles, but there is something in the way her lips stretch that makes goosebumps stand straight up all over Ayumu's body. "Honey, are you awake?" she asks him, reverting to Japanese, and Ayumu nods, but his eyes flutter, he is close to dozing off.

He feels a light touch on his cheek, forcing him to open his eyes again, and he is met with the icy blue eyes of the nurse. "Do you feel any pain?" she asks, her tone rising as if she is nervous, and Ayumu doesn't understand why she looks so anxious but he nods nonetheless, reminded of his aching pain.

As if waiting for this answer, the nurse takes the needle Ayumu has got so used to seeing over these past few days. "A light tug and then you won't feel a thing," she reminds him just like all the other times, and Ayumu doesn't even think about protesting because he knows after the needle comes nothing but relief from the crushing pain in his bones. As he feels the needle stab his skin and the medicine flow through his veins, his eyes start to feel heavy once more and only seconds later he sees nothing but darkness.

He's woken up again by a harsh jolt; he feels his body jump upwards in the air. It takes him time to process his whereabouts, but as his body shakes violently he realizes that he's lying on an emergency bed and the inside of a car slowly comes into his vision.

His eyes roam around in a search of familiarity and instantly feels calm when he sees the nurse again. She quickly notices that he's awake and with a smile rubs comforting circles on his arm. "We will take you to a much better place," she says through a gentle smile, and tenderly brushes the hair from his forehead while slowly closes the door with her free hand, but Ayumu notices her startled by something.

Soon Ayumu is also aware of the cause of her disturbance, a noisy sound that pains his ears. The sound of a siren rings through the street, and Ayumu, physically forcing himself to stay awake and full of curiosity, peeks outside the car. He sees an ambulance steer speedily into the hospital grounds and come to a full stop.

"Hurry! Call the nurses!" someone shouts. "A boy is in critical condition!"

Ayumu watches the boy, who looks the same age as him, being carried on a similar emergency bed to his own. He looks familiar, he thinks. Ayumu observes the lifeless pale skin and black hair that flutters in the wind as he is rushed inside and when his eyes dart to the boy's hand, which has dropped outside the bed, and sees a heart-shaped ring placed prettily on his pinkie, he unconsciously touches his similar-looking pendant.

Just when he feels like he's close to solving the conundrum he hears a loud gasp next to him and in moments the door is swiftly shut, erasing the boy from his view, so Ayumu closes his eyes again, lulled back to his dreamland as he feels the pain winding its way back to his bones, much more forcefully this time.

The last thing he remembers is the sound of the engine starting.

As the car rushes along, a poster slips onto the ground. On it is a photo of Ayumu and Genji smiling, with the words 'missing children' written above.

II

Sometimes I feel like I'm standing on a bridge. The bridge is old, covered in cracks and moss. I can hear bricks of the stone fall deep into the river beneath.

The river my eyes can never reach.

At the end of this bridge, I can see sunlight showering people, beautiful scenery unfolds in front of my eyes, everyone seems to be so merry – it's a feeling I don't recognize. Every time I make a step, I feel the ground shake beneath my feet and huge thorns split the stone in two; they rise high into the sky and their spikes shadow me, leaving me in the everlasting dark.

Even if I cut my flesh open I can never leave the rejected side of the bridge.

A scream, a wail, followed by continuous sounds of crashing and items breaking.

Moments later a young woman emerges from the locked room, uniform untidy, hair sticking up in every direction, looking drained and dishevelled, and her tired eyes roam around pleadingly in search of a helping hand.

"Is everything okay?" A soft voice rings out from behind, making her whip her head swiftly. Her eyes immediately soften as she recognizes the familiar face of her colleague.

"Felix is acting up again," she explains breathlessly, and as if to demonstrate, the kid screams behind the closed door, louder, more desperate this time.

"Xaria, please help me out!" The caretaker takes the startled woman's hands in hers, gazing at her with begging, wide eyes. "He scratched me all over, I can't calm him down, please do something!"

Xaria sighs, but flinches when she hears yet another loud thump. She throws a tense glance at the wooden door before her eyes shift towards the young woman once more. Nervously she adjusts her uniform, nods, and with timid steps walks towards the door. Her hand lingers on the door handle for a second longer and she gives a last glance towards her colleague who just frantically shakes her head, gesturing her to open it.

Drawing a deep breath, she opens the door with a loud crack.

What she finds inside the basement is the kid throwing a plate against the wall, breaking it into small pieces.

She jolts, swiftly closing the door.

The sound makes Felix turn his face in her direction and his face darkens into a mixture of fear and pure hatred. His eyes glow in horror even in the dark room.

With trembling feet, she makes the first step, but the child wails and his hands fly out in search of something to throw. The sharp movement knocks his petite body off balance, causing his injured right leg to buckle and stagger, but the woman is quick to catch him before he falls on the floor.

She huffs, holding the child tight to her chest, and for a moment little Felix falls quiet, only his ragged heartbeat cutting through the silence, but it doesn't take long before the kid is snapped out of his daze by yet another head-splitting screech, and the caretaker yelps in pain as his sharp teeth dig into her skin and gnaw on her arm.

Reflexively she yanks her arm away and pushes the kid on the floor. She squeezes her eyes in pain, rubbing the wound in a soothing manner. Irritation and fury cloud her senses as she glares at the culprit with an enraged look, but her eyes soon soften when she catches teary eyes gazing back at her, his stare showing more hurt and betrayal than any words could describe—more than anything, it's the fact that he doesn't look surprised to be treated this way that makes her heart clutch with unfamiliar guilt and sorrow.

She can't understand why the kid is so agitated—no one knows anything about him, not even he himself.

One day he didn't exist, then the next day he appeared out of nowhere, falling into their arms to be taken care of, bringing nothing but confusion to everyone in the orphanage. He doesn't have a real name, an age, or anything to prove his existence—to show that he's not a figment of her imagination, that he really draws breath.

She's oddly afraid of this nameless human being sitting in front of her, gazing at her with unsaid dubiety. "I'm sorry," she croaks through trembling lips and tries to move closer to him, but Felix flinches, backing into a corner. "Are you hurt?" She tries again but the answer never comes, he just stares at her.

He doesn't speak either, hasn't muttered a single word for the past weeks he's been there—every time he opens his mouth to talk, something always holds him back, muting him completely.

She doesn't get a chance to ask any more questions because Felix leans his weight onto his arms, forcing himself to stand up even if his leg bends painfully. Without a word he stumbles towards the door, the previous anger and agitation completely erased from him.

He's an unexplainable phenomenon, bizarre, one of a kind, and Xaria worries that they will never be able to understand the complexity of this child.

She doesn't know how much time has passed and how long she has been sitting on the floor but when she finally jolts herself awake from her thoughts, panic overtakes her and she rushes out of the room in a search of the kid. She runs into his bedroom, her eyes shifting from one sleeping kid to another, but the familiar curly locks are nowhere to be found. He has tried to run away previously but luckily the guards caught him before he could leave the gates and she can only hope that he's not already out of their reach. She bursts through one room to another, getting more anxious as time passes by. He couldn't have gone far, or so she hopes.

Only the garden is left as the last option, so with shaky fingers she opens the door, letting in the cold night breeze, making her shiver. She fixes her jacket around her shoulders, holding the fabric firmly to her frozen body, and walks outside.

The silver moonlight is enough to guide her, landing on earth with velvety grace and lighting her way. She huffs agitatedly as her eyes roam around in desperation, but no one is there, and before long her eyes are wet with tears of annoyance. She walks towards the gate, planning her next move, when from the corner of her eye she sees a small figure lying in a foetal position on the muddy ground, wrapped in a thin blanket which surely wouldn't be enough to shield him from the cold air. She exhales the deep breath she has been holding this whole time and allows the tears that had stayed glued to her eyes to fall freely.

With tired steps, she moves closer towards Felix, who's sleeping peacefully in front of the gate, as if waiting for someone to come.

It breaks her heart knowing that no one will come, but what hurts the most is that the kid himself probably knows this too—and yet he still waits.

Gently she takes him into her arms, careful not to disturb his deserved slumber after so many sleepless nights. She doesn't forget to put the teddy bear he takes everywhere with him back into his arms and he embraces it gladly in his sleep. Then, with soft, soundless steps, she walks inside.

His eyelids flicker, the touch of wet coldness awaking his senses, and with a squeeze he forces his eyes open. At first, he sees nothing but whiteness—blanched, toneless scenery where the only permanent host is snow and everything else has disappeared under layers of frozen powder.

Felix blinks repeatedly, trying to make the ghostly place in front of him disappear, but no matter how hard he rubs his sore eyes, he stays lying in the same place. And when the coldness of the land makes itself apparent—the glacial wind sweeps against his skin and creeps under the thin fabric of his shirt, making his body shake uncontrollably—he instinctively wraps his trembling arms around himself in search of warmth and exhales his heated breath, watching as the small cloud of fog fades in front of him.

Felix looks around and realizes that he's probably not leaving the forsaken area anytime soon, so with his frozen limbs and fingers that have lost their senses, he leans his weight onto his palms and tries to stand up from the slippery, icy ground.

He brushes the white powder from his clothes and turns his head upwards, trying to search for any guidance out of this abnormal place, but he finds nothing but sky painted in shades of red and blue, perfectly melding with one another, leaving a line of purple in between, just above where he stands, and he's left with no other option but to gaze at the beautiful yet sinister sky that contrasts so sharply with the bleached land underneath as the snowflakes fall and weigh down his eyelashes.

Out of the blue, a glowing white butterfly wings its way towards him, faint and transparent. It dabs airily against his cheek but enough to burst sparks inside his veins, filling him with warm sensation in this frigid place. Then it continues on its way, heading towards the mountains, and as his eyes follow its odd form, something in back of his head screams at him to chase it, so Felix does as his heart tells him.

He quickens his pace, even though his legs are aching, and for a while nothing changes, there is nothing but snow surrounding him, but he's only focused on the gracious butterfly in front of him, swaying calmly through the air but still fast enough to remain out of his reach.

After a while of mindlessly wandering the soulless land, he finally sees something resembling a tree, standing alone and sticking out with its darkened branches. He frowns as he stands in front of the lonely dead plant, bare and raw but still standing confident in its hideous glory, any colour of life wiped away, leaving only awful tones of foul brown; its naked twigs, seared and tottering, still stretch upwards as if trying to reach the beautiful sky above.

A loud screeching cry makes him flinch and when he looks up he sees a raven sitting comfortably at the top of the tree, staring back at him, its huge, crystal-clear eyes mirroring his reflection back at him. They gaze at each other for a moment before the bird screams at him once more, flapping its dark wings and showering him with snow, and with that it flies high into the sky, disappearing from sight.

Before Felix can understand what has happened, he feels the ground shake beneath his feet, sending vibrations through his whole body and, in the seconds before the bravely standing tree collapses to the ground, layering him with white powder. He quickly shakes the snow from his already frozen body and with timid steps walks closer to the fallen tree. But his feet slip, sweeping him off balance and sending him stumbling face down onto the ground.

At first, he senses the ice eating his skin where his palms linger, and with a few sweeps of his arms his eyes are met with a solid layer of ice—a frozen river perhaps—but what takes him aback are the two raven eyes ogling him from beneath the glaze. He jolts back, afraid. For a moment he doesn't dare to look, just listens to his hammering heartbeat, but soon his curiosity gets the better of him and he peeks once more, hoping that whatever it was his mind imagined will have disappeared, but to his dismay he catches those same eyes once more.

And the more he looks the better view he gets.

There is a boy trapped beneath him, looking up at him eagerly as if expecting something. He leans further down and his trembling fingers dig into the ice as he continues to gaze at the mysterious kid. The boy glances back and forth at his face and his palm resting on the icy glass, and the next moment he is pushing his hand upwards, right beneath Felix's own, warming his frozen limb. His breath catches soundlessly, and he blinks once, twice, not believing his eyes. When he opens his eyes again he finds that he is now the one trapped in the glazed glass and the boy is looking down at him, still with as much curiosity, but to his surprise he doesn't feel afraid, he feels oddly content floating in the abyss. He closes his eyes as a buzzing sensation of serenity washes him over, leaving him feeling the most rested he has ever been.

He then feels a light tap on his shoulder and as he turns, he finds the boy now much closer to his face, his eyes still fixed directly on him. He gasps, jerking his body backward, but the boy is quick to catch him by his hand, swiftly intertwining their fingers but saying nothing, just gazing at him with those big, sad eyes.

Felix blinks, not understanding the bizarre situation he has caught himself in. He feels a stinging sensation above his collarbone, burning him softly, and as his eyes drop down he sees his necklace glowing white, weakly lighting the darkness surrounding him. Then, when his eyes dart back towards the boy, he catches the boy's ring glimmering with same amount of brightness. They look identical, his necklace and the boy's ring, shaped the same, glowing the same, but when he looks at the boy in search of answers, all he receives is a knowing smile, confusing him even more.

For a while, they float in the darkness where the only source of the light is their own jewellery, but then the light dims, consuming them into blackness, into nothingness.

When Felix returns to reality, the first thing he notices are the tall trees towering over him, murky in the autumnal fog; he sits up, runs his fingers over the moss and bark on the moist ground, and scents the aroma of earth.

"Are you okay?" he hears someone speak and flinches once more when he catches the glimpse of the same boy, sitting right beside him, playing in the dirt with a stick. "Do you know who I am?" he asks and turns his head towards him, gazing at him with eager round eyes that sparkle even in the dark night.

He shakes his head rapidly, still feeling out of place. "Why don't you speak to me?" the voice wavers, sounding hurt, and along with his tone his eyes drop drown as well, filling with unsaid pain and immediately making Felix feel guilty.

"She... She gets sad when I, when I speak," Felix stammers, unable to find the right words, but the boy in front of him doesn't seem to be startled, he just stares at him, the knitted furrows between his thin browns becoming tighter.

"Who does?"

"The nurse... I mean, my mom." He panics, his voice trembles.

"Your mom would never get angry at you."

The sentence is enough to knock the air from his lungs and he jumps forward, grabbing the hands of the mysterious boy.

"Do you know my mom?"

"Of course I know her! I'm your..." He pauses, averting his gaze as he nibbles on his bottom lip, not speaking for a while. "I'm your friend."

"But I don't have any friends." Felix declares in a matter-of-fact tone.

The boy grimaces, his face pinches as if he'd been punched, and Felix doesn't understand why he looks so hurt. "You have me now. I will always be your friend," he mutters under his breath, and as the grip on his hand tightens, he looks down and finds their fingers intertwined once more. "I'm Genji."

"Who am I then?" He asks the question that has kept him awake this whole time but the boy, Genji, just sighs and drops his head down.

"I can't tell you that even if I wanted to."

And so he nods, not asking any further questions, and turns his gaze to the ring decorating the boy's ring finger instead. Out of habit, he touches his own necklace, which still feels hot to the touch, even though it is no longer glowing. They sit in comfortable silence for a while, their hands glued desperately together as if they are afraid that if they let go they will disappear from each other's consciousness. And maybe they will.

Felix's eyes roam around aimlessly, observing the area he has found himself in this time. "Where are we?" he asks, feeling the boy's eyes fall onto him but not daring to look.

"In the forest... In our forest." This makes him look at the boy, who just sadly gazes at the ground.

"Our?"

"Everything started here, in this forest, so it's ours now. Well, until we leave," Genji mumbles, trying to explain, but Felix doesn't understand, and maybe it's for the better to know less so as to have less to worry about.

He musters his courage and puts his head on Genji's shoulder. It doesn't feel out of place, quiet the reverse, it feels like the right thing to do. His eyes fall once more onto their intertwined fingers, and he allows himself to play with the latter's paler and colder ones.

And when Genji wraps an arm around his shoulders, the feeling of being curled up in his arms—with their fingers interlaced and the soft beat of his heart ringing like a lullaby in his ears—can't be put into words.

As he closes his eyes and falls asleep in his arms, forgetting the world, he can tell that this is where he belongs, that in these arms he feels at home.

And when later in the night Felix is awakened by the loud wailing of a kid in their shared room, although he feels the coldest he ever has lying in his empty bed, the sizzling warmth still lingers on his skin.

Starving for tenderness he grabs his toy, squishing it against his hollowed chest where his heart pangs in pain, beating for someone whose name he doesn't remember, and with that he lets his eyes close as silent tears roll down his cheeks.

And as I was left alone in the dark shadow of the bridge, I felt the penetrating cold devouring my soul, the painful numbness that made my heart ache every day as I watched people continue to live on the other side.

Felix sits at the noisy table, observing the room, and watches as the caretakers rush from one room to another, some holding plates, some tidying the tables, some calming down the crying kids who never stop wailing, but as he watches life unfold in front of him, something dies deep down inside him.

The delicious aroma makes his stomach grumble in hunger. He doesn't even remember the last time he ate—or forced food down his throat. His eyes follow the plate full of food that one of the caretakers puts down right in front of him, but the moment the plate is placed down, it is emptied by hungry hands.

And now he's left gazing at the empty plate.

He bites down on his lip, holding the scream inside, but he can feel his hands shaking and anger taking over his senses. He wants to cry, from hunger or from disappointment he doesn't know, but as icy tears well in the corners of his eyes he feels a slight nudge from his side, and when he turns his head he recognizes the caretaker from yesterday, smiling tenderly at him and holding out what looks like a sandwich. "Here, take mine," she says, shaking the food a bit and reaching closer to his grasp. He gazes at her and the food for a while, knowing that if he takes it she will be left with nothing to eat, but the hunger inside of him gets the better of him and he quickly grabs the food and eats it in one go, afraid that it will also be taken away from him.

And when he looks at her, feeling guilty again, she just smiles at him reassuringly, making him feel less bad.

"Was it good?" she asks and he can only nod in response, still not mustering a word, but she doesn't show her disappointment, she just continues to beam at him. "My name is Xaria, but you can call me Auntie if you want to."

Auntie…

"Auntie Moriko?" he gasps, immediately clapping his hands to his mouth when he realizes that he has spoken. Xaria seems equally as surprised to finally hear him speak.

"No, it's Xaria, my name is Xaria but you can call me whatever you like." She quickly gathers herself, her previously perplexed expression fades away from her lovely face and she puts a gentle hand on his shoulder, comforting him.

Felix doesn't notice the silence that has fallen in the room and only when he feels eyes burning into his skull does he turn his head towards the other people in the room. Unwanted attention immediately makes him meek so he jumps down awkwardly from his seat and rushes towards his room to hide from so many eyes.

"He's finally spoken," whispers one of the caretakers while looking blankly into space. Xaria just smiles.

Clear as day I can see Auntie Xaria standing on the other side of the bridge. She has always been generous enough to show me love, to try to fill the void inside of me, but the void is never filled and my pain only grows.

Maybe I'm too greedy by nature but all I ever wanted was to be loved, a soft demand; but there was no one in this world to love me. Because at the end of the day, it was her job to love me, it was what she was paid for and I think both she and I knew that from the start, so there were no misunderstandings between us. I knew she would never be able to give me motherly love and she also knew that at the end of the shift she would be giving her love to her own son, not to me.

"Here, all done!" Xaria chirps, albeit somewhat nervously, as she fixes the uniform on the petite, fragile body of the kid. "Felix, are you excited for your first day at school?" she asks even though she already knows the answer.

Felix just drops his eyes to the floor, focusing on his dirty shoes while his small fingers fidget unceasingly, rumpling his newly ironed clothing. Although he wants to say no, he nods hastily while the lip caught between his teeth loses even more colour. The tears that are so close to spilling stay secure inside the corners of his eyes but glisten with unsaid worry.

He feels a light pat on his head. "Will you be a good boy? You won't worry auntie, right?" The grip of Auntie Xaria's hand tightens unconsciously as they walk towards the bus and Felix once again nods, still not looking up from the ground. He blinks the tears away and takes a sharp intake of breath in an attempt to calm down his raging heart, which is ready to jump from his ribcage.

He notices the hand slip out from his hold and only then he realizes that he's already standing in front of the bus. Letting out yet another shaky breath he stays glued to his place for a moment. "Felix?" The caretaker now sounds worried.

Inhaling heavily, he juts out his chin and with trembling legs makes the first step inside the bus. The impatient driver doesn't wait for him to sit down and sets off the moment he steps inside, making Felix lose his balance and slam against the seat. It's not enough to injure him but he feels pain nonetheless. Even so, the agony of his heart quickly makes him forget about the soreness of his limbs. The bus takes off towards its destination rather quickly and Felix hurriedly stumbles towards the window to see Xaria walking slowly towards the orphanage.

He wishes she would stay for a second longer. He wishes she would be there to watch him leave, but instead it's him who witnesses her walk away.

He decides to ignore the light tug on his heartstrings and slumps down onto his seat.

He's used to it.

The agitation as he waits outside the classroom is tearing him to pieces, he is full of curiosity and angst as he watches the teacher speak. His bottom lip is already split in two, darkened a rich red. He wasn't lucky enough to have other kids from the orphanage with him in the same class; not that he particularly wanted them to be, but at least he wouldn't feel like the elephant in the room if he had another atypical kid like him to accompany him.

"Felix?" After what feels like forever, the teacher finally calls out his name, and Felix sprints inside, almost stumbling in the process.

Now, standing at her desk he notices everyone's eyes focusing only on him, he averts his gaze to the floor, but the feeling of being burned by looks lingers on his skin.

"This is Felix," the teacher starts, and Felix feels a strong grip around his shoulders as she forcefully hugs him. "The boy I've been telling you about." She says it in such a threatening manner that even Felix understands that something meaningful hides behind it, but he isn't able to comprehend what so he ignores the uncomfortable tension that has fallen inside the classroom. "Want to add anything?" And even if Felix had wanted to, she makes it sound so troublesome that he decides it would be better if he just shook his head. "Okay then, sit next to Eva. Eva, please raise your hand!"

A short girl with a ponytail raises her hand and Felix walks slowly towards her and falls onto the seat, only then letting out a breath he didn't even know he was holding.

"Hi, I'm Eva, nice to meet you," she says through a beam and holds her hand out.

Felix hesitates for a second before taking her hand in his and shaking it nervously. He hopes his hands aren't clammy. "Nice to meet you, let's..." He hears a few soft snickers coming from behind him. He violently champs down on his lip before mumbling "Let's be friends." He finishes his sentence just above the hush, but the girl already looks uninterested and, removing her hand quickly as if disgusted, she averts her gaze.

Felix's eyes dart onto his lap as he fidgets with his fingers, scraping the skin off, but he doesn't care, not even when he tastes the disgusting taste of iron on his tongue as his lip starts to bleed.

When the bell rings the kids rush outside the room in bliss, although not forgetting to give Felix looks of pity and dismay, which together look much like fear, as if Felix is some kind of contagious disease.

"Felix, right?" He hears a squeaky voice to his side and when he finally manages to look up he's met with blue eyes and freckles. "My name is Anne." Felix nods, not daring to respond this time, but she doesn't seem bothered by his lack of answer and sits down in front of him.

"It's lunchtime, why are you still here?" she asks as she puts her chin in her hands and gazes at him curiously, as if Felix is some kind of mystical creature.

"I will eat here," says Felix. Again, though, the girl doesn't seem to care, she just hums as she takes a lunchbox from her bag. She nods towards Felix's bag, gesturing him to take out his food as well and Felix obliges, too afraid to mess up the unusually smooth conversation.

"Wow, an Aero bar?" she exclaims while gazing at the chocolate bar with wide, twinkling eyes. "They're my favorite!"

Felix glances back and forth at the bar and Anne before handing it over to her, saying "I'm not hungry." She pouts, debating for a while before giving in and taking the bar excitedly.

"Let's switch! Do you like jellybeans?" He doesn't, in fact, but he nods regardless.

"Thanks," he murmurs as he takes the bite of the candy and grimaces. But he's too thrilled to care about the sour taste the candy leaves in his mouth.

"Auntie hurry up!" Felix whines as he tugs on the sleeve of Xaria, who with a chuckle follows the overexcited kid. "Did you buy me an Aero?" Felix asks for the ninth time, and with a fond smile the caretaker once again says yes, that she indeed did, making Felix beam from ear to ear.

"You know I can't take you to school every day, right? Don't get too used to it," she scolds him playfully, making Felix pout and swing her arm side to side, and Xaria can't help but ruffle his curly locks. "We're here! Now go and be a good boy!"

Felix tugs on his backpack straps and waves at her before rushing inside the building.

He runs towards his classroom, his heart beating excitedly for the first time in a long time, eager to meet his new friend. Standing in front of the door, he gazes inside through the small window and can't help but yelp in enthusiasm when he notices the familiar face talking to another classmate. They're laughing at something and Felix doesn't mean to eavesdrop but he can't stop himself from leaning his ear against the wooden door. Their voices are muffled but just about audible. He hears loud giggles, and as he touches the door handle, he hears that familiar squeaky voice.

"He even tried to be friends with me." Felix frowns, his hand freezes on the spot.

"And the way he looked at me? So creepy." An unfamiliar voice rings inside his ear which he then recognises as Eva's. His fingers start to tremble and his heart throbs painfully. He feels his throat go dry and all the air is knocked out from his lungs with a violent punch. There is no air to breathe. He feels like he's suffocating and he knows he has to leave, nothing good will come of him staying and listening to all the terrible things they have to say, but somehow he can't force himself to move, he is totally paralysed, and he continues to listen even as he feels his eyes water.

"Ah right…" Anne says softly. "What a freak." And this is when Felix can't hold back a broken hiccup that escapes his bruised lips. He feels as if his insides are on fire and his heart is burning to ashes as the tears finally spill from his red eyes, stinging his face. He sniffles, rubbing his sore eyes, and soft sobs scrape painfully inside his throat as he tries to muffle the sound, too ashamed to be heard. But his cries don't go unnoticed, and when he opens his eyes for a second he sees the girls looking at him with cold looks that make Felix stumble back in mortification, and before he knows it, he's already sprinting away.

I just wanted a friend…

He doesn't know how long he has been running or how fast his short legs are moving but he can only hope and pray that auntie hasn't left yet.

Breathless from running and crying at the same time, he tries to puff out the last bits of air inside his exhausted lungs as he carelessly crosses the street, which is blurred by the hot tears that keep on flowing. He hears a car honk in the distance, followed by annoyed cussing coming his way, but he has no time nor the strength to care.

A relieved sigh leaves his throat when he finally notices the familiar figure walking slowly down the street, unaware of the inner turmoil going on inside the kid, and with all of his might he forces his legs to run faster towards the only source of comfort he's left with. Even if auntie will never love him truly, never see him as her own, even if she doesn't care that he will cry a river, he has no one but her and so he rushes over to her as fast as he can.

"Auntie!" he wails through his sobs, and his hoarse voice is so loud that the caretaker turns her head back from the end of the street and Felix observes the worry painted all over her face, but he has no time to think about it, he just wants somebody to hug him.

"Felix?" She doesn't get to finish as she's cut off by her own soft yelp as Felix grabs onto her leg with full force. "What happened? Felix?" She tries again but the question quickly dies on her tongue as Felix lets out a throaty cry. She looks around and notices the unwanted attention they are gaining from strangers, so she carefully takes the kid into her embrace. Felix instinctively flings his arms around her neck, nuzzling his head into her chest as he continues to sob.

"Hey dear, what's wrong? Why are you crying?" she asks tenderly, already walking towards the bus station. Felix doesn't answer, his only responses his loud sobs.

"Take me home!" he bawls, tightening his arms around her, and sobs once more but chokes on a dry cough that makes him go into a gagging fit. His voice sounds so worn out, so rough that Xaria almost doesn't recognize him.

"I'm taking you home dear, don't worry." she assures him, bouncing his tensed body up and down in an attempt to calm him down, but Felix just shakes his head, staining her blouse with salty tears.

"No! Take me to *my* home!" he yells, which is quickly followed by yet another wet snivel. Her grip around his body tightens, but she says nothing, and Felix feels disappointed for the second time that day.

That day, the first day of my elementary school I saw the bridge crack more than it ever had before. I think that was the day I realized that maybe I would never be able to reach the end.

And maybe that day the last string of hope was sundered.

With small steps he walks inside the police station, feeling unbelievably tiny around the tall men hovering above him and rushing towards different corners of the building. The room is filled with noises of laughter, the phone ringing non-stop, heavy steps, anxious conversations, and much more. Some of the policemen stop to absentmindedly ruffle his hair, already used to seeing him hanging around.

His grip on his backpack strips tightens as he turns his head upwards towards the familiar policeman. "Where is Detective William?"

The officer is caught up in his work and doesn't answer immediately, so Felix with trembling fingers gently pulls on his shirt in an attempt to gain his attention. "He's in his office," the policeman says in a bored voice, and with a sigh, Felix lets go of the fabric that he's been holding on and with even smaller steps walks towards the room.

He knocks politely on the door and steps backward, fixing his backpack on his shoulders, just to soothe his nerves. A moment later the door opens, revealing a detective who doesn't notice him at first, but after looking around confused for a while, the detective's eyes drop down to see Felix gazing up at him expectedly. William's face loses its previously bewildered expression and breaks into a beam. He opens the door further, giving Felix more space, and with yet another quiet huff Felix walks inside the big, dull room.

The first thing he notices is the desk covered by hundreds, if not thousands of sheets of paper, scattered around messily. He also notes the coffee cups in every corner of the room, telling him that the officer must be busy. But he doesn't have a lot of time for observation as he's suddenly lifted into the air, strong arms holding him in place, and when he looks at the man, he finds him smiling at him. "What are you doing here kiddo?" William asks, seeming genuinely happy to see him, but Felix can't maintain the mood; he drops his head down and chews anxiously on his bottom lip. "Is everything alright?" asks the officer, his tone softer this time, even concerned.

William carefully sits him down on the chair in front of his desk, which is too high for his short legs, leaving them dangling in the air. He fidgets with his fingers for a moment, and the pressure on his lip increases, turning it from cherry red to white.

"Do you remember when you told me to ask you if I ever need anything?" he mumbles as his fingers scratch more deeply into his skin, peeling it off from the corners of his fingernails.

William looks surprised for a moment, his brows hidden behind his hairline but then he nods, although the worry between his wrinkles never disappears on his dark skin. "Felix, is everything really okay?" he tries again, more demanding this time yet gentle. Felix nods without thinking.

"Do you know what day it is tomorrow?" he whispers through tight lips, almost inaudibly.

William, more confused than ever, throws a glance at the calendar hanging on the wall. "June 15th, why?"

Felix huffs in irritation, now fumbling with the fabric on the sleeve of his torn hoodie. Another minute of silence falls over the room as William patiently waits for the kid to speak and Felix tries to find the right words.

"It's, it's fathers' day."

And when the detective stays silent, Felix panics, staring up at the man with shameful, wide eyes.

"I know, I know you're not my dad but..." His voice breaks, so he clears his throat, his fingers digging deeper into his skin. "But the teacher, she, she told me that I could ask someone important to me to come and you, Detective, you're the one I could think of..." His voice wavers at the end; he bites down on his lip to stop himself rambling and drops his head down low once again.

For a moment William says nothing, and Felix takes it as the rejection he had always expected, feeling stupid for thinking that he would ever agree to that, but then, like a mantra or prayer, a voice rings in his ears, saying "Okay, no problem, I'll come." And this one sentence is enough to fill him with hope, fill him with something warm; he doesn't know the name of the sensation so he chooses to call it happiness.

"Really?" He whips his head up, his face glistening with the light that burns inside him, his every nerve tingling with a fuzzy feeling that is new to him. "Will you really come? Do you promise?" He searches for any doubt to wash over the detective's face but William just smiles and nods his head softly. Felix whips his pinkie finger in the air, reaching towards the officer who chuckles at his childlike actions. The officer gently entangles his own finger with the child's. "I promise."

And suddenly the room looks much brighter than it did before.

"And then he went inside and saved the dog, even though the captain was yelling at him," the girl standing in front of the desk chirps, standing next to her dad who just to brag has taken his fire-fighter's helmet with him. Felix anxiously taps his feet on the floor, glancing towards the door every second. He pinches the scar on his leg, still gazing worriedly at the door—maybe if he stares hard enough, William will magically appear in his vision.

He won't come, he doesn't care, the devil hidden in the corners of his brain whispers into his ear, its voice mocking. *But he promised,* he fights back, forcing himself to believe the voice in the back of his head, but he knows he doesn't sound confident, and the devil senses that and Felix can hear it cackle.

Promises are sweet lies; they aren't made to be kept.

His legs tremble and he pinches the scar even more forcefully, almost opening up the healed injury once more.

Deep in his haze, he doesn't even realize that the girl has stopped talking and is walking back to her seat. He's thrown back to reality again when the teacher's voice rings into his ears. "Is anyone else left?" she asks as she reads through the list of the students. "Felix," she starts to say but cuts herself off, giving a quick glance towards the distressed kid, and clears her throat. "Right...I think we're done for today, thanks for participating, and a big thanks for parents who found time to visit us today." She finishes her speech but Felix isn't listening anymore.

With a loud thud, he bumps his face onto the desk, arms wrapping around his shaking body. And he ignores the snickers coming from different sides of the room. He fights back the tears from slipping from the corners of his eyes, he doesn't want to give them the satisfaction of seeing him cry. The only thing he wants is to go back to his empty bed and sleep his pain away.

The bridge cracks once more, a few piles collapse into the river beneath, and Felix feels something break inside of him as well, not strong enough to kill him but painful enough to leave a scar. And when later in the evening William barges into his room, apologising profusely, Felix just pretends to be asleep.

Even though he doesn't get even a blink of sleep that night.

Sitting on the grass, Felix's short fingers lazily play with the dried, dead-looking daisy as he softly hums a melody he doesn't know the name of. His gaze never leaves the lifeless flower, its rotten petals now painted nasty brown, looking anything but pretty and filling Felix with a sickening feeling of revulsion.

The flower will never bloom again, never raise its crown from the grass, eager to reach the light of the sun after being trampled upon. It is unsightly and plain, it won't catch anyone's eyes as they walk by, everyone will stamp the plant into the ground, finally ending its suffering.

Felix feels so much hatred for this sapless flower, a flower that lets others walk over it, so he rips the plant out of the grass cruelly, with no remorse, and watches it bleed till the last drop of green liquid pours down to the ground. He harshly throws the flower away into the distance where no stranger's eyes can reach. He pulls his bruised legs closer to his chest and continues to hum the melody. Closing his eyes he lets the sun soak him with rays of sunshine whilst he listens to the other kids' screams of joy in the distance, kids he has no desire to befriend.

Suddenly something blocks the sun from his view, casting him in shadow, so he squeezes open an eye and is met with the beaming face of Hotaru.

"Here, it's for you!" he chirps through a smile, thrusting a bouquet of wildflowers at Felix. Felix's eyes dart towards the flowers, alive and dazzling, brightening the scenery with their petals, all of them painted in different vibrant, eye-catching colours. He hates them for looking so beautiful, nothing like the daisy he threw away a while ago. He looks back to the boy, who is gazing at him with a peeved look on his face.

And then the sound of a loud slap makes the kids stop playing around, and a momentary silence is followed by a full-throated wail.

"Why did you do that Felix?" Auntie Xaria grills him as she tugs him roughly by his arm, dragging him through the mighty hall, but Felix couldn't care less about the punishment he has to face for smacking Hotaru. "He said that he gave you flowers because the other kids said you looked sad, don't you feel even a bit bad?" Her voice rises, she can't mask her disappointment, and she shoves Felix inside his bedroom and with folded arms waits for his response.

But Felix doesn't even spare her a glance, he just gazes outside as he slides his finger across the windowpane. The irritation bubbles up inside her, and before she can control oneself, she's already pulling Felix's face away from the window, digging her fingers into his flesh as she holds him firmly by the chin, and staring at the kid intensively, as if to show her authority, to somehow make the kid speak. But Felix just gazes at her soullessly, no trace of guilt whatsoever in his empty, glassy eyes as he answers calmly, "The flowers were beautiful. I *hated* them."

The flowers were too pretty for me to hold, they wouldn't flatter me anyway so I've decided I hated them.

Ugly...

The word brings much familiarity to my heart—finding its home in my mind. Along the way the word made a permanent wound on my soul, and I started to believe that I was utterly ugly, inside and out, so each time my eyes ever lingered on something beautiful, I was filled with rage and resentment, with bittersweet envy. And even if I could rip the ugliness from my skin, I knew the ugly stayed within me.

Sometimes I wonder why my classmates, my peers, my teachers, why did everyone despise me so much? What did I do to deserve their resentment? Was it because I was ugly? Was I so revolting to look at?

Ugly...

Unloved...

Unwanted...

All of these words found their way to the depths of my skin, they left claw marks and no matter how much I scrub my flesh, they linger, reminding me of my hideousness.

"Why don't you go and meet them?" Xaria asks as she sits next to Felix, who is looking into the distance, gazing at the couple that have come to pick up their future child. A child that he never will be. A feeling of revulsion fills him as he watches the kids make fools of themselves, losing their last bits of dignity as they try so hard to be the ones to be chosen, to be the ones going to the warm home.

"No one will adopt me anyways, so why bother?" he whispers under his breath, leaning further against the tree from behind which he's peeking.

"If you continue to think so negatively nothing good will come of it."

But if he believes in broken promises the disappointment will bring so much ache in the end, he doesn't know if his heart can bear it.

He never mutters his thoughts out loud; he just continues to gaze at the couple playing with the kids. They would never be able to love him as much his own, real parents would—the ones who abandoned him.

A slap from the back of my head.

Look ahead, they may be a threat.

A foot sinks me to the ground, weightless and soft, and I wonder if there will be an end to the fall. Someone kicks me in the shin, where it aches the most. One slap, two punches, hands lingering, leaving marks around my impure body, dragging me to the dark corners of the school.

One heartbeat I'm drowning, my body shivering with cold, the next I can smell my flesh burn as the cigarette butt digs deeper into my skin, decorating my already scarred skin and bones.

I can feel someone watching, someone who isn't there, glorying in my sorrow. But maybe it's me, thrilled to see myself die.

Truth to be told I don't remember when exactly all of this started. When mean words turned into punches and bruises. Maybe the day I was born… Maybe I was destined to suffer in this joyful world. Maybe I never had an easy life, I can't tell because I'm left with no memories of my woe.

But I remember by heart the day the flames of hell started burning. It was the first day of middle school. The day when I first saw him, standing next to the teacher, smiling. And his smile seemed so sweet at the time.

"Hello! My name is Noel Fournier," the boy, Noel, beams, gaining everyone's attention, including Felix, who just observes him through frowning eyes. The reason he's staring at the boy is that the name sounds familiar but he can't pinpoint from where. And the more he gazes the faster the realization settles in.

Noel Fournier of the Fournier family, one of the biggest funders of his orphanage—he's sure he's seen him around before, peeking out from an overpriced car, dressed in nice, new clothes and holding onto expensive toys. He stands out in a place full of low-class orphans, making him easier to remember.

He sighs, making a mental note not to get into trouble with him.

Caught up in his thoughts, he doesn't notice the sound of loud steps coming towards him and only when he hears the low screeching noise does he turn his head towards the sound, finding Noel sitting in the row next to his empty seat. He doesn't realize that he has been staring but when the boy waves at him with a timid smile, he quickly averts his gaze.

To his dismay, he waits for him after lessons—Felix always preferred going outside last so no one would bother him. He hangs back, trying to dry off his soaked notebook that somehow found itself being drenched in the fountain right outside of the school, but eventually, with a low groan, he drops the damp journal onto his desk. He hopes he has an unused notebook somewhere back in his room. Then he hears a soft yelp, and when he looks up he is met with the towering figure of the new kid.

"I didn't see you there! I thought everyone had already left," Noel says, rubbing the back of his head awkwardly. In response Felix just nods—he has no desire to continue the conversation, and with a quick movement he throws the notebook in the trash can. It's useless anyway.

Unconsciously he grips the straps of his backpack as he makes his way out, but a rough hand is there to stop him at his tracks, dragging him back into the room. A dreadful feeling of worry makes itself apparent inside of his guts.

"What happened to your notebook? Why did you throw it away?"

"You'll find out soon enough," he answers before heading towards the exit.

"Hey, you seem familiar, have I seen you before?" Noel shouts from behind, still not finished with the dry conversation, and Felix can feel his legs shake, buckle in fear, even if there is nothing to be scared of, at least for now.

"Probably from 'Miracle Children'," he mutters bitterly. He'll find out at some point or another, so it's probably better if he gains this information from Felix himself, but suddenly all the air is knocked out of his lungs as he feels his body thrown backward, and he can only pray that it won't hurt too much this time, that Noel won't be careless enough to bruise him in places that would be easy to see. He squeezes his eyes shut, his head bowed as he waits for the punch.

But it never comes.

Instead, he finds the boy beaming warmly at him, completely oblivious to his distress.

"You live there? No wonder you looked familiar! My name is Noel if you don't remember! I'll make sure to tell my parents that you're my classmate." And the way he smiles at him so sweetly brings an acid, bittersweet feeling to his chest, because he knows it won't last long.

"Please don't talk to me," he whispers, trying to get away from the hovering body blocking his way.

Noel is taken aback as he stands on his way. "Why? Did I say something wrong?"

"Please..." he begs, his voice wavering with tears that slowly choke him, demanding to be let out, and even if Noel seems as dumbfounded as before he still steps aside, giving Felix the space to walk, and it doesn't even take the blink of an eye for him to sprint out of the classroom.

He didn't learn as fast as I thought he would. The next day he came to greet me again, asked me to hang out after school, and the day after that as well, and soon the days turned into weeks and Noel still seemed as unbothered as ever, grinning at me, trying to start a conversation with me.

And I would be lying if I said I didn't like the attention, the generous kindness that I'd never received from my peers before. Even if I saw him hanging out with the students that tormented me the most, I decided to turn a blind eye – in the name of 'hope', the hope that he maybe I deserved a friend like Noel too.

But hope is a dangerous thing, it either delights your soul or devastates it – you have to remain aloof to hold on to hope.

"Why are you doing this?" he wails, but his wail is choked down by a yelp before he can even finish the sentence as he's shoved down on the cold floor. He watches as the light slowly fades from the room, and as the door closes with a loud thud he registers the shadows coming from different sides of the room, filling it with sneering laughter. Noel's cackles echo through the room, penetrating his ears. And he can feel his eyes well up with hot tears that burn inside of his skull, but he doesn't know the reason for his unshed tears. Is it because of his knowledge of his impending fate? Or is it because of the disappointment that aches his heart so painfully?

But he isn't given too much time to think as he feels hands wrap forcefully around his legs, dragging him across the room, and the last thing he registers is the screeching sound of his fingernails scraping against the porcelain floor, and before he can even cry for help, or beg them to stop, he finds himself gasping for air, but nothing but icy cold water stabs into the back of his throat and nose, sending burning pain through his body.

He screams, his arms and legs kick out desperately as he tries to break his head on the surface, but Felix never learned how to swim, and the more he struggles the worse it gets.

With an effort, he breaks the surface again, desperate for air, but then with hopeless gasp, he is under again. This time he sinks further and the terror has his heart hammering against his ribcage – anguish has consumed his heart and his head is pounding, every cell in his brain is begging for survival. His lungs feel as though they've been set on fire. Slowly, black begins to seep in at the edge of his vision. He tries to open his mouth to breathe but takes in only chlorine water. He can't hear the laughter and chatter of the carefree students inside the room anymore, the sound drowned out to buzzing in his ears, gradually turning into silence. His legs are tired and struggling to bring him back towards the surface, so he grabs onto the corner of the pool, his fingernails bleeding.

Suddenly the sound of a flowing river pounds inside of his skull, and he can taste it, a dirty river, foul and unclean. He can feel his body smashed against the stones in between the emerging waves. He hears someone wail out his name. The cold settles inside his bones; the darkness envelops him. As if he had been there before, as if he had already drowned once in that river. With a strength he had never felt before, his limbs learn to move all over again, crashing his head through the surface, and with a long gasp he fills his lungs with air and his whole body wobbles upwards, coming crashing down onto the floor once again. He coughs onto the loathsome taste of the water, gagging and choking. He's left shaking, his body bending in every direction as he tries to breathe.

And the sound of laughter echoing in the room slowly fades away into silence; he doesn't recollect how long he stayed shivering on the floor.

And when he's sitting on his seat, still trembling in both terror and cold, he hears someone laugh behind him.

"God, it stinks in here." Followed by yet another mocking cackle, and he can do nothing but judder uncontrollably and watch with shaky, crazy eyes as the dirty droplets of water drip on the floor.

And at that moment the only thought that corrupted my mind was why? Why me? What was the unforgivable sin I had committed to deserve this eternal punishment?

And it hurts. Hurts so bad. I can no longer bear this constant pain, so I let the ghosts in my chest plant dead flowers in my heart.

And the flowers are thorny, wild and violent and I can feel their spikes of hatred piercing through my weakened heart.

"God has a reason for allowing things to happen. We may never understand his wisdom, we simply have to trust his will."

Felix allows himself to secretly open his eyes, peeking around yet still holding his folded hands tightly across his face. He observes the crowded church, where everyone has their head down and their hands in the air as the pastor continues the sermon.

"Have patience, God isn't finished yet."

He can hear something, or maybe someone, in the back of his head. The sound is buried deep but he can hear it loud and clear, enough to send shivers down to his spine.

And how much longer should I wait? I've waited long enough. I've waited my whole life. For seconds, for minutes, for hours, for days and years, I've waited. But all I have is wordless silence.

The voice wails, sounding much like him, but there is something sinister in the way its tone breaks, sounding drained and torn in between the screams and cries.

""For I know the plans I have for you," said the Lord, "Plans to give you hope and a future. There is surely a future of hope for you, and your hope will not be cut off.""

Bored, he gently puts his hands down, detached from the preaching spewing out from the lips of the pastor behind the pulpit, who is reading joyfully from God's words, which sound nothing but a buzzing silence in his ears. He looks around, feeling like a ghost trapped in a room of people full of faith, belief and *life*, but one particular boy gains his attention, a boy with knitted brows and hands clasped so tightly together that the pressure shakes his limp arms. He is chanting something soundlessly under his breath, lips barely moving, but he seems flustered, agitated even, and when everyone else raises their heads again at the end of the prayer, he continues to murmur to himself, his expression cramping and his limbs shaking more forcefully than before, as if he's afraid that time is slipping away, not giving him enough moments to finish his prayer.

Felix tilts his head to the side, observing the boy from afar, only to find him already staring in his direction, his eyes wide, glassy with unshed tears as he gawks at Felix, making him shift uncomfortably under his heavy gaze, but even so he can't take his eyes off of him, and the more he watches the better look he gets of him. He looks about the same age as him, he has big, round eyes, pellucid like a sheet of glass, giving them a limpid look. His skin is waxen, making him look like he hasn't seen sun in years. His sunken eyes heaved down with eyebags no kid his age should have. His cheeks hollowed. He resembles a ghost more than an actual human.

"God promises to make something good out of the storms that bring devastation to your life."

But before anything can come to his mind, he feels familiar, rough palms squeezing his shoulders from behind. He doesn't need to turn to know who is digging their fingers painfully into his skin.

He doesn't need time to remember what comes afterwards. Still, he flinches, never getting used to the ache that follows their words.

"Felix, I'm bored! Let's have some fun, shall we?" Noel whispers in his ear, only for him to hear, awakening goosebumps at the thought of the terror that awaits him.

He squeezes his eyes shut and dropping his head down he gulps heavily, but the lump inside his throat stays put. He can feel his body wet with sweat, his limbs start to shake; in a panic he looks up, searching for a helping hand, and for a second his eyes catch a woman staring in their direction with her brows raised, so Felix frowns, biting his lips, but she looks away, not sparing a single glance thereafter.

Like they always do.

They look at him and decide he's not worth of their worries, only because they're not the ones getting painted black and blue, and people have seen him, seen him being dragged along the floors of the school, outside of school, in the dark corners of the classrooms, but they never do anything, neither his peers nor adults, and it gives Noel more power, knowing that even no one dare touch him.

And so Noel grabs him by his arm, getting impatient at the lumpen form of the boy sitting next to him, and forcefully hoists his body upwards, dragging him towards the door, he lets Noel shove him around like a doll.

But something forces him to turn his head back, and when he does he gets a final glimpse of the shimmering black eyes that have never stopped gawking at him. Felix just shakes his head and closes his eyes, not fighting his fate, because what comes next is unchangeable.

"No need to panic...Because god will be right there with you, he'll keep you safe and sound."

The last thing he registers is the priest's voice chanting inside his ears before green scenery comes to his vision as he is thrown onto the ground.

But who will save me?

He wonders as the first kick goes through his ribcage, plunging him deeper into the grass.

"What are you staring at?" Gregor, Dylan's father, asks when he catches his son staring blankly at the empty seat in front of him.

"Ayumu was here," Dylan murmurs in a daze. He blinks once, twice before finally looks at his dad, his fingers finding their way onto the man's arm, tugging him urgently. "Let's go, I want to see Ayumu," Dylan declares, louder this time.

Something flickers on Gregor's face, something resembling disappointment or even vexation, and it needles an ugly feeling inside Dylan's heart, squeezing it and making his blood go cold. "I'm not lying, he really was there!" His voice wavers, breaks at the end as he feels wetness flood his throat, making it hard to speak. He feels tears sting his eyes as he takes in the doubtful expression on his own father's face. "Dad, I'm not crazy, Ayumu really is here! You don't believe me?"

His dad doesn't respond and looks around, noting the unwanted attention as people start to gaze in their direction, but Dylan couldn't care less, not when his dad is piercing him with accusing eyes. He hears him sigh, making flames blaze inside him.

No one believes him anymore, the trust was broken the night he let go of Ayumu's hand—even his own father, his parent, looks down at him with cold, unforgiving eyes.

Everyone hates you.

The voice rings in the back of his head, releasing the tears from the gates of his eyes, and he gazes at his parent as the waterfalls roll onto his cheeks. "I'm not crazy, dad, I'm not," he cries, tugging harder at the fabric.

Images of doctors, their faces covered in masks leaving only their dead eyes visible, their cold fingers holding him tightly, burning his skin, and shoving pills down his throat—all of this, every moment spent inside the clinic comes to his vision.

I'm not crazy.

Gregor inhales deeply once more, patting his son's shoulder in a comforting manner, but that's not enough to bring peace to his burning soul. "I believe you, Dylan, Ayumu is here, I see him too." And as he watches his dad playing tricks on him, pretending he's looking at Ayumu, he feels acid pour through him, leaving him in indescribable agony.

His own father takes him for a fool, no, as an idiot—everyone thinks he's a lunatic blabbering aimlessly. His words have lost their value, there is no one left to believe him.

What did you expect? You're crazy, you killed Ayumu.

The voice cackles at his misery, making his bones shake so much that he thinks he's on verge of breaking.

I didn't kill him. I didn't kill Ayumu.

He's not dead.

He's here.

He tries to force himself to believe his own words but he can't tell the difference between reality and delusion anymore. He can't trust his own words, he doesn't know what's real and what's not.

Oh, but you killed him. You killed that poor kid, you pushed him off the cliff and now he's dead and it's all your fault.

"I didn't kill him!" he wails out loud, successfully gaining everyone's attention. Even the pastor is looking at him with judging eyes, making him burn with shame. He feels every gaze on him in his core, making shivers go down his spine as eyes filled with judgment and disgust follow him.

Everyone hates you.

He sobs, hot tears pour down to his face as he wails once more, "I didn't kill Ayumu, he's alive!" His weeping echoes through the mighty walls of the church, and his dad, having finally had enough of him, swiftly grabs him by his arm and hurries out of the holy place.

But Dylan never stops crying, wriggling from his father's grasp as he tries to set himself free. "I'm not crazy! I am not," he sobs between throaty, wet coughs, and when he rubs his teary eyes he sees a boy lying on the field. "See, he's there! Dad, Ayumu is here! Please stop! Dad!" He screams and yells but his dad just keeps on walking towards the car with big, harsh steps, dragging Dylan with him. "Dad, please believe me," Dylan croaks, punching his parent with the little energy he has left.

Someone, please believe me.

Something snaps in Gregor, and startling everyone around he roars, "Stop it, will you?! Ayumu isn't here, he is gone! How many times do I have to tell you?"

And for a moment the whole world falls dead silent, even the birds stop chirping.

Felix gazes at the scene unfolding in front of him, the sudden outburst successfully saving him from his upcoming beating, giving him a minute to catch some fresh air before he is shoved into the ground with nothing but dirt to fill his lungs. He feels his own tears well as he watches the boy being dragged towards the car, staring back at him just as intensively, his eyes flooded with yet to be shed tears. He feels oddly relieved, comforted to be seen, his pain acknowledged and to see the boy cry for him, or with him—he doesn't really know but he's thankful nonetheless that someone has finally seen his sorrow.

He watches as the boy is thrown inside the car, sees the wrinkles appear on the man's sour expression as he himself climbs in, and he sees the boy's face glue to the window, still staring at him from the behind the glass, tears continuously dripping down one by one from his shimmering eyes. Felix drops his own head down, his own tears wetting the land as he sobs quietly, and in the distance he hears a youthful hymn, angelic voices escaping through the thick walls of the church mixed with the soothing sound of the organ that rings out, enlivening his senses.

Amazing Grace, how sweet the sound
That saved a wretch like me.

He hears the car start but he doesn't have the heart to look up, to watch the first and only person to share his pain with him slip away from his reach as fast as he appeared, and so he keeps his head down as his body shakes, pouring hot tears onto the grass.

"What are you crying about?" He hears them snicker, and then comes the familiar ache as Noel's feet press on the back of his head, pushing his face into the dirt. "Did you think they would help?" The feet weigh on him more forcefully. "There is no one who would save you."

Through many dangers, toils, and snares
We have already come

Felix doesn't answer, doesn't muster a sound, he just continues to weep quietly, irking the boy standing above him.

"Don't believe me? Then scream, scream, and see if anyone will show up!" he shouts, grabbing him by his hair and yanking his head upwards, and Felix gasps for air, finally able to breathe again. "I said shout!" he yells again, now straight in his ears, making his eardrums throb in pain, and truth be told he wants to shout, to scream, to yell for help, but he knows that it's not worth of trying, that even if he tears his vocal cords apart no one will come, so he bites his tongue, blocking any sound from leaving his throat, even if it aches.

Clicking his tongue Noel pushes him to the side and with a nod, he gestures his friends over to the limp body. Like loyal dogs they quickly grab Felix by his arms, dragging and scraping his skin against the ground, and pull him into a dark passageway where the sun barely reaches.

T'was Grace that brought us safe thus far

After one punch and another Felix lays down onto his back, his eyes trying to reach the sunlight that peeks through cracks on the ceiling, and he listens to the choir that continues to chant the carol, lulling him to sleep, or is he losing consciousness? He lets his eyes close as his body bounces to the ground from one kick and another. With no further protest he lets his body turn blue, leaving him with permanent scars. He doesn't scream, nor cry, the pain crushing against his bones is barely noticeable. He senses his mind flagging, covering with a haze. The only thing he can do is to lie flat on the earth beneath and listen to the mantra.

And Grace will lead us home

He doesn't know how long he stays lying there or how much damage has been done, but the last thing he registers is one of the guys shouting something in a frantic tone, followed by loud footsteps that throb right into his head. As he's left lying there in the all-consuming darkness he notices that the singing has stopped and the world has fallen silent. He closes his eyes and lets his battered body rest, and with short breaths that sting his lungs, he tries to calm his soul down. As he feels the familiar tears in the corners of his eyes, he closes his eyes and wishes to be dead.

Later in the evening, he doesn't even try to fight for the food, he lets arms be shoved into his bruised sides, moving him away from the feast, and just sits there, swaying from side to side as he feels nothing but coldness in the core of his bones, nothing but a hollow in a place where his heart belongs. He sees caretakers running from one corner to another, he watches the kids delightfully devour the delicious-looking food that smells so, so nice but brings nothing but revulsion to his ravenous stomach.

Life goes on and everyone is too occupied with their own misfortune to notice that it has finished for one of them.

"Felix, dear, are you eating well?" Auntie asks as she brushes her fingers through his messy locks. "You seem to be losing weight," she says, sliding her hands over his tanned skin and letting her palms linger on his hollowed cheeks where the dry, patchy skin scrapes the pads of her fingers.

For a moment Felix gazes at her, his lips turned into a thin line as his eyes glisten in the dark. The bruises underneath his shirt sting more as he nods, lying both to her and to himself.

Looking unconvinced she nods, letting her hand drop down. It makes Felix wonder what would happen if someone looked at him closer, or longer. If someone ever heard his wordless pleading and cared enough to reach out a helping hand, maybe then…maybe then everything would turn out differently. Maybe it wouldn't hurt so much.

But it's too late to dwell on something that won't ever happen so he steps aside and walks towards the bathroom. He looks closely at the reflection of a boy he doesn't recognise, no matter how many times he looks, but he can never recognise this boy because it's not him.

He slowly strips down, noticing every curve of his body, every movement of his muscles, and when he stands still, naked and raw, he can't help but feel repulsed—his body is covered in bruises and scars, his ribcage is bursting through his skin, his arms are lanky. He is totally and utterly ugly.

He gently brushes his fingers through his hair, lifting the locks enough to show the scar that hides right above his left brow, the reason for his doom.

The scar remains but the memories have forever vanished.

He despises his scars but he cherishes them as well, in an oddly twisted way, because they're proof that his pain is real. They decorate his flesh like a souvenir of his past, a reminder that he continues to exist.

He claps his hand to his mouth, muffling the quiet sobs that leave his bruised lips, and slowly he slides down on the floor, wrapping his arms around himself and letting the tears slip from his eyes to burn his skin as they roll by.

When I think about it, I was only a teen and yet I already wanted to die, I was and still am just a kid but somehow I feel so ancient, and so youthful at the same time.

But that night the devil came crawling to me, whispering in my ear that he could take my pain away and since then something else is haunting my body, something fierce and terrible, desperate to burst forth. I dare not say its name because I'm terrified it will be my own.

It did not kill me or make me stronger, it made me venomous and callous, it made a home in my pure mind and rotted it away.

Felix fixes his hair and jumps out of the window, cutting his hand on the broken glass in the process.

He hisses as he gazes at the blood that seeps from the broken skin. He throws a quick glance back, checking whether anyone has seen him, but all he sees is the lonely piano standing in the centre of the room—the abandoned music room is the only place where he can rest in peace and have time to eat without being bothered by anyone.

Putting pressure on his newly formed injury he walks out of the school, just to catch a bit of fresh air before he is suffocated in a room full of people who are waiting patiently for him, but he doesn't get far before he's dragged to a dark corner beside the school building.

He knows there will be a lot of witnesses, seeing him being mercilessly punched and kicked, but he also knows there won't be anyone who would dare to help him, so he doesn't even try to fight back. These days he doesn't even bother to take a guess at how many bruises will appear on his tanned skin by the end of the day. And these punches? They don't hurt as much as they did before, either.

"Nice to see you here, Felix." Noel chirps as he throws the butt of his cigarette onto the ground.

Felix knows it was stupid of him to walk so close to their secret hiding space, where they smoke before lessons.

But he would end up beaten up no matter the circumstances.

He doesn't flinch, nor does he run away, he just glares at the older boy.

"What? Are we playing brave now?" Noel asks teasingly, jumping down from the stairs and walking up to him with slow steps. He exhales in Felix's face, and the disgusting smell of nicotine makes Felix cough.

Noel's eyes drop down onto his hand, which has not yet stopped bleeding. Felix can hear him chuckle and the next moment his hand is whipped in the air and he feels indescribable pain as fingers plough right into his wound, ripping it open and making even more blood spurt out.

"What? A failed attempt?" Noel laughs, making Felix's blood go cold. "What a shame, you should've finished what you started. *Waste of air.*"

The words make his heartbeat drum into his ears, he can feel his pulse racing in his veins and suddenly he has an urge to vomit. His jaw tightens as he clenches his teeth, trying to hold back the scream—he wishes to howl in pure rage.

"Forgot how to speak, freak?" Noel kneels in front of him but Felix never spares him a glance, his eyes stay glued to the ground, shaking in wrath. "Look at me when I'm talking to you!" he shouts, gripping his hair painfully and forcing him to look up, and something like fury washes over his face as he catches Felix looking at him with dull, emotionless eyes. He punches him right on his cheek, making him crash against the coarse concrete beneath, but Felix just lies in the same position, eyes closed, trying with all his might to stay calm and not let his devilish thoughts get the better of him.

Then he is forcefully grabbed by his collar, making him squeeze his eyes shut and wait for another punch to colour his skin. But the punch never comes.

When he dares to open his eyes a little he finds Noel gazing at something, something on his neck, and a sudden feeling of dread sits inside his lungs.

His necklace.

"What is that? I've never seen it before," he says as he softly touches the pendant, getting a better view. Felix flinches, jumps back, which he recognizes as the wrong move when he sees the crooked smile stretch further on Noel's face, giving him a sinister look. Before he knows what's happening he feels a strong grip on his neck again, leaving him breathless.

"Is it important to our Felix?" Noel asks, and within seconds he breaks the necklace off his skin.

The last thing he registers is the ringing sound of the chain splattering onto the ground—then his mind goes blank.

"What is that?" Noel laughs. "Who is that boy?" He cackles mockingly but Felix doesn't react. His sense of reality fades away, settling into nothingness, and his mind goes blank.

Gaining no response Noel glances at him curiously, his brows raised upwards, but Felix stays sitting there in the same place. His hands are balled into fists and his knuckles are white as his whole body shakes with hysteria. He feels the last crack on the bridge, the very last crack that makes it collapse into the void, and then he hears something break, something cracking, his sanity perhaps.

Then something snaps in him and everything becomes a blur.

Without even realising, he roars through gritted teeth, leaps up, and tackles Noel to the ground. He continues to scream as he punches the boy in front of him, scratching him till he feels blood fill the corners of his fingernails. Noel seems frightened for a moment and Felix realizes he likes this look on the boy better, to finally have that smug, arrogant smile wiped off his face, and he decides that he wants to see him wear this expression more often so he hits him again, harder this time, smashing his head against the block. His hands are coloured by a mixture of blood and tears.

He feels someone grabbing him from behind but he just digs his teeth into the flesh so deep that he feels iron on his tongue—the monster inside him has been unleashed and now there is no turning back. He is lost in his fury.

He doesn't know how much time has passed, how many times he has hit him, how much blood has been spilled—he just yells as he continues to punch the lumpen body beneath him. Blood pours out from the nose of the lifeless boy, and as Felix pounds his face with his blood-stained fists, his eyes roll back in his head.

Noel soon gives up trying to fight back the raging male who more closely resembles a rabid animal, thirsty for blood, than an actual human. Felix can feels bones crack under his fingers. Control over his body has long been lost, his hands move on their own, diving into the flesh of his classmate as forgotten animal instincts awaken in him, killing the last bits of humanity left inside him. At the same time, he's afraid, afraid of himself, afraid of the monster he has become and what he will look like when he sees himself in the mirror, but there's nothing he can do about it—the anger and anguish that have built up inside him over so many years have finally clawed their way out.

No one would dare to say that Felix didn't try to keep them locked inside the dark, unreachable corners of his being, that he didn't ignore the darkness consuming his soul each time someone stabbed incurable wounds deep into his heart with every insult, with every false promise, but it's always been him against the world, and now his demons have entirely filled the void of his empty heart and started to spill out, flooding him the poison that all the others poured in. He didn't jump, he was pushed and shoved until his legs finally gave up and the ground slipped beneath his feet and he was thrown down into a dead abyss, and as he gazed into the abyss, the abyss began to gaze back, enveloping him in an affectionate hug as he dived deeper and deeper into the darkness, washing away the fear and worry his demons brought so that he stopped fighting them and slowly learned to accept and love them as his own.

Since his mind is entirely out of his control, he doesn't notice when Noel's eyes roll back down, now glowing in fury, and it takes only a single kick to the stomach to make Felix stumble back, causing him to bend his wrist in a way that will for sure leave a wound. He gasps for air as he feels his insides squeeze in pain. As Noel kicks him in the back of his head, making sparks fly from his eyes, he feels like his body has been set on fire, and the next moment Noel is the one sitting on top of him, diving delightful punches into his skin, making his eyes tear up in agony.

And yet he can't make himself care. This is the most carefree he has ever felt—even with his face covered with blood—and so he laughs and laughs until he can feel his lungs bust, and when Noel looks taken aback for a moment, he spits blood in his face.

"I'm going to fucking kill you!" Noel roars, putting his hands around his neck, slowly but surely squeezing the air from his lungs. But Felix yet again just guffaws.

"You think you can scare me with that?" he mocks him. "I'm not afraid of death." And he brushes his bloodied fingers against his skin, painting his face with his own blood, playing a sick game to see how long it will take to crack him, to force him to show that same frightened expression. And it works because Noel jolts back, his eyes wide with both fear and confusion, too dumbfounded to comprehend what has happened.

Felix grins, enjoying every second. The realization that he holds the power to induce fear in a person is addictive.

He tries to stand up but his legs buckle so he leans against the wall, leaving blood marks all over it. He is breathing heavily, but there is nothing but blood to fill his lungs, and this is when, from the corner of his eyes, he sees a shard of broken glass shining in the light. He slowly leans down, feeling every bone crack inside his body, and gently takes the broken piece in his hand.

"If you want to kill me so bad, then kill me, I have nothing to live for anyway," he says nonchalantly and stumbles closer towards the boy, who retreats into the corner, his eyes wide and full of terror. Felix is enjoying it way too much. He grabs Noel's hand and puts the glass in his grasp, cutting his skin in the process—he feels the warm blood drip onto his own fingers. Then he slowly guides his hand towards his throat.

"Kill me," he says, leaping forward and feeling the glass pierce his skin. "Come on kill me!" he yells again but then he feels something hard coming crashing onto the back of his head, making him flee and crash against the wall before his lifeless body finally slumps to the ground.

Then the only thing he remembers are the images blurring with one another at the speed of light, followed by the loud screech that leaves Noel throat. "Is he dead?" But he can only groan in pain as his heavy eyes shut down, finally bringing peace to his mind.

Felix flickers his cold eyes as he feels a touch of coldness on his warm, bloodied skin, and when he finally regains consciousness, he finds himself still lying on the hard concrete ground. He can't move, his body feels heavy, weighing down his bones that ache in pain, so instead he decides to watch the snowflakes fall swiftly past the glow of the streetlight—all different types to look at, different shapes, different sizes, large ones and small ones shimmering like stars. They stick to the ground, covering it with a velvet flow and melding with his hot poured blood, turning it a pretty rosy colour.

His eyes flicker shut again and he listens to the sound of the falling snow, a quiet, soft, and precious sound that comforts his sleepy soul, so he continues to lie there as the snowflakes flutter, leaving icy, wet, cold kisses all over his face, melting on his tanned skin. He smiles, his bruised lips stretching so that the dry, blood-stained flesh breaks, letting more blood flow, and with that, he falls into a deep slumber again.

He doesn't know how long he has been unconscious, but slowly Felix opens his eyes, the persistent harrowing pain emerging from the depths of his bones once more. The only thing keeping him conscious is the sound of cars passing, but every drop of sound hammers inside his skull. It takes a while but eventually he manages to put himself in a sitting position, his bones uncomfortably touching the hard, cold ground. He moans weakly, gently touching what looks like a sprained wrist, and he can only hope that it's not broken. He tries to open and close his palm but the stinging pain is like a dagger slicing through his nerves, and so with an exasperated sigh, he carefully rests his hand on his knee. He scoffs at the thought of a new wound to add to his collection of injuries, but at the same time he wonders how much his body will be able to take before all of his bones shatter to the ground. His body feels too heavy to move and even if he could he's afraid that his bones will break merely by trying.

He inhales deeply and tries to put his feet on the ground, but immediately he squeals in pain. And yet he has to get up; he has to protect himself.

Somehow he manages to stand up and he stumbles into the street, still covered in dried blood, almost crawling as he drags his legs across the heavy cement, scraping his skin even more and opening newly healed scars.

His body sways, rocking back and forth as he tries to keep his balance, but as he holds his hand out to catch a passing taxi, he loses his balance and ends up stumbling face down onto the ground. He groans as he feels the pain eating him alive, but then he hears a frantic honking that throbs inside his head and forces himself to turn his head upwards.

"Are you okay?" the driver shouts from the window, not making any move to help him. Felix can't really blame him—he wouldn't jump to help a person covered in blood from head to toe either.

"Never felt better," he yells back, and digging his fingers into the metal, he leans his weight against the car and with great difficulty, his bones creaking, pulls himself back up into a standing position. "I just need to go to the police station, you know the one, next to the big park, I think, but I really need to, I just really need to get there," he blabbers through slurred speech as he feels himself on the brink of losing consciousness again, and just as his eyes are about to close, he hears the driver talk to him once more.

"Do you even have money to pay?" he asks. Felix only nods, too tired to muster a sentence. He feels high, a calming buzzing sensation spreading through his veins and making him doze off into the unconscious. He drops his head against the cold window and watches as the colours blur into one another.

How long it takes him to arrive at the station he doesn't know but he somehow manages to stay awake the whole journey, in spite of his body screaming at him to shut his eyes. He doesn't even bother to stand normally, just drops his weight down onto the ground.

"Please wait here, I really have money to pay," he says, and the driver grumbles something under his breath but Felix decides to ignore him.

Too tired to walk, he decides to crawl up the stairs and as he gazes at the light coming from inside the building, he knows that the moment he steps inside, his whole life will change.

When he finally shoves the door open with the last of his energy, he hears someone gasp. The next moment someone is holding him up and he screams, feeling every inch of his wounded muscles stretch.

"Oh my God! Felix? Is that you?" shouts the man, who sounds like Logan, and Felix can only nod as he squints against the brightness of the room.

"The taxi, the driver," he says. "Please pay him."

"What? Forget about the driver! What happened?" screams Logan, gaining the attention of the others around him, which Felix can tell because he hears the frantic sound of footsteps approaching him.

"Please. I want William, call William!" he wails, the pain slowly becoming unbearable as each minute trickles by.

He hears someone talk in a panicked voice, he makes out someone calling for William, and after a few minutes he's wrapped in protective arms, holding him in place and not letting his wounded body move.

"It's okay, I'm here now." He hears the familiar voice of the officer so he lets himself weep and wraps his trembling arms around him, probably dirtying his clothes. "Can you tell me what happened?" he asks softly, holding him carefully, as if afraid to break him.

"He, they, they've been hurting me for so long and I, I didn't know what to do!" he hiccups. "They, they threatened me and beat me, every day, every single day and I, I…" He never manages to finish his sentence because he breaks into a fit of sobs, drenching William's uniform with his tears.

"It's okay. Don't rush yourself," he assures, trying to sound calm but his voice breaking in angst.

"And I didn't want to bother you, so, so I, I tried to ignore them but he…"

"No need to say more," William stops him, sounding on the verge of tears himself as he holds Felix closer to his chest, and Felix lets himself be enveloped by the tall figure and lets his shoulders shake.

Yet only he knows that his shoulders are being shaken not by quiet sobs but by the laughter that he has been holding onto. He finds it comical knowing that he has probably just ruined someone's life. He doesn't know whether he should feel concerned that he feels no remorse in doing so, but the decision is already made. If he is going down, he's dragging everyone down with him. Even so, when William moves back a bit, his pleased smile turns into a pained expression once more and he allows more tears to pour from his eyes.

"Can you tell me who did that?" He likes how rigid William looks right now. It's all thanks to him that finally his pain isn't being taken for granted.

"Noel, Noel Fournier…"

"It's okay, he won't hurt you anymore, I promise." And even though Felix finds it hard to believe the detective's promises, which have been broken before, he nods nonetheless. As he watches a few of the policemen rush outside and feels someone gently helping him to stand, he can't help but let a content smile play on his lips and let his eyes close, feeling peaceful for the first time in a long time.

Then he passes out for the third time that day.

He's woken up by the shrill voice of a child. His eyes open quickly, with surprising ease, and he sits up, feeling the cold beneath him. As he digs his fingers deeper into the ground he senses the wet touch of snow.

He scans his surroundings; somehow the crushing pain in his bones is all gone. He finds himself in a wooded area, in a dark forest where the snow forms a perfect blanket over the ground. Not even a blade of green grass is visible, every twig is laden with snow, looking soft and white.

The scenery, idyllic as it is, induces an unpleasant feeling in him, and he is suddenly suffocated by an overwhelming feeling of dread. He's been here before, he's sure of it. He has seen this forest before but now he can't place its whereabouts. He tries to think, but where he is won't come to his mind. The scent, the touch, the atmosphere and the air are all too familiar—they awaken every sensation in his body, his mind and his heart, trying to tell him something he's unable to understand.

"Is anybody here?" he yells, but the echo of his own voice, filling up the air and resounding from different sides, is the only response. He catches his breath and takes one step back, his feet slowly sinking in the cloudy snow.

Am I dead? he thinks as he scans the soulless forest, devoid of life, forlorn, cold and dark.

He starts running. He has no destination in mind, but the urge to get away from this forbidden place takes over his sound mind. As he goes deeper into the woods he soon find himself lost, in a place where not even moonlight reaches. He sees darkness and only darkness, but it doesn't stop his legs from moving forward. He doesn't even stop when his legs slip on the frozen surface. Doesn't stop even when the bushes dig deeper into his skin, cutting his flesh.

As the tears come, so does his sense of déjà vu. He has been here before. He knows the stinging feeling of the thorns scraping against his skin and his feet getting tangled in the mud. Suddenly he's knocked off his feet by a weight crashing into his legs, and he collapses into the gloomy whiteness. As his head comes into contact with a hard surface beneath the snow, he squeezes his eyes shut and groans, the familiar feeling of a headache filling his senses.

When he manages to open his eyes again he's met with ogling black eyes staring intensively at him. He lets out a little yelp, swiftly moving to a sitting position, and stares right back at the child sitting on front of him and gazing wordlessly at him.

"Hello?" says Felix, his voice unsure, his tone weak and full of confusion.

The kid just stares at him through his knitted brows for a moment, looking oddly angry, but then his chin wobbles, so do his lips and his eyes glisten in the moonlight with fresh tears and the next moment Felix finds himself being wrapped in a suffocating embrace, the short arms of the kid wound tightly around his neck. "I missed you," the child croaks, burying himself deeper into Felix's warmth.

"I missed you so much." He nuzzles his head into the crook of Felix's neck, leaving Felix with no other option but to rub comforting circles on the child's back, feeling his petite body shake as quiet, wet sniffles ring in his ears.

He exhales, still bewildered by the whole situation, but continues to rock his body back and forth, humming a melody he doesn't know the name of while his mind tells him he is doing the right thing.

After what feels like hours, the kid finally calms down and lifts his face off Felix's shoulder. He gazes at him with unsaid pain in his eyes and Felix stares back, counting the rose splotches on the little boy's face as the aftermath of his tears.

"Are you okay?" he asks, continuing to rub the child's back as he chokes out the last unshed sobs before sniffling a wet snort and nodding.

"Where are your parents? It's dangerous to be out alone in the woods."

Felix thinks he may have said something wrong because the kid's eyes start glistening with tears once more, so Felix pulls him into yet another hug, resting his chin on his small shoulder and sighing with worry as his eyes dance around the corners of the woods where small cottages can be seen in the distance.

"I know it's dangerous," the boy whispers, his voice muffled against Felix's body. "But I was waiting for you."

"For me?" Felix squeaks, unable to mask the surprise and confusion he feels.

"You don't recognize me, I know," the kid mumbles against his skin and he sounds so sure yet so sad that Felix wants to do nothing but to take the little boy's worries away.

"I'm Genji."

"Okay, Genji, I'm Felix, it's nice to meet you but we really need to find your parents," he says as he gently nudges the kid by his arm.

The kid, Genji, purses his lips, thinking deeply before glancing at something behind him, and when Felix follows his gaze, he finds something lying on the ground covered in snow. He gasps in horror when he realizes it's a human body.

"Who is it?" he asks in panic as he jumps up from the ground, letting the kid fall into the soft blanket of snow. He tries to make a step but something holds him down, not letting his limbs move.

"Oh, it's me," Genji says in a matter-of-fact tone, leaving Felix gawking at him for a moment before he shakes his head and tries to move once more. "It's no use, you can't save me," he adds, now clinging to Felix's leg. "And you can't leave either."

Felix feels a sudden dread take over his senses as he tries but fails to move his legs, but the kid remains unfazed, peeking up at him from the ground.

"We, we can't leave him, we, I need to help him!"

The kid wails, "No! Don't leave me!", his screams echoing through the empty woods. "Don't leave me again, please!" But Felix finally manages to make a step forward, and as he walks into the snowstorm, the kid never stops weeping, begging him to stay.

"I'm not leaving you Genji!" Felix shouts, cutting the kid short. "But we need to help him, or you, I don't know!" He drops down onto his knees as he checks the body lying in front of him. He quickly brushes off the snowflakes covering it from head to toe and shakes the cold, lifeless form, but there is no response. He curses under his breath and tries to lay the body on its back to check for possible injuries, but as soon as he touches it he feels the touch of the body's cold skin on his fingernails and he flinches. When he focuses his blurred vision, his breath catches in his throat, momentarily cutting off his airways.

It's not Genji, it's him, Felix.

Well... a younger version of him, glaring at him with furious eyes.

"What the fuck is going on?" he whispers under his breath and turns back to Genji in search of answers to his many questions, but Genji is just sitting next to him, calmly making snowballs.

"Today we're going to die." Genji mutters, smashing the snowball against the ground and watching it scatter into small bits of snow. "And we're going to stay here forever and nothing will be able to separate us anymore."

"What the fuck... What are you saying? I can't die, you, he, we can't die!" Felix yells in despair but the kid seems unfazed. He nudges the unconscious boy once more. "Hey! Hey! Can you hear me? Please wake up!" he yells so loud that he feels his vocal cords scrape, but he keeps on shaking the body, even when tears start streaming down his face. "Please wake up, we can't die like this," he begs. Then he rests his face against the chest of the body, praying to feel or hear a heartbeat, but to no avail. He sobs as he shakes him weakly.

"I want to stay here." Suddenly he hears his own voice ring in his ears. "I'm happy here, I want to be with Genji forever."

And as Felix observes his own small face, full of scars and bruises, his heart clenches with pity and rue—guilty because he wasn't strong enough to protect the innocent kid.

"Please, we must leave, I promise I will be strong for you, okay? I will never let anyone hurt you, so please, let's leave." He reaches out his hand to touch the boy's cheek but the boy's head jerks back and Felix hears him shouting "We can never leave the forest!"

Suddenly the boy's brown eyes morph into black emptiness, and as he roars his voice drops an octave lower, sending shivers down Felix's spine.

He knows that the time is ticking as he sees his fingers glow and then fade into the air. "No! No! No!" he wails, wrapping his arms even tighter around the boy, trying everything in his might to warm up the frozen form.

"Please, Genji or whoever you are," he begs. "Please open your eyes!" He hears kids screaming and feels their small hands wrapping around his arms, trying to force him off the boy, but Felix uses his superior strength to his advantage and stays glued to the boy's chest.

Miraculously, his prayers are answered as he hears the soft, almost inaudible beat of a heart, and he jumps back, cupping his face in his hands as he tries to get a better look of him.

"Please stay with me, okay?" he says. "Open your eyes." And slowly but surely the boy's eyes flutter open, unfocussed but so beautiful that Felix bursts into tears as he gently drops his forehead onto the boy's and his lips let out a relieved sigh.

He sees a white fog rise up and begin to consume the whole scene and with a last glance he looks at the kids, who are now gazing at him with tear-stained faces, wordless hurt written all over them. "I promise I will protect you, you will never feel pain anymore, I promise!" he says sternly, gently patting his younger self's head, and with that everything washes away into whiteness.

The white light vanishes into thin air, revealing the washed-out walls. The only thing keeping him awake is the sound of ringing as each bell hammers inside his skull. It takes a while but eventually he manages to pull himself into a sitting position, his bones uncomfortably touching the rough hospital bed. He grimaces as the familiar, sharp, medicinal scent tickles his senses. He looks around, observing his setting as the distinct sounds of people's laughter and weeping morph into a single noise, flooding his ears.

He checks his sprained wrist which has been neatly wrapped in bandage, and suddenly he has an urge to smash his hand against the wall—he feels nothing and all too much at the same time—but his internal thoughts are cut short as the nurse walks into the ward, holding a clipboard and scribbling something on paper.

"Hello Felix," she says in an uninterested voice.

Irritated by her arrogance, Felix rolls his eyes and averts his gaze, but due to the lack of response she comes up close to Felix and he is forced to nod.

"So how are you feeling?" she asks, clearly wanting to leave, and even though he is still in too much pain to ignore, he physically forces himself to bend his lips into a deceitful smile.

"I'm feeling fine, can I go home now?"

She raises her brows, checking something on her papers again.

"We can't let you go without permission."

Right...

William had probably had already left—no doubt something else had come up, something more important than Felix. Auntie Xaria had probably made her excuses too. But somehow Felix doesn't feel hurt at all, for the first time the heaving disappointment doesn't sit inside his stomach. It's a weird position to be in, to feel nothing, to have every emotion wiped away with no trace. And as the anomalous sensation spreads through him, he realizes that something has changed. He can't put his finger on what it is, but he feels delighted to have the crushing weight of worries lifted from his shoulders. And so he just hums disinterestedly and, with a small, careful movement, places his feet on the ground.

"I'm giving myself permission."

As he softly hops down from the bed he sees panic wash over the nurse's face, wiping away her previous indifferent expression, and once again is overpowered by a feeling of self-satisfaction.

"Wait!" she says. "You can't leave like this. You have to wait till we call your parents. It's the rule."

Felix crooks his lips into a devilish grin and with a carefree voice deadpans, "I don't have any parents, I live in orphanage."

The nurse flinches, guilt written all over her face, and Felix can't help but savour the irresistible feeling of overthrowing the rule of the disrespectful nurse. It's an addictive sensation.

Without giving her a second to gather her thoughts he stumbles outside the ward only to be stunned by the strong chemical aroma of the hospital. The white walls bring back nausea and with sluggish steps, he walks through the crowd. Hordes of nameless people pass by, bumping and shoving his scarred body, and for a moment his fingers tremble, the familiar feeling of fear almost overtaking his senses. But then he lifts his chin up and crawls his way through with more force and determination.

Caught up in the moment he doesn't notice a hospital bed rolling towards him at full speed, and only when it almost crashes into him does he manage to jump out of the way. From the corner of his tired eyes he sees a boy lying on a white sheet that contrasts with his grey skin and blue lips, and for a moment time slows down as Felix watches the corpse-like boy being rushed towards the emergency room, but then his view is blocked by a middle-aged man sprinting towards the bed.

"Dylan!" the man weeps, trying to grab the boy's hand only to be stopped by doctors who drag him back with force. "Please! Doctor, please, please save my son!"

The man collapses on the shining floor as the boy disappears from sight, and Felix stares, unable to take his eyes off the poor parent who continues to blabber pleading words to no one.

That must be nice, he thinks. To be loved like that boy.

Felix hopes he doesn't take it for granted.

Suddenly the man looks up, probably sensing the eyes on him, and Felix jumps, taken aback to be gazed at with such wide, helpless eyes that reflect familiarity, gazing at him as if they had done so a million times before.

"Ayumu?" the man croaks, and Felix frowns, not recognizing the name thrown out at him, but then the man shakes his head and with sad laugh murmurs, "I must have gone crazy." But Felix heard him loud and clear, and an uncomfortable feeling settles inside him, pressing on his heart.

As he continues staring rudely at the distressed parent, a girl of around the same age as him comes rushing towards the man and jumps into his arms.

"Where is Dylan? Is he okay? Please tell me he's okay!" she sobs into his shoulder, and the man hugs her closer, now being the one comforting the girl.

"I don't know when he took the pills…" she says, her words cut short by a loud sob. "I looked around and he, he already was on the ground and…"

"It's okay Sophia, it's not your fault," the man assures her even as his voice breaks. "Dylan is going to be okay."

And Felix hopes he will be okay too, he wishes nothing but the best for a boy who was lucky enough to have so many people caring for him.

And with that he makes his exit, whistling a melody he doesn't know the name of.

How cruel life can be for young people like us.

Noel was expelled the very next day. So what if I ruined his life? So what if I don't feel any remorse for doing so? If a thought of hurting me ever crosses one's mind, I want them to be hurt deeply.

I did not want the poison they filled me with to start to spill, destroying everything around me. But since the very beginning everyone infected my body, they made me contaminated, unsuited to live among them. So, I will play the role I was given – a deadly, wild flower that will not hesitate to kill anyone who will be foolish enough to come closer to it. I will thrive on distant adoration and immerse fear that my existence will bring to others.

In the end the only thing I have understood is that the thorns in front of me on that bridge weren't there to block my way. They were protecting me. And as the last bits of the bridge have fallen, I will now be able to keep myself safe.

And perhaps I wasn't able to protect my past from the scars and bruises, but I hope that I did some good for my future, and I hope the future me lives a life he can be proud of.

If not, I hope you have the strength to start all over again.

May 5th, 2009

A letter to myself

Later in the night, Felix dreams about the beautiful, terrifying forest again.

It is snowing and it is so quiet that he can hear his own breath mixed with the sound of the snowfield susurrating beneath his feet as he marks the untouched white expanse of pliant land with his footprints. As he walks through the quiet snowstorm the moonlight brightens, displaying everything to him: the naked trees and brave flowers peeking through the iced powder, giving a soft touch of colour to the whitewashed scenery; witch hazel, flashing bold yellow, looming up even through the snowflakes and the darkness of the night; golden daffodils, petals bright with power, stretched in a never-ending line beneath the trees, dancing in the breeze; the glory of the snow lighting his way; and the azure petals peeping up along the road. As he follows their lead the earth beneath him stiffens, feeling rougher than the soft touch of the snow.

He stops in his tracks and looking around he finds himself at a dead end at the edge of a cliff. He tilts his head down, studies the scenery below but sees nothing but indigo sky splattered with thousands of shining stars twinkling on the Milky Way and the crooked, waxing crescent moon. As odd it may sound to look at the world turned upside down, he doesn't feel unsettled even for a minute. He knows he's deep in slumber, that he has landed on the wonders of his dreamland, the only place in the world where he feels at home.

He closes his eyes and breathes in the night, feeling the stars fill up his soul. He savours the feeling of being nowhere and no emotion weighing down his heart because he knows that once he wakes up this sensation of pure peace will be forgotten, put in the drawer of memories that cannot be remembered.

Soon after he feels a light needling touch on his shoulder, and when he turns around he's met with two familiar kids sitting behind him. They don't even spare him a glance but seeing them brings a smile to his lips regardless.

Then the younger version of himself looks up from the ground, stopping whatever game he was playing with Genji, and tilts his head to the side, signalling something to him. Following the line he finds a boy sitting on the edge of the cliff, gazing into space with his legs calmly dangling in the air and humming something under his breath. With slow steps he walks towards him and sits down carefully beside him. He peers at him for a moment, notices that his skin is still pale but not as pearly-like as it was on the hospital bed—some colour has been splashed onto his cheeks, making him appear more alive.

Not knowing how to jumpstart the conversation, he settles on simply asking, "So you woke up?" He realises he is dancing around a topic he isn't sure if he even wants to bring up, but he hopes that the fact that the boy—Genji, or Dylan, he doesn't know what to call him—is right next to him means that he's alive.

The boy nods blankly while staring into space, but it's enough to summon a buzz of something resembling relief inside Felix's chest.

"Are you... Are you feeling okay?" Felix asks. He is trying not to come off as demanding but he needs to be sure the boy is safe and sound, so he lowers his tone, makes it softer than before, trying to sound as gentle as he can as he continues to look worriedly at the boy's profile. Another beat of silence rings through the quiet forest, only the sound of the breeze rustling through snow interrupting their senses, but then finally, albeit painfully slowly, he turns his face towards him. His round eyes are the first thing that catches Felix's eyes. They have a sheen to them, they brighten his existence the same tender way they did when he first dreamed of him, lost in the dusky woods, awakening unfamiliar sentiments in him. They are the same dazzling eyes that absorbed him at the church, revealing untold truths, and yet they are also the same eyes through which he saw his life wasting away the night before, glasslike and gleaming, transparent even, reflecting his own bruised and bloodied face back to him but dimmed underneath.

Felix closes his eyes softly, amazed at the way he remembers him: body, soul, and all.

It would be great if he could remember it all once he woke up and left the heavenly state of his dreamland, but he knows it's too much to ask, he knows that the universe, his doomed fate, isn't on his side.

"I will, as long as I'll be able to meet you again," says Dylan all of a sudden, instantly stopping the trainwreck of Felix's thoughts.

"But will we?" Felix asks, unsure, his voice quavering because he's afraid of raising his hopes too high. Dylan just nods in response. "How do you know all of this?" He is curious now because no matter how many times he has landed on the wonders of this forest, he has never been able to make sense of it, and Dylan seems to know this place very well.

"Because you visit the forest when you need it the most and me…I'm trapped in here, I'm forbidden from leaving, I come here every time I close my eyes, some nights I remember some I don't. So I've learned how everything works in here." As Dylan mumbles, he leans his chin on his knees, again gazing in the distance whilst his fingers play with the snow beneath him.

"Can you tell me when we will meet?" As soon as the question leaves Felix's lips, Dylan flinches, hesitation written all over his face as he throws a short, nervous glance towards the kids who are now glaring in their direction with wide black eyes.

"I cannot." He says breathily, looking at Felix with shameful eyes. "But even if I told you, we won't remember each other. Even though the answers will be right there in front of our faces."

"Just like in the church and at the hospital," muses Felix, finally understanding a small part of this universe.

"Sorry," Dylan says suddenly, his chin wobbling, and as Felix notices his eyes glisten with wet tears he feels something break inside his heart.

"Can you tell me about me? Who am I or what kind of person I was?" he asks, even though he knows the probable answer.

Just as he thought, Dylan whispers a broken apology and hides his face in his knees, rubbing away the few tears that managed to escape. "Everything is my fault," he adds, and his voice sounds so small, so broken that Felix doesn't even care to find out what he's apologizing for.

"You're struggling no less than me, there's no need to blame yourself," he says as images of him lying on the hospital bed come rushing back to him, making it hard for him to breathe.

"How can you say that? Everything turned this way because of me!" Dylan yells, looking at him with wide, bewildered eyes, but Felix just smiles, gently patting him on his hand, which is clenched into a fist filled with snow.

"Searching for you is also the only thing that keeps me going, so don't you dare die!" he says. "Be strong, so we can fix the chaos we've made."

But Dylan doesn't answer, he just looks at him with his tragic eyes, and Felix can feel the nausea coming, the feeling of worry forming like a lump in his throat. "Promise me that you'll stay strong for me and for us, Genji." Dylan flinches at the name and Felix guesses he doesn't want to be addressed by it so he tries again with "Dylan." He speaks more sternly this time and finally Dylan nods again, but his gaze is averted and Felix isn't sure if he feels relieved at all. "I can always meet you here, right?"

"Well, it's a dream state after all, nothing here works logically, but we will always be here as a reminder that we still exist, that we all are waiting." Dylan gestures towards the kids, who are once again consumed in their own little realm, ignoring the two boys' existence.

Felix sighs. "It's nice," he says sadly through a forced smile, "to know that there is at least one person who is waiting for me."

Dylan falls silent for a while but then dares to speak up again, his voice more confident this time. "Do you see the houses in the distance?" Felix watches as the cottages in the distance light up one by one, resembling fireflies. "Everyone there is waiting for you to come back, some passed away waiting for you to knock on their doors again, some are scarred so deeply that they forbid their own kids to go into this forest, and some went on living their lives, but the existence of yours stays somewhere in their minds. Not only me, your parents, my parents, our friends and neighbours, countless people are waiting for you to come back. Never forget that."

And the way Dylan speaks so confidently, so truthfully, brings tears to his eyes because he wants to remember every person he has named, he wants to remember his past, every small and meaningless memory, he wants to recollect them all. "Dylan, I don't know, I don't know what kind of person you knew me as but I, I'm changing, and I know that I'm changing but I don't think for the better..." He clears his throat as the tears that flood his throat make it harder for him to speak "So please bear with me when we meet, alright?" And Dylan smiles so sweetly, so gently that it makes the tears finally pour down his cheeks, and he drops his face into his hands, trying to hide his horrendous state.

But then he feels fingers lightly brush through his hair and a soft weight rest on his ear, and when he looks up he sees Dylan putting a small, pretty daisy behind his ear. "I will never give up on you, and you know that."

"Do you promise?" Felix croaks as he waits for any uncertainty to wash over Dylan. But it never does. He just beams wider and gently intertwines their fingers.

"I promise."

III

On a warm summer night, on a bronze soft sky, the moon shines over the hill, pouring out gentle moonbeams, making nature fairer, flooding the forest and field with magical light. The trees, the vines, the flowers are astir with tender serenity as Genji and Ayumu lie on the rough bark and leathered leaves, gazing at the stars that have become old and dim, glimmering above Genji's front yard.

Ayumu, feeling weary and drowsy after playing the whole day, lets his eyes rest and savours the feeling of the warm and shadowy breeze coming from the deep, gloomy forest and the smell of the trees, but then a gentle nudge startles his senses, waking him up from his short nap, and he frowns but forces his eyes open, only to see Genji pointing his finger at something up in the sky. Following the direction, he catches sight of something gold-bronze, fluttering and wriggling down the sky. It's summer now, the season of fireflies, and he sees them, dancing orbs of light, stirring and glowing brightly, being effortlessly beautiful.

Charmed by their graceful glory, Ayumu desires to catch them one by one to keep his own little pieces of stardust at home, but he knows they shine brightest when they're in the wild, so instead he makes a wish on the fireflies striving to outshine the stars above on this warm, dark summer night.

"Want to hear a story?" Genji whispers excitedly yet tiredly, and Ayumu just murmurs groggily in response. "Do you know how fireflies were born?"

Ayumu rolls onto his side, now gazing bleary-eyed at Genji, who is blinking lazily. He nods his head softly and Genji's own dozy eyes light up. "My mom told me that once upon a time there were two sisters living with their dad." He yawns, cutting his sentence short, but after shaking the sleepiness away he goes on. "One day their dad didn't come back so the older sister went to find him in the forest and her younger sister followed her."

"I would too," Ayumu interrupts absurdly, and after shifting about for a while, he finally finds a more comfortable position next to Genji. He closes his eyes again as Genji's voice lulls him into dreamland.

Genji huffs exasperatedly and clears his throat before opening his mouth once more. "But it was very dark and the younger sister got lost." Ayumu frowns, listening more closely now. "So she started praying that God would give her light to find her sister."

Genji looks up, pouting as he tries to remember the story, and Ayumu whines softly and pinches him on his arm, making him yelp. "And then?" he complains impatiently.

"I think what happened is the next morning others found her in the lake but there were shining orbs around her! And this is how fireflies were born!" He finishes enthusiastically, waving his arms in the air as if to explain better.

But Ayumu just stares at him unimpressed. "So what happened to her then? Did she find her sister?"

Genji scrunches his nose and looks up at the dark sky once more, taking in the sight of glimmering orbs that shine in the night.

"I don't know, I guess the fireflies are still searching for her," he whispers, stretching his arm into the sky as if trying to catch one of them.

Ayumu follows his idle gaze up towards the fireflies, but now with a sour, bittersweet feeling forming inside him, and with a sigh he lets his weight drop onto Genji's shoulder. Genji puffs in pain but does nothing to get away from his grasp. And so they go back to their original state, lying on the grass and gazing aimlessly at the dark, navy sky.

"I hope she'll find her soon," Ayumu whispers and lays his head comfortably on Genji's arm as Genji instinctively wraps his lanky limbs around him. Feeling ever so content and safe in a warm embrace, Ayumu's eyes flutter shut once more and he doesn't even register when his mum calls out his name from the distance.

Dylan watches the raindrops slide down the window as his body bounces, hitting his head lightly on the glass. He sighs as he closes his eyes, unable to concentrate on the music playing in his earphones.

He sits quietly on the bus, watching the world move at an unstoppable speed, but it's not easy to follow the world unfolding before him as he relives the conversation from before.

"I just miss my son," his mum croaks through a broken voice, squeezing Dylan's heart till it shatters.

"I'm sorry, I…" he groans, rubbing his temples in torment as he listens to his mom's uneven breathing through the end of the phone.

"I just want to see you in person, Dylan, it's been years," she whispers, unable to tone down her sniffles. "Can't you come this one year? It's been fifteen years Dylan, no one is blaming you…"

"I can't mom! I, I just can't." Eventually Dylan's voice breaks.

Now the Eguchis' house is empty, with a missing soul inside, he doesn't have the heart to go back. He couldn't bear to sit and gaze at the empty room from his window, foolishly waiting for the light to turn on in Ayumu's room and his head to pop out into the night, just like the good old times when, on sleepless nights, Ayumu would talk to him about nothing, with his eyes reflecting the stars above, shining brighter than any of them.

Besides, Dylan is a coward by nature; he's not courageous enough to face Mizuki either.

"I'm sorry mom but I can't come back," he whispers, rubbing his face furiously as he feels the dread crawling back towards him.

He inhales, squeezing his eyes shut. He can feel a headache coming on, and as he lightly bumps his head on the window, suddenly everything feels too much. Once again he feels caged in the prison of his mind.

He misses his mom too, a lot, he misses her to death, but how can he go back when he knows meeting with Mizuki will be unavoidable? How can he face the woman he has taken everything from? The woman he made stand in the rain in front of the police station every day with that goddamn sign, "Please help me find my son", with a picture of Ayumu grinning like the happy soul he was. He doesn't know if her hatred towards him has died down over years or if she still blames him, or if she will also lie to his face and tell him that it wasn't his fault, that it was just an accident that a kid couldn't prevent.

He hopes she will never forgive him because he is no place to be forgiven.

Grief is an odd concept. Some days it seems to have been departed from you, and you don't notice it lurking behind you, following your every step until one forgotten memory makes you sink into the ocean of truth. If you're lucky, you manage to swim successfully to shore, but sometimes you drown in the depths of the darkest corners of your mind as you feel your lungs fill with regrets and guilt.

Dylan senses that today is one of the latter, but he knows that the next day he will wake up again, maybe with a tear-stained face, but he still will open his eyes, and as a fresh tear or two falls out from his sore eyes, he will force himself to stand up, get washed, dress and continue floating through the streets like a lost ghost, trapped between worlds.

But until then all he can do is wait and surrender; the more he fights the deeper the trap will shove its daggers into his flesh. The pain will only get stronger. And so, he continues to breathe as a reminder that he's still alive, that he still exists and that maybe the ghost someday will find its home again.

"Should we do a DNA test just to be sure?" Her voice is gentle but filled with tentativeness.

The story is simple: they both know the horrible truth that the only thing shared between Felix and the woman sitting in front of him is the pain of helplessness.

"I don't think I'm the one you're searching for," Felix mutters barely above a whisper, his voice strained, and he hangs his head low, not daring to look up from the floor and watch the disappointment wash over her face. "I don't think I'm your son."

She's such a lovely woman, he thinks, she doesn't deserve to go through this heartache alone.

If only they could help each other out somehow. If only this was the happy ending he has been waiting, yearning for his whole life.

But life, it seems, delights in watching him die. It is never satisfied, it demands more slaughter, more tears and blood.

Felix wants to cry so bad, and his tortured lip is close to being slashed in two as his teeth continuously gnash on the flesh to somehow stop tears from flowing, because he knows that if he lets his emotions pour, he won't be able to stop. He squeezes his eyes for a moment, savouring the feeling of wetness in his sore eyes, and tries to calm himself down with a shaky intake of breaths.

The moment he steps outside, he rushes towards a nearby alley, towards any secluded area, safe from judging eyes. His head is spinning, blurring the entire world and making his head throb in indescribable pain, fogging his mind and senses.

He throws his head down and gags on saliva alone, there being nothing else to eject from his empty stomach. He coughs, choking on his dry throat and struggling to breathe, and after a few more pathetic retches he lets his body slide down onto the ground.

His chest heaves with each intake of breath; he wheezes and bumps the back of his head on the concrete wall.

For a long while he just stares blankly into space, watching as his whole life spiral out of control, but he doesn't pay much attention to the way his heart howls in pain—his life has crumbled many times before and as always, he will collect the broken pieces and craft his life from the scratch once more. But the heartache is persistent. His shoulders begin to shake, and his body trembles as the tears crashing against his ribcage demand to be freed, and all it takes is one breath for the walls built inside him to collapse. His whole body trembles with each silent sob as he squeezes his eyes and allows the tears to flow.

Truth be told, Felix is tired, *so tired* of every day crawling back to empty home defeated by fate, with no one there to console him. He longs for it, each and every shattered piece of his heart is starving for love. For who is Felix? He is a nobody. A boy with no parents and no real name. Nothing about his life feels raw and valid. With his head buried in knees, he continues to wail silently. The need to call out to his mum is suffocating—no matter how many times he cried for her, she never came, never held her crying kid in her arms. She left him to sob alone.

Do his parents even want him to be found?

He has wondered about it a lot, spent many sleepless nights thinking about it. Even if they hate him, spit on his face and beat him to death, he needs to know. He's so tired of searching and finding nothing at the end. He needs to find closure, needs to finally be able to close this torn book of his life, filled with pages covered in nothing but blood and tears.

He rubs his palms painfully against his sore eyes, just to feel something, just to remind himself that this is the life that was gifted to him. Gazing blankly at the horizon he watches the lights swirl in pink and orange, fading into blue and purple as his body sways against the wall. He feels nothing, thinks about nothing, his mind is a blank sheet of paper waiting to be filled with more words of despair.

He stays in the empty alley for a while longer, the fear of stepping inside the soulless house bringing dread to his tired soul.

He closes his eyes and wonders about his past—what kind of person was he? What was his name? How old is he? What did he dream about as a kid? He wants to know it all, wants all of his stolen memories back, and he will go through the flames of hell to return them.

But all of a sudden, he hears something—a weak, scared meowing coming from the far end of the alley. He rubs his swollen eyes, trying to see through his bleary vision, and with shaky legs he lifts his body up from the wall and follows the desperate screeches.

What he finds is a box hidden under some rubbish. "Please take care of me" it reads, and when he peeks inside he sees a kitten, small, vulnerable, its tiny body shaking with cold, its fur drenched in mud.

"They left you too?" Felix asks through a bitter, forced smile as he leans in closer, scaring the poor animal. "They didn't want to take care of you. How selfish of them." He gently lifts the box, observing the adorable kitten.

He knows it's a bad idea; he knows he can't bring a cat to the dorm, but he doesn't care. It's as if he wants to prove to his parents that he can take care of and love something.

"Don't worry, I'm going to take good care of you," he smiles as the kitten gazes at him, its round green eyes watching him curiously. "I'll be your family."

Dylan stumbles up the stairs, his limbs weighing him down, too heavy to move. The thought of his bed waiting for him is strangely alluring.

"I'm going to feed you so well." He hears the familiar high-pitched voice, making him stop in his tracks. "What should I feed you, tuna maybe?" The question is followed by a faint meow. "Aren't you adorable?" He hears Felix coo, giggle softly, and before long the same boy shows up in his vision, holding what looks like a dirty box. Felix doesn't notice him at first, too enticed by whatever is inside the box.

"Is it a cat?" Dylan can't help but exclaim and rush towards Felix, startling him in the process.

"Oh my god, it's so cute!" he yells overly enthusiastically as Felix eyes him in surprise, taken aback by the sudden outburst. "Can I hold it?" Dylan looks at him, his eyes wide, twinkling with happiness, making Felix grimace.

"Stop screaming! The landlord can't know!" he hisses, looking around, making sure all is clear before again glaring at the boy, who just beams apologetically. Felix sighs but nods regardless, handing him the box as the kitty watches both of them curiously.

"Oh my god!" Dylan whisper-yells, bouncing about like an overjoyed kid, and Felix can only stand there with folded arms and watch. "I'm going to die, it's so fucking cute!" And the way he says it sounds just a bit too aggressive, threatening even.

To their dismay, they hear the sound of short steps coming down the stairs. They share equally panicked looks for a second before they bolt, and without thinking ahead Felix throws himself and Dylan inside his room.

They stay attached to the door for a while, their chests heaving with each breath as they calm the adrenaline pumping through their veins. With an elongated sigh Felix opens his eyes, immediately checking the kitten, which thankfully is sitting inside its box safe and unharmed, looking at him more confused than scared.

"So..." Dylan clears his throat, making his presence known, and Felix eyes him, only now realizing that he has let Dylan inside.

Felix's eyes are comically wide as he looks around the room, which is in its natural state—chaotic and filthy. "Where should I put it?" he asks casually as he clings onto the box for dear life.

Felix doesn't answer. He observes the papers scattered around, the empty boxes of food thrown in every corner of the room, the dirty clothes on the floor, and as his face pinches in disgust he hears a soft chuckle coming from the side.

"I mean, we are men living alone so don't worry about it." He glances at Dylan, who is doing a terrible job of being subtle while checking out his room.

Felix sighs, too tired to argue. "Put it on the table." This itself is a hard task, however, because said table is filled with unfinished food, but Dylan being as polite as ever just nods, carefully moving the dishes out of the way and placing the box.

As he does so he notices a paper with a printed picture of a kid, and he frowns softly. When his eyes read the words "missing child" above, he feels his blood go cold and his heart skip a beat or two before pounding at full speed. He hears nothing but his frantic heartbeat thudding inside his skull as images of posters of Ayumu, plastered everywhere his eyes reach, come rushing into his brain.

This doesn't go unnoticed by Felix, who moves swiftly into his way, covering the papers with his body, full of shame. He bites down on his lip as he tries to gather up all the papers, feeling his blood boil in mortification.

They stand there like this for a while, both lost in their worries before a displeased meow snaps them out of their thoughts. They stare at each other for a moment, not comprehending what has occurred before Dylan finally soothes his nerves down and, clearing his throat, dares to speak.

"I think the kitten is hungry," he says, looking at anything but Felix. For a moment Felix doesn't respond, but then he jumps, finally registering Dylan's words, and rushes towards the box. He gazes at the cat, his fingers gently patting its soft fur, and with a sigh he murmurs, "I have milk."

"No!" yells Dylan suddenly, making Felix flinch as he glances at the now embarrassed boy with wide surprised eyes. "I mean, milk is bad for cats, they can't digest it," Dylan says timidly, embarrassed at having screamed.

Felix's brow rises, he's genuinely surprised but says nothing and nods. "I have a can of tuna?" He tries again, unsure, waiting for Dylan's approval.

"Do you have bread? You can soften it in water, that will be more suitable." Felix gazes at him in confusion before nodding again, and when Dylan's lips stretch into a bright grin, Felix ignores the uncomfortable tug on his heartstrings, trying to tell him something.

When he doesn't move from his place, Dylan raises his eyebrows and tilts his head to the side, taking in the uncertain state of the boy, and he murmurs carefully, "Or...I could do that?"

The moment Dylan puts down the bowl the kitten sprints towards it, munching on the food, and he can only watch it with a fond smile.

After giving the kitten one last gentle pat, Dylan looks at Felix, not speaking for a moment, his black eyes glistening with unsaid words. "Anyways, I should probably get going, sorry for coming in uninvited," he says, his lips flickering into a faint smile that doesn't quite reach Felix's eyes.

He turns around painfully slowly, an invisible thread dragging him back, begging him to stay. Felix flinches, his arm hangs in the air, almost touching Dylan, and he bites his lip as a feeling of uncertainty fills him. His body is pushing him towards Dylan, swatting away the balance from his legs just to force a step out of him.

Maybe tomorrow morning he will blame it on how terribly and utterly lonely he feels at this moment, how terrified he is to be left alone on yet another dark night, and so before he can stop himself he yelps weakly, "Do you want a cup of tea?" He grimaces at his poor attempt at an invitation and he can only hope that Dylan won't be able to see his true intentions through his bloodshot eyes.

Dylan whips around, standing there wordlessly, blinking at him with his perplexed, glimmering eyes. Felix fidgets nervously, terrified that he has probably made a fool of himself and Dylan will laugh in his face, mocking him for even daring to think that he wanted to stay in Felix's presence, but then Dylan's face breaks into a huge, sincere beam, "Sure! Why not?" he chirps enthusiastically, not even trying to hide his excitement.

"So what are you going to name her?" Dylan asks as he blows on his hot tea. He takes the first sip, still gazing at Felix.

"I haven't thought about it yet," Felix answers truthfully, looking down at his feet, now deep in thought.

"What about Lucky?" Felix peeks at Dylan in confusion, his brows knitted and a small pout forming on his lips. "You know, because of your name? Like it would match and stuff, I mean that would be cute?" Dylan rambles, feeling embarrassed all of a sudden, and the blush only darkens on his cheeks as Felix continues to stare at him weirdly.

"I guess Lucky will do then," he murmurs, his fingers playing through Lucky's soft fur as the cat sleeps contently on his lap.

"How come you know so much about cats anyways?" he asks, more to himself, accidentally voicing his thoughts out loud.

"I took care of a stray cat when I was a kid," answers Dylan, and Felix notices him smile fondly at the memory so he nods with understanding.

"What was its name?" Felix lifts his face up, looking genuinely interested.

Dylan flinches, an uncomfortable feeling knotting inside him as he bites down on his bottom lip, chewing in comfort. "Dream, her name was Dream," he whispers, almost inaudibly, and although Felix may be timid around him he has the eyes of a hawk, immediately sensing the heavy aura creeping into the room. He frowns at the distress of the raven-haired boy sitting before him.

Dylan raises his eyes from the floor only to look down at his watch. The knitted brows, shaky eyes and clasped lips—all of his body language screams nervousness and agitation and Felix doesn't know what he's done wrong.

"Look at the time, I probably should get going," Dylan declares, his voice uneven, and when he smiles at Felix it looks painfully forced. "Thanks for the tea." His smile is lopsided, nothing like his usual genuine, bright one, and as he slowly walks towards the door he turns one last time only to find Felix already staring at him. "See you next time?" he asks uncertainly—it almost sounds like a plea—but Felix doesn't respond, he just averts his gaze, his eyes concentrating on the pet on his lap instead, reverting to his normal demeanour, so Dylan shakes his head and walks outside, pondering the meaning behind Felix's actions. After he closes the door behind him, he rests his head against the wall by the door and a heavy, tired sigh leaves his lips.

Dylan stands in front of the mirror, eyes fixated on his reflection, watching his every move as he gently takes a finger to his lips and stretches the skin upwards, forcing himself to smile. He waits, thinking that if he keeps looking, maybe he will learn to smile again. He glances quickly at his phone lying on the floor and he knows he can call Sophia, or even his mum. He knows they will understand, they will listen to his heart, even when he stumbles over his words, but he's enough of a burden as it is.

For a heartbeat Dylan's eyes linger on the bottle of pills that he has thrown in the bin. He feels his mind rot, consumed by the familiar yearning to self-destruct into oblivion. Then he shakes his head and with a groan he slides down on the floor, staring blankly into space as a hurricane of thoughts take hold of him.

How weak of him to be still haunted by memories that linger like a tender curse. He hates that his eyes have never dried from the tears that pour like poison even after fifteen years. But what is grief if not a good old friend—familiar but unpredictable at the same time.

At first, Dylan tried to hide himself away from the grief as it brought nothing but agony to his wretched soul, but over time he learned to welcome it as his only loyal companion in life. For what is grief if not desperate hunger to love? To keep loving the memory of someone, someone who is long gone? And all the love you beg to give overflows your broken heart before pouring out from each unhealed wound.

And Dylan foolishly refuses to let go, he chooses to stay hostage in the forest of their memories.

You make me happy when skies are grey

As Felix blinks he recognizes the familiar touch of the beams of sunlight, stinging his skin softly, colouring his cheeks in deep rose. He becomes aware of the unidentifiable aromas of wood, moisture-laden air, soggy grass and wildflowers. He stretches his arms as he becomes one with the field, and after staying in that position for a few more seconds he finally forces himself to sit up and look around the empty forest in a search of the velvety sound of the melody.

He sees two kids leaning against the age-old oak, their backs turned to him, but he quickly recognizes them. Genji is the one holding the guitar. It is too big for his little body but he continues to sing to the younger one, who has placed his head on his shoulder.

Please don't take my sunshine away

To Felix's utter bewilderment the kid turns his face back to him as he sings the last sentence, his eyes begging, pleading for something Felix has no way of knowing.

He notices his black eyes glisten, filling up with unshed tears.

"Please don't leave me again," he whispers with a strained, broken voice which quickly chokes down a dry sob, and Felix is left wondering the meaning behind his plea, but he is not given enough time to think because to his astonishment his young self turns his face towards him and scowls at him furiously.

Felix frowns as he stares at the kid, but suddenly a drop of wetness makes his eyes flutter. When he looks up his vision becomes bleary as rain starts to pour down on the ground.

Darkness falls, turning him blind as everything goes black outside, leaving no grey, no white—not a single ray of light to find in the sky above, which was baby blue only a moment before. Hesitatingly, Felix closes his eyes, and he prays that when he opens them everything will turn back to normal, but when he blinks he sees nothing but a black sky covering the cloudy night, no stars, no moon.

The air hangs heavy, without even a slight breeze. The birds have fallen asleep on the high wires—no sound can be heard in the meadow. It is as if life has been momentarily put on hold, as if nature is holding its breath. Chaos rises inside Felix. Doubts and losses revisit him and fear rises in his belly. As the memories start to close in, terror surrounds him and slowly his final scrap of courage dies, losing the fight against despair.

He turns his head in search of the children, in search of answers, but they are long gone, vanished in thin air, leaving Felix lost in the cool, dark night and the icy rain that chills him to his very marrow.

He looks around for help but there is no clear view for miles as the fog quietly embraces nature in a hug. He can only pray that the dawn will arise soon but until then he has to make it through the night.

Suddenly a faint shimmer breaks through the blanket of darkness, shining ever so slightly but enough to be seen. Felix peers up at it, trying to get a better view, and soon he notices that it's a single lonely firefly marching towards him.

The firefly flutters weakly, its light fading, flickering away with each bat of its wings, but somehow it manages to land gently right on his palm. He stares at the fly, his eyes reflecting its frail shimmer, making them glimmer in the dusk, but then it suddenly turns and feels swiftly into the woods, shining brightly enough to illuminate the mighty trees around it.

Felix doesn't think twice as he strides into the blackness—the light guides him more surely than the light of midday towards the place where *he* is waiting for him. Moving the dry branches out of his way he comes face to face with a sight he surely didn't see coming, freezing him in place.

A door, a simple wooden door has been purposefully placed in the centre of the lifeless field.

Felix, confused, walks with timid steps towards the wooden frame. He circles around it but finds nothing behind it, and yet there it stands. The firefly lands gracefully on the handle, twinkling and flickering, gesturing to him. He inhales shakily as a feeling of dread finds its way inside him and he senses that whatever awaits him behind the door, it's unlikely to be pleasant.

With trembling fingers, he grips the handle but then lets a few seconds pass as he squeezes his eyes shut and listens to his raging heartbeat hammering inside his head. Then, inhaling heavily, he opens the door and allows the darkness to consume him whole.

At first, it's nothing but a void of nothingness. He looks around blindly in the hope of seeing something, anything. Through the blackness surrounding him he spots the firefly in the distance, still glimmering faintly, giving him a sense of comfort. Then he catches his breath as fireflies start to appear from every corner, twinkling like stars in the night sky so that little by little, small details of his whereabouts come into his vision.

He blinks in confusion as he finds himself in an empty room. He doesn't know this place. He knows he should remember the room but no memories come rushing towards him, so he lets himself wander around in the hope that he will find something that will help him to remember.

The house seems old, built on ancient love and happiness. He brushes the dust from an old portrait hanging on the wall. Yes, it's a picture of him, it's the same face, but why is he scowling down at him with such a look of wrath?

His palm lingers where the walls are finger-marked with colourful dried paint. The fingertips are much smaller, easily hidden beneath the pads of his fingers. The whole wall is covered with ruined, wrinkled papers scrawled with pencil marks. He must have treasured them for years. The ugly, childlike doodles are drawings of him and Genji and he can only guess that the others must be scribbles of their families.

In the very corner of the wall, he sees a calendar hanging down. He reads 2000 written in big numbers, and underneath it he reads May, where four days have already been crossed out in red marker.

This old house keeps brief sense of joy alive. His innocent tears soaked in every crook and corner of this house. *His* old house keeps the memories unharmed. Even with no memories of the home, he understands that once he was living his life at fullest in this house.

Suddenly a sweet aroma wafts up into the air—the familiar smell of homemade biscuits made with love and care, awakening Felix from his thoughts. When he looks around in a search of the scent he sees a short hallway he hasn't noticed before, so he timidly walks towards the next room, the wooden floor cracking beneath his feet with each step he makes, making him even more anxious.

He peeks inside the room and quickly realizes that it's supposed to be a kitchen—worn and old just like the house, but still cosy, filled with familiarity and warmth. He notices two women sitting in front of the table, drinking tea in silence. A dim, weak lamp placed on the table is the only thing there to illuminate the room, making it hard for Felix to make out their faces.

"It's getting late, maybe we should check up on them?" one of them says, gently placing the cup on the table and looking up worriedly.

"I'm sure they're fine, the older kids always take care of the little monsters," her companion chuckles, gently patting the concerned one on her shoulder.

"But it's already past eight, they're never late, you know that."

"Oh come on, you know my Ayumu always listens to Genji and Genji would never do anything reckless," she says in a reassuring voice and pours more tea into her cup. "Stop worrying. Your wrinkles are showing!"

The woman doesn't seem convinced but she doesn't say anything for a moment, just gazing blankly out of the window where the darkness has fallen outside. Then she sighs heavily and leans further back on the chair.

"Even so," she says. "It's getting late. Let's go find them, I've got a bad feeling about it."

"If they don't show up in ten minutes then let's go and find them. Why are you so antsy anyway? They always come home around this time."

But when she just exhales heavily in response, the woman places her cup on the table with a loud thud and says, "Okay, let me finish the tea and then we can go."

Finally, the lady smiles but it doesn't bring ease to Felix's heart. Instead he feels a growing sense of dread. He looks worriedly at the clock that says fifteen minutes to nine, but as soon as the minute hand moves, the clock suddenly stops working.

He frowns as the uncomfortable feeling inside him gets stronger, heavier, and when he looks at the women sitting in front of him they have also frozen in time, not moving even slightly, not even breathing. He feels his heartbeat jump and quicken, and suddenly the clock starts to run fast, the hands flying round so quickly that his eyes can't even follow. The rapid ticking rings in his ears, throbbing in his head as he gazes at the clock with wide eyes and feels sweat gather in the corners of his temples.

And then, for some reason, it stops exactly at midnight. Too dumbfounded by the bizarre encounter to move, he finds himself frozen in place, gawking at the wall where the clock has started to work normally again. Before he can comprehend what has happened a sudden, white light flashes, blinding him momentarily, stinging his eyes and making them squeeze shut in pain.

When he blinks his eyes open he finds himself in the same place, but it feels different. He can't breathe, the smell is horrible, and nor he can see—once again he finds himself in total darkness.

The old house now stands alone and abandoned, destroyed by years of devastating heartache and grief. The roof is open to the sky, letting cold droplets of rain drip onto his skin. The rooms that once echoed with lively laughter now lay silent. Overgrown mould and moss turned the house into the graveyard of his memories.

The core of house remains the same but this is not where he used to live—his house was beautiful, full of joy and love.

He can feel dread swell in his lungs as he observes the old, torn house he used to call his own, but then a familiar voice awakens his senses. "Did you finally come back?" He looks up and finds Dylan sitting on the table in front of him, carelessly swinging his legs back and forth.

"What is going on?" Felix croaks in a mixture of yelling and desperate crying, but Dylan doesn't seem affected, he just gazes at him wordlessly.

"You still don't understand, don't you?" He tilts his head to the side, jumps down from the table, and moves unhurriedly towards him. "You told me to wait, so I've waited. You told me to be strong, so I did." He speaks sternly, coldly even, but then he sits on the floor next to him. "I did everything you asked me to…" Dylan's eyes drop down onto Felix's hand, which is still balled tightly into a fist, and with a gentle touch he starts to play with Felix's fingers, easing the tension away. "But we don't have much time left," he murmurs, still aimlessly tracing shapes on Felix's skin with his delicate fingers.

"What, what's that supposed to mean?" Felix mutters when he finally forces his eyes off their intertwined hands.

Dylan's fingers freeze for a moment before he sighs and unclasps their hands, leaving Felix feeling cold once more from lack of affection.

"I'm, I'm not strong Felix…," he says breathily, his voice wavering, "I'm weak and I'm a coward."

Felix shuffles uncomfortably on his seat and angles his head to get a better view of Dylan and try to read the unreadable expression he's wearing.

"But you promised me, don't…" His voice breaks as the lump grows in his throat, making it hard to breathe. "Don't you break your promise too." He is almost inaudible now, almost as if he's afraid to voice his thoughts.

"Only if I can be with you again. But it's hard… It's so hard without you," Dylan murmurs sorrowfully, his eyes glimmer with tears and he quickly wipes them away before they can fall and take him down with them. "It's up to you now how this story ends." Only then does he dare to look at the younger boy with his glassy, grief-stricken eyes that hold so many untold stories.

"Why me?" Felix utters throatily, sinking deeper into the floor as he gazes up at the young man with vexed eyes. "I can't Dylan, it's hard for me to, to…" His voice wavers at the end and he gulps, his throat dry.

"Because you have to make a choice." Dylan looks down at the floor again, playing with his fingers nervously as he chews on his bottom lip. "Do you want me to stay?" he murmurs almost in a whisper, his voice so weak and small that his question almost goes unnoticed by Felix. Felix winces, his mouth so dry that he has lost the ability to speak, and he looks at Dylan, completely speechless. Dylan lifts his gaze back up to him again, his eyes hopeful yet mournful.

"I want you to stay."

Felix sighs breathlessly.

"I want you to stay so bad."

He clings to Dylan's hand in a search of some familiarity amongst the chaos that they've created. Dylan falls naturally into his arms, like the moon chasing the sun, as he wraps his arms around Felix so tightly that it's almost painful, desperately trying to cherish the brief moment of eclipse.

"I wish I learned how to stop myself from missing you," Dylan wails, his hands roaming desperately over Felix's body, trying to bring him closer than is physically possible—he wants to reach into his soul to feel complete again. "I wish I could get rid of the guilt that kills me slowly." And he shakes violently, shattering in Felix's arms. "I wish for so much that I end up wishing for nothing."

But Felix just shushes him, rubbing his shoulders gently to help him cough out the words he has choking on for so long.

"Let's end this meaningless war of pain, okay?" Felix says, feeling his fingertips sting as he wipes the hot tears from Dylan's eyes. "I think we stayed on the battlefield for too long..." He stops to look out of the window and notices the sun rising up from the mountains, washing away the dark sorrow surrounding them. "I think it's time to go home now."

Dylan gazes at him for a heartbeat, blinking the tears away before he lunges into his arms once more and feels Felix's welcome arms wrap themselves around him. Felix rests his chin softly on Dylan's head and watches the stars fade away in the violet sky with crimson clouds. It's oddly calming to watch the sun reach the skies, and he feels light-hearted as he closes his eyes, treasuring every sound of quiet Dylan's heartbeat. He doesn't even feel sad when the weight from his arms is suddenly lifted as he watches him fade away in the rays of sunlight.

IV

"My dear child," she speaks softly as she leans closer towards him, taking in every inch of him with her cold, blue, dead eyes that are always shaking with unexplainable disquiet. "How are you feeling?" Her tone is calm and sincere but her voice is trembling with hidden trepidation. "Do you feel any pain?"

He shakes his head daintily, even though the clothing that is too small for him scratches against his skin and blocks the air from his lungs. The pain in his bones hurts even more...

Her grin widens, stretching unnaturally across her wrinkled skin, and he feels the icy touch of her fingers as they glide across his bruised cheek. "That's good, I will take your pain away," she says and grabs him painfully by his arm, tugging him closer to her chest and leaving him breathless. "You won't feel the pain anymore, mommy will take care of you *this time.*"

She gently massages his skull, which is constantly throbbing with an insufferable headache. He feels cold fingers tap against his lips, jolting him in surprise, but he quickly recognizes the familiar bitter aftertaste of the pills. With no protest, he opens his mouth willingly, letting the tablet melt onto his tongue. Even so, he can't help but grimace at the bitterness of the medicine—he is not yet used to the burning sensation it leaves in his throat—but when he feels a slight nudge on his shoulder, he forces himself to swallow the pill.

And with that, a lulling sensation of dizziness takes over his mind, forcing his heavy eyes to flutter shut. And even in the pitch-black room, he can see her smiling, and the thought of making her proud makes it easier for him to relax and allow his eyes to close completely.

He hears the light sound of footsteps so he peeks through half-closed eyes and sees her lingering in front of the door, just looking at him. The light shining from the corridor envelops her in shadow, making it hard to see her.

"I'll be back soon, *Theodore,*" she assures him as she slowly closes the door whilst still staring at him, and so he nods to himself and allows his weary body to drift off to dreamland.

Only she never came back…

Silence embraces Felix as slowly but surely his brain shows signs of life, and with a groan he presses his body against the blankets. After letting his sore eyes rest for a minute longer, he arises from his empty bed in the morning, alone.

The soulless house creaks awake and slowly the sounds of reality start to register in his hazy mind. He forces himself to get out of bed, just like he does every morning, to face the same things over and over again.

"At least I have you now," he whispers as he pats the kitten gently, careful not to disturb its sleeping form in the corner of his bed, still wary of him.

Humming, he flits around his soulless apartment as he performs his banal routine. His light crooning is the only thing to break the silence of his four walls.

He munches on a toast as he adjusts his shirt in the mirror, carefully tucking it into his trousers without wrinkling the fabric and puts jacket on. He turns his body around, evaluating his appearance for a minute before groaning and picking up his backpack off the floor.

"I'm going," he shouts into the empty room, and when he gets the usual soundless response, he exits his cold apartment.

Outside he catches Dylan and his friend, Sophia, laughing about something. He stays standing there for a moment, gazing at the male through knitted brows and mulling over his next step. Dylan looks happy as he giggles at something his friend has said, and Felix wonders if he should interrupt the cheerful atmosphere, but instead he winces and takes a step back as the voices in the back of his head plead with him to run, to get away from the implicit threat. Shaking his head, he hurries towards the bus stop. In the end, Dylan is a stranger to him and he prefers to keep it that way—he's not worth getting heartbroken over.

Felix decided long ago that he will live in comfortable solitary, never again he will let someone waste his trust. He has learned his lesson, there is always someone waiting for the best moment to stab him from the back, and often enough it's the person you least expect it to be.

He prefers to believe humans are inherently evil until someone convinces him otherwise. It's safer that way—if he expects nothing but the worst from everyone, he's never sad or disappointed.

On the bus, he places his head against the window and watches as the world starts to spin, an acoustic melody accompanying him in the background.

He scrolls through his phone, searching for any possible missing person's files and checking the news just in case anyone has come up with any helpful information. He doesn't know what else he can do—the finish line has never seemed so far away. Every time he thinks he's close to understanding it all, to solving the mystery of his doom, he is pushed back with more force each time.

He exhales heavily and drops his head back onto the seat, every inch of his body aching. He feels burnt-out and lethargic, and his brain thuds in relentless pain. Every so often he dozes off into a slumber, his eyes too heavy to stay open as the world, so full of life, unfolds through the glass.

"Morning Felix," Dylan exclaims when he catches sight of Felix walking with Nathan along the hallway. Felix momentarily freezes and glances at Dylan with uncertain, narrowed eyes, but Dylan's eyes just widen in expectation, twitching with anticipation to see what will happen next. He hopes, no, he wants Felix to let him get close to him, to let him pass through the barriers he has put in place for everyone else, but Felix just stands there, staring into Dylan's eyes, searching for something he himself doesn't know, while Nathan, still holding onto Felix's hand, looks up at the two of them, his curious gaze shifting from Dylan to Felix.

What lasts only a second feels like an eternity for Felix as thousands of thoughts overwhelm him.

To trust or not to trust?

A threat or a friend?

Danger or serendipity?

As the contradictory urges of his fight-or-flight response torment him, the wailing in his head grows louder, too loud to be ignored, and the voices beg him to escape, blurring the lines between actuality and unreality. He shakes his head, snapping himself out of the momentary haze, and with short, hasty steps walks away from the scene.

Something tugs on Dylan's heart, saddening him as he watches Felix hurry away. He hears a voice telling him that "*this isn't the way it's supposed to be."* But that's how it is—once more he's back to the familiar state of being one of many strangers around Felix.

Oddly enough, he catches the kid looking back at him as Felix drags him away. There is an unreadable expression in his round, clear eyes, as if he's hiding something beneath them, but when Dylan smiles at him he just averts his gaze back to Felix, looking up at him with an expression full of fondness and enthusiasm.

"Felix!"

In a blank state of mind, Felix lets his weightless body sway from side to side, the listlessness in his aching brain the only sensation keeping him conscious. His head bounces up and down, dropping harshly as he snoozes on and off.

"Felix!" The voice calling out for him sounds so distant, and as his eyes begin to slide closed and he feels himself losing touch with reality, it morphs into a muffled buzzing in his ears. His legs feel like giving up—they are shaking beneath the pressure of his tensed body, and as he squeezes his eyes shut, trying to soothe the stinging headache, he collapses against the wall in search of support.

"Felix!" The ear-splitting voice now comes ringing from right beside him, making him jolt in fear and almost sending him keeling over. When he finally manages to open his eyes halfway, he's met with an angry colleague of his.

"I've been calling you for ten minutes!" she says, but it takes a while before her words finally register. With a pained groan he shakes his head and rubs his temples.

"I'm sorry," Felix mumbles, slurring his words. "You were saying?"

"Take the food to table two, it's getting cold," she says, shoving the food tray into his hands, and it takes everything in Felix's might not to drop it right there and then. With shaky fingers and halting steps and an anxious heart, he shuffles towards the table, praying for his shift to be over. His eyes never leave the clock on the wall and the uneasy feeling spreads inside him, making his body shake even more violently.

Up in the grey sky one golden listless leaf travels through the air like a small, lonely firefly and guides Felix on his way as his footsteps ring through the frozen alleys where the naked trees accompany him whilst the crisping wind snaps sharply at their leaves. He shudders, sensing a shiver on his skin as frost forms on his face, and exhales a warming breath through his numb lips.

The moment he steps inside, though, he's hit by a wave of warmth enveloping him in a welcoming hug. He gently takes off his coat and wraps it around his arms, and as he walks, the faces looking down from the missing persons' posters follow him, watching his every move.

"Felix!" He hears the familiar voice and he's soon shadowed by the towering figure in front of him. William gives him a tender smile, his eyes sparkling with nostalgia, and Felix counts one or two new wrinkles on his face, only then becoming aware of how many years have passed since his last visit.

"What brings you here?" William asks as he carefully wraps his arm around Felix, guiding him inside. "We don't have any news. You know I would inform you immediately otherwise." He gestures to Felix to sit on the chair across from him and, carefully setting his fresh cup of coffee on the desk, he also flops down onto the seat.

Felix nods, eyes darting back to the hundreds of posters plastered all over the wall, so many unfamiliar eyes piercing through his skull.

"I'm not here for any missing kids' files," Felix mutters through the sandwich William has kindly offered, his eyes still focused on the posters. William leans back, arms crossed as he lets out a low hum, curious to hear Felix's explanation. His eyes linger on one particular poster of a child a second longer before he turns his attention back to the officer. "I have a few questions about, well, about *them*."

William breathes out heavily, melting even further into his seat. "We still haven't found any new clues," he informs Felix, his voice coming out quieter this time, filled with shame and unsaid apologies. Felix just nods, he wasn't expecting a different answer anyway.

"I know," he says quietly. "I just, there are a few things I can't understand and you're the one who knows the case best." He places the food down, now gazing at William with full attention. "Can you tell me what happened that day?"

"Well, it's been more than a decade since," William murmurs, blinking at the ceiling, trying to squeeze the memory out of his brain.

"I'm sure you remember more than I do," Felix responds sternly but it sounds more sad than strict.

William rubs his face before clapping his palm against his chin and dazing blankly into space.

After a long, stretched-out silence, Felix starts to shuffle on his chair, getting impatient from the lack of response from the detective, but William just groans softly before gazing at Felix with sad, shameful eyes.

"I'm just a useless old man now," he chuckles bitterly, and before Felix can muster a response he is already standing up from the chair and stretching his back, his bones cracking unpleasantly loudly. "Let me find the report for you and let's grab something to eat, shall we?"

"Is it...legal?" Felix asks, his brows perked up as he watches William walk away.

"I'm the head of the office; I can make exceptions here and there." He smiles faintly and tenderly ruffles Felix's hair, and with unhurried steps he disappears between the high shelves.

The Gauthiers
Name: Verlee Gauthier
Date of birth: 02/07/63
Occupation: Critical care medicine specialist

Felix's eyes linger on the official photo of the woman for a moment longer. His fingers start to tremble and his grip on the file tightens, crumpling the paper. Despite how many years have passed, he still shudders under the cold gaze of her piercing blue eyes, and he feels a cold sweat drench his skin and the familiar feeling of dread weigh down his lungs as images of those eyes flash in front of him, ogling him with the same unsettling sense of mania.

There was nothing sane about those blue eyes. They always quivered vigorously, with mortal terror beneath, like a feral, injured animal looking in the eyes of death. And even when her stare was fixated on him, her chilling eyes always looked past him, as if gazing through him into nothingness, at something that didn't exist and something that he wasn't. She never looked at him; her eyes never recognized him as a solid form. He doesn't know if she even perceived his existence or if he was just a façade of something she was trying to find beneath.

She's smiling in the photo, like she always did—her grin outstretched unnaturally wide like whenever she gripped his arm a bit too hard and pulled him so close to her chest that he found it difficult to breathe. She was always smiling, even when tears poured down from her crazy eyes onto her wrinkled, greyed skin. Felix is sure that this very smile will haunt him in his worst nightmares until his final breath. Shaking his head, he tries to discard the dire images from his vision and with a shaky sigh he flips to the next page.

Name: Damon Gauthier
Date of birth: 10/11/59
Occupation: Anaesthesiologist

He has no solid recollections of the man. He was...he was just there, lingering in the corners, behind her shoulder as he gazed at him with droopy eyes, heavy with shame and remorse. Like a puppet in a dollhouse, he was bound by the strings she held in her claws, governing his every step so as not to let the house of nightmares she had built fall down.

Below, there is a note pinned to the paper and jotted with messy, barely legible scribbles that have been clearly written in a rush. Felix's frown deepens, wrinkling his skin further as he tries to read through the smudged words.

As Felix goes through William's transcripts, he views the family in a way he has never had the chance to. He learns that they were an ordinary middle-class family, working at the same hospital, and from the brief interviews with neighbours he gathers that they were nothing but generous and friendly and that they were people of faith and regularly went to the local church. At first glance they looked like a normal, loving family, but Felix guesses it's true when they say that curtains were invented for a reason. You never know what hides beneath the vibrant walls until it's too late.

What particularly catches his attention is a circled sentence written in darker ink and bigger letters, standing out like a sore thumb.

Issues with relatives.

There is no explanation for the sudden shift of tone from the "perfect family." The sentence doesn't look like it's directed at the same family he was reading about a moment ago. With confused, wide eyes, he whips his face round towards William. "Did any of the family members speak about their disappearance?"

William takes a sip of his coffee, raises his eyebrows and waves his hand in a gesture to wait, and so Felix does so, shifting impatiently on his chair.

"Only after they disappeared," says William, wiping his lips with a napkin. "They lost touch with their family members and if it hadn't been for their neighbour, God knows how much longer it would have taken for the police to find out about their disappearance." With a sigh, he leans back onto his chair, his arms crossed. "We called them in for the investigation afterward, and also to..." He cuts himself off mid-sentence and sneaks a nervous, hesitant look at Felix.

"We had to discuss your custodianship," he whispers almost inaudibly, sounding out of breath.

They stare at each other for a spell before William's words finally register in Felix's ears, making him freeze momentarily and tighten his grip on the worn-out file. He knows that by law the first place he would normally have been taken into would be his parents' relatives, so logically they had to have declined the offer, because who is Felix to deserve a loving family anyway?

Uncertainty and confusion must be visible on his face because William hurriedly tries to clarify his doubts. "Because we couldn't find any documents about your adoption, they weren't legally required to take you in."

His suspicions are once again proven right. Felix was an unwanted child, undeserving of love, with no place to go, and even if he had, he doubts he would have been welcomed. He gulps, his throat suddenly dry, unable to form a sentence, and it takes him a moment or two before he's able to choke out words once more.

"In your notes, it's, you say that..." He shakes his head, trying to get hold of the hurricane of thoughts fogging his mind but his fingers just shake more viscously. Unable to stop shaking he wraps his cold fingers around his knee, pinching his scar in comfort. "It said that they had issues with their relatives," he manages to blurt out through gritted teeth, trying to keep his chin from wobbling.

William eyes him sadly, shame and pity visible behind his kind, honey-coloured irises, which only agitates Felix even more strongly. He doesn't need William's pity. He squeezes his scar so hard that he's afraid that the wound will be reopened and bleed once again.

"They didn't approve of their marriage, that's why they cut their ties," William starts to explain, keeping an eye on the boy, taking in his expression, and when he notes nothing but a spirit of inquiry allowing himself go on. "Verlee was infertile and Damon's family didn't want them to get married because she couldn't have kids, which put a strain between the families."

Felix gazes blankly for a long moment, corrupted by his thoughts, before he draws a heavy sigh and with a nod goes back to reading the file.

Theodore

He gasps a lungful of air, and suddenly everything feels unbearably heavy, an overwhelming feeling of dread burning up his insides and sizzling his nerves. The closer he looks at the photo of the tombstone, the more he feels like he's choking on his own blood flooding his lungs, blocking the air, leaving him breathless and drained.

May 5th 1999-May 11th 1999

He feels punch-drunk. His mind is hazy and his vision blurry as the letters on the grey stone meld with one other and the sounds of carefree laughter and a soft piano playing in the background buzz like white noise in his befogged ears, hushed by the ear-splitting ringing coming from somewhere in his mind and piercing through his skull. He blinks rapidly in the hope that by blinking his eyes the image will vanish out of his sight and become yet another dream. He hears her strident voice calling out for him by the name that doesn't belong to him. She has never left, her presence is forever imprinted on his rotten brain.

"Premature birth." William's thick voice rings in his ears, his explanation short and dry but enough to explode the tumult inside of him. Trying to show nonchalance on his expression, he just hums in response, masking his raw nerves, and continues to read with wide-open eyes, afraid to miss anything important.

Change in Verlee's behaviour.

Neighbours hear them fighting more often.

The handwriting gets messier and messier as the reports escalate to the climax, and Felix can't keep up with his own eyes as they flitter over the page at a rate of knots, skipping from one sentence to the next in a desperate race to the conclusion.

Breakdown at the hospital.

Suspended from work for one week.

He perks up, his eyes wide with confusion as his gaze lands on William once more in a search for answers, for clarifications to his never-ending questions.

"She tried to attack a pregnant woman but no complaint came forwards," William says tiredly, sounding out of breath, as if it's too exhausting to even think about this case. Like Felix he wants nothing but to finally close this chapter of theirs lives. Happy ending or not, everyone deserves closure.

After reading that the couple went as volunteer doctors to Japan, Felix notices a question smudged with black ink, barely visible in the corner of the page.

May-September???

Troubled, his eyebrows rise up in confusion. There is no explanation, no additional note, and as he continues to read attentively it seems like from there on, William has more questions than actual answers.

Where did the $100.000 go?

Felix quickly shuffles through the official report of the bank account, his fingers sliding over the documented data before landing on a cash payment that does indeed read one hundred thousand dollars, which is undeniably an extraordinary number in comparison with the previous tight-fisted pay cheques.

"A hundred thousand dollars," he mumbles under his breath, bewildered to see such a huge number.

"The withdrawal was made in cash, so it was impossible to track the payment receiver," William explains, interrupting his thoughts. He lifts his face and gazes at him with frowning brows, and as William watches the disappointment wash over the boy's face he quickly adds, "Also we're dealing with a different country with different laws, which made everything more complicated."

Felix nods even though he can't wrap his mind around the fact that a middle-class family could afford to let such a huge amount of cash go to waste. There must be a reason and he now understands why William's journal is filled with nothing but question marks.

Nothing in this story makes sense.

On 24th September 2000, they went back to Canada.

And if he thought that the story couldn't get more outré and outlandish, he is proven wrong as more question marks come into his vision, smudged by ink.

Change in behaviour.

Isolated from neighbours.

They stop going to church.

Leaving the house only at night.

It's baffling how the story of a seemingly normal family could turn so quickly into something sinister, something he would never wish on anyone.

But what really makes a breath hitch in his throat is the next sentence.

The next-door neighbour catches a glimpse of a child from her window.

No mentions of adoption.

Felix's fingers start to shake. He holds onto the papers for dear life in an attempt to ground himself, to not let his thoughts go haywire. He gulps, but the lump stays scraping against his throat, and with an uneven intake of breath he continues to read.

Illegal adoption? Trafficking? Kidnapping?

Slowly but surely, everyone started to notice the weird behaviour of the couple. Felix reads the interviews with their co-workers, neighbours who before had nothing but compliments for the pair but later can only describe them as "looking unreasonably anxious all the time", as if two totally different people had come back from Japan.

People who were previously outgoing and kind had completely isolated themselves from the world, only leaving the house at odd hours. People of faith had seemingly forgotten about the church, and on the corner of the wrinkled paper he catches yet more smudged words, clearly written in a rush.

Father Thomas (Hiding something)

Felix looks up at William, whose eyes have been following the pages. With a sigh, William leans further back on his chair.

"She told him something during confession...," he says, and Felix blinks, not catching the reference, so William drops his head in shame and whispers barely audibly, "He's a priest, he's forbidden to say."

Felix huffs in a terrible imitation of a laugh as he gapes incredulously at the police officer in front of him, who hasn't dared to look into his eyes yet. He shakes his head, dumbfounded by the ridiculousness of the situation; how one event after another is stopping the case from being solved, as if the universe were indulging in foul play, doing everything in its might to prevent Felix from reaching the finish line.

Bone surgery on the leg.

Broken arm.

Fractured ribs, neck, and head.

Newly healed. Less than a year ago.

High doses of TCA and Z drugs in blood. (Purchases of sleeping pills and painkillers)

The handwriting gets even messier on the torn and wrinkled paper, words squiggled illegibly, clearly written erratically in urgency and fury. Felix's heart sinks the more he reads about the injuries. He sometimes forgets how severe they were. How someone could go through such a wounding experience that caused so many injuries and yet not remember any of it is beyond Felix. In all honesty, he doesn't know whether to feel blessed or cursed that his brain has decided to permanently delete the memories.

Memory loss? The boy doesn't speak.

He visibly stiffens. His teeth start to chatter and chills shiver him to the marrow. The tone of the jotter falls into defeat and disappointment even as the words continue to be aimlessly splattered around the paper.

The boy doesn't remember anything.

There is no document about his upbringing.

No official document of adoption.

Felix feels his heart sink deeper and deeper as the last string of hope is ripped out mercilessly. The story, *his story*, doesn't even feel real—it reads more like a piece of fiction because how star-crossed can someone be? How destructive and fatal can his destiny get? As if every event, every choice was made just to afflict him with even more bad luck.

No official files found of missing children in Japan around that time.

The Japanese government isn't cooperating.

Who is this boy?

Who am I?

Felix doesn't even comprehend that he's already on the last page of this anecdotal excuse for his life story. His story really is something for the universe to laugh at.

Last seen around March 17th 2001, leaving the house in the evening as witnessed by the next-door neighbour.

They made small talk with the neighbour at around 8 pm.

Witness says they didn't act out of the ordinary and seemed in a good mood, saying they went out for groceries.

After three days the car didn't show up, and the neighbour called the police after she heard a child's cries.

Felix lets out a dumbfounded, breathy laugh, because this is how the story ends and this is how his eternal nightmare started.

May 5th, 2001

The kid will be taken to the orphanage before the family will be found.

Only they never were found even after years for Felix is sitting there and reading about people he has no recollection of nor connection to. With a heavy sigh he leans back, averting his eyes from the files and gazing blankly into nothingness, blinking rapidly as he tries to ink each and every word deep into his brain so as not to let any important information ever slip away again.

"So...," he starts, his voice uneasy, wobbly, and with a quiet cough he tries to steady his tone whilst gripping his scar for dear life. "Can you tell me about the day you rescued me?"

William has never spoken about that day, no matter how many times Felix asked him to, but now he thinks he's probably mature enough to learn about it, especially since his memories are becoming hazy and unclear with time.

When Felix catches the uncertainty wash over William's expression, his heart sinks, and in a meek whisper he begs, "Please?"

William closes his eyes and exhales heavily, having no desire to let past memories haunt him once more, but Felix deserves to know, and so with a thick tone he starts.

"Well, it was early in the morning when we got the call. The neighbour was complaining about cries coming from the Gauthiers' home and asked us to do a welfare check." William licks his dried chapped lips and after a bat of silence takes another sip of coffee. "So we go there and nothing seems out of the ordinary at first but my partner, Logan, he then also hears the sound of cries as well, childlike cries." William puts his chin in his palms and peeps at Felix through his long lashes, but Felix just nods, urging him to go on. "We knock on the door but there is no answer. The car isn't parked in the driveway either, so at first we think that they must have just popped out and left the kid at home alone. But when we knocked again you immediately stopped crying. I don't know, you were probably scared."

Felix watches the way the frown in between William's brows tightens, his resentment of the memory exposed for Felix's eyes to witness. William massages his temples as if to force the memory to re-open. His eyes are closed as he continues.

"The permission for a warrant takes time and we couldn't just barge in without any solid evidence, so we waited for a while, but when you didn't make any noise afterwards we got worried that you were in danger and called the boss." He chuckles bitterly, his lips hidden behind his cup again. "I remember how angry he got. He cursed us for wasting so much precious time, but I blame my recklessness on being a newbie."

Felix shakes his head without batting an eye, wordlessly disagreeing. He knows how much blood and sweat William wasted on helping him and he can appreciate the effort no matter the outcome.

"So we tried to find a way inside..."

"We won't get in trouble, will we?" William whisper-yells, looking worriedly at Logan who's mimicking the same anxious expression.

"Boss told us to do it, right?" Logan replies with another question, not sounding even slightly confident.

They tip-toe around the house, trying to make as little noise as possible. William loyally traces Logan's steps, looking around for any sign of danger, gun already on display in his trembling hands. Logan tries to find an open window so they can get inside without too much fuss, but when he can't find one he exhales a defeated sigh. William and Logan look at each other, exchanging words through their eyes, and after a second or two, Logan smashes the glass with his elbow. "We had no other choice," he says, and William doesn't know if he's trying to convince him or himself.

William doesn't have time for second-guessing as Logan hops inside gracefully, leaving him with no other option but to follow him with a sigh.

They stand in the main room for a few minutes, looking around. Nothing seems out of the ordinary, the house is in a good state, with no sign of forced entry or struggle. The main room is clean and tidy, and William can only hope and pray that the family won't sue. They walk around the living room, scanning every corner, and just as they are starting to feel defeated, William's eyes catch something out of the ordinary and he frantically nudges Logan.

They both gaze at the plateful of rotten food, ants already finding their way all over it. William frowns—it may not seem worth bothering about but something in his gut is telling him that something's wrong, very wrong. It's a small detail but one that knocks a seemingly normal house out of order, and to William it is a red flag. What could possibly have happened to put the family in such a rush that they didn't even finish their food?

"Let's go," Logan's hushed voice snaps him out of his thoughts and with a stiff nod he pushes the even more hesitant Logan towards the stairs.

William grips his gun tightly—a little too tightly—as he wanders around the ground floor, trying as hard as he can not to make any noise. Nothing grabs his attention, but as he stands in front of another closed door—to a basement perhaps—and grips the door handle with his free hand, he feels something irritating his skin. He inhales deeply, trying to soothe his raging nerves. He doesn't know what could be waiting for him behind the wooden door but if his gut feeling is accurate, it's something that will strike terror into him.

Face twisted in anxiety, eyes squeezed shut, he finally musters the courage to open the door.

And he's met with…nothing.

Deprived of sight he enters a chamber of darkness. With shaky hands, he tries to find the switch to gain his vision back, but when he fails to, he takes the first step into the blackness. As he shakes his flashlight weakly in the darkness, he yells, "Is anyone here? It's the police!" He tries not to let the terror he is feeling inside seep into his tone. "It's the police, come out!" he shouts again but gets only silence in response, making him sigh in relief.

With no desire to stay longer he quickly checks over the room, and it's not until he is already stepping on the stairs when he hears a faint sound of wood creaking. The sound makes his blood run cold and freezes him in place.

"It's the police! Put your hands up!" He yells in a wild voice that reaches even Logan's ears, and in the blink of an eye Logan comes bolting down to the basement, gun pointed at nothing.

"Come out!" William snarls again, flashing his torch around the room.

They exchange looks once again and with slow, short steps walk closer to the wooden furniture. Soon another creaking sound disturbs the silence, curdling William's blood as adrenaline pumps through his veins as he grips his jaw, sweat dripping from his forehead. With shaky fingers William opens the closet, gun quivering in his hands, and shouts "Freeze!"

What he finds in the old, dusty closet is a small child paralyzed in fear, shaking like a leaf at the sight of a gun and with tears in his terror-stricken eyes.

After that everything blurs and William only manages to let out a small gasp as the kid tears his dewy-eyed gaze from the firearm and makes the choked sound of a muffled scream as his eyes open wide in horror before he lets out an ear-splitting screech, shaking the walls around him. In a flash, the boy's skin grows dull and his eyes roll back, but William is quick to react this time and he manages to catch the kid before he falls. With uneven, short gasps he gulps air into his lungs as he holds the kid close, gripping tightly onto his limp body in both fear and relief. Then, letting out a shaky breath he whispers weakly, almost inaudibly, "Call the ambulance."

"And that's it," says William, sounding out of breath as he finishes retelling the story. "Sadly, we don't have any developments in the case," he adds timidly, his tone full of shame.

Felix doesn't speak for a few seconds, too lost in his thoughts, trying to commit each and every word to memory so that he will be able to keep hold of them forever this time. Then he nods and, leaning back, he crosses his arms, still gazing at nothing, and mumbles through pursed lips, "Thank you for your time."

William only shrugs because both of them know very well that it's the least he can do.

"How about memories? Do you have any memories?" he asks carefully, afraid to put Felix off his stroke, but Felix clams up, dropping his gaze to the floor, catching his bottom lip in between his teeth, and nibbling it softly before he sighs and his shoulders drop in defeat. "No, I still can't remember anything."

An uncomfortable silence washes over the table, the light tune of the piano still playing somewhere in the background, and neither of them dare speak.

Felix shakes his head and rubs his clammy hands nervously on his clothes. "I should probably get going, I have to go to my nightshift," he says, quickly gathering his belongings.

Felix slides the file towards William but the man just shakes his head, confusing Felix. "You can keep it," the officer answers shortly.

Felix gazes at him with raised brows for a moment before he sighs and nods. "I'm going then, thanks for the report." He tidies the stack of papers and offers a small, timid smile before putting his coat on. William stays in place, not daring to say a word, his eyes fixated on the floor, but the moment Felix steps away, William decides to speak up.

"I will find them," he says. "I promise."

This forces Felix to turn his head back, and for a moment he stares at the hunched-over policeman who still doesn't have the guts to meet his eyes. With a sigh, Felix speaks. "There are tons of unsolved cases only in this town, detective William, don't feel obliged to waste your time on mine."

Felix blinks rapidly and waits for a moment or two for the detective's response, but William stays frozen in his place, not looking at him, not particularly looking at anything, and when the silence stretches for too long Felix shakes his head quietly and steps away with a heavy heart.

"I'm glad." Felix stops in his tracks, not bothering to look back this time. "I'm glad you grew up so well Felix. I'm proud of you." His words make Felix's heart clutch uncomfortably tight, taking his breath away as he feels his fingers start to tremble.

William finally lifts his gaze at Felix, staring at his back with sorrowful eyes. And William means it wholeheartedly. He has witnessed many other ill-fated kids stumble down the wrong path—kids he once rescued but ended up putting them behind the bars years later. But Felix is different, *he always has been*, even with his star-crossed fate, even after going through so much suffering and pain, even if once he was bleeding to death in William's arms, even when the life was being wiped away from the boy's eyes, he has always stayed as strong as ever. It's a shame, really, that the detective wasn't strong enough to help and ease the kid's heartache.

For a long moment, he stays watching Felix's back, picturing the younger Felix who with slow steps walked inside the orphanage where William himself took him to, holding onto the teddy bear William had given him as a gift, before glancing back at him, his eyes wide, full of hope and trust.

This time Felix doesn't turn around.

"Goodbye detective William," he mutters dryly without sparing him a second glance, and with that he walks away.

Once Felix has completely disappeared from sight, William exhales the breath he didn't know he had been holding this whole time. A smaller, more selfish part of him wishes that the kid would have turned around one last time and given him that same look of faithfulness and dependability, but this Felix doesn't need him anymore, doesn't trust him anymore… Some mistakes can't be fixed and William has to accept the fact that the kid who once depended on him doesn't exist anymore.

Outside, he lights a cigarette and lets the smoke out from his lungs with a heavy sigh, enveloping his surroundings in misty fog. He watches how the smoke fades into thin air, gradually displaying the serene moon for eyes to view once more. He gazes aimlessly at the dark, starless sky for a while, and images of the past roll like an old movie in his brain, taking him back down memory lane.

William's head is pounding. He massages his temples, trying to lighten the headache that hasn't stopped throbbing since the start of the whole ordeal. Every time he closes his eyes, images of the kid, of his frightened doe eyes looking at him with so much terror, return to his vision, making his heart squeeze with shame each time.

His rueful musings are quickly interrupted when he senses a featherlike tap on his shoulder and, lifting up his head with a languorous motion, finds Logan sitting on his desk, his expression indecipherable as he gazes blankly into space.

"The kid doesn't remember anything." It's the only thing he murmurs, still without meeting William's eyes, but it's enough to re-spark the twinges of conscience and heavy-heartedness. William lets out a strained groan and drops his head onto his knees, letting a feeling of hopelessness taunt his thoughts, but Logan keeps going, even if his voice gets unsteadier and shakier with each word. "He has head trauma." Logan clears his throat and stops speaking for a moment, withholding information. "Severe head trauma," he adds, just above a whisper.

Sick at heart, William sighs with closed eyes, trying to ease his devastated spirit. A million thoughts, assumptions, and theories spin together like a hurricane in his mind, putting his soul into a storm. But then he hears something drop onto the table which makes him peek through his lashes, and he finds Logan placing a set of photos neatly down.

"A skull fracture," Logan remarks, pointing at one particular radiograph and trying to sound level-headed, but his voice wavers at the end, revealing his raw emotions. "It's already healed."

William carefully takes the picture of the skull X-ray and sees the fracture line going across the temporal bone, making his heart drop.

"Doctors think it could be a reason for his memory loss," says Logan, clearing his throat once more. "Along with whatever mental trauma he had to go through."

He's just a child.

He should be running around the fields, playing with his friends, in the embrace of loving parents, not lying on a hospital bed with permanent scars on his tiny body.

"Are we dealing with a case for CPS?" William whispers carefully, loath to voice the dreadful truth because he still hangs onto a final string of hope that not everyone is evil, that there is still some good left in humanity.

"According to the doctor, it couldn't have been caused by the hands of a person, because..., because the injuries, they..." Logan laments exasperatedly while vigorously shuffling the photos around the desk, putting the countless X-ray pictures on display. "Look how many broken bones he has!" he shouts in both fury and disbelief, although it sounds muffled to William, who is fixated on the photos. Bone after bone, each and every bit of the kid has been broken, fractured, or injured, and he feels revolted just by the thought that there is no unmarked part of his body left.

He's just a kid.

"What? Who? What kind of monster could have done this?" Logan murmurs defeated, his shoulders slumped as he balances his elbows on the desk, breathing heavily. Meanwhile, William remains silent, shaken by the sight of the pictures, his pulse ringing loud in his ears.

"What the hell are we dealing with?" Logan whispers, his voice panic-stricken.

"I don't know." It's the only thing William blurts out. He really can't wrap his mind around who or what kind of brute could have the heart, the pure determination to put a child through something like that.

The very next day William dashes through the washed-out hallway, struggling to keep his balance as his feet slip over the polished floor. He almost trips over when he eventually gets to the reception, but fortunately he manages to hold onto the desk, startling the nurse behind the glass in the process. He hunches over, breathing hard and erratic, puffing and panting, fighting for air, and the nurse is left with no other option but to watch before the policeman finally regains the ability to speak again. He gulps and leans over the desk, lifting up his badge.

"I'm here to see the kid that was checked in yesterday," he says hoarsely, and when he takes in the confused look the nurse is giving him he elaborates with a sigh, "He doesn't remember his name."

The nurse blinks, still looking a bit bemused before realization lights up on her expression and she looks down at the papers.

"He's in room 108," she replies gently, offering him a timid, yet polite smile.

William nods and sets off at a slow pace to search for the patient's room, gripping tightly onto the plastic bag as he walks. When he finds the room, he stays outside for a moment to soothe his agitated nerves—he doesn't know what state the kid will be in, or how he'll react when he recognizes him and it brings nothing but trouble to his heart. He inhales heavily, rubs his clammy hands on his trousers, and with a shaky breath opens the door.

The first thing that catches his eye is a petite figure sitting on the corner of the hospital bed, gazing outside through the window and holding and rubbing something in his palms. When the figure hears the door creak he quickly hides whatever it was he was holding beneath the white sheets, but William notices a necklace glisten in the sunlight.

When he turns his head back to William, the policeman's heart twinges in pain as he takes in the melancholic gaze the kid is giving him. He looks fatigued; it's the first thing William thinks. His eyes are droopy and sorrowful, any childlike glimmer dimmed as he observes William's every movement. There is an undeniable sadness in the way the boy is staring at him, an utter hopelessness in his eyes, resembling prey trapped by a predator and coming to terms with dying.

With a sigh and a heavy heart, William sits down on the chair across from him while the child watches him with his dull eyes.

"Do you remember me?" he asks, forcing a cheerful tone in the hope of instigating small talk, but when he notices fear wash over the kid's face, his heart starts to race and he stutters in panic, "I'm a policeman, I won't hurt you." He tries to assure the kid by showing him his badge and the boy calms down, finally looking free from strife as his narrow shoulders slump down in relief.

An uncomfortable silence settles inside the room as they both remain silent, not breaking their shared gaze. Truth be told, William doesn't know what to do, how to talk to the kid, or why he even showed up, but the one thing he's confident about is that he wants to help the child so with a sigh he sits more comfortably on the chair.

"Do you know why I'm here?"

The kid lifts his gaze up to the ceiling with pursed lips, looking deep in his thoughts before he shakes his head blandly.

"I want to help you." The kid blinks, uncertainty and dubiety in his eyes. "But we need your help too, is that alright?" William asks carefully, attentive to not upset the boy. The child nods, still looking suspicious of the policeman, and William lets out a heavy breath, trying to find the right words.

"Do you remember anything?"

The boy frowns, his bottom lip getting caught in the gap formed by his freshly removed front teeth, and he drops his head down, fumbling with his fingers before he barely shakes his head.

"Can you, can you speak?" William asks the question everyone is curious about.

The kid flinches, peeling the skin off from next to his nail "I…" He makes a strangled noise that quickly gets caught in his throat so he just settles on nodding.

William sighs in relief, that's good, at least there is some positive outcome. He shuffles around on his seat a bit, trying to sit more comfortably, when he hears a crunching sound and he's reminded of the gift he almost forgot about.

"Hey, I have a present for you," he whispers through a lopsided smile.

The child visibly perks up on the mention of a gift so William carefully places the bag on the hospital bed and watches the way the kid's eyes stare at it curiously yet doubtfully, and how haltingly his short fingers touch the bag, testing the waters before he finally rips it open and his eyes immediately flood with light like a Christmas tree as he eagerly takes the toy out, holding it tight to his chest.

"Do you like it?" William asks tenderly, letting himself lean in closer to the boy. The kid nods frantically, gripping onto the toy as tightly as if it were his only source of comfort. William watches with a fond smile as the kid caresses the teddy bear affectionately, his fingers lazily playing with its fur. It's a painful reminder that he's just a kid, a small, soft-hearted and well-behaved kid, and it makes William's heart clutch with an unbearable feeling of sadness.

"I really want to help you," he whispers, his voice unsteady and shaky, ready to break any second.

The child stiffens. He stops playing with the toy and just looks down blankly at his fidgeting fingers, and William's heart breaks into two as he takes in the helpless state of the kid. Even though he's still not sure what to do, he sits next to the child and gently pats him on his slumped shoulder.

"I know it's hard but let's at least try, alright?" The boy nods without lifting his gaze.

"My name is William. Do you know yours?"

William feels the boy's shoulders start to tremble beneath his palm so he tilts his head to the side, trying to get the best angle to read the kid's expression only to lock his eyes with the boy's. William wraps his arms around the child without a second thought, bringing him close in a comforting hug.

"It's okay if you don't," he says as he gently rests his chin atop the messy locks of the nameless boy. "I told you I'm here to help, didn't I?"

He hears the kid sniffle softly, wiping the unshed tears with his white-knuckled fists, and William is able to breathe out in relief. He shuffles around a bit, trying to reach for his bag without disturbing the boy lying comfortably into his arms.

"Let's play a little game, shall we?" This somehow catches the child's attention so he turns his round face towards him and stares at him with wide, curious eyes. "The policeman's going to show you some photos and you just have to answer a few questions, do you understand?" The boy nods eagerly, without tearing his eyes from him.

William gently lays out the pictures of the couple's relatives.

"Do you recognize any of these people?"

The boy gazes at the photos for a while, full concentration visible on his adorable features, with his brows knitted. He lifts his face towards William again and with a pout, he shakes his head, but William just offers him a small yet genuine smile and delicately ruffles his hair.

They go on like this for a while, William pulling out photos of the couple's friends, colleagues, people close to them, and the child wrapped safely in his arms, dangling his legs in the air from time by time, moving around and humming melodies under his breath, and all of it is enough to swell the man's heart with affection towards the kid. But every time his heart swells he is reminded of all the pain and suffering this warm-hearted, pure soul has had to go through, and if William had a little less self-control he would probably break down in tears there and then.

The boy, oddly enough, doesn't recognize any of the faces and William tries as hard as he can not to show his deep disappointment and upset the kid. But then, when he lays down a photo of the couple, the kid's breath catches in his throat and he visibly stiffens, ringing an alarm in William's already heavy heart. "You remember them?" he queries, but his voice comes off louder than he intended, which makes the kid tremble even more viciously, so William quickly tightens his grip around him and caresses his hair with his fingers, trying to alleviate the child's understandable distress.

"Are they..." he coughs, the lump in his throat not letting him voice the words that make him so uneasy in his heart. "Are they bad people?" he whispers weakly, just the thought of his assumptions being proven true casting a heavy gloom upon him.

The kid stays quiet for a moment that feels like eternity to William, but then, confusingly the boy only shrugs, stunning William. Utterly flabbergasted, William stares at the kid with wide, perplexed eyes, trying to catch any uncertainty wash over the boy, but the boy stays still in the same position, staring back at him just as intensively.

"So, they are good people, then?" This time the boy's grimaces, displaying a disagreeableness that makes the policeman's senses tingle. "If they're neither bad nor good... Then maybe you're scared of them?"

The kid breaks away from William's grasp and turns his body fully towards him. Sitting cross-legged, his gaze shifts to the toy as he blinks his tear-logged lashes. The sight of the defenceless and child eats William's heart out, making him feel wretched and defeated, and although he realizes that he has to say something, to do everything he can to comfort the troubled kid, no matter how hard he ponders he can't find the right words, and even if he could he doesn't think there is anything he could say that would make the child feel any better. So he settles on gently poking the boy's face with a toy, tickling him, making him scrunch up his button nose but with a hint of a smile breaking out on his chubby face. Regardless of the heavy mood still lingering in the room, William takes it as a small win. With a sigh, he gently puts the plushie within the kid's reach again and for a while the child just stares at the teddy bear.

"You know, sometimes parents..." But he doesn't get a chance to finish his sentence, not when he sees the boy flinch at the last word, spreading a hair-raising feeling of dread right through him and washing him in cold sweat.

Now it is William's turn to lose his cool, his brain going haywire as the realization finally settles in, making his heart sink into his shoes and his blood run cold through his veins.

"Are, are they..." He chokes on his own words as he eyes the kid with huge, horrified eyes. "Are they even your parents?" His voice drops to a whisper as air is blocked from his lungs.

The room is spinning and William feels his skin cover in goosebumps. Suddenly it feels freezing cold in the room, and yet the boy, completely oblivious to the disturbance of the policeman, just shrugs.

"Where did you first meet them then?" he rasps, his voice thick with tension as he waits for the dreadful answer.

The kid, still oblivious to the heavy air that has settled in between the officer and him, circles his finger around, making William's face wrinkle with a mix of worry and confusion.

"You met them here?" William asks with no confidence in his tone, but the boy just shakes his head, quickly disagreeing.

"So you met them at the hospital?"

The child whips his head up, eyeing him with so much melancholy that William bites his tongue and avoids his heavy gaze. The kid nods.

"In the hospital where the doctors were treating your injuries?" William's heart tightens at the memory of the kid's wounds, the thought of the awful pain his small body had had to go through.

It's unfair really, how life chooses to bedevil the kindest souls.

When he catches the boy's chin tremble and his teeth dig deeper into his lips, wiping the rosy colour from their skin, his heart sinks to his gut, shattering into pieces, and he's ashamed that the only thing he is capable of is opening his arms awkwardly in a welcoming hug. The kid falls easily into his arms, not wasting a second in jumping into William's embrace, clutching onto his uniform with his tiny fingers without ever letting the toy go, holding it behind his broad shoulders. William chokes out a breath, pulling himself together and trying to calm the million thoughts reeling inside his mind. He grips the boy close yet stiffly, holding the child securely and rocking him back and forth. The boy seems unfazed by the tense form of the officer—he just nuzzles his head deeper into his chest, staining his uniform with his hot tears.

When his petite and bruised body starts to tremble, following the strangled sounds of sniffles that have managed to escape through the thick fabric of the policeman's jacket, William tightens his grip, patting him unsurely on his back. "It's okay, I'm going to help you no matter what," he mumbles against his locks and closes his eyes, radiating as much content and comfort as needed for the kid to soak in, to bring even a little peace to his wretched soul. The boy's trembling fingers crumple the fabric between his pads, and this is when he lets himself bawl his eyes out, melting into William's arms and causing the policeman's eyes to well up with fresh tears. William's heart bleeds each time another devastating whimper leaves the kid, and with his eyes squeezed shut, he holds him tight, safe and sound. His heart has raced in fear too many times to count, but he has never felt so helpless and powerless as at this very moment, with a defenceless kid crying in his arms.

With a last sniff, the boy moves back, leaving the warm embrace with a choked hiccup and wiping his running nose with his forearm. He drops his head in shame, tearing William's heart to shreds.

"It's okay, everything is going to be okay," he tries to assure the boy and takes the toy from his limp grasp. "This old man will help you."

William starts to squeak, talking in a high-pitched voice and making gibberish noises to entertain the child, and a small smile makes its way across the kid's face without quite reaching his eyes. Next William tries poking the boy's sides with the plushie instead, tickling him and successfully making the child giggle through a lumpy throat.

With a fond smile William lightly prods the boy once more, making him laugh louder this time. The boy twitches away from the teddy bear but to no avail as William continues to jab his sides until he fully guffaws, filling the room with his clear laughter. Taking pity on the kid, William puts the toy back into his arms and ruffles his hair gently, and their eyes lock for a long second, observing each other before William stands up with a sigh and stretches his back.

"I need to go now, thanks for helping me." He caresses the kid's full cheeks, pinching them lightly, and the boy just gazes at him wordlessly with round, doe eyes full of admiration.

He's already standing in front of the door, his fingers lingering on the door handle, when a weak voice breaks the silence, making his gut churn. "Will you come back?"

Momentarily his heart skips a beat, before rising to a ruthless speed and throbbing against his ribcage, and he drops his weight against the door, all the balance swept from his legs, because even one sentence is enough for him to catch the heavy accent of the kid, tightening the uncomfortable knot inside his stomach. His gut feeling warns him that something is wrong, that he is dealing with something much bigger than he can handle. With uneven breathing, he forces himself to turn around in the direction of the kid, who is already gazing at him anticipatorily, his honey eyes full of hope, making William's heart sink. The realization of his amateurishness comes crashing down like waves on a stormy night, and so he lies through clenched teeth.

"I will, and I will bring your parents back," he declares with no real confidence. He doesn't have the heart to crush the little kid's hopes, especially not when he sees his eyes light up with awe. William will do anything to stop those glimmering from turning dim all over again.

"Do you promise?" he croaks, his voice weak and uncertain, and William can't help but grimace to be so undeservedly viewed like some kind of wonder, but he nods, ignoring his self-loathing, and pronounces, "I promise."

"What do you mean you're changing my district?" William yells, gnashing his teeth and not caring that the person sitting in front of him is his boss.

With a sigh his boss rests his face on his palms. "We talked about this last year, officer," he answers sternly.

"But the family," William shouts again, his voice breaking from the tension. "The case I'm working on!"

His boss groans and closes his eyes, completely ignoring him. "The boxes are already on your desk, just collect your belongings."

William feels unexplainably small and powerless for the second time as his shoulders drop in defeat.

"But I..."

But I promised.

With a last blow of smoke, the cigarette burns down, and without taking his eyes away from the glowing moon, William drops the butt on the ground and steps on it harshly. "I promised."

Felix reads the document over and over again before he feels his eyes sting painfully, spreading the migraine inside his skull and blurring his vision. With a strangled groan he drops his head back, staring blankly at the ceiling, suffocated by too many thoughts at once.

No matter how many times he reads the same sentence, no matter how much he thinks about it, he still can't make sense out of his doomed fate. How can someone forget their whole life without any memories left behind? He's tired of facing the uncertain world with no memories of him being born.

Is there any real purpose to his torment? Does he, Felix, a nameless, homeless boy deserve a happily ever after? Will the book of his life end with a warm epilogue that will all the pain, blood and heartache worth it? Just like for the countless other questions in his life, he doesn't have an answer.

Who was I?

Who am I?

Who am I truly?

He often asks himself who exactly he is. Which parts of him are raw and real? But there are no answers. He's a stranger haunting someone else's body.

He is at constant war with himself, slaughtering weak parts of him to survive this horrific reality but this genocide to rebirth only led to murdering who he truly was because you can't pick and choose which piece of you will be kept before you turn into some monster, a creature poorly mimicking a human.

Caught up in his own raw feelings, he jumps from his seat. He needs to get away, he needs to get away from himself. Thirsty for fresh air, he staggers outside onto the balcony and leans his body against the railing, gasping for breath as the emotions flood his senses and suffocate his entire being.

He is in a state of torment between his past and his present, and he wishes that at least one of them didn't bring an ache to his wretched soul. He wishes he had been happy at least at one point in his life because the future looks just as dreadful as the past. And the heart-breaking part is that there is nothing he can do to fix it. Event by event, everything has been lined in a way to make him suffer as much as humanly possible.

He muffles his whimper with his hand, covering his face with his cold palms to try and make the headache go away. He is tired, *so, so* tired, both physically and emotionally. He doesn't know how much longer he will last—he just wants everything to finish soon and with as little pain as possible. There is a limit to how long he can hold back the flood of feelings, and when that becomes impossible, he must decide if he will let go or drown.

"Felix?" The raspy voice calls out a name that doesn't truly belong to him, and with an effort Felix turns his face, only to be met with the familiar sight of Dylan gazing at him with an unreadable expression. "Are you okay?" Dylan asks with a hint of worry in his voice.

Felix stares at Dylan through narrowed eyes, paying intense attention to his expression. If he focuses carefully, he can clearly see the pity in his glassy eyes. It's enough to drive him up the wall and make his blood boil with utter rage. How dare he pity him? Is his existence so pathetic that he only deserves to be looked at through woeful gaze? Before he can control himself, something snaps in him.

"Felix..."

"Can you just shut the fuck up already?" he screams, his voice echoing on the thick walls surrounding them, making them shake, and Dylan jolts back, surprise and fear washing over his face. This fills Felix with more confidence—this is the expression Felix wanted to see. This is the way he wants to be viewed.

"What do you want from me? Why do you keep bothering me?" he yells before his voice gives up, his fingers clinging to the cold metal of the railing as he keeps an eye on Dylan, who is gaping at him from the corner and looking taken aback and hurt, his mouth opening and closing but no words coming out. Felix's shout once again pierces the uncomfortable silence. "Is it fun for you?" he snarls through gritted teeth. "Are you enjoying the show?"

"No, I..."

As Dylan croaks meekly it just enrages Felix more, clouding his senses. "No what Dylan? What the fuck do you want from me?" He lunges forwards with his hands balled into fists, ready to attack as his eyes shake with unrestrained rage and madness.

"I just...," he gulps, making his Adam's apple jump, "I just want to be your friend."

Felix's breath catches in his throat, making him wince. He has stood in front of his bullies, gone through flames of hell, and has not faltered; but at that moment, his legs shake as he musters the courage to whisper a small and confused, "What?"

Friend? That's a word to bring hope to one's heart, and God knows how many sleepless nights Felix has wished upon a star for a friend, but now hearing the word doesn't bring the feeling of euphoric relief he'd always thought it would.

It's too late.

Maybe, just maybe, if their paths had crossed before Felix's feet slipped and he fell into the abyss of nothingness, maybe then Felix's life would have turned out differently.

But Dylan was too late.

Felix is broken beyond repair, and instead of bringing peace of mind and sparking joy in Felix, Dylan's words only get under his skin, inflaming him more. All they do is remind him of his wasted lives, of what could have been if his life had been oriented in a different direction.

He chuckles, leans his back against the wall, and glares at Dylan with crossed arms. "Friends? And who said I want to be friends with someone like *you*?" Felix spits bitterly, his rash words dripping like poison from his restless, evil tongue. The words thrust like a sword, stabbing Dylan in the core of his heart and making him flinch and wrap his arms around himself, enclosing himself within protective walls that keep him safe as Felix's eyes remain pointed at him like a sharp knife, ready to wound his scarred soul.

They all hate you.

Everyone hates you.

No wonder Felix doesn't want to be friends with a murderer.

There was one person who cared about you and you killed him.

With trembling hands Dylan covers his ears, trying to stop the screams inside his brain, but they only get louder, consuming his senses entirely.

"What? Cat got your tongue?" Felix snarls, a devilish grin spreading over his face as he watches the boy in front of him break. "I'm not sure what you've deluded yourself but I've never shown any interest in being your friend! So maybe see a doctor since that one-sided friendship of yours doesn't seem to be coming from a sound mind!"

They all hate you. They all hate you. They all hate you.

Dylan's legs buckle, knocking the air out from his lungs as he staggers back, and Felix is addicted, intoxicated by the feeling of being in power, being the one who induces terror in others. Not the other way around.

"Aren't you going to speak?"

"Stop screaming at me!" Dylan shrieks, on the verge of tears as the ringing in his head thuds against his skull, fogging his mind. Felix shuts his jaws with a loud click, stopping more venom from pouring out of his mouth.

You should have been the one to die, not Ayumu.

How long are you going to be a burden for everyone?

How come a murderer can walk freely when a child's body is rotting somewhere in the woods?

"I..." Dylan's voice breaks as he fights for breath, suffocated by the overwhelming flow of emotions. "I didn't..." He clears his throat and steps back, again enveloping himself in a hug. "I didn't know I made you so uncomfortable," he finally whispers weakly, his tone filled with unshed tears. "I'm sorry."

"I'm sorry I shouted at you."

Felix sighs exasperatedly, slowly coming to his senses as he watches the trembling man before him, and suddenly he feels a painful tug on his heartstrings, taking his breath away. It doesn't feel as good to view someone as nice as Dylan be ripped to shreds as it normally would. Now he has noticed Dylan's doe eyes glistening in the moonlight, he knows he won't feel any satisfaction in finally being able to wipe away the warmness and fondness reflected in them.

No, it feels wrong to watch the heartbreak behind those tender eyes. It feels so, *so wrong*. His heart sinks and all at once he's consumed by an irrational feeling of dread and fear, his head buzzing as the hissing in his ears grows ever more tumultuous, pounding in his skull.

"You always will be my number one best friend."

He squeezes his eyes shut and hunches over, covering his ears, but the ear-splitting bleeps won't stop.

"I will always protect you."

He is shaking in agony as he tries to muffle the scream trying to push its way out through his clenched jaws. He digs his fingers into his skin, feeling the wetness of the sweat on the pads of his fingers. The electric wave of sound becomes unbearable, spreading to every tip of his nerves, urging him to rip his skin off.

"Please let's go home, I'm so scared."

The terrified weeping of a child echoes in his brain, making his teeth chatter and his body shake uncontrollably as the thin line between reality and illusion begins to blur.

"Please don't leave me again."

He gasps, the sound stops as quickly as it started, and he can't stop himself from falling to his knees, still in a state of nerves as he stares into space with crazy eyes that twitch restlessly in horror. Blinking rapidly, he regains what's left of his sanity and quickly whips his head up, only to be met with a familiar emptiness. He feels a familiar pang in his heart as he gazes at the empty space where Dylan was standing a moment ago, shaking and with tears in his eyes. Tears that he caused to flow. His heart races, pumping in his ears as the feeling of numbness lays a claim on him, suffocating him and holding him in a death hold.

This is it... This is how the story ends.

But Felix doesn't feel relieved, not even for a bit. Instead, he chokes on dry tears and with short steps walks inside his soulless room, holding onto the door frame in search of a sense of balance.

He slowly crawls into bed and pulls the sheet over his head. But even that doesn't shut out the world, so loud and so painfully silent at the same time. So he buries his head under the darkness of the pillow. And he falls asleep whispering *"I am safer alone."*

But solitude is not safety, it is death. If no one knows that you're alive, *you aren't.*

V

Eyes puffed red from staring upwards at the waning sun, he observes the way the colourful carp-shaped windsocks whirl in the gentle breeze, swimming through the clouds as if marching with the untameable stream of waves, heads ever so proudly tilted up towards the sun, which slowly drowns beneath the mighty mounts. Addled by the tender clucking sound of dragonflies lulling nature to a slumber, he is briefly startled by a sharp knocking on wood.

Genji glances up at his mother, who with a final blow of the hammer lets the last blue wind cone wing its way towards the sky beneath the black and red windsocks, all tied together by the thin strings hanging from their roof. After ruminating about it for a while, Genji eventually asks the question that has been bothering him the whole evening.

"Why are we doing this?" he asks, holding the kabuto origami unskilfully made by Ayumu close to his chest.

With raised brows, Moriko looks down at her son from high on the wooden ladder. She wipes the sweat from her forehead, removing the strands of hair that cling to her rosy sunburnt skin. "What do you mean why? Because it's children's day tomorrow."

Unsatisfied by her answer, he drops his gaze down, aimlessly poking a hole in the sodden ground and muddying his new shoes.

"I thought we didn't believe in things like this…" he mumbles through a pout, conflicted by the doubts which have been bubbling up in him the whole day. His mother sighs heavily and puts the hammer in her back pocket, and with slow, gentle steps she climbs down the rickety ladder, shaking from side to side. She blows the dust from her hands and kneels down at her son's level, holding his face and playfully yet softly pinching his cheeks.

"What I believe in is that no matter the belief, parents will always do everything to protect their kids." A loving smile adorns her face as she rubs her son's full cheeks with care and affection.

Lips set in a tight line, Genji keeps his eyes down, tracing amorphous shapes onto the ground.

"Then why don't I..." he begins, but with a sudden change of a heart he backtracks, vacillating over whether to display his worries. He shakes his head, slumping further down until his chin touches his chest.

"Why don't you what?" Stumped by the atypical behaviour of the child, Moriko tilts her face to the side, trying to read the heart of her son through his fretful eyes. She blinks rapidly when the realization sets in. "Do you want to go to *kodomo no hi* too?"

Hearing the question, the kid visibly perks up, hope setting light to his guileless eyes. "Can I?" he squeaks happily, yet still with a touch of hesitation.

Moriko chuckles and playfully pinches her son's nose, making him yelp but simultaneously soothing his deep frown away. "Of course you can," she says with a grin. "Why didn't you tell me before?"

Genji's face contorts into a grimace; his prior sullen expression reappears, forming wrinkled lines of worry on his frail skin. "I didn't want to make you sad," he says quietly, his faint voice almost stifled by the way his head is bowing down, reluctant to meet his mother's gaze.

Genji almost jumps out of his shoes when the lilting tittering tickles his ears, but before he musters the energy to lift his face, he can't help but notice his own monstrous, shapeless reflection as Moriko brushes her fingers through his tangled hair, kneading his skull softly, unlacing the knots of worries.

"You can never make me sad." Her seraphic voice is in tune with the wildlife that is bursting into a serenade for the night: frogs chorusing croaks beneath the wild grass, the grass rustled somnolently by the cooling breeze, and the monotone chirping of the crickets. It's all too soporific, lulling Genji to sleep. "You make me happier than anyone." She kisses him on his temple before standing upright. "Now let's go see Mizuki, we need her help."

Through the dark, unlit street, the light slowly lures him in as Moriko opens the door to the house of the Eguchis'.

"I told you not to eat so much." Genji hears the familiar nagging of Mizuki, probably scolding Ayumu.

In the entrance, his gaze lingers on the new painting that Ayumu has drawn, and with an appreciative smile he reads the word "Genji" written beneath the green stick figure.

"You can barely fit into your kimono now." He sees Mizuki exhale in frustration as she gently pinches Ayumu on his tummy. Ayumu is standing proudly in his blue kimono with the same crude helmet on his head, sticking his tongue out and holding a cookie in his other hand despite his mother's nagging.

"I see you guys are getting ready," Moriko chuckles, finally gaining the attention of the busy family. "Well, I came prepared too." She shakes the bag in her hand and winks. "I made mochi and chimaki for tomorrow."

Mizuki's body falls with a deep sigh. "Thank God," she says through closed eyes. "I forgot to make them."

Genji's eyes dart from one person to another. Even to his child's eyes, the house seems fuller, livelier now the missing members have entered.

The carp streamers are higher than the roof
The biggest carp is the father
The small carp are the children
Enjoying swimming in the sky

Ayumu sings the song he learned especially for *kodomo no hi*, swaying from side to side.

"Stay still!" his poor mother demands, helplessly trying to calm her agitated child down.

"Leave that poor kid alone and help me with something." Moriko ruffles Ayumu's hair and gently places the bag on the table. "Genji wants to attend *kodomo no hi* too."

It's the only thing she says but it's enough to brighten Mizuki's face. "Really?" she asks, looking delighted.

Moriko nods. "But we don't have a kimono."

Before Genji can listen to the adults further, Ayumu tugs him by his arm, taking him away from their parents.

"Cool, right?" Ayumu asks as he circles around, showing off his new kimono, and Genji nods, humming in approval. The smile from the compliment sours quickly on the kid's face. "You're not wearing your helmet," Ayumu says through a pout, having noticed that he's the only one wearing his blue helmet.

It takes a moment for his friend's words to sink in, but then Genji quickly takes the crumpled paper out of his pocket and puts on his head.

"That's better." Ayumu nods with his nose in the air.

The doorbell interrupts the familiar harmony of the families. Mizuki slowly walks to the door, and her eyes dart down when she opens it. Akiko is standing outside with her usual big yet polite smile.

"We are playing hide and seek, can Genji and Ayumu play with us too?"

Mizuki clicks her tongue as she gazes at her son, who is vibrating in excitement.

"Pretty please?" the girl begs.

"But it's getting late," Mizuki says, looking at the clock showing that it's already past seven.

"Mum, please?" Ayumu runs toward Mizuki and grips her arm. "Come on, it's my birthday!" he whines.

"It's not your birthday yet," his mother argues back, making the kid groan and jump in frustration.

"Please, auntie." Genji joins in, although he is not often one to complain. "I'll take care of him."

Mizuki sighs again, letting her son shake her arms from side to side as his whining gets progressively louder. "Okay! Okay but be back before nine, got it? We need to wake up early tomorrow."

"Yes, ma'am!" The kids' chant in chorus, and they are ready to bolt outside when Mizuki catches Ayumu by his collar.

"Change into normal clothes! I will not let you ruin this kimono."

"But I wanted to show the others..."

"I said change," his mum commands, looking so grumpy that Ayumu stomps loudly up the stairs and bangs his door shut with a loud crash. The mothers exchange looks and shake their heads tiredly.

After only a heartbeat, Ayumu emerges from the room wearing his usual red striped shirt, a gift from Moriko last year.

"Wear this when you have a rest so you don't catch cold," she says, but Genji is the one who takes the green jacket that matches his blue one, knowing it's going to be him who will force Ayumu to wear it.

"Come back soon, alright?" Mizuki repeats as she stands by the door, worriedly watching the kids running towards the gate.

"Alright!" they yell as the fireworks go by, painting and shaking the sky above.

I am a child of the sea.

The tuneless lilting of high-pitched saccharine voices engulfs the grim silence, but beneath the cloying tone of the caterwauling dwells the soporific shade of plaintive lamentation.

On a pine-covered seashore which white waves wash up on.

The unmistakable melody of his beloved song is distorted as the squeaky voices break into bloodcurdling howls.

There is a humble home, and smoke is coming out of the window.

The cacophonous, gravelly, and almost haunting hubbub of the hellacious carol is enough to send terror racing through his body, forcing him to snap open his eyes.

That is my dearest old home.

With a short gasp, Dylan jolts awake but finds it hard to move due to the moss that has crept over his body, bogging him down to the gloopy ground and wreathing him so that he is one with the sodden land of the inescapable forest. He retches, repulsed by the smell of the rotting green and the foul earth that is so nauseatingly soft to the touch, and he desperately tries to disentangle himself from the web of the grass.

Filthy from head to toe he stands on his feet, gazing into the depths of the dormant woods that have faded into pitch blackness.

Shielded by withered boughs, high above in the black velvet sky, the moon begins to shine again, but now it is nothing more than a slim, silver crescent, almost invisible, crooked and scrawny, shedding a sleety glow across the leaden, starless night sky, like the pretentious grin of a Cheshire cat, looking down upon the shrouded forest where the heft of the silence is so great as to be almost tangible.

Freed from the morass, Dylan stands bent, just like the crescent moon, alone in the malevolent woods. His heart comes to a halt when out of the corner of his eye he catches sight of two foredoomed kids running towards the cliff.

"Stop!" he cries out, rushing towards the children with the brimming desire to intervene, to change their fate even within the dream and not be so cowardly and helpless. He shoves Genji roughly to the ground, keeping a tight grip on Ayumu's wrist, and glares with unspeakable loathing at the murderous kid of his own self.

"Why?" Ayumu cries as his body softens, wasting away through Dylan's fingers and forcing Dylan to dim the hellfire in his eyes as he glances at the child. It's like looking into the eyes of death, and his breath catches in his lungs as the kid's skin pales, blends into the shades of grey and green. Ayumu looks back at him, his eye sockets black voids with no trace of the eyeballs, and the skin on his face starts to melt like an old candle, revealing blinding white bones through the layers of decaying flesh. "Why didn't you find me?" His wail shakes the whole forest, making Dylan stumble back, his body set alight by a torturous feeling of dread.

The fear comes as fast as it goes, stealing away his vision and his sound mind.

"Defendant."

Undertones of scarcely audible muttering chime out of earshot. His brows twitch and he squeezes his eyes even tighter, determined to keep them shut whilst the loud silence clings to his senses again.

"Defendant."

The voice rings out again, sharper and more traceable this time, alarming him and causing his nerves to spark and his heartbeat to race. Desperate to cling to the unconsciousness of slumberland, where he can stay in a state of numbness for just a little while longer, his body moves spasmodically, wriggling from the grasp of the real world stirring him awake.

"Defendant Yamaguchi Genji!"

The vexed shout coincides with the short-winded gasp Dylan chokes out as he springs up onto the wooden seat and comes to his senses. His eyes, wide and witless as per usual, are now dilated with fear and confusion, tainting their shimmering black-pearl allure with wild bestiality.

The quiet noises start to reach his ears, and one by one he hears unfamiliar sounds of whispers and hisses, whooshes and swishes, whirs and soughs, and rustles and buzzes. All too many prying eyes leech onto him, leering deeper than his flesh and bones, looking right through him, all vulnerable and defenceless. The susurrations turn into incomprehensible chattering which is then taken over by the chaos of mass yelling and shouting.

His eyes, still out of focus, shake with confusion, and the view in front of him remains opaque. Even when his numbed body leaps forward as numberless fists and fingers dig into his back, he stays frozen in place with his head hung low. A heavy knocking sound echoes around the place, ploughing right into his skull and sending waves of white noise painfully through his ears, making him wince in pain. Then silence settles again and the world goes mute, only an incessant piping filling his hearing.

"Defendant Yamaguchi Genji."

Dylan flicks his eyes open, although his birth name sounds as foreign as ever to him, and as his sight returns, he notices the rusty handcuffs around his wrists, scraping his skin red. His blood freezes, chilling him to the bone and sending him into a cold sweat. The eyes burning into his iced flesh make his skin crawl, and he longs to ease the insufferable itch, but the solid cuffs, like thorns in his flesh, restrain his movements, sending him into a rage. He springs his head up, causing the heavy chains around his ankles to chime in the silence.

The old-fashioned, airless room spins round in a blur as Dylan scans each corner of it. As he fights for breath, his heavy breathing and his raging heartbeat thumping in his ears are the only sounds he can hear, alongside the whispers of strangers muttering in his ear, suffocating him and making him feel crumpled from inside.

He stops dead when he comes face to face to Sophia, who is dressed differently to her normal outfits, wearing a formal dress instead of baggy sweatpants and a worn-out shirt. As if turned to stone, Dylan gawks at his friend, who is giving him a displeased look and shaking her head from side to side in frustration.

Before a thought can pass through his mind, Dylan hears the ear-piercing knocks again, making him instinctively turn his attention towards the source of the sound. He gapes, shell-shocked and terror-stricken. He feels rotten—his stomach is in knots and his knees feel weak.

"Yamaguchi Genji, are you going to cooperate or not?"

And there he is, Felix, leering down at him from the judge's bench with a stern expression. His heart sinks the moment his eyes meet Felix's judgmental ones, and he's left hanging, open-mouthed and shaking in his shoes. Felix's eyes narrow, piercing right through him. "What is your answer?" he asks, terrifying Dylan even more.

Numbed with fear, Dylan gulps for breath as the cold sweat rolls down his cheek. Felix's gaze makes his skin sting and he has to avert his eyes, but the sight before him makes his blood go cold and his insides twist: Ayumu is sitting at the table to the side, crying on his mum's shoulder.

The yowl that breaks out from Dylan's lungs strikes like a peal of thunder, shaking the walls around him and deadening any other sound in the room. He springs up, knocking the chair on the floor with a loud thud.

"No! Leave me alone!" he hollers, his voice so tight that his skin turns red and his veins burst out. He feels the eyes burning into his skin once more, but the moment Ayumu turns his head towards him his nerves shatter, making his knees go weak and his legs tremble. He staggers and trips over the chains that ring out as his head crashes onto the wooden surface before toppling onto the floor.

For the first time, there is a heartbeat moment of complete tranquillity, the noiselessness of the cosmos and his mind in perfect harmony, with only a static thrumming sound tingling his ears, making him blink. However, the momentary peace quickly comes to an end when he is blinded by the sharp lighting of the chandelier, and again the subdued murmurs become distinct.

"Dylan!" He hears Sophia shout amongst the many disembodied susurrations whispering in his ear at once, their poisonous words knifing his wretched mind for new scars to bleed.

"He was such a nice kid, what happened to him?" A strident voice hisses in a gloom-filled tone.

"I heard he went insane." Like venom dripping from a snake's fangs, another taunting voice flickers its tongue.

"Oh god!" A grating voice jumps higher with exaggerated worry. "Poor Moriko, her life was already tough to begin with."

"Don't feel sorry for the mother of a murderer," laughs a wicked voice, its tone dropping lower so that it sounds almost hellish.

I didn't kill him.

I didn't want this to happen.

I didn't cause this.

"But you did." The voice chortles again, causing Dylan to open his eyes in alarm. As his blurred sight comes into focus, he registers two faces looking down at him.

"No!" he shrieks as the men pull him by his arms. "Let me go!" he chokes out, his eyes welling with tears as he tries to fight back, twisting and turning and helplessly kicking his tied legs.

"I'm sorry." His voice is brittle and his limbs sore. He moves convulsively, exhausted from trying to break free from their grasp. "I'm so fucking sorry," he croaks, strangled by his pent-up tears.

When the policemen push him down on the seat again, he doesn't dare to lift his head. Looking down at the floor he continuously mumbles "I didn't kill him" over and over again while rocking his limp body back and forth.

Filled with fury, Sophia jumps up from her chair.

"Your honour," she says, "Mr. Yamaguchi Genji is struggling with a severe case of PTSD. His treatment is unacceptable!"

"He's the one to blame!" someone shouts from behind.

"He's at fault for this tragedy!" agrees another before the room turns into chaos once more with everyone shouting over each other, blaming Dylan and tarnishing his name.

Felix bangs the gavel once more, silencing everyone. He clears his throat while arranging a stack of papers.

"Ladies and Gentlemen, the case for your consideration tonight is Yakushima Island in Kagoshima Prefecture, Japan, representing

Yamaguchi Genji. The defendant is charged with the manslaughter of Eguchi Ayumu."

"I didn't kill him," Dylan murmurs under his breath, his voice shaking both from the anger of being accused of such a heinous crime and his own uncertainty in his innocence.

"On May 5, 2000, the victim Eguchi Ayumu died as a result of criminal negligence by the defendant," Felix reads laconically without a slight waver in his voice, only a perpetual stoic tone and a blank and apathetic expression, not even twitching a brow, making him appear inhuman and soulless.

"I didn't kill him!" Dylan howls, hammering his cuffed hands on the table and quietening the room.

Felix leans his head down; he peers at Dylan with a razor-sharp gaze. "Defendant…"

"It wasn't my fault!" he squeals again, successfully interrupting Felix and leaving him with no other option but to stare at Dylan stony-eyed.

Dylan feels caged in his own skin—his body convulses, sending papers and objects flying up from the table. Twisting and turning he desperately tries to break free from the heavy chains nailing him down. Once again the guards come rushing towards him but their hold is more violent this time, almost bruising as they snatch him off the ground by his arms.

"I said it's not my fault!" Dylan continues to holler, kicking the air pathetically. "Please let me go!"

"It's your fault!" Ayumu screeches into the room, which is now rowdy with whispers and chatter. He wriggles out from his mother's secure embrace and with a struggle he stands on the chair to make himself appear taller. Then, looking straight into Dylan's eyes, making Dylan wince and stop struggling with the guards, he shouts, "It's your fault that I died!" His immature voice sounds thin and brittle.

Each word feels like a stab, and each lunge of the trenchant blade leaves an open gash on Dylan's already torn heart. He is barely aware of his limp body being pushed down onto the chair again. He continues to stare at Ayumu with eyes that have already welled up with tears and filled with the gamut of emotions from mawkishness to lament, and most importantly, betrayal.

When Ayumu doesn't budge from his place, Dylan closes his eyes to keep the tears to himself and takes a deep breath.

"I loved him," he croaks shakily, grimacing as he gently opens his eyes. He finds Felix staring at him with an arched brow, looking suspicious but unable to mask his surprise. Dylan gulps but the heavy lump stays lodged in his throat.

There are too many skeletons and ghosts hidden in his wretched soul, and he wants to talk about the demons that haunt him, but there is so much to speak about that he can never find the right words, and even if he could he doesn't think they would express what his heart desires to confess.

A heartbeat of nervous silence passes by and Dylan bites his tongue, but Felix nods at him, urging him to continue, and so, with an intake of shaky breath, Dylan faces Ayumu. For the first time, he doesn't avert his eyes from Ayumu's empty eye sockets directed towards him.

"I loved you more than anyone in this world, even before I knew what love meant."

Like waves crashing against the shore, the hushed gasps from the spectators waft across the walls, leaving the room calm like after a storm.

"I wanted nothing more than to protect you so I could spend every moment and second with you." He gazes at the kid with beseeching, pitiful eyes, exposing the earnestness of his heart in its raw and naked form.

"There is so much I wanted to do with you, so many things I wanted to experience with you." Like a sinner before the gates of heaven, Dylan drops his head in shame and in sorrow for all that could have happened and what the future was holding for them if he hadn't been so careless.

Ayumu's brows knit together, wrinkling his wilted, sage-green skin. His scarred lip starts to tremble and tears start to gather where his eyes are supposed to be. He staggers back, almost stumbles over, but his mom is there to catch him this time whilst she glares at Dylan with silent resentment.

"But…," Dylan chokes on the tears that are demanding to be given free rein. "But I just fell asleep." He whimpers just above a whisper, finding it brutally painful to open the scars that are yet to be healed. "And when I woke up, you were gone and I can still feel the fear that went through me at that moment."

"Is he blaming the victim?" someone shouts in anger and the sour words are enough to open the gates of Dylan's swarming emotions and let the memories once again cut him open for everyone to see the vulnerability of his state.

But before the chaos can occur Felix puts his hand up, silencing the spectators.

It takes a moment for Dylan to speak through his hot tears; only the sound of him sniffling echoes on the thick walls.

"I'm sorry that I screamed at you," he mewls through his wobbling lips, and his chains clang through the silence as he raises his cuffed hands in an attempt to spread his arms and prove the genuineness of his words. "I shouted from fear of losing you and yet that's what eventually made me lose you."

A moment of silence settles in the courtroom, as if to mourn not only the lost soul but the souls that have died with him but continue to exist in the world where Ayumu has no place anymore.

"But he trusted you!" screeches Mizuki in a strained voice. "He trusted you with his life!"

She jumps up awkwardly from her seat, knocking the chair down with a loud thud that makes Dylan flinch, but not even fear can force him to lift his head up and face the grief-stricken mother.

"I trusted you!" she screams, smacking her chest till it seems her heavy heart will explode.

"I'm sorry…" is the only response Dylan weeps through lips wet with tears that fall from his glassy eyes like sharp raindrops on a storm-tossed night.

"Every day I ask myself…" Mizuki chokes on the tears that burn her skin, and no matter how violently she scratches and rubs her collarbone, trying to tear off the flesh that has been carrying this agony for so long, the pain stays undying, making a permanent home for itself along with regret and guilt in her heart. "Why did it have to be my son?! Why Ayumu?"

She drags Ayumu to the floor in an embrace, holding the living corpse of what is left of her son for the last time. Ayumu hides his face in his mother's neck, unable to watch the suffering of his loved ones. "My sweet little Ayumu." Mizuki continues to sob into the rotting skin while caressing her son's thinning hair.

"Don't you dare look away from us!" she yowls through gritted teeth, looking feral, all geared up to protect her child at all costs. "Look at me when I'm talking to you!"

Dylan shies away, shrinking further down into his seat, and his soft cries soon turn hysterical when the woman he once loved as his own mother continues to scream at him. "Look at us! Look what you have done!"

As he continues to choke on his sobs, he understands that in the end, in his heart, he's still the same frightened and guilt-ridden Genji. He may not live in the past but the past lives within him.

"Face the people you've caused so much pain!" Only then does he dare to drop his armour and peek up. Following his gaze to the side he comes upon the dishevelled state of Kuragari, sprawled in the corner with a reeking bottle of cheap alcohol in his hand. He snivels, quickly squeezing his eyes shut in the hope that this image won't find a permanent place in his brain, but before long curiosity gets the better of him and he half-opens one eye. Sitting on chairs of shame are his parents. Their heads are hung low in embarrassment, mortified to be the forebears of a murderer. As a broken-hearted scream dies in Dylan's throat, Mizuki's yell shakes the walls once more.

"Why didn't you die instead?!"

Before Dylan can apologize for his sins, Sophia, having had enough of her cousin's humiliation, springs up from her chair and says, "Your honour..."

"Cascading failure," Felix answers rather dryly, looking lasciviously at Dylan and taking in his every physical response, every slight movement of his muscles. Dylan lifts his head, gazing open-mouthed at the judge with eyes filled with unshed tears and perplexity.

"Do you remember what it means?" Felix leans his head on his hand, trying to look indifferent but unable to conceal the flames of zeal glowing in his eyes. Dylan glances from side by side and looks at the crowd, waiting for an answer. He blinks the tears away before laying his eyes on Felix once more.

"Cascading failure may occur when one part of the system fails," he mumbles almost inaudibly, uncertain of his words.

Felix nods firmly before sighing heavily and fixing his posture. "When this happens, other parts must then compensate for the failed component. This, in turn, overloads these nodes, causing them to fail as well, prompting additional nodes to fail one after another."

Their intense gazes are fixed on each other, but Dylan continues to gawk with no hint of comprehension behind his naïve, doe eyes. Felix exhales in exasperation while pinching his nose.

"You aren't *arche*, Yamaguchi Dylan."

His breath catches in his throat when he hears his present-day name rolling from Felix's tongue in a dream where he's supposed to be Yamaguchi Genji, the little evildoer. Receiving no response, Felix snorts ominously.

"What? Did you really think you could get away from your past by changing your name? Do you think that just by pretending to be someone else your sins would go away?" Dylan shrinks back and the chains once again fill the room with silvery clanking. "You can't escape from the roots of the forest that have grown so deep inside of you."

The menacing look on Felix's face quickly changes back into the usual stoical one as he puts his papers neatly together whilst continuing to speak in a monotonous tone.

"You weren't the first and only cause that led to this tragic event because every moment, minute, and second led to the decisions which finally failed the system. The fact that you chose that exact forest to hide in, even the fact that you agreed to play hide and seek that very night." Felix tidies his desk, putting everything in its place, appearing to be getting ready to leave. "We can go as far as to say that the circumstances in which you two were introduced to each other, the fact that you were neighbours—these are all the occurrences that brought you two to be standing on that particular cliff on that exact day.

"And besides, it may be that you didn't kill Eguchi Ayumu, because he has yet to leave the land of the living." Irritated, Felix raises his hand to cut off the wave of gasps echoing from the bewildered crowd. Aghast, Dylan searches for Ayumu in the mass but only finds Mizuki standing on all fours on the floor, looking as perplexed as him, with wide red eyes.

"And although you couldn't have been the origin of the failure, you, Yamaguchi Genji, were the last node to fail before the catastrophe that sparked the loop of your cyclic life."

Felix, without any hurry in the world, removes his robe and drops it behind the chair. "This is exactly why you're the one who has to take the blame. Because of your failure, Ayumu spent his last moments in pain and fear before he was thrown to the wolves and reborn as a new person, but just like in your case, flipping to the next chapter doesn't blank out the previous pages of the book." He takes the gavel and strikes it hard three times. "Instead of breaking the loop of suffering, you desire the suffering, and so, before you continue to fear the tragedy that has already occurred by holding on to the past while waiting for your future, I, Felix, charge you, Yamaguchi Genji, with the involuntary manslaughter of Eguchi Ayumu. However, I shall accept a plea of insanity."

"What?" Dylan croaks, but before he can comprehend the severity of the situation, he's already being dragged away by the guards. "No! I'm not insane!" he screams, desperately trying to wriggle out from their rock-hard grasp. "I'm not crazy, please!"

"Yamaguchi Genji will be serving his sentence in a psychiatric hospital," declares Felix, and on that harsh note, he stands from his seat and bows to the audience who clap eagerly for justice served.

Dylan's pleas go unnoticed as they drag him outside the room, and just before the towering wooden door closes, Dylan glimpses Ayumu and Felix standing together behind the judge's bench, their eyes fixed on him, watching him go.

The thunderous wail strikes terror into Felix, making him jump out of his skin and his bed.

Lethargic from sleep, he stays on all fours on the floor, his eyes half-open, and it takes a heartbeat for his dreamy mind to get the drift of what is happening, but then a loud crash momentarily stops his heart, jerks him awake and finally forces him to jump up. Like a deer helplessly watching the oncoming blinding lights of a car, he fixates on the wall that parts him from his neighbour, from where the booming sounds are shaking the walls of the whole building.

"It's not my fault," Felix tells himself silently, but his wounded heart is telling him otherwise. Unable to face the truth, he rushes frantically towards the door, not wasting a moment as he leaps outside, where spectators have already gathered, watching the show. Their hubbub is almost loud enough to cloud the continuous screaming coming from inside. Some are standing by their doors, still sleepy and complaining silently about the disturbance with slurred mumbles. Some are not so sanguine, swearing and cursing out loud as if trying to drown out the person in distress.

"This is not my fault," mutters Felix's irredeemable brain, vexatiously and begrudgingly. "What's happening?" he asks a passing student who is rubbing the sleep away from their eyes, but they just shrug their shoulders, as ignorant and lost as Felix.

Everyone instinctively bends their knees when the blaring sound of a smash shakes the walls within. Uneasiness is heavy in the air, forcing a moment of a dead silence to bed in before someone with some sense shouts, "Call an ambulance, for fuck's sake!"

Felix never learns what comes next or if the ambulance was ever called—instead his legs drag him down the stairs, taking his heartstrings with him and not giving his mind a place to hold the fort. Abruptly he missteps and stumbles, landing on all fours as his clear view of the concrete stairs distorts into an old, wrecked wooden stair, whittled away by worms.

"Come back!" He hears an unfamiliar male voice.

"Theodore, stop!" And by the name, he remembers it all.

Damon Gauthier is yelling at him through the past.

With the shouts and the sound of the rain breaking against the ground comes the familiar head-splitting pain, crashing into his skull like waves on the seashore and bringing back bits of stolen memories. He groans, leaving red marks on his skin as he squeezes his temples where the core of the pain resides, right above his brow, the place where the scar remains like an old friend from the past.

He slowly rises from the ground and only then becomes aware of how cold the floor can actually get as he stands there barefoot. The guilt is rooted in him, stabbing him all over with a poisoned blade, urging him to go on, and so he rushes onward, shaking his head, battling against his agonizing headache and ignoring the coldness on the floor. Only when he's standing in front of the black metal door does he realize that he has reached Dylan's friend's doorstep.

His mind is bemused by the lengths he has gone to for a person he should care nothing about, and it's almost enough to make him turn away and go, but the heavy pang of remorse in his heart stops him in his tracks, and before his brain can change his mind, he bangs impetuously on the metal door, disturbing an already tormented night. After what feels like a trip to hell and back, the door finally opens, displaying a languid-looking Sophia trying hard to stay conscious.

"Felix?" she asks, mystified and suddenly looking more awake. "What are you doing here?"

Felix stands there like a statue, not knowing how to get the words out when he doesn't have a clue what has occurred.

"Dylan...," he starts with a whisper, the words sticking to his tongue. "Dylan, he..." But the sentence remains unfinished as Sophia shoves him aside and sprints towards the stairs.

In somewhat of a daze, he is left alone, surrounded by the cold, concrete walls which never stop whispering untold secrets.

By the time he walks upstairs towards the evidence of his act of wickedness, he finds the hall of shame emptied of the nosy crowd but still full of wails coming out through the open door. Like the proverbial cat, curiosity kills Felix the moment his eyes lock onto the heart-rending sight of Dylan wailing in harmony with Sophia, manhandled by people in white, twisting and bawling in agony like a wounded animal trying to escape the grasp of the nurses. He isn't sure how long he stares, but at one point someone feels the prying eyes of an onlooker and slams the door shut in front of his nose.

He stands there in the soulless hallway, with the flickering, weak light keeping him company and the unbroken cries chiming in his mind.

"It's not my fault," he whispers meekly, trying to convince his mind that he is saintly when he is all too aware that he is the devil in disguise.

Dylan didn't punch the clock in the hospital, nor the university the next day.

Or the day after.

Nor all the next week, but the imprint of guilt remained inside Felix's mind like the ghost-shell of his face, taunting him even in his dreams.

Slowly the resounding cries of his brain insisting on its innocence dimmed down like the flames of his anger, and maybe the incident was the last blow towards the already wilted candle which Felix named hatred. The anger will set your heart ablaze, burning the life inside of you, but the smoke will suffocate you faster, dirtying your vision in grey and leaving you nothing but bygone ashes.

As he stashes the boxes he scattered back on the shelves, he whispers under his breath, "I'm losing control."

The control he worked through bloodshot eyes and tears to sculpt with his bare, raw hands, shaping and curving it out of the rot, but the flames he himself set free, and they have spread like hellfire, burning him inside-out.

And there are no tears left to shed to quench the flames now.

With staggering steps he drags his feet towards the door when suddenly the door next to him opens, revealing Sophia walking out of Dylan's room carrying some untouched, mouldy food. She looks drained, with heavy, dark circles under her eyes which are filled with gloominess and despair. Engrossed, she doesn't even notice the witness to her poor state.

"How is he?" Felix asks before he can stop himself.

Sophia flinches, almost dropping the food. Her wide eyes soften when she recognizes the familiar face, unaware that the person standing in front of her is the reason for her dolour. She smiles sadly through trembling lips. "He'll be fine," she whispers, with a little uncertainty between each word.

With a heavy sigh Felix closes the door, resting his head on the cold metal to cool his burning mind where the fatigued image of Sophia nests. Lucky meows, making his presence felt through the mist of Felix's worried mind. Felix turns his gaze on the kitten, his eyes red with a dim spark.

"Do you think I'm a bad person?" he asks the cat, but the kitten just bumps its head affectionately on his leg.

They say cats can split hairs between good and evil.

Must be a lie.

His eyes stare at the butterfly on the thin glass, fluttering its wings so slowly that it looks almost ghostly. Yet again, everything seems otherworldly within the isolated walls of the ward.

The butterfly doesn't move, sitting comfortably outside the window even as the shadow of the spider crawls closer, and Genji feels envious of the helpless butterfly, mocked by its freedom compared to the imprisoned patients inside the white walls. In its luxurious cage, the bird is jealous of the butterfly that wanders freely outside and maybe deep-down hopes for it to be killed by the approaching spider.

His eyes wander away when the spider jumps on the beautiful butterfly, embracing it in a slow death. He feels the familiar warm touch of his dad through the thin layer of the hospital gown that barely protects him from the evening cold.

"Genji," Sophia starts carefully, talking as if to a bird with the broken feather, helpless and all too dependent on her. "We're ready to check out."

He looks down at the paper bracelet on his thin wrist, and only when his father's warmth leaves him does he nod, slowly heaving himself up on the softly creaking hospital bed.

Before he leaves the room he gives a last glance towards the window, where now only the shadow of the spider lingers, but even then he feels jealous of the short-lived freedom of the little butterfly, a freedom that will never be his even when he returns to the outside.

The silhouettes of moths decorate the gloomy moonlit room, flying from one corner to another, hunting the helpless, smaller flies, and just like the layers of food decaying on the table the rotting body lies still in the bed, lazily following the trace of the shadows. His vision is blurry, strained even by the slightest movement. How quickly the body forgets to move—it feels like he will have to learn to walk all over again.

The door creaks and like a mouse out of hiding, Sophia walks inside the dungeon, squeaking like a wounded rodent.

"I brought food," she says as she gazes at the piles of homemade food littered all around the cave, knowing all too well that her words will fall on deaf ears.

The body, shackled with abstract chains, doesn't budge, continues to melt and spread like a wax candle all over the bed that has become his coffin. Sophia inhales a shaky breath, momentarily disturbing the deathly quiet room, and with small steps she walks backwards, closing the door.

When Dylan hears the click of the door he swings around on his back, gazing aimlessly at the intimate four walls of his room, knowledgeable about each and every crook and empty gap. He sees what a mess his room has become, clothes and empty cans thrown in every corner and a smell that he can't tell if it comes from him or the rotting food. He heaves himself up, but a feeling of weight pushes him back down, further and further into the bed, paralyzing his whole body.

As the shadows continue to fly above his head, the darkness starts to creep in, surrounding him entirely, and from the corner of his eye, he catches the usual white robe floating just above the floor. Dylan doesn't need to look to see the faceless figure of Ayumu, standing in the corner of his room, wearing a worn white kimono with an equally pale triangular hat on his head.

When he feels the bed creak, he closes his eyes, succumbing his fate easily. Soon the weightless body lies on his chest, hugging him, reminding him that he has never left, that he will always be there to catch him in his short, weak hands. And with that he knocks himself uncurious, once again running away from reality like a fool.

"Where is it?" Felix groans as he scatters the papers all over the floor, digging deeper into the piles of boxes, whilst Lucky follows the frantic movements of its owner.

With a groan he falls back onto the floor, eyes glued to the ceiling, the tattered notebook nowhere in sight. As if to mock his worry, obnoxiously mirthful music plays from the TV, his ill-fate once again reminding him of its presence with a sneer. His breath gets tangled up in his lungs when a heavy weight drops onto his chest as Lucky gets comfortable for a slumber.

"I'm getting a bit too careless, aren't I?" he asks the kitten, patting its soft fur. Its small presence is enough to bring some peace to his disturbed soul.

"Jack Baker has been arrested for armed robbery."

The words immediately knock the sense out of him as he leaps up from the floor, causing the cat to roll down onto the floor with a thud. Eyes stretched wide, he stares at the screen, watching the footage of someone from his past getting dragged away by police officers.

Jack was a bad lot—he brought even more trouble for the caretakers than Felix himself. Felix doesn't remember how many fistfights he had gotten into with him, how many bruises coloured his skin just because of him, all because Jack always started quarrels, couldn't go a day without starting an argument with someone. He wasn't always a brawler, though—his full-throated sobs disturbed one too many nights.

In the end, no one is surprised when a lowborn cracks. Such people have only two options in life: reshape the pain so it can be hidden or be thrown behind the bars. No one seems to care enough to stop the Ferris wheel full of low-lives—no one ever gives them chance to jump.

He bites his nails and his brain quivers with angst.

Felix marches up the hill he has been defeated by so many times. The road where so much of his tears and even his blood has been spilled makes him one with the place. No matter how hard he tries to break away from the roots, the trees have grown tall from his blood and they will always stand proud.

The whispers of the autumn wind welcome him back to the place he used to call his own. "Miracle children" reads the moth-eaten wooden plaque, the tiny colourful handprints washed away by the past, leaving only memories. Felix puts his hand on an empty grey spot once decorated in red with his handprint. He lingers there for a heartbeat with his eyes closed, picturing all the distaste and sorrow the plaque holds. He knows that if his hand lingers a tad too long, all the evil of his past will come rushing to take him back, just like Pandora's box.

With a sigh full of dread he opens the door, entering the past once more, the familiar doorbell ringing in a bitter reminder of all the parents that have walked in and left without him.

"Welcome!" The familiar voice is almost expected and so when Felix's gaze catches upon the sleety, brown eyes, he doesn't even budge.

Tiptoeing through the night, Felix sneaks out on the balcony used as a hiding spot by the tempestuous teenagers. With a cigarette in his mouth and a lighter in his hand is when he first notices the silhouette sitting on the floor and for a heartbeat he feels nauseous, thinking he has come face to face with one of the caretakers, but he sighs in relief when he recognizes the familiar face of Hotaru sitting on the wooden floor, legs dangling in the heavy summer air with his usual bouquet of flowers next to him—this time plain white ones. Since Hotaru was a kid he has had an unusual fascination with flowers, and Felix couldn't understand what exactly was so captivating about plants that could be killed so easily.

"Why do you like flowers so much if you can't see them?" Felix asks as he lights the cigarette, sitting next to Hotaru and fixating on the bouquet.

"I like the way they smell, the way they feel to the touch, and the delicate meaning of each of them." Without missing a beat Hotaru gives his usual answer, gently playing his fingers through the bouquet. "I don't need eyes to understand the beauty of living," he adds while closing his eyes. "Or the ugliness."

Sensing the curiosity in the warm air, Hotaru blinks, turns his face to Felix, and with an unchanging serene expression says, "I talked with my mum today."

Felix nods, knowing that the boy isn't finished with the story yet. "She's in jail and she may or may not have said she wishes I was never born. She blames me for her problems."

The smoke gets caught in Felix's lungs, making him gag. Even if the boys don't have the perfect relationship, he has some sympathy left in him so he pats Hotaru aimlessly on his back, but the boy just shrugs him off, turning his attention back to the starless sky.

"I know she's ugly," he says, "even if I can't see her face talking to me."

Felix clears his throat, uncomfortable with the heavy atmosphere between them; he drops his weight on his elbows, turning his face upwards towards the crescent moon. "So..., what are these flowers for?"

Hotaru chuckles at the poor but welcomed attempt to make him feel at ease. "These are Alyssum, they mean worth beyond beauty."

"Oh,", says Felix, mimicking interest as his eyes cast back the silhouette of the golden moon, reflecting the thin line of a smile. Wild cicadas are crying somewhere far away, rattled by the silence of the night.

Felix grips the metal bars of the balcony, gazing at the forest surrounding them beyond the locks that prevent him from leaving or anyone taking him away.

"Do you think I am ugly?"

"Not yet," Hotaru answers quickly, as if he has heard the question before, "but you're blind to the goodness of people who care about you, and that makes you ungrateful and selfish."

Felix snatches the cigarette from his lips with a loud pop, exhaling the smoke with building anger.

"That's the only way for us to survive."

Hotaru once again turns back to him. "We're not the same." The stabbing words fall gracefully from his chapped lips.

Felix doesn't know what it is that's causing the distress in him, the coldness of Hotaru's words, the empty gaze directed only at him, or the cutting truth thrown at him.

So he does what he's best at, he runs away.

He throws the still-lit cigarette in the air so it lights up the sky like a lost firefly, and with that he stands up, but bends down close to the boy, to make sure Hotaru will feel his words just like his reeking breath.

"We're the same," he says. "You're just a better liar. That's how you got adopted."

Before he walks away through the glass door, he throws a last glance at the boy with his back to him. "I may be ugly, but at least I can admit to it."

"I see you still have a thing for flowers." Felix sneers, looking around the place that never changes.

"I see you're still an asshole," Hotaru gently bites back, never losing his temper, always keeping up the façade, never displaying the cracks.

"I heard about Jack." Felix ignores him, continuing to wander around until he catches sight of the new innocent kids running carelessly around in the backyard, not realising how close they're standing to the cliff and how little time is left before one of them slips, falling deep into the cruel abyss of life, with all the others following behind like black sheep.

Some chat jovially with the caretakers, others are more reluctant, sheltering in the corners and wrapping their arms around their frail bodies, and a few of them cut themselves off from the whole group, shutting out the big bad world altogether and paying no mind to the present moment. They seem so different and yet so similar: bounded up in their sinless little hearts, which have already begun to spoil prematurely, blemished by rotting spots and ripened with pain even before they have learned the rhythm of the heartbeat of life. They are divided by the roles they have chosen to survive—the stalwarts, the cowards, and the wicked. While their tainted hearts are already foul and will never beat in tune, it's what grows from the rotted seed that matters, a dazzling flower or the thorny bush.

"I can't say I was surprised," Felix says as he rests behind the crystal-like garden laboratory, waiting for the flowers to bloom, wondering which twig bristling with spikes will make to his side—wizened by hatred and anger.

"Why? Are you any different?" Hotaru snarls back without taking his eyes from the table, completely ignoring his presence.

The words boil the leftover anger in him as he abruptly turns to face his nonchalant friend.

"I've changed," he announces.

Hotaru only chuckles while his fingers dance through the lovely shades of green.

"It's this place and the people here who don't change."

"And how is your life going to turn out?" asks Hotaru. "Working a minimum wage job? Running from one part-time to another trying everything to make ends meet? You're no different from the rat beneath the train rails thinking it is exploring the world." His words pierce Felix's hollow heart like arrows. "You and I can never be like the people on the train."

"I'm not like you." Felix grimaces, his hands balled into tight fists. "I'm not like any of you."

Hotaru sighs and, putting away the bouquet, turns to him with an unimpressed expression. "Is this what you came for?"

His eyes remain cold and empty as the years pass by, always filled with antipathy towards Felix.

Felix fixes his gaze on his red-stained palms, the hair dye dripping like blood, tainting the bathroom in claret, just like the hidey-hole at school yesterday. Is it his blood on his hands or Noel's? He can't figure it out. Before he can cast the die or wash off the hair-dye the bathroom door is kicked open.

Hotaru stands there enraged, his stare burning with wrath. "Are you happy now?" he snarls, closing the door with a loud crash.

Felix avoids his heavy gaze, unable look into eyes that always have saw through his hidden parts.

"I'm not in the mood to talk to you," he says.

"But you were in the mood for breaking the nose of the son of our biggest funder," Hotaru yells, his voice breaking with pure rage as he throws the shampoo bottle at Felix's direction, adding injury to his shattered heart.

Much to his annoyance, Felix feels tears start to fill the cracks in his soul and his eyes. "Is that the only thing you care about?" he tries to scream back, but it only comes off as a broken croak.

Hotaru's face pinches, and his eyes are closed tight as he speaks. "Listen," he starts, walking closer to the darkness where Felix remains unmoved. "Me and you have it hard." He nudges Felix's shoulder with his finger, prodding him further into the void of light. "But you can't be so selfish."

"Selfish?" The howl breaks through him like blood from his palm, mixing with the red dye. "What do you know about my pain?"

He slaps the defenceless Hotaru across the face, leaving a red handprint on his face. "What do you know about the pain?" Felix pounces on the boy who has been handed everything on a silver spoon, while he had to lick the crumbs from the floor. Rashly, in the heat of the moment, his fingers dive towards the eyes of Hotaru, making him yelp in pain. "Should I be like you?" he bawls, digging his fingers deeper into the source of the sympathy of all. "Should I stab my eyes for someone to feel bad for me?!"

Once again, Felix can't tell whether it's his own blood or Hotaru's smeared all over the weeping boy's face—or maybe it's just hair dye.

The answer seems so close, but before Felix can uncloak the true identity of the villain once and for all, the caretakers barge in on the desperate cries of Hotaru, snatching the helpless victim off Felix and out of his reach. He watches the eyes fall onto him, the fear and disappointment flying over the faces of those who have stayed in the light, drawing a line between them and Felix, who remains in the dark. If there is any sadness left in him, he's numb to it; instead, their ghastly expressions just ignite the fires within him.

And with that, Felix signs a pact with anger that bursts out like flames from his heart.

He runs faster than the rain shattering against the concrete with red dripping from his head, leaving blood traces on the road that form a crime scene after murdering his past self. His veins char with the fuming blazes that his heart pumps within him, burning him like a lump of coal and setting his legs on fire as he sprints through the dire night. The fumes of his withering soul befog his sound mind, unaware of the destination of his heart.

Only when he's standing in front of the glassed building does he recognize the restaurant owned by the Fourniers'. The flames ignite him as a whole, spreading to his mind as the tantalizingly lit surname unhinges him. His addled brain cries "Do it!" and Felix slowly takes a rock from the ground. "Do it for yourself!" It screams again, tugging at his senses. Taken by his anger and his headache, he wails into the soundless night and throws the rock at the window, breaking it easily and setting off the alarm.

He doesn't know how far his screams reach, how many ears they fall on or how much more destruction he brings, but he eventually comes to his senses when someone tackles him to the ground, scraping his face against the concrete.

"What do you think you're doing?" the policemen shouts in his ear, but Felix continues to yell even when he's being dragged to the police car. He only stops when his face is smashed against the cold metal and they put the heavy handcuffs on him. But his anger praises him as he's shoved inside the car, assuring him that it's what they deserve.

Xaria jumps from one corner to another, like a rabbit dancing with death as she collects all her belongings.

"Mommy." A kid walks inside, rubbing his drowsy eyes. "Where are you going?" he asks through a yawn.

Panicked, she accidentally kicks the pile of papers onto the floor, letting them scatter around.

"I'll be back soon, alright?" She holds her kid's face, kissing him aimlessly on the temple as her eyes shake with alarm. "Just go to sleep."

With that Xaria springs out of the room, not giving a final glance at her kid reaching curiously out towards the papers, where all the information gathered about Felix remains.

She scuttles down the stairs but taken over by fear she misses a step and collapses onto the floor.

"Are you okay?" The child rushes towards her, grabbing her with his small hands, but Xaria shrugs off her son's touch, haltingly lifting her body as the pain in her bones grows. Her raging heart tries to conquer the ache as she fumbles with the keys, failing to open the door with her trembling fingers.

"Just go to sleep." She shouts once she is finally outside, her voice muffled by the merciless rain falling down on her.

She sprints through the night in thin layers of filthy, wet clothes as the rain continues to pour down on her, raindrops flowing through her bones. Her sight blurred by the rain, she fails to notice the incoming lines of light of the car, and only when a loud honk shakes the ground beneath her feet does she jump, falling backwards as her dress gets tangled in the mud.

"Are you alright?" The stranger jumps from the car, gazing at the deer caught in the headlights.

Xaria looks around, her eyes wide and full of tears, and starts to shake with helplessness.

"Can you give me a ride?"

In a stupor, Felix gazes with eyes drunk with enmity at the metal bars surrounding him. How tarnished he feels is enough to make his body shake with rage. There is a monster inside of him demanding to be freed, to destroy with its deadly claws anything that stands in its way, but no matter how overpowered he feels by the malign presence, physically he's too weak. Still, though, the gruesome images continue to paint his brain with ink red as blood, and somewhere in his putrid soul, his bruised heart—all too small, all too frail—is doing everything in its might to stop him becoming one with his fulsome malice.

But when the sound of jangling keys registers in his mind and he sees William's disappointed face entering the cell, fate pushes him down to the arcane, dark parts of his essence. His mien changes in a blink, a devilish grin sprawling over his face as his baleful gaze burns into the policeman.

"You've finally come," he snarls wryly. "So you give a half-shit about me then?" he asks without any real expectation of an answer, remembering all the years he longed for William to come back for him. Now he has finally arrived, Felix doesn't feel any tug on his heart-strings. Instead he is numbed with anger.

"Why did you do this?" William avoids the question, closing the door and walking closer to the teenager lying on the floor.

"Did it bruise your ego?" Felix tilts his head to the side, his face blank of any trace of emotion. "That the almighty saviour William couldn't save a piece of shit like me?"

William's brows furrow as he stares down upon him through narrowed, lost eyes, looking at him as if he were stark staring mad. "What are you even talking about?" he sighs deeply, bending his knees as he squats down to Felix's eye-level. "Do you know how much trouble you're in? You could go to jail!"

Felix doesn't know what leads to his heart bursting into flames again, burning up the last bits of amity in him—William's disparaging tone or the sheer unfairness of his life—but something inside him cracks, letting out all his darkest thoughts that he has kept to himself for years.

"What if I wanted to?" Felix mumbles with eyes glued to the floor, all the weight of the pain he has carried all these years bearing down on him at once. "What if I want to go to jail?"

He knows something has to change. He knows that the longer he turns a blind eye to his situation, treading water, gazing aimlessly at the same crossroads of the future, the more fate will continue to torment him, shredding his heart to bits. Maybe he swam for too long, or maybe he marched against the waves too hard, for now he's too exhausted to look up at the blue sky from the sea of impiety.

In the end, not every carp surpasses the stream, some are left behind to rot in the waters. Felix is tired of living the same old day every day, taking one step forward from the crossroads but always coming back to where he started.

He pounces on William, stabbing his face with his fingers. "Isn't it a crime?" he shrieks, holding him in a death grip, just like an animal piercing flesh with its fangs. "Arrest me then!" he shouts as he kicks the policeman who groans in pain.

The thrilling feeling of elation is back, and his anger watches him act with a Cheshire grin, praising him.

"Take me to jail!" No matter how hard other officers try to enter, William holds a shaky hand around the bars, stopping them. "Come on! Arrest me, dear policeman!" Regardless of how much Felix hits him, scratches him, despite the red lines being painted on his face, William doesn't fight back, allowing the kid to relieve his rage on him.

"Please, just arrest me!" he wails through angry tears that burn his skin.

Just get me away from this place.

The metal bars finally get unlocked and the crowd of officers barge in, snatching Felix by his arms and pinning him against the floor.

"Take me! Please take me away from here!" He bites back, gnawing at the policeman's hand and receiving a punch to his skull in return. "I hate you!" he wails as blood drips down from his opened scar, letting the memories flow out. "I hate all of you!"

William stays on his knees, his head hung low in shame as the kid continues to bawl hot tears while battling against people he can't beat. And with the pill choked down his throat comes the longed-for somnolence of his mind.

Lulled by the drugs, Felix rests his head on William's shoulder, after all these years looking serene at last. Dazing into nothingness, William traces shapes on the kid's palm and remembers his small, puny fingers that almost fitted around William's one finger but are now bloodied and covered in scratches and bruises.

He knows he has failed the kid again, for the second and certainly the last time. He squeezes his eyes shut and exhales shakily through his gripped jaw, trying to hold his anger inside.

"His caretaker's here." Logan's voice drags him up from the sea of regret, with waves of resentment and pique filling his entire being. He nods and gently takes Felix's head in his palms but the sudden movement awakens the boy. With blinking eyes, he observes the position he's sitting in and quickly flinches away from William's reach, burned even by a slight touch. William's eyes droop with sadness, but Felix continues to avoid his gaze.

"Felix, Xaria is here." Logan offers a helping hand but Felix stands up on his own, even though his legs are shaking, still frail from the pills.

"Felix!" The sweet-toned voice of Xaria turns to despair as she howls out for him. "Where is he?" she shrieks while wriggling out of the grasp of the policemen stopping her from entering the forbidden place. When her eyes finally land on the teenager she rushes towards him with unstoppable force, dropping all her belongings as she takes him in her protective arms, shielding him from everyone's eyes.

"Are you okay? Are you hurt?" she asks as she searches his face for any signs of pain, raindrops falling like tears from her wet hair.

Felix nods as he gazes at Xaria with blurry eyes.

"What did you do to him?" Her yell shakes the limp body of the boy.

"We..." William coughs, ashamed of what needs to be said. "We had to give him a sedative."

Hearing this, the woman's face breaks into a frown as she hastily brushes Felix's hair with her fingers. Her embrace feels so odd to his skin, galling his clouded mind. Half of him wants to pull away and rip off the flesh where he has been brushed up against by the person he was starving to be hugged by all these years.

But just like before, he will never get the thing he desires, unless he changes...

For a brief moment, Felix wishes Xaria had embraced him more in the past, not only when he cried hot tears but with a genuine love—if she had, maybe he wouldn't resent her touch so much now.

Forcing some sense of strength into his weakened muscles, he briskly shoves Xaria away, and with that the itch inside his skin calms down. He feels the heavy baggage of the past part from him.

The room falls quiet, and since Xaria's heart-wrenching expression brings nothing but vexation towards the boy, he avoids her gaze.

"Okay, the most important thing is that you're okay," she whispers as she rubs Felix's shoulder. Felix still isn't meeting her eye, afraid that he will fall back into the pits of fires of the past if he does. He has burned enough. This time, instead of burning his flesh, he will burn from the inside, with unyielding flames of vengeance.

The rain is heavy outside, crashing loudly against the concrete walls. William and Xaria guard his sides, holding the umbrella over his head, protecting him. And yet Felix knows the care is temporary; he won't fall into the same trap twice because the pain of the let-down aches more with time.

This time he will be the god of his own life, and so he walks away through the merciless rain and doesn't look back even when the people from his past call out to him.

"Do you think she needs a ride back?" he asks as he watches the scene unfolding through the rain that blurs the outlines of people through the incoming lights of the cars.

The woman runs downstairs, carrying an umbrella loosely in her hands and chasing the indiscernible silhouette of the boy.

"Let's just go home now, you're tired," the man says as he winds the window up, muting the sound of the rain.

"Dylan, how are you feeling?" Sophia asks as she turns towards him from the passenger seat, gazing at him with undeniable worry.

"Fine, I guess, a little sleepy," he answers, staring into nothingness as he plays with the thin paper bracelet on his wrist.

"It's just sedation, you'll be fine," Gregor mumbles through a yawn, sounding as frail as Sophia looks. Meanwhile, Sophia just gazes at him with sleepless eyes that have shed too many tears.

Dylan gnaws at his lip, biting the apologies down, too ashamed, too afraid of their response. In the end, he has always been a coward, always hiding from the truth. He wordlessly takes the bracelet off but he knows the label of insane will always be burned onto his skin.

He shoves his hand out of the window, letting the feeling of the rain dropping onto his skin bring some sense of reality to him.

The reality of the oath that lets his loved ones hurt him continuously.

His fingers let go of the paper, letting it fly into the stormy night, and with that, he breaks the spell of the malediction that is hurting everyone around him.

His past.

"You never took your belongings before, so why now?" Hotaru asks as he puts the box onto the table, thanking the kid that has helped them to find it.

"Research," Felix answers dryly as he opens the file, his eyes reading carefully through the scribbles of his check-in report, the reason why he has come to this dreadful place.

First name: Unknown

Last name: Unknown

Date of birth: Unknown
Parents: Unknown
Place of living: Unknown
Taken in: 05.05.01

No matter how much he tries to change, he always stays the same, just like the walls surrounding him, and the story gets awfully boring if it repeats itself too many times.

In the end, no matter how much skin you shed, it's what is deep within you that matters. If the heart stays rotten, so does the flesh outside, because no matter how much you try, you can't bring the dead back to life.

Again and again, though, dried flowers also get framed on the walls because beauty can be found even in ugliness, depending on the eye of the beholder.

He walks down the hill, crushing the dried leaves beneath his feet while feeling a certain empathy with them. He too, like a trembling leaf in an autumnal wind, scared of falling onto unknown ground, kept tight hold of the branch, but in so doing he ended up alone on the naked tree, gazing down at all those who had fallen down to eternal slumber. At that moment he wished he had someone next to him, sharing the same grey shades of death, but instead he was left hanging alone on the mighty tree.

Dylan sits alone on the lonely swing as the summer breeze carries his body up into the blue sky. He gazes at the families gathered together at the table; kids playing round, high with joy, and he feels so bleakly lonesome amid so much life. He hears the metal swing clang next to him but doesn't have the heart to look up.

"Hello Genji, I'm Sophia." The girl, Sophia, his cousin, chirps gleefully as she swings her body into the air whilst keeping an eye on him.

"Don't..." Dylan murmurs through tight lips as he feels a dreadful feeling of inquietude settle heavily inside his worn heart, making him cautious to speak. "Don't call me that."

Sophia momentarily stops swinging and gazes at him with a worried expression.

"I'm sorry Dylan," she says earnestly and Dylan just nods, still not brave enough to take his eyes off the fresh grass beneath him. "But I wish I had a Japanese name too," she adds suddenly, swinging herself up into the azure sky once more. "I don't know anything about Japan; my parents never tell me anything."

Dylan stays silent but peeks at her through his lashes as the sense of malaise he has become wise to grows greater into his soul.

"Can you tell me something about Japan?" She sounds so keen to listen to Dylan that he hasn't the heart to disappoint her. Or maybe he's afraid to.

"Well...," he starts, just above a whisper, his lips unused to speaking. "It's a beautiful country with kind people. It's beautiful even in winter."

"Did you have a lot of friends?" The question stops Dylan's heart, and he feels his bones shake as dismay settles in his soul.

"I'm back." The devil laughs loud and clear in his ears. "I never left."

Dylan squeezes his eyes shut, listening to his raging heartbeat pound against his ribcage, demanding to be freed as the cold sweat starts to roll from his glistening forehead.

Sensing the distress in the boy, Sophia gazes at him with troubled eyes, sincere apologies hidden beneath her gaze. "Did I say something wrong?"

"I didn't..." He tries to erase the image of Ayumu that has reappeared before his eyes. "I didn't have any friends," he lies through gritted teeth as Ayumu scowls at him, shaming him with a mere glance.

For a while Sophia watches him silently and Dylan feels the weight of regret slowly press down on his frail heart. He sees the terror-stricken eyes of Ayumu accusing him from afar, flames of hatred in his honey eyes.

"Then I will be your friend," declares Sophia with ease, finally gaining Dylan's attention as he gawks at her with wide eyes and an open mouth.

"Do you want to be my friend?" Sophia looks embarrassed this time—her glimmering eyes have dimmed down.

"I...," Dylan mumbles, lost in thought, his voice quivering, ringing with uncertainty. "I..." His voice slowly drops down an octave lower, sounding unnatural, sinister even. "I...," he blabbers, sounding raspy and out of breath.

Sophia looks at him through knitted brows, but her eyes stretch wide as the pills start to fall out from Dylan's mouth, splattering the ground. Dylan coughs, choking on the pills as his skin pales, turning a deadly grey, and his eyes roll back in his head, and with that his body slumps to the ground among the piles of colorful pills.

"No!" Sophia wails, destroying the tranquility. With a shriek she jumps from her bed, her breathing uneven, consumed by a sense of panic that sends her heart haywire. Not thinking straight, she leaps up and rushes out of her room in her nightgown. With each step she takes, she hears her heart shatter into a million pieces, causing her to stumble down the concrete stairs. An unknown fear is making itself at home in her mind, shaking her to the core. The way to Dylan's room has never felt so long.

Without knocking she unlocks the door with shaky hands, letting it fly open with a loud crash. Her eyes roam helplessly around the room, but she sees that it's just the way she left it—filthy and filled with despair.

From the corner of her eyes she sees a figure slumped on the bed, which brings both relief and wrath to her torn soul. She slowly walks towards Dylan, who hasn't changed his position, still molded to the bed. She stands at the corner of the bed for a heartbeat before tugging the bed sheet from his body.

"Come on, get up," she says calmly, gazing at Dylan who stays lying in fetal position as his unfocused eyes gaze aimlessly into nothingness.

"Get up!" she exclaims louder this time, swinging the dirty bed sheets over him. "Dylan, get up!" she roars, latching onto him and shaking his limp body. "Come on, get up!" she begs as her fists dive into the cold skin of her friend. "How long are you going to stay like this?"

She pleads to be seen or to be heard, but as if dead, Dylan stays frozen in place, blinking slowly with bleary eyes.

"How long..." she murmurs through tears and the lump in her throat. "How long are you going to blame yourself for something that is not your fault?" She throws a final, feeble blow at Dylan.

"It is my fault." He speaks for the first time, still gazing into the unknown. His voice is forceless as he tries to roll the words over his tongue. "It's all my fault."

Sophia groans, falling clumsily onto the bed and holding her face in her palms. A heartbeat of silence settles within the walls.

"When will you move on?" she asks as she rubs comforting shapes on his leg, gazing at him with glistening eyes. "It's time to move on."

Dylan just shakes his head and nuzzles his face into the pillows, hiding from her troubled eyes.

"He's not coming back, Dylan." Sophia turns her gaze to the wrinkled fabric of her clothing, gently smoothing the creases. "He's dead."

"Don't say that!" Dylan jumps up from his bed with a howl that shakes the walls. "Please don't say that...," he whispers, his tone pained, full of sorrow.

Sophia sighs, letting her gaze drop onto Dylan's eyes, glimmering with tears. "You need to let go of the past, you can't let it keep chaining you down."

Dylan just shakes his head and drops his weight down on the bed once more, gazing wordlessly at Sophia.

"I'm not ready yet..."

"It's time." Her gentle whisper caresses his senses, bringing some serenity to his troubled mind, but the nauseating, reeking smell of alcohol punches him the moment he blinks his eyes, making him grimace and scrunch his nose in aversion.

The darkness of the house engulfs him in a hug, welcoming him back home.

From the corner of his eye Felix catches the lucent silhouette of the cat, lying right next to him. Bewildered, he blinks his eyes, now fully aware as he gazes at the cat passing through thin air. His mesmerized eyes reflecting the glow of the creature slowly start to fill realization.

"Dream?" he whispers in the dark, where the only source of luminosity is the cat which, when called by its name, wakes up in the instant, gazing at him with beaming eyes.

"It's not fair!" Ayumu pounds feet on the ground, tramping down the fresh grass. "Why does she like you and not me?" he complains as he tries to touch the kitten once more, but the feral cat just hisses at him, even though when Genji was doing the same thing, it remained calm.

"Cats like me," mumbles Genji, continuing to tease the cat with a leaf.

Ayumu pouts in annoyance, avoiding looking at the serene duo who are having the time of their lives.

Sensing the sadness of his friend, Genji looks at him.

"If you want we can name her Dream," he says. Ayumu turns his attention back to him, looking intrigued at the offer. "So you can share names, maybe she will like you more then."

The purring of the cat brings Felix back to the present, making him aware of the sight of the kitty lying on its back, showing its belly in a sign of trust. He chuckles with melancholy and carefully skims his hand through the gleam. "I missed you," he whispers, rueful of all the memories they could have made.

They stay like this for a heartbeat, savouring the moment of re-familiarizing themselves with one another, satiating the longing that has followed their hearts all these years.

Everything is so familiar, and yet it is so strange to be inside the house again; the house that was once beautiful but has been filtered through grief that can be seen in the broken glass scattered around like traps, the papers filling every corner of each room, the empty bottles of alcohol and the dirty clothes.

The house reeks of desperation. Felix gently picks up one of the crumpled pieces of paper from the floor, and the moment his eyes land on a photo of himself, his breath becomes tangled in his lungs.

"Have you seen me?"

He reads the words above the childhood picture of him, smiling so widely he's almost unrecognizable to himself.

Age: 6

Last seen: May 5th, 2000.

With tears gathering in his eyes, he touches the paper, caressing the photo of the once happy child, but the sentiment is cut short when Dream starts to run up the moth-eaten stairs.

"Dream!" he yells out. "Dream, wait for me!" He chases the cat up the old, creaking stairs.

The hallway is shrouded in the familiar darkness, the only thin line of light coming from the door open ajar. With fearful, short steps he walks towards the light where the cat is waiting for him in front of a wooden door.

Slowly he opens the door, which he quickly recognizes as his own, and there he sees the toys he used to play with, his old clothes, dozens of untidily drawn paintings decorating the walls. But the sense of familiarity is tarnished by the filth that has become his room, the muddied footprints leading to each corner, the dirty clothes and unfinished plates of food scattered around, the pure despair that has crawled its way even into his room.

Looking around, from the corner of his eye he notices a shadow crumpled up uncomfortably on his child-sized bed. He walks closer to the silhouette and recognizes a woman's face. With his breath caught in his lungs, he staggers back, holding for life onto the door frame, his fingernails scraping the wood as an unstoppable stream of emotions cascades over him.

Tears glimmering in the dim light, both petrified and anticipative of his fate, he utters weakly, "Mum?"

The noise stirs the woman awake and she rolls onto her back and opens her eyes. "Ayumu?" she says, a sweet smile brightening her face, washing all the sorrow away.

Felix hiccups, flinching from the moment he has been yearning for his whole life. Astounded and rooted to the spot, he stares at his mother open-mouthed, feeling his legs go limp and his heart go numb, nonplussed by the emotions consuming him all at once.

Mizuki rises from the bed, supporting her weight on her elbows as she takes a good look at her son.

"What's wrong, dear?" she says.

Even if the words sound foreign to his ears, his mother's fond tone, the tone he's been ravenous to hear one more time, is enough to bring Felix to tears, and he sprints towards his mother, enveloping himself in her embrace.

"Mommy!" Like a child he wails out through a waterfall of tears. He is still just a child in need of his mum, just what the mirror on the wall reflects him as. "I'm sorry!" he apologizes through a choked sob, knowing all too well what the years of yearning must have been like. "I'm so sorry!"

Mizuki holds him tenderly by his face, wiping the starry tears away. "Where have you been?" She faintly discerns the line of the scar and with a feathery touch caresses it with her thumb. "You made mum so worried."

The tragic realization that he can't understand the words coming from his mum's mouth makes him cry only harder, turning him hysterical as he sobs on her shoulder. Mizuki gently brushes her fingers through the strands of his hair, soothing the lifelong heartache away. "It's okay." She kisses him by his scar. "You're with me now." But the moment is abruptly stopped when light strikes the room, revealing a man by the entrance.

"Dad?" Felix sniffles, wiping his persistent flow of tears. However, he quickly becomes aware that his father isn't looking at him, nor is his mother anymore.

"Come on." He walks closer to them, bringing with him the smell of alcohol. "Let's go to bed."

"I dreamed of him again," Mizuki whispers bitterly, gazing at her palms through raw tears as if she can still feel the cold touch of her son's tears. "It felt so real."

Rubbing his face, Kuragari sways from side to side, stumbling into the wall. "Don't worry, I'll find him," he assures her through fuzzy speech.

"How?" Mizuki screams, jumping up from the bed all of the sudden. "When all you do is drink all day, instead of searching for your son?"

Caught in between them, Felix's eyes dart from his dad to his mum. Never in the past had he had to face a situation like this.

"Why are you so useless?" she yells as she throws the mud-covered flashlight at her husband. "You call yourself a policeman?" Before she can grab any more items to throw, Kuragari holds her by her arms, but Mizuki doesn't back down.

Fresh tears start to gather in Felix's eyes as he watches his once beautiful family crumble.

Because of him.

He led to the failure of the serene harmony. He was the first particle to fail, dragging everyone after him.

"Why is no one doing anything but me?" Mizuki shouts and kicks the table over with a booming crash, making the posters wheel in the air like falling confetti, but her howl dies down quickly in her throat when a thunderous wail strikes the night.

"Yonaki baba!" a kid in the distance cries, disturbing the village. "She's back!"

Through narrow ed eyes, Mizuki throws a resentful glance towards the window showing a house with only one room lit inside.

"Why him?" she spits, her words dipped in venom. "Why him and not my son?"

"Enough!" Kuragari shouts, punching the wall, making Felix flinch and whimper through his sobs as he holds his palms to his ears. "How can you even say that?" Kuragari trembles with rage as he shakes his wife by her shoulders. "Genji is as much our son as Ayumu!"

"You watched him grow!" he cries in both rage and sorrow. "Hell, you watched him being born!"

Having no desire to watch his parents in such a raw state, Felix leaps up from the floor and runs away from the scene, his tears falling like raindrops. On his way he crashes into a person in white, evidently a nurse, rushing into the room behind him.

Then the entire story repeats itself as Felix peeps inside only to see before him the heart-rending sight of Genji wailing while being manhandled by a number of people in white, twisting and bawling in agony, trying to escape the grasp of the nurses.

Felix isn't sure how long he stares but this time he locks his eyes with Genji, whose eyes are wide with fear as he lets out a penetrating screech loud enough to make the door shut in front of his nose with a bang.

"He's here!" The sob shakes the walls within. "Ayumu is here!"

Heart pounding rapidly in his chest, Ayumu takes to his feet and bolts away from the crime scene, devastated to hear the child's cries once more.

He chases Dream around the draughty house, stumbling and tripping over the things scattered on the floor. He slips on a book and his body slams against the door, opening it easily, and he tumbles out onto the grass. Dream meows, urging him to go, but the pain quickly crawls through his nerves, eating him inside. "Wait a bit," he croaks, holding the weight in his arms as he slowly tries to stand up.

As he turns his head up towards the sky, he sees an extraordinary sight: the sky is split in two, one side lambent with loud sunshine and the other pitch black with soundless night. In the middle there is a line carved where Felix is standing, as if stamped just for him. Spellbound by the world he has been dropped into, he stands where the two worlds meet, and only when Dream meows once more does he comes to his senses.

His eyes dance around, not knowing where to land. He watches a crowd of people wearing kimonos of a type he remembers seeing in a children's book and prancing unhurriedly through the night with lanterns in their hands—they appear shiftless and vapid, lifeless, just like the colour of their skin.

He walks along the thin line between life and death, not belonging to either side, and with keenness in his eyes, he examines the two intermingling worlds.

A pallid man dressed in white stands in front of the glowing lights, his eyes reflecting the sunlight from the other side and his gaze fixated on a woman sitting at a bus stop with a baby in her arms. Over there people in everyday dress go about their hectic lives, just like the life that once belonged to Felix. He takes a look at the woman, her ash-black hair falling ungracefully as she balances her phone on her shoulder.

The emotionless face of the man remains still but his eyes glimmer with a different story—a sad story, a tiny beam of woe. He waves his hand in the air, carefully touching the wall dividing him from his loved one, and with a gentle push, a white butterfly is birthed on his palm. It flies lightly towards the woman, who flaps it away irritably with her hand.

Felix flutters his eyes like the wings of the glimmering butterfly—the more he gazes, the more recognizable the woman gets.

"Auntie, I told you I'll be back at noon!" Akiko complains, and her whiny voice drums in his ears, bringing back the memories.

Caught up by the pain, he loses track of time, and watching the lively girl he used to play with, the realization of missed opportunities hits him in the heart like an old song. Giving her a last glance, he sighs, walking down the line where he belongs. Not quite dead but not alive either, lost somewhere in the middle. He blends perfectly with both sides, dead and alive, humans stuck together in two close worlds, yearning and silently grieving for one another. Who are more selfish, the ones that don't let go or the ones that decide to stay, bringing sweet pain to another?

"Ayumu!" Someone disturbs the silence, but he can't see anything except a glowing lantern floating in the night sky and creeping closer and closer to him. "Where are you?" echoes the howl.

Felix narrows his eyes at the lantern; a dim silhouette slowly starts to paint the air behind the glow, and before long a familiar face comes into his vision, knocking him senseless.

"Dad!" he wails. He tries to move his feet towards his father, but something is stopping him—Dream gnawing at his trousers, pulling him to the other side. But Kuragari just runs past him, continuously chanting his name with an undertone of pure despair at the thought that he will never find his son.

"Dad! I'm here!" Felix sobs, reaching his hand out towards the man who has disappeared into the night, leaving behind only the sound of his cries.

"Dad..." he mewls, standing alone on the thin trail as people move by him, never noticing the sorrowful boy in their midst.

The cat continues to tug at his clothing, urging him to move, and so, rubbing his tears away, he gives a last glance to the tiny gleam of light in the far, dark distance before the skies turn black, engulfing everything into the void. With wide eyes he watches as the worlds get sucked in, disappearing from his sight as if they never existed.

Dream bites his skin, meowing over and over again in desperation, and eventually his feet start moving on their own, forcing him to run away as he continues to look back at the abyss creeping closer to him and demolishing everything in its way.

The road narrows into a corner, and the moment he reaches the very end, everything else disappears around him. He heaves a shaky sigh as a new sight appears before him: heavy trees looking down at him with care, shielding him from the malicious grin of the crescent moon. Dream bumps her head on his leg, making him stumble back, but what catches his attention is the stone he has been standing on.

Eguchi Ayumu

05.05.94-05.05.00

Gone but not forgotten

The breath catches in his lungs, making him gasp as he jumps back, burned by the sight of his own gravestone.

Not yet dead, but for everyone else he's long gone.

To think of all the people waiting in anguish for him to return, and all the tears that have been spilled because of him and all the grief this place holds, is enough to make his weakened heart ache. Ache for the people he never had the chance to exchange last goodbyes with and would never have the chance to share laughter and tears with.

So many missed opportunities and for what? Before the answer dawns on him, he notices an intruder into his doleful state: an old woman sitting by the grass, gently caressing the stone right next to his whilst humming a melody from his past in a creaky voice.

Yamaguchi Genji

03.18.92-05.05.16

A carp that swims up waterfalls in the rapids and reaches the top

Will immediately turn into a dragon

A song his mum had tried to teach him days before he vanished, but the old dear singing is certainly not his mother. Walking carefully, he takes a better look at her, his gaze falling onto the corner of her cheek.

"And then suddenly the ring falls from her finger," Moriko chirps as the kid on her lap gnaws lazily at the apple, gazing at her face. "Are you listening?" she chuckles, pinching Ayumu's cheeks gently, but the kid continues to fixate on the corner of her cheek.

"Heart," he mumbles with a mouth full of apple.

"What?" Moriko giggles more, now putting away the book.

"Your mole." He lifts his tiny finger and carefully tracing the mole on her face. "It's a heart."

"Yes, it's heart-shaped because it's full of love for you," Moriko guffaws as she jumps in for a surprise hug, leaving kisses all over the complaining kid's face.

Even if the skin has wrinkled, the heart has stayed pure, looking as lovely as before.

Tears start to flow once more as Felix sprints towards Moriko, now old and frail, not as full of life as before. He hugs her from the side, not caring that she can't sense his presence.

He looks at the little figure Moriko is putting on his gravestone, a statue of a frog. "I missed you kids," she says, and although she says it with a shy smile, her voice is filled with rue.

Felix rubs his face on her shoulder, hiding his tears, pained to see her so wearied. Through blurred vision, he sees a soft light soaring towards him and, narrowing his eyes, he spies thousands of fireflies floating through the dark and blinding him with their light. When he opens his eyes again, he finds himself engulfed by the fireflies, illuminating a path through the gloomy forest that he knows all too well by now. The fireflies have become bigger, mightier, more profound—they resemble the shapes of lanterns, shining so brightly they burn his eyes.

"Ayumu!" someone yells in distance. "Genji!" yells someone else. "Where are you?"

Felix looks around, desperately trying to catch sight of the visitors of the night, but his vision is misty and the images blur with one another.

"Genji!" he hears Moriko wail. "Come back!"

"Ayumu, dear!" his mum follows shortly after. "Where are you?"

The lanterns slowly approach him, as if searching for him, but before he can be found, he stumbles over a lump on the ground. When he looks down, he sees Genji lying on the muddy ground, his clothes covered in filthy muck and his body shaking violently. At first Felix thinks it's because he's cold, but then he hears a heart-wrenching sob leave the kid's lips as he tries to stand up but fails, the slippery ground making him fall once more and smearing mud all over him.

"Hey, are you okay?" Felix kneels closer to him and gently touches his shoulder, but to his surprise, and terror, his hand goes right though the child who just continues to weep. He jumps back, falling onto the ground as he looks at Genji with wide, horrified eyes. Thunder roars through the sky, painting everything in shades of purple, and both of them are jolted by the penetrating sound. Meanwhile, the rain just gets stronger, piercing painfully through the skin.

Genji tries to stand once again, his tears mixing with the mud as he tries to rub the tears and raindrops away, and before long he's rushing deeper into the woods, even while the people behind him continue to call out their names.

For a while Felix is left sitting there gawking, his mind hazy, the rain hitting the ground the only sound buzzing inside his ears, but then he sees the firefly again, its light even weaker in the stormy night but still flickering ever so softly, guiding him towards the direction the kid went. And so, with all the energy he has left he forces himself off the ground and speeds into the wooded area, ignoring the heart-breaking sound of the mothers' cries.

"Ayumu, please!" He hears Genji weep. "I'm so scared, let's go, Ayumu!" Felix curses under his breath as he desperately tries to push the bushes and branches out of his way. The terrified weeping of the child echoes in his brain, making his teeth grind with angst.

"Ayumu, please move, it's too dangerous!" Felix stops in his tracks and almost falls face down on the ground when he finally sees the familiar petite figure standing at the edge of a cliff.

"No!" the younger him, Ayumu, shouts, holding tighter onto the tree beside him, the roots of which are hanging over the cliff. "You're mean! I don't ever want to see you again!"

"Ayumu!" Genji croaks through a sob, his voice jumping as he bounces up and down in agitation. "Please, I'm sorry..." He hiccups as he angrily rubs the tears away. "Please let's go home, I'm so scared." He clutches onto his filthy clothing as if to stop his body from trembling.

"No! Leave me alone..." Both of them squeal when yet another thunderbolt crashes through the dead sky, mercilessly shaking the ground. Ayumu jolts forward in fear, and for a second he loses his balance, making Genji screech, but he quickly grabs a branch of the old tree. "Leave me alone! I hate you so much! I, I hate, I hate you more than you do!" he yells, but he himself sounds unconvinced as his voice wavers.

Felix looks around, his jaw still closed tightly as his whole body shakes with both angst and adrenaline. He quickly moves towards the kid in an attempt to get them out of there. Even though he knows it's impossible.

"I don't want you to get hurt and I'm sorry that I shouted at you," Genji mewls, making a step closer to the younger one, but Ayumu just stumbles back but gasps when he almost slips again. "I promise I will never shout at you again." He weakly lifts his pinkie up. "So please let's go back, okay? I will give you all of my toys! Just please let's go, I'm very scared." His sentence breaks at the end as he cries louder this time, more and more fresh tears rolling down his cheeks as he gazes with terror-stricken and pleading eyes at his friend.

Ayumu, still frowning and pouting, is deep in thought, but it does seem like he's starting to give up. When he makes the first step forward Felix lets out the breath he has been holding, heavy with relief, and although Genji's sobs continue to fill the forest, he doesn't sound as scared as before—he is probably even more relieved than Felix himself.

But then like a curse the loudest thunderbolt cracks the sky in two and Felix lunches forward, his eyes opening wide in horror, as he sees Ayumu jump in fear.

"Be careful!" he yells and for a moment he swears the kid catches his eye, looking at him with pure horror, but then only the sound of a quiet yelp is heard as his short legs lose their balance, launching him backwards and the branch he was holding onto breaks, and with that he slips away from his vision in mere seconds—one moment he is there and the next he is gone.

And only the quiet echoing sound of screaming can be heard from beneath the cliff before the river splashes loudly with its guest.

For what feels like forever he stays in the same position, his hand weakly hanging off the cliff as he gazes blankly into space with crazy, shaky eyes. He can't move, can't hear anything, sees nothing at all, as if everything has stopped and only the sound of rain has stayed. He feels his eyes water as his tears blend with the raindrops that have never stopped pouring from the pitch-black sky.

Then he hears a quiet thud behind him, a sound of grass rustling hesitantly, and when he turns his trembling head behind him, he finds Genji collapsed on his knees, his wide eyes shaking, gazing at nothing as the rain mercilessly pours down on him. He isn't crying, he isn't screaming, he isn't moving, he isn't even breathing as he sits there with tears rolling down his face. Felix sees something break behind his eyes, his previously twinkling eyes dimming to nothingness as he continues to gaze, his body swaying back and forth.

Felix tries to stand up but his arms can't hold on to the slippery ground and his body sinks deeper into the mud.

"I need to find him," Genji whispers to himself, making Felix whip his head back. "I need…" He staggers, trying to get up. "I need to protect Ayumu," he mumbles but his eyes are still staring blankly into space.

He leans all of his weight on his arms and somehow manages to stand up. "Ayumu! Genji!" The voices can still be heard from the distance, but they sound so far away, and Genji's chin wobbles as he listens, trying to hold back his tears. Still stumbling he moves to the other side of the cliff and looks down to see if there is solid ground beneath. He holds tightly onto the old tree.

Felix tries to get up again, his limbs going in every direction as he desperately tries to find his balance. Genji is already making a first step forwards, his knuckles turning white as he grips the wood.

"No! Stop!" Felix begs as his legs give way once more, leaving him kneeling on the ground. "Don't go there! Genji!" he yells full-throated as he lunges forwards to try to catch him, but Genji is already stepping down when he finally manages to get within reach, and when he tries to grab him by his arm, his fingers once again go through the child's body.

Genji's leg wobbles, becoming swallowed up in the mud, and Felix doesn't even have a chance to blink as the kid goes flying down towards the ground. He quickly claps his palms against his eyes, but he still hears the loud thud, and he's sure he will forever be haunted by the sound of the cracking bones.

After what feels like forever, he peeks through his palms, and when he sees an outline of a hanging leg he quickly squeezes his eyes shut and mewls pathetically. Finally the tears march out from the corners of his eyes, and he drops his head down into his palms and weeps.

For the first time, Felix wishes he could forget everything. He squeezes his eyes harder and harder in an attempt to forever erase the images from his brain. As the tears roll down, each drop morphs into a faint speck of light as it hits the ground.

"Let's play, Felix." Noel's droning voice ploughs into him like a kick in the head, and his breath catches in his throat as he shuffles back, looking around wildly, his arms already wrapped protectively around his shaking body.

At first he sees only the mighty trees sheltering him from hazard, but then his howl strikes through the woods as Noel's shadow appears before him, creeping up at a familiar, taunting pace.

"Go away!" Felix wails, taking the broken branch in his hands. "Leave me alone!" He swings the bough around as he slowly creeps towards the cliff.

One by one the shadows of his past start to appear: William, Xaria, they're all there to taunt him once more.

"Why can't you just leave me alone?!" The past always comes back to haunt him—no matter how much blood his past selves have shed, the past remains the same.

His whole body leaps as he swings the branch, and when he staggers back he yelps, the cold air embracing him from behind as he slowly dives into the void below. But before he can fall, Xaria is there to catch him by his wrist. Eyes wide with terror, he gazes at the woman, silently pleading for help, begging her not to let go of his hand ever again. But suddenly a voice breaks in, crying "Mommy!" and gaining her attention, and with that her grip softens as well.

"No, please!" Felix howls, feeling her slipping out of reach once more. "Don't let me go again!"

But Xaria will never choose him over her own son, he has learned that one too many times, and with that he feels the air engulf him in a freezing hug. The fall isn't painful as he thought—his body feels weightless as he prances through the sky. It's when he crashes against the unmerciful waves of the river that his bones ache. His whole body shakes and his limbs flail helplessly as he tries to stay above the surface of the water.

Felix never learned how to swim.

Exhausted from drowning in the same river twice, he lets fate take over and gazes at the grinning moon beneath the waters as his vision grows hazy with the bone-crushing tiredness he feels.

But then, when he feels someone grab him by his feet, he gasps, letting water into his lungs. And here are the same old blue eyes that have never stopped taunting him, lurking from the darkest depths of the river. He screams, ripping his lungs apart as he struggles to free himself from her reach, but Verlee has always been more powerful than him, her grip has always been as suffocating as a snake's.

Lightheaded, Felix isn't capable of staying conscious much longer, so he lets her drag him into the depths of the river, and with that he is surrounded in darkness.

VI

The red door of his nightmares comes to greet him once more.

"Felix!" The voice fades within the air, caressing his senses breezily but not quite reaching his ears.

Felix is bewildered – there is no real focus in his bloodshot eyes as his gaze moves towards the door.

"Felix Scott!" The professor shouts his name once more, finally shaking some sense into him.

As his hazy vision slowly comes into focus, reality mingles with the sight of the red door, and he sees nothing but red as the blood continues to drip onto the floor. Once again he's perplexed – does the blood belong to him or someone else? He looks down at his sinful palms, searching for the blood of another victim of his unsettling anger, but he finds that his hands are painted only with his own blood. Alarmed, he jumps from his seat, leaving a trace of blood behind him.

"Are you okay?" The previously stern voice of the professor changes into a tone of worry, making Felix feel even more agitated.

Without answering, Felix pinches his nose to stop the waterfall of blood and marches out of the lecture hall in disgrace with a heavy feeling of the eyes following him from behind, holding nothing but pity for him.

As the water starts to drip from where he has splashed it on his face, he lifts his gaze up to the mirror and observes his reflection breaking through the glass, watching his every move.

He has shed so many skins that he has lost his true self in between. Is he a coward, hiding from space? Or is he vulgar, taking everyone's place?

The anger he sealed the deal with laughs down at him.

"You promised to help me!" he cries, falling to his knees.

"But I didn't say for how long." The chortle rings in his ears, making tears stream down his face. He is all too weak now, beaten in his own war.

And yet no evil thing lasts long, and the ending brings much more pain than before, taking its sacrifice and leaving him shattered on the floor, gazing at his palms where bloodstains remain in the cracks of his skin as the seal of the deal.

"Look what you've done!" Xaria exclaims, snatching the ruined toy from his tiny, wicked hands.

The woman examines the damage with a deep knot between her brows, and with a sigh looks down at the kid who hasn't raised his gaze from his palms, the palms he ripped the toy to shreds with. "Why did you do this? You loved this toy."

He loved the toy because it was the only gift he had ever received, but not the toy itself, no.

"But William doesn't love you." The chilling voice cackles in his ears, taunting the unloved kid.

Loving something unlovable brings embarrassment to the kid, and his shame has turned into a fit of unstoppable anger that he feels day and night. That's why his little fingers were tainted by the malice of destroying something he used to love. It is only when the bell rings that he comes back to earth from the clouds of gloom, and he needs to force every muscle in his body to stand up from yet another battle he has lost with himself.

Felix roams through the colorless, lusterless hall, carrying piles of boxes in his hand, towards the room of Dr. Luis.

"We need to talk to his parents." He hears the familiar raspy voice through the thin line of the door open ajar. "His attitude towards other kids is getting out of hand."

Felix's brows crinkle as he gently puts the boxes down next to the door without making a sound. He leans his ear through the thin open line, clandestinely listening to the voices chant.

"So you're suggesting that Nathan should move to another facility?" The nurse's voice engulfs Felix in the death grip of a snake, making his last breath catch with a gasp.

He steps back, holding for dear life onto the bleached wall, and soon his breath becomes erratic as he sprints, heart racing, towards the playroom where he's sure the kid remains.

Felix has long held that with enough watering, even from a thorny bush a lovely rose can break through the spikes. He may not be strong enough to cut away the past agonies suffocating the flower, but he will do all he can to keep the fresh growth pure. He isn't like them, the people of his past, flinching when the thorns prick them.

Even if his whole body is covered in cuts and scars, he will continue to embrace the flower.

He almost breaks through the glassed door separating him from his own little flower that he planted. Ignoring the concerned looks of the witnesses to his fall from grace, he searches for Nathan with wild, shaky eyes. When his eyes land on the kid, he catches him holding a plastic toy high in the air, aiming it at one of the kids.

"No!" Felix shrieks, sprinting towards the kid before he can do any more damage with his bad-tempered ways. He tackles Nathan to the ground, wrapping protective arms around his little flower.

"Felix!"

"Theodore!"

Verlee chirps whilst swirling around the crestfallen wooden tabletop, splinters jutting out and nothing but time-worn, grimy toys seated around it, with Felix sitting in the center with a paper crown on his head.

"Happy birthday to you!" she croons, approaching with an untidy homemade cake in her hand.

Before the woman puts the cake on the table, Felix grabs the food with his hands, gnawing hungrily and smearing the foul-tasting cream all over his wasted body. The woman laughs, lifting her hand up to pat the starving child. "Good boy," she murmurs with no real care in her voice, and Felix flinches, forcing Verlee's hand to freeze mid-air.

The glum tone of the room is tainted with darkness, and now ominousness is added to the gloom. The heavy air in between the kid and the woman makes Felix shrink down further into the chair, fixating his shaky gaze on the smudged cake, with fearful eyes.

"Why..." she starts with a menacing whisper. "Why did you flinch?" She shrieks, throwing the plate of cake at the wall.

"Did I ever hit you?" she yells, now throwing everything her hands can reach and ripping up the toys one by one. "Am I a bad parent?"

The sob he has been trying to secret away finally breaks from Felix's throat, making him choke as he wraps arms around himself, trying to bury himself away from the booming sounds that hurt his ears so much. He yelps when the woman grabs him by his shoulders forcefully.

"Tell me, am I bad mother?" she screams into his face, making him wince both in pain and fear. He frantically shakes his head as the fingers knife deeper into his skin, coloring him with pretty bruises.

"Then why did you flinch?" she roars in his face, spraying him with her venomous spit.

"Tell me, why did you flinch?!" Then comes the long-awaited slap across his face, stinging and burning the place where her wicked hand lands and leaving a mark. The wailing of the kid shakes the walls within as Felix falls onto the floor, holding the place that still aches with familiar pain.

"Oh god," Verlee exclaims, also landing down next to the kid who is crawls away, trying to get away from her reach. But Verlee always has been fiercer than him, so she easily pulls him into a forced embrace, dragging him across the floor. "Look what you made me do." She hushes whilst patting him on the head with no real fondness in her fingers.

She joins Felix in crying as tears start to well up in her eyes. "I'm sorry, alright?" she mewls through trembling lips. "I love you," she says as her hands wrap around his neck like a snake around its prey. "Do you love mommy too?" Her grip tightens to almost suffocating, allowing Felix only to choke out a soft "Yes."

As the memories flash by, his whole body tenses, shaking with the fear that has been burning inside him for so long, fogging his mind for years and poisoning him with each breath he takes. Memories can be forgotten but they're never lost—they hide somewhere in the depths of the mind despite its best attempts to erase the pain from your soul. Once tainted, the soul will always be tainted.

"It hurts..." Lost in his memories, he hears a choked mumble, forcing him to crash back down to earth. "It hurts." He looks down to find Nathan slowly turning red due to his grip around his frail neck.

"Good boy." He feels the cold touch of Verlee on the back of his head, making every hair on his body stand up. "Just like mommy."

Rashly, he throws the kid onto the floor, but this time Nathan doesn't yell or cry, he just gazes at him with sorrow-stricken eyes as the nurses embrace him.

Felix opens and closes his mouth, trying to twist an apology out, but the images of the past remain still in front of his eyes, making him somewhat irrational.

"Felix." He hears Dr. Luis speak from behind. "We need to talk." He says it calmly yet sternly, making Felix's heart wrench.

"Am I fired?" Felix asks the moment he closes the door, leaning his back against it for some balance, steeling himself for what is to come.

"No, of course not," Luis answers composedly as he shrugs off the white coat from his shoulders. "Think about it like a small vacation." He adjusts his black tie in the mirror before locking eyes with Felix's own bloodshot, haggard ones.

He turns around to face Felix, who stays glued to the door, head dropped in shame. "You need to rest." Luis puts his hand on his shoulder, making him look up. The doctor gives him a tight, yet earnest smile. "You're only a student."

"Can I ask you for a favor?" Felix asks as he opens the door, leaning against the door frame.

"Sure thing." Luis chirps as he gazes at him expectedly.

"Can I take care of Nathan by myself?"

Whilst collecting his belongings, he feels how the dried branches of the tree of hope he once so desperately reached towards have started to break one by one, and how he can't do anything but witness it all. But sometimes an old, wearied tree needs to be cut down so a fresh one can arise.

His eyes linger a tad too long on the shattered glass of the pendant that has stayed with him throughout it all, the shards of the past he searches for like a lonely sailor in an ocean of memories.

The smiling boy stays with him, even if the broken glass distorts his innocent grin.

It's painful for him to think how many skins he has shed, how many past selves he has murdered in cold blood, just to have a normal life. The necklace is the only source of consistency in his life.

Downhearted and full of gloom he carefully caresses the cracked glass that distorts the cheerful expression of the nameless boy, and with a sigh he slips the necklace safe back in his pocket as if to hide what's left of his past from the destructive present.

A heartbeat of tranquility shatters when he walks outside the changing room only to come face to face with Dylan, gazing at him with that familiar pair of pure eyes. All Felix can do is stare back, switching roles so that Dylan avoids his heavy gaze and walks inside the room without sparing Felix a last glance.

Dazed, Felix stands there as the guilt comes back like a storm, snatching him from the seashore and drowning him in a sea of rue. But the thought doesn't last long as he feels a weight come crashing down on his leg, and when he looks down he catches sight of the familiar blond locks swirling into the air.

"Hey!" he forces a cheerful tone as he kneels down on Nathan's level. "What are you doing here?"

The pout on the kid's face swells before he jumps into Felix's arms, nuzzling his face into his neck.

"You didn't say bye."

Wide with surprise, his eyes quickly crinkle into a genuine smile as he chortles and takes the kid in his arms.

Felix's fingers dance through the blond curls of the kid bending down towards the piece of paper that he's scribbling on. Felix's gaze lazily follows the movement of Nathan's smaller hands.

"Is that me?" he asks, carefully putting his finger on the taller stick figure with a wide smile, contrary to the smaller one who has a crooked, upside-down grimace.

Nathan nods without raising his head.

Felix sighs and, untangling his fingers from the kid's hair, he gently takes the paper in his hand and turns it upside down to see the drawing of Nathan grinning at him.

"Much better," he says.

Nathan peeks up at him through his lashes, head still hung low.

"I know you're hurting," Felix observes. "But hurting others won't make your pain go away."

Dazed, the kid flutters his eyes in confusion.

While trying to twist his words so the kid will understand, Felix catches sight of the bruise on the Nathan's arm and gently takes the little boy's palm in his.

"Looking at this bruise makes you angry, am I right?" The kid turns his attention to the fading wound and nods slowly. "But pressing your fingers into it will just make the bruise last longer."

He brushes his hand through the messy hair of the kid again, moving a few locks that have fallen onto his forehead to the side.

"Be kind, alright?" he says. "Anger will just make your pain live long."

The innocent kid blinks at him, still tangled in wonder, but the time has come and Felix stands up, ready to go. Seeing him stand, the kid jumps up on his chair and tries to reach Felix's level in order to hand him the drawing. Felix snorts, ruffling his hair some more.

"Thank you, kiddo, be nice before I come back." The kid nods firmly, sealing the promise.

He's already at the door, hand around the handle, when the kid decides to speak again. "Do you promise?"

Momentarily his heart skips a beat as the all too familiar atmosphere lands in the room.

"Do you promise to come back?"

He feels certain that if he turns around, the room will be painted the blinding white of hospital walls, with Nathan sitting on the hospital bed instead of him and him playing William's role. Unlike William he has no heart for telling lies, so he stays with his back towards the kid. "I promise."

He will never hurt Nathan the way he was hurt.

The languorous darkness that had been pressed against him like a cocoon, sheathing him from the coldness of the grave of the seven seas, is cleft by the waltzing gleam, defeated by the dim glow of the sea. The stubborn lights never stop dancing against the ghastly void, steadily growing in power and size before the stream of the unstoppable glimmering shoal of carp sprints up from the darkness, pushing Felix upwards towards the sky where the crooked moon has never stopped watching over her son.

In the arms of Morpheus, Felix is kidnapped from the waters where he belongs.

"The river flows in you, Ayumu." The voice of his mother echoes like a forgotten lullaby.

His eyes flutter, letting the bubbles pop, and as he's being lifted in the air, the only thing he chooses to see is the mighty moon watching over him. Like a fish out of water, the first gasp of air lunges inside his lungs like a knife, making him gag on the seaweed that has made a home inside of him.

As he continues to choke on the salty waters, the unmerciful stream of waves crashes against his ribcage, banishing him out of the land of the sea. The second his leg lands on the sand, he runs towards the shore even as the sea tugs him by his feet, begging him to stay. His whole body collapses onto the ground the moment he escapes the hands of the sea, and with choked, short breaths he learns to breathe all over again.

The waves of the sea continue to caress him by his head, welcoming him back to the underwater kingdom. On all fours he continues to stare at his reflection, distorted by the sea, displaying little Ayumu to his sight.

In the end, the only thing that separates him from the child is the skins he has shed, but from the inside, the innocent yet defeated heart of the kid has never stopped beating.

From the corner of his eyes, he catches sight of Genji, and with a gasp he looks back, only to find Dylan sitting there languid, gazing at the horizon where the sun has started to colour the sky with warmth. With a sigh, Felix crawls backward, falling next to Dylan, where he truly belongs.

"So, we're back where we started," he whispers bitterly, watching the sun rise for a new beginning.

"There is no new beginning for what's already been finished," Dylan answers wryly, never gifting him a return glance, always afraid.

"There must be a way...," Felix bites the words out, sounding as uncertain as he feels. "There must be a way to fix everything..."

The images of his tarnished house, the sound of the desperate cries of his dad all come together to taunt him.

"You can't fix the unfixable." Dylan again cuts him off with his pessimistic tongue.

"You know, you're big with words but you can't even look at me," Felix snarls, the evil inside of him lit for a moment, but Dylan just shakes his head, shrinking further down into the sand.

"The system has already failed," he says. "We can't fix it."

"I think you're the one who doesn't want to fix it," says Felix, and with that Dylan finally looks at him with an ugly grimace on his face.

"You don't get it, do you?" Dylan growls through gritted teeth. "We're not the same."

Felix turns his head towards him, all ears to hear what Dylan has to offer.

"I see you falling off the cliff every single night!" Dylan leaps forward as if showing his heart, scattering the sand around. "I can hear your cries, see the fear, the resentment in your eyes!"

Felix keeps his face calm, watching the agitated man. "I remember everything!" He bangs his fist against his chest. "You remember nothing." He accuses with a finger in his face. "We are not the same, we're like..."

"Begging and the end," Felix mumbles through a daze, staring at the ground as if the earth will lend him the answers.

"What?" Dylan asks, thrown off balance.

"I'm arche...," Felix murmurs to himself, steadily getting up from the viscous wet sand. "And you're the end." As if remembering he's there, he looks at Dylan with eyes inexpressive of the deep thoughts behind them.

"Everything starts and finishes with us." He walks towards Dylan, who flinches back, trying to get away from the heavy aura that surrounds Felix. "We need to fix ourselves first and then the other particles separating us will follow through."

"What are you talking about?" Dylan whispers.

"But how?" Felix just ignores him, gnawing at his bottom lip with an austere expression.

The healing starts with acknowledging your inner child.

The sentence from his workbooks starts to form before his hopeful eyes.

"Ayumu!" he shouts, startling the other. "And Genji. We need to find them." He tugs Dylan by his arm, silently begging him to stand up, but Dylan just shoves him aside.

"Come on, Dylan." Felix pleads, trying to reach towards him, but Dylan just moves away.

"I...," Dylan starts, but his voice breaks. "I can't."

Felix gazes at him with his breath held in his throat, tamping down the anger inside because the last thing he can do is force someone to heal when they're not ready to.

"Okay..." is the only thing that comes from his mouth in the end. "I'll be waiting for you."

For in the end, Felix is best at waiting for someone to come to his side.

With that, they quietly say their farewells, and with no real desire to, Felix turns his back towards his friend and walks across the seashore as the sand sucks his legs in—the sea trying everything in its might to hold him back, to make him stay a bit longer. But Felix has been running away all his life, too proud to face himself, and for once he feels that he's in control of his fate and so, although he stumbles and staggers, he never looks back.

His pace is broken when he catches a glimpse of his mum; already aged, gazing at the kids running carelessly around, knowing deep down she wishes he was one of them.

"Just wait a bit longer, I'll come back," he shouts to no one as his mother remains with her back to him, but the promise is sealed nonetheless.

His feet feel the familiar touch of the grass as he enters the ungodly forest where he first lost himself. For the first time he feels sure of himself as he walks through the great woods, he feels at home surrounded by the naked trees and thorny bushes that bite into his skin. Destination unknown, he prances through the forest, trying to find the child of his soul that has been abandoned by himself—because in the end no one has hurt him more than himself. He's tired of going to sleep and waking up in the past. For once he's hopeful to be awake in the future.

Lost in thought he doesn't seem to notice the shadows that crawl beside him, slowly craning up next to him, and only when he comes face to face with the hollow expression of Xaria does he jump back in surprise to see that the uninvited past has come to see him again in a last attempt to beat him down. This time, though, he is not afraid, although his fist still jitters at the sight of Noel blocking his escape route. The ghosts of his past have all gathered around, circling him threateningly.

"I'm not afraid anymore," he declares through trembling lips. He gasps when from the corner of his eye he catches a glimpse of the broken bridge that he now realizes he himself cracked, and Ayumu sitting at the edge, still waiting for him to come. Now he understands that he has left the kid hurting alone on the lonely, crooked bridge. He inhales a shaky breath and makes a first uncertain step towards Noel.

"I'm not afraid of you," he snarls but Noel doesn't even flinch or look inside his eyes—he just stands there gazing into nothingness.

Felix blinks, and with a last intake of breath he moves forward, making Noel disappear in thin air. Stunned, he looks back, only to find the forest abandoned of any soul. Shaking his head of any thoughts, he runs towards the old bridge but finds the other end sheltered by high thorns, preventing him from linking with himself. He peeks through the bush to find Ayumu sitting on the other side of the bridge, his legs dangling into the void that surrounds them from below.

With no other option, Felix inhales deeply and dives his hands into the bush. He hollers in pain as the thorns gash through his flesh, tearing his skin apart and slitting his palm in two, causing blood to spurt out of his veins like a river, staining the spikes in drops of red. He doesn't stop ripping the thorns from the ground even when his fingers go numb, deprived of sensation as they latch onto the prickles. With a huff, he throws away the last thorn, and with his chest heaving up and down he gazes at the end of the bridge where the familiar figure is sitting at the edge. He rubs the sweat away from his forehead, coloring his skin in bloody red while still gasping for air.

"Ayumu!" he gasps, sounding done in, the words barely slipping from his tongue. Ayumu lifts his gaze up to him, catching him with his persistent, grievous eyes. His heart guilt-ridden, Felix offers Ayumu an apologetic smile without breaking his gaze from the dejected expression meant for him and only him. The melancholic look knocks the air from Felix's lungs, crushing his soul, and in utter shame he drops his head down.

"I'm sorry I've made you wait so long," he mumbles through tensed jaw, his lips barely moving and his hands clasped into white-knuckled fists.

A heartbeat of complete silence settles between them, dividing them farther from each other on the fallen bridge. "But I promise you..." Felix tears his face from the mud-spattered ground, and his eyes again fall naturally on Ayumu, who is glowing in the soft indigo moonlight, brighter than any of the stars above, but the moment their eyes connect, the moment Felix takes a look at Ayumu's glossy, honey eyes, all his words are stolen away. He gulps, his heart caught in his throat. "I won't hurt you anymore." He finally breathes out the words, barely audible.

For a moment Felix wonders if his words have gone unheard as Ayumu gazes upon him wordlessly, his expression unreadable, and Felix is ready to repeat himself, to declare his devotion, when Ayumu stands up and dusts the dirt from his clothes, ready to listen to Felix's demands.

"So come to me, okay?" Felix says with a tender voice, spreading his arms for a much-needed embrace.

Ayumu gives a quick glance into the black nothingness beneath their feet, looking doubtful.

"I will catch you, I promise." The kid looks up at him, with no conviction in his eyes. "I promise," he repeats, opening his arms and heart to the kid.

Ayumu squeezes his eyes shut and with closed eyes jumps from the edge of the bridge, falling into the abyss, but his scream gets tangled in his throat when he feels two secure arms engulfing him in a long-awaited hug.

"I'm here," Felix shouts as they fall deep down into the unknown. "I will never leave you alone."

A wholehearted cry that he has secreted away for so long finally breaks through Ayumu as he wails and clutches tightly onto Felix's clothes, finally feeling at home within his own skin, and when they fall into the all too familiar river, neither of them seems to be surprised as Ayumu looks around the gloom with fright-stricken eyes. He yelps when Felix lets go of his hand and tries to swim towards him, but Felix just smiles.

"The river flows in you Ayumu," he says, swirling around the lake that is his home.

And one by one the loud carp start to appear in their vision, dancing gracefully against the river current. Awestruck, Ayumu looks at the fish and gently yet carefully touches one of them. As the fish wobbles around, a laugh finally breaks from the child, and Felix watches him with a tender grin. The more he laughs, the higher they rise up into the blue sky, and when they eventually reach the river bank with Ayumu still giggling to himself, Felix takes his hand and they walk around the dry bank of the river. Standing in front of the wrathful river doesn't bring as much as fright as Felix thought it would. He isn't afraid of drowning anymore.

Suddenly a woman's laughter joins theirs, and Felix looks around through a frown, gripping the kid's hand a little tighter.

"So have you chosen his name?" Moriko asks as she jumps down, giving a hand to Mizuki whose belly is round and full of life.

"Yes…" She croaks as she tries to crawl down. "I'll be naming him Ayumu."

"Is there any reason why?" Moriko asks whilst putting the blanket on the ground.

"Because of a dream I had," she says gloomily, and when Moriko doesn't speak up, waiting for her to tell the story, Mizuki shakes her head. "Oh my, it was so unpleasant I don't even want to remember."

"Come on, I'm interested." Moriko bumps her shoulder against Mizuki's as she lays next to her on the blanket.

"At first there was nothing but the darkness surrounding me, my sense of reality had gone but the cold touch on my feet grounded me to actuality. Slowly but surely a sensation of wetness came along, I realised I was standing in the river in my bare feet. Suddenly a cry burst through the dead silence, and as I narrowed my eyes, soft moonlight slowly crept around me, lighting my way, but the cries didn't stop."

Moriko tilts her head in confusion and Mizuki just shakes her hand, gulping down the food. "And here I was holding in my arms a newborn whose wail shook the ground beneath my feet. I was surprised, but I knew the child was mine so I gently started to sway him."

Mizuki sighs heavily, not looking too well and not wanting to continue telling the story. "But the blissful moment didn't last long—the weak rustling of the leaves grew louder and more aggressive, and before I could blink I heard a loud growl "Appossha" coming from the woods. Before I could react, a monstrous red face emerged from behind a tree."

Mizuki covers her face with her hands, shaking with fear. "Its long black hair was like a tangle of seaweed stretching from the ground into the icy river. "Appossha!" it demanded again, but this time I regained my senses and started running against the merciless stream. I could hear the water break and splash onto my skin as the monster chased me down. All I could hear was the sound of the river and the child's cry. I didn't even realize how deep into the water I'd got." As Mizuki retells the unpleasant story, Moriko pats her on the shoulder in sympathy.

"Only the face of the child was showing. All I could see was his pinched expression as he sobbed in fear, so I raised my arms up and continued running, and when even my nose was beneath the water I sensed the tight grip around my feet, pulling me deep into the river, and before I could blink the kid was gone and so was the river around me."

"Oh my," Moriko exclaims, pouring some warm tea for her friend.

"Then, as I was digging in the mud trying to find my baby, I heard the rustling of grass once more, so I looked around alarmed, this time only to find Kawa-Otoko sitting on the stone, waiting for someone to talk." With a heavy sigh, she lifts her face from her palms. "So I crawled over and sat next to it."

As Mizuki tries to gather herself and find the right words, Moriko continues to rub her friend's back. "Without turning to me, he asked "Do you want to hear the story of the little leaf?" And so I nodded."

"There is a story about an old oak tree that had loved one little leaf, the youngest one, but vibrant with rich shades of red that outshone any other leaf. Strangely, the other leaves didn't envy the eye-catching colors of the younger one, they loved it as much as the oak tree. But the twig of the leaf was weak, perhaps too thin to bear so much life, and so one spring rain the raindrops shook the leaf and no matter how hard the tree tried to hold onto the leaf, it fell, too fast, too early, before it had had a chance to mesmerize the eyes of passersby. The oak and the leaves mourned for a long time until all the leaves fell the following autumn, and after that, the tree slowly dried up, but in the place where the little leaf fell, a small, almost invisible twig sprung up from the ground.

"Nothing disappears with no trace left behind, even a small leaf can bring back a stolen life. I'm sure a beautiful tree grew from that leaf, carrying the ghosts of his past loved ones. Just like that leaf, your son hasn't disappeared either. When you feel heavy of heart, just for a moment close your eyes, and when you open them I'm sure you will find him in everything your eyes reach."

But without any warning Mizuki yelps in pain. "What's wrong?" Moriko jumps towards her, holding her secure.

"My stomach...," is the only sentence Mizuki croaks, still holding tight onto her stomach.

"Oh god!" Moriko exclaims as she notices the wet stain on Mizuki's dress. "Oh my god." In a state of panic, Moriko leaps from the ground. "Your water broke."

As Felix stands with Ayumu's hand in his, he watches the water creep from the riverbank, sealing a deal with the river and making the water in which he was gifted life one with the water that took that life from him. When the last drop of his blood drips into the water, the ground beneath his feet starts to tremble in fear as the merciless river breaks through its cage. In sheer alarm, Felix snatches Ayumu from the tremulous earth and starts to run with the kid attached to his side as the river destroys everything that stands in its way. Even in the roar of the deadly stream, he can hear the cries of the child he seeks, and soon enough he catches a glimpse of Genji crying alone as the river creeps closer towards the defenseless kid. In a moment of chaos, Felix sees Dylan standing at the top of the mountain, looking over them, and Felix prays silently for a helping hand, but Dylan just turns his back to them. And realizing it is down to him to save both of the kids, he tugs Genji by his shirt and runs with them both secure in his arms as the river chases them down, begging them to stay.

Consciousness comes back like waves, bringing bits of reality with it and taking away the memories.

With a low groan, Felix returns from the land of dreams. He takes a few moments to step out of the warm bed, sitting up while rubbing the remnants of the dream away. As his brain starts to rage with thoughts he hears a forgotten melody ringing in the back of his head and soon enough he hears foreign words fall onto his ears.

I am the child of the sea.

Curious, he walks towards the balcony from where the song is playing and it takes a heartbeat before he realizes that the voice belongs to Dylan. With a short gasp he jumps back, causing him to stumble and hit his back on the piles of books so that they scatter with a loud thud. He holds his breath, afraid to make any more noise, but then he hears Dylan speak from the side.

"Felix?"

With no other options on the horizon, he sighs and walks outside into the chilly night. He finds Dylan sitting on the ground with a guitar in his arms, gazing at him with pair of innocent eyes filled with shame.

"Did I wake you up?" he asks.

"Of course," he spits before he can stop himself displaying his old, wicked ways, but having someone finally to talk to he settles down with a sigh. "No, you didn't, I just can't sleep."

Dylan nods with pursed lips, biting down on the words he wants to speak. The silence stretches awkwardly between them, and so clearing his throat, Felix speaks.

"What were you singing?" he asks, forcefully spitting the words out due to being unfamiliar with chit-chat.

"Oh," Dylan squeaks embarrassedly. "A Japanese folksong, it was the first song I learned to play on the guitar."

Felix nods whilst biting his lips, seeking for words to get the conversation going again as the guilt settles in his war-stricken heart.

"Why..." He clicks his tongue, forcing himself to speak. "Why did you stop?" He shakes his head with eyes squeezed shut with embarrassment.

For a while there is only silence between them and Felix wishes the ground would swallow him up whole, but as Dylan starts to sing again, his heartbeat starts to beat in tune.

On the pine-covered seashore that the white waves wash upon.

Felix slowly lifts his head from the floor and rests his gaze on Dylan, who is gazing up at the crescent moon while singing his heart out.

There is a humble home, and smoke comes out from its window.

Felix closes his eyes and lets the night consume him with the soft melody playing in the background.

That is my dearest old home.

And for the first time, his heart doesn't feel heavy in his chest.

VII

One by one the dainty snowflakes float through the sky, covering everything in a dazzling white that is oh so soft to the touch.

The joy of merry children warms up the cold air, their rosy cheeks and noses tinted with the crisp night.

"Ayumu!" shouts Genji standing in the middle of the white field with his palms cupped to his mouth. "Where are you?" But the only response to his cry is the sound of the snowflakes settling on the empty ground. With a huff of frustration, he kneels on the ground and collects a handful of snow, adding it to the snowman he is building. A sudden yelp leaves his lips when the coldness embraces him in an unwanted hug.

"Gotcha!" shouts Ayumu as he throws more snow onto his friend, dusting him in white.

"Stop!" cries Genji, trying to fight back with his lanky arms but only getting covered in more snow.

Somehow amid Ayumu's giggling Genji tugs him by his arms, engulfing him in the snow beneath him, but the heartfelt laughter doesn't stop, filling the field with its joyous melody.

"What are you doing?" chuckles Genji, dusting the white flakes from his wet clothes, but Ayumu just continues to cackle from beneath the soft blanket of snow.

Shaking his head Genji wobbles towards the unfinished snowman once more, rolling snow in his hands to add to his creation. He hears the snow crunch from behind and soon enough Ayumu appears at his side, kneeling and giving a helping hand with a grin that outshines the sun.

"I love snow," Ayumu mutters after a spell of silence, still smiling from ear to ear.

"Me too," hums Genji under his breath, and with a devilish grin he collects snow in his palms and throws it in Ayumu's direction, earning a heartfelt laugh once more.

The evening breeze carries her out as her hair twirls wildly in the blue, pellucid sky. With frantic steps she emerges through the gathered crowd, all too busy with their own lives. Even when they shove and bump, Xaria continues to walk with a stack of papers held tightly to her chest. The air smells like summer, like freshly cut grass and it's humid around even without so many people squeezed together. With a quick glance, she checks the address once more, and finally, at the end of the road, the small glass-fronted building of the police station appears. With a last breath she quickens her pace.

She opens the clear door and the moment she steps in she's overwhelmed by the chaos surrounding her. With shaky steps, she walks towards a chair and sits down with a thud. Her heart comes to a halt when a door suddenly whips open, almost breaking the glass, and from the corner of her eye Xaria sees a man being manhandled by a policeman as they barge inside.

"Fuck you!" The man roars, making her jump in the air. "Fucking let me go!" But the policeman just shoves him further inside.

She shrinks into her seat, crumpling the papers in her tight grip, and her heart loses its rhythm, beating erratically in her ears as the fear slowly takes over. She looks around, only to find a man sitting next to her with handcuffs around his wrists, further igniting the flames of terror inside her, and horrified she averts her gaze, staring down at the floor as she feels her body dance with each heartbeat.

"Next!" Xaria hears a policeman shout out from the reception so with frantic steps she walks towards him.

"How can I help you?" The man asks while typing something into the computer.

"I'm searching for these people." Xaria slides a photo of the Gauthiers towards the policeman.

The man looks down from his glasses and gives a mere glance at the photo before returning his eyes to the computer.

"Are they filed as missing?" he asks.

"Yes, but I would like to know if maybe they're here, or if your district knows anything..." she replies through a shaky voice as the hectic sounds around her consume her senses.

"I can't tell you that," the policeman says sternly, without lifting his eyes from the computer screen.

"Please, it's important," she begs him, leaning her full body against the table as she shoves the picture in front of his face. "Do you recognize them?"

"Ma'am, it's private information. We can't tell you anything."

Xaria groans and bangs her palm onto the table. "You didn't even look at the photo!" she exclaims but her voice quickly dies on her tongue when she feels a pair of arms around her shoulders.

"Ma'am, you need to go." Another policeman speaks from behind.

"I need to find them!" she announces as she tries to get away from the man's grip. "Please tell me!" But the hold just tightens and bruises her skin as she wiggles desperately from every side.

"Please calm down." The man speaks but Xaria just seethes as the fingers burn into her skin.

"Let me go!" she screams then, forcefully shoving the policeman with her arms. "Let go of me!"

And in a moment of chaos, the policeman accidentally gets hold of her, throwing her against the floor and scraping her skin bloody red.

"Are you okay?" He rushes towards her, helping her to stand up.

Xaria grimaces as the pain in her leg slowly burns through to the bone. She looks down to find her knee bleeding forcefully, and with a sigh she staggers away, limping as she walks towards the next police station.

A low groan leaves her lips as she collapses onto a seat in the park. For a heartbeat, she just gazes aimlessly at the birds eating crumbs of bread from the grass. Life seems so joyful today but Xaria doesn't replicate the jovial mood as she reads through the papers, crossing off the names of the police stations she has visited today.

"What are you doing here?" She hears the familiar deep voice of William, and she doesn't even need to look up as she feels him sit next to her.

"Trying to find them..." Xaria answers simply, putting away the papers as she looks at William, who is lighting a cigarette.

"Did you come to our police station?" She nods and William puffs smoke from his lips.

"There is no news about them yet."

A handful of silence falls over them as William slowly smokes his cigarette and Xaria just gazes into the nothingness, lost in her thoughts. But then her shoulders start to tremble as the tears well up in her tired eyes. "It's unfair," she croaks as she drops her face into her palms.

All the pent-up strife comes undone at once as the waterfall of tears drips to the ground. "It's so unfair."

William just pats her on the shoulder, giving her silent encouragement. "We'll find them, don't worry."

"What time is it?" she asks suddenly, ignoring his words as she harshly rubs the tears away.

"Half past seven."

"Oh god." Out of the blue Xaria jumps from her seat. "Felix's play..."

"What?" But William never finishes his question as Xaria is already rushing away.

With a sprint, she runs inside the empty hall. No one is there, everyone has already gone home and the hall is dim, with only the stage lights still lit up. She looks around in hurry, through the empty seats and finally notices a figure sitting on the stage, dangling his legs into the air.

"You're late," Felix murmurs without looking at her face.

"I'm sorry," Xaria starts but Felix just scoffs, standing up.

"You promised!" he shouts, letting the echo buzz against the walls. "Don't make promises you can't keep."

"Wait!" she calls out as she runs towards the stairs, but she ends up twisting her injured leg, opening the fresh wound. "Wait for me!" Too consumed by sadness she doesn't notice the pain settling inside her bones.

The boy seems to be slipping away from her reach with each passing day and the distance between them grows as he walks away.

"Stop!" She catches him by his shoulders, forcefully making him turn around.

To her dismay, Felix is already crying, a river of tears streaming down his face as he glares at her with pure mistrust. "I have no one but you but you don't even care about me!" he wails, angrily rubbing away his tears, but fresh ones are ready to roll from his cat-like eyes that glimmer with pure despair.

Xaria collapses to the ground, holding his face in her palms as she gazes into his limpid eyes. "No Felix, I love you..."

"Don't say that!" Felix shrieks, harshly shoving her hands off his face "I hate that word. Don't say it unless you mean it." And with that he sprints away into the dark, leaving Xaria on the floor.

The lights dim.

Lovely birds sing their hearts out towards the sun bathing the world in warm auburn. The woman sitting by the window croons quietly and watches nature lulled to sleep by the rowdy birds.

The moment of quiescence is broken by the ugly creak of the door displaying Felix standing by the door with a huge smile adorning his face.

"Missed me?" he asks as he dangles the plastic bag in his hand letting the sweet aroma settle inside the room.

Xaria just smiles at the young man and nods her head to the side of the empty seat.

"How's studying going?" she asks while running her fingers through his messy locks and nudging him.

"Good, everything's good," Felix answers through a timid smile but drops his gaze onto his fidgeting fingers. "A potential family called, but..." He sighs, scraping the skin off his fingertips. "They weren't mine."

Xaria hums, wordlessly tracing her palm along his cheek, her touch lingering for the space of a heartbeat.

"Enough of me." Felix sluggishly turns his head up towards her. "Tell me how your life is going."

"Well, there isn't much to do," she chuckles, giving her all attention towards the window once more. "I play poker with the others every night, I've made a few friends here and there."

For a while, blinking lazily, she stays silent, lost in her thoughts as her eyes fill with unsaid woe.

"I get it now..." she murmurs through trembling lips and turns her gaze towards Felix. "How lonely it gets to wait for someone to come." Felix, never having learned what the appropriate thing to do is, swiftly grabs her hand in order to comfort her.

"Does your son visit you?" he asks meekly, yet intrigued.

"Not as often as you do," she says dolefully, albeit with a dazzling smile decorating her wrinkled face.

Felix hates him for that. How ungracious can one get to not appreciate a loving parent? If only he could call Xaria his own.

But then gently her expression becomes gloomy, the shimmer in her eyes dimming down as she watches Felix with growing delirium. "I'm sorry...," she whispers through tight lips, and her fingers start to shiver while her somber eyes never leave Felix.

"I'm sorry I didn't take good care of you." She opens her heart, the raw guilt she has had to carry all these years. "I've tried my best, but it wasn't enough."

Wordlessly Felix gazes at the woman, the flowers inside of him starting to bloom. The apology doesn't feel as magnificent as he thought it would – rather it feels like the waves simmering down after the storm, resembling a gleaming pacific mirror reflecting the blue sky above.

"I tried to help, help to find your parents, I really did but I feel like I've failed you as a caretaker." She shakes her head, shedding the regret away.

Felix gently taps her hand, interlacing their fingers he just hums quietly, accepting her awkward words.

"I never asked you to give me more than you could." Felix finally speaks up, swaying their interlaced fingers from side to side. "And you gave me enough."

Xaria just closes her eyes, shielding the welling tears, and shakes her head in disagreement. "I could have done something to help you, to ease your pain..."

This time Felix shakes his head and with a smile, he speaks. "You were the only person who ever loved me and so I appreciate the effort."

With a sigh, and with some trouble, she stands up from her seat and with sluggish steps walks towards the drawer next to her bed. Felix watches her eagerly as she shuffles through her belongings.

"Here." She stretches her hand out with a stack of papers in her palm. "Here is all research I've done and all the police stations I've checked so you won't have to do the same twice."

Felix's brows perk up as he gently takes the papers in his hands. "Police stations? Why did you go to the police?"

"I thought I would find your parents there, where else could they go?"

He blinks lazily, still fixated on the hard work of Xaria. "I don't know...," he says honestly before turning his head in Xaria's direction. "Where can they be?"

"Keep fighting and one day I'm sure they will show up. A person can't disappear without a trace."

With a dreadful feeling of uncertainty spreading inside him, he nods nonetheless, gently putting the papers inside his bag as he stands up. "I must get going now, I already skipped one lecture."

With timid steps, he walks towards the door, and when he's already out of reach he turns around one last time. "I'll come back soon."

The smile spreads on her face as she weakly waves her hand before turning her back on him and gazing outside through the window once more.

Walking through the hall, Felix carefully avoids bumping into someone as the room slowly fades away into obscurity and the faceless, nameless students pass him by. He doesn't need to know their names—if you don't know someone's name you don't give them the power over you. Life feels dull, and his sight greys before he sees nothing but black as he desperately tries to get away. From every corner he feels eyes throw daggers at him, finding their homes in his skin, and it all starts to feel too much with so many eyes on him so he runs inside the cafeteria.

With a sigh he looks around. Everything is pitch black to his vision, but he sees Dylan with a friend embraced by streaks of light. Felix still isn't sure if he can trust him, but with timid steps he approaches, something dragging him back and something pushing him forward at the same time.

"No! Don't do that!" screams the devil inside him, setting his nerves aflame. With each step, he hears his heart break, weighing down on his wretched soul. If he makes another step he surrenders himself to fate, and he will lose all control of what's to come. It's scary, this plethoric sense of uncertainty—the future seems terrifying when you live in the past. But Felix is sure the present will bring him to a much brighter future. For the first time, he wants to feel hopeful for tomorrow. He licks his dried lips and with gathered courage, he speaks.

"Dylan," he says, interrupting the conversation between Dylan and Sophia.

Dylan tilts his head upwards towards him, and it takes him a heartbeat before realization settles between his round eyes. "Yes?" he asks hopefully, unconsciously leaning closer towards him.

"Well, I...," Felix starts, but the bravery inside his heart quickly dissipates, leaving him with ashes. "I skipped the first lecture and I was thinking maybe you could lend me your notes?"

Dylan blinks at him, no thought traced on his face as he gazes at him. The attention makes Felix shrink, and he clumsily plays with the strings of his backpack. "I'll get them back to you today."

Finally, a familiar grin stretches out on Dylan's face as he jumps up from his seat and runs towards his bag. After shuffling around for a while, he pulls out a notebook and hands it to Felix. "Take your time, I don't need them."

Felix nods, carefully taking the notebook in his hands. "See you then," he adds, his voice hoarse from pressure.

"Yes!" Dylan exclaims enthusiastically before clapping his palm to his mouth, his voice having come out louder than he intended.

As Felix walks away, Dylan watches him go with a fond smile playing on his lips.

"Are you friends with him?" Sophia's voice rings inside his ears, intruding into his train of thought.

"No, why?" He turns around towards her direction, his eyes still twinkling with excitement.

"Good. You know what people say about him," she says as she tucks into her food, now looking less tense.

"I don't care," Dylan answers with a frown, gazing accusingly at his friend. "He's nice."

"Well, ask anybody else around then." Her voice is dripping with irony, and her sarcastic tone makes Dylan's blood boil. He scoffs and leans back with his arms crossed. "They don't know him."

"And you do?" She looks at him through her lashes, her brows crooked.

Her words make his heart sink and he darts his eyes to the ground. "No, I don't," he mumbles through gritted teeth as a feeling of uneasiness settles in.

"Now roll everything in seaweed but be careful not to crack it," Moriko yells through the phone which Dylan is desperately trying to balance on his shoulder as his hands get messy in the food.

"Got it," he answers back in Japanese, the calls with his mom being the only time he speaks his native language.

"Why did you suddenly want to make food? I know you've been living on nothing but junk food, don't even try to deny, I talk to Sophia." she asks then, her voice filled with curiosity.

"Homesick." Dylan lies as he tries again to roll the ingredients in the seaweed.

"Are you making it for Sophia?" She doesn't back down, her voice rising in irritation.

"No," Dylan answers dryly but curses when the roll bends, causing the rice to spurt out.

"You cracked the seaweed, didn't you?" Moriko chuckles from the other side, entertained by her son's misery.

"It's not funny! I'm trying!" he whines like a child, starting all over again.

"So who are you making this if not Sophia? You know I'll be happy if you've made a friend." Her voice is gentle and sounds earnest.

"We're not friends," he huffs as he successfully rolls the dish. "Not yet."

"I'm glad," she whispers, almost inaudibly. "Glad that you're opening up."

It brings chaos inside him that they think so little of him and treat him like a wounded child. He sighs, unable to muster the energy to give voice to his worries. But then suddenly, the doorbell makes his whole body jump so he quickly says goodbye his mom and rushes towards the door. He takes a deep breath before opening the door and revealing Felix on the other side.

"Hello." Dylan forces a nervous smile as he opens the door wide.

Felix just nods and leans his arm towards him, handing him his notebook.

"Thanks for that," he says and takes a step back, ready to turn around before Dylan yelps "Wait!"

Felix's brows perk up as he waits for Dylan to continue.

Dylan rubs the back of his head awkwardly and smiles a crooked smile. "I made too much food. Do you want to maybe stay for a bit?" Felix blinks stupidly for a moment, the words not sinking in.

"I don't want to leave Lucky alone for too long," he says. It sounds like an excuse, but it isn't—Felix is sincere in his words even though he would like to taste some real homemade food after years of surviving on instant ones.

"Then bring her with you." Dylan tries again, nervousness settling in as he desperately tries to hang on to the last thread of hope of making a new friend.

It takes a moment before the doorbell rings again, now revealing Felix in a loose hoodie with fur showing from its pocket.

"You look like you're about to rob me," Dylan jokes, giving him space to walk inside.

Felix moves in with short, languid steps, still uncertain about his decision. When he comes to the centre of the room he lets Lucky jump out from his hoodie. He looks around, taking note of every corner of the room—it's no different from his own, maybe a bit tidier, but all the rooms in the dormitory are basically the same.

"Here, sit down." Dylan points to a chair at the table that is filled with homemade food.

"You didn't lie when you said you cooked a lot," Felix murmurs as he sits down with Lucky on his lap, his fingers dancing gently through her fur.

Dylan just giggles as he puts some more food down on the table.

"What is it, is it sushi?" Felix asks as he observes the dish, not daring to touch it yet.

"It's called ehomaki," Dylan explains as he sits down. "It's a traditional Japanese food."

"Are you Japanese?" Felix asks as he takes the first bite, letting the flavors spread over his tongue. He hadn't realized he was hungry until he had something to fill his ravenous stomach.

"Yes, both of my parents are." Dylan offers him a smile and it's all too bizarre for Felix to have someone to talk to, although to be honest he can't say he despises it.

"What are you doing in Canada then?"

For a moment the question takes Dylan's smile away, but before the guilt can settle in, his lips point upwards once more.

"My dad is from Canada."

Felix nods with a hum and cleans his fingers with a tissue. "The food is delicious."

The grin on Dylan's face just widens and his eyes sparkle with a familiar shimmer. "You know, it's believed that ehomaki wards off evil and brings good luck." Felix›s brows perk up as he listens. "But you have to eat it whole in one sitting without leaving a single grain of rice behind."

"That's interesting," Felix muses as he rests his face in his palms. "Japanese culture is interesting in general."

Dylan nods in agreement, with a fond smile on his face as he goes off on a path of nostalgia.

"What about you?" he asks. "Are you from Canada?"

The dread quickly finds its way into Felix's heart and he is overtaken by gloom. The room starts to spin and cold sweat starts to gather on his forehead as a nauseous feeling settles in his bones.

"Felix?"

"Yes, my parents are from Canada, I'm Canadian," he lies through gritted teeth—but maybe it's not a lie, he doesn't know.

Dylan seems oblivious to Felix's distress. "That's cool, I like Canada too."

Felix just nods, and to soothe his nerves he strokes Lucky, desperate for a sense of comfort.

Clearing his throat, he tries to speak again. "So... What was it like in Japan?"

Dylan's face pales and his gaze drops down, not meeting Felix's eyes. "I don't really want to talk about it," he admits shamefully, and truth be told Felix is taken aback, but he nods regardless with curiosity lit up in the corners of his heart. Suddenly they're both startled by a booming sound coming from the television.

"The remains of James Taylor, age six, were found this afternoon..."

But before Felix can focus on the voice, Dylan quickly turns off the television. Felix slowly turns his head towards him only to find him hunched down in his seat, his eyes shaking as sweat drips from his face. This time it's not Felix's fault.

"Are you okay?" Felix's hand itches to touch the troubled boy, but Felix is unintelligent when it comes to affection and his arm hangs uselessly in the air.

"I'm fine," Dylan whispers, but color is yet to return to his skin.

They stay in silence for a bit with Felix gazing at Dylan full of unknown worry for him. He has never felt like this before, the urge to help is consuming his sound mind. Never in his life has he wanted to save anybody but himself, but this time his body begs him to do something, to comfort the unnerved young man.

"I must get going." Just like all the other times, he runs away from his feelings.

He gently takes Lucky in his arms and stands up, but Dylan doesn't bother to look up, his shaky eyes still glued to the floor.

"Thanks for the food." He staggers towards the door, something holding him back, willing him to stay.

"Goodbye." When he is already standing by the door he tries again to get Dylan's attention, but Dylan stays still, his body shrinking into his seat. With a sigh Felix opens the door, letting the cold breeze cool his hectic mind.

"Did I do something wrong?" he asks Lucky on his way to his room.

Because it's all new to him, he has never learned how to be a human. There was only darkness in him before, and now a small light has finally appeared in his life, he doesn't know how to react to it.

Gazing at the waxing moon he lets himself get lost in his thoughts, planning his next move. From time to time he throws a glance towards Dylan's room, where the light is still on. He gnaws on his lip as all the possible outcomes gather inside his mind. He's uncertain about what awaits him next and it scares him to the core. He's afraid of the fall, even though he has fallen so many times before and knows that there is an end to every fall. But this time he wants it to work out right. He's giving away his last chance, the chance to rebuild the broken bridge, and if it fails, there goes the bridge.

And so, drawing a deep breath, he shouts, "Dylan!"

With each passing second, his heart hammers in his chest and it only takes a moment before Dylan peeks his head out. "Did you call me?"

The relief hits him in waves, but this time the sea is calm.

"How are you?" he asks.

Dylan visibly flinches before an awkward smile plays on his lips as he rubs the back of his neck. "I'm fine, sorry about that."

Felix just nods his head, uncertain what to say next. "That's good." He settles on a simple answer.

And for a while they just gaze at the navy, starless sky whose only host appears to be the crooked, silver moon, engulfing everything in its soft light. But then, like magic, the world fades into white as fair snowflakes start to dart away from the sky.

"First snow," Felix mumbles as he gazes at the sky that has turned white.

"Let's go." Suddenly Dylan speaks, making Felix's brows rise in confusion.

"Go where?"

"Let's go outside, it's the first snow." Dylan grins at him, already walking outside and leaving Felix perplexed

That night Felix learns that friendship can't be determined or predicted—it comes slowly but naturally and you just need to let it come, let it guide you to the right path.

"It's cold." Felix croaks through chattering teeth as he rubs his arms over his body in a desperate search for warmth. But Dylan isn't looking at him—he's gazing at the sky, awestruck, and letting the snowflakes decorate his skin—so Felix closes his eyes, savoring the feeling of the cold on his frosted flesh. His cheeks are dusted in pink and the snowflakes cling to his eyelashes as the moonlight embraces him in its silver hue. For the first time in forever, Felix feels at ease with his soul.

"Mind if I ask you something?" Dylan's voice interrupts the sense of complete tranquility, fluttering his eyes as Felix gazes expectantly at him.

"Can we...," Dylan starts but bites his lip, blinking rapidly as he tries to come up with the right words. "Can we be friends?"

The words strike Felix like thunder in the calm sky, stealing away the balance from his body, and he staggers back.

"I'm not a good person, Dylan," he answers honestly.

In the depths of his wicked mind, he knows he isn't kind, that he has destroyed any good in himself and is left with only anger as a friend. He can admit to his evilness, and he's afraid his touch will rot someone as pure as Dylan away. He has stayed in the dark for so long that he's afraid he will be blinded by the light if he leaves the cavern of despair.

"I'm not a good person either," Dylan says with a tight smile, his eyes telling stories Felix is yet to hear. "I must also have a dark side if I am to be whole. As Jung said."

For a heartbeat Felix just blinks, words falling mute on his tongue no matter how much he searches for the right ones.

"Let's stay bad together and maybe we will find some good in us." Dylan stands there in the rain of snowflakes, his whole body covered in white that he doesn't bother to dust away, and gazes at Felix with eyes begging him to stay.

Gulping, Felix drops his head down low, his heartbeat raging along with his turbulent mind, making him buzz in his own skin. He feels like he has to make a profound decision, to rewrite the stars in the sky and finally turn to the next page of his book of life.

So he nods firmly, not yet mustering the will to speak.

"Let's be friends then," Dylan says through a smile that is all too proud, all too joyous to be directed at Felix.

And as the snow settles so do the two bent souls.

VIII

"I can't do this!" Ayumu screeches as his hands turn red from gripping the handlebars too tightly.

"Come on, it's not hard." Genji tries to push the bicycle but Ayumu just shrieks in response.

"No! It's scary!" His legs start to tremble on the crank, taking away the balance of the bicycle, and he falls over with a loud thud, bringing the bicycle crashing down on top of him.

"Are you okay?" Genji immediately rushes towards his friend, helping him to stand up from the spiky grass.

"I told you it's scary!" Ayumu whines as he gently rubs the scraped skin on his knee that has started to bleed.

"Okay then," Genji murmurs as he walks towards the bicycle. He stands it upright and quickly jumps on it. "Ride with me then."

Ayumu stands pouting for a while before nodding his head and walking toward his friend. Carefully he sits behind, his hands hanging awkwardly in the air. With a groan Genji guides Ayumu's arms to his waist, holding him close. "Hold on tight!" That is the last thing he shouts before taking off.

Ayumu squeals as he holds onto Genji for dear life, digging his frail fingers deep into his skin, but Genji just chuckles as he rides towards the shore.

The stream of rain is unmerciful as it pours down onto the earth, stealing the life away. Its raindrops, sharp as razorblades, stab into the skin.

"It's all your fault!" Damon's holler fills the air, muffled by the sound of the rain pouring down onto the ground. He tugs at his hair, as if trying to rip his flesh open, ruffling it aggressively as the raindrops pierce through his drenched skin.

"Everything is going to be fine!" Verlee screams in harmony as she holds her doused jacket closer to her chest in search of warmth in the coldness of the night.

"How?!" Damon's scream strikes once again through the rain; as he stomps closer with heavy steps, Verlee flinches and slips to the edge of the cliff in an attempt to get away from the enraged man, but she is left with nowhere further to go. "How's it going to be fine?" He digs his fingers deep into her skin as he shakes her limp body by her shoulders. "If we get caught we can go to jail!"

"We just need to bury the body and I will take care of the rest," she tries to reason with him but Damon continues to push her frail body back and forth, guiding her further towards the hill.

"You don't understand, do you?" His howls shake the earth beneath them, and his feet are soaked in mud as he drives her closer to the edge. "We committed a crime! And it's all your fault!"

Gregor taps his fingers on the steering wheel as he croons along with the music playing on the radio. Everything is hazy in the heavy rain, but through the bleary view he catches a glimpse of a parked car with its doors open wide, and squinting his eyes he sees a couple standing outside in the pitiless rain. He leans closer to the window, trying to get a better look at them, and he sees the man shaking the woman by her shoulder and screaming at her face.

Clicking his tongue he averts his gaze, looking down at his phone where he reads that it is 11 PM on the 17th March. He groans as irritation builds inside of him. How could he forget?

When he looks back up he sees only the man this time, standing alone at the edge of the cliff with his head hung low as the rain claims him for itself.

Curiosity getting the better of him, and with a sense of unease spreading through him like wildfire, Gregor stops his car in front of the man and rolls down the window.

"Is everything okay?" he asks, but the man stays still in his place, his eyes shaking vigorously.

"Everything is fine," he whispers almost inaudibly in the heavy rain.

Gregor gazes at the man for a moment longer but left with no other option, he turns the car engine back on and drives away, not wanting to intervene. What he doesn't notice is the shoe tangled in the moss at the edge of the cliff.

With a quick movement, he taps a number on his phone and waits for someone on the other end to answer.

"Hello, Gregor," Moriko exclaims happily, but he can tell it's forced—her voice lost its spark a long time ago.

"Hello, please pass the phone to Genji," he mumbles as he balances the phone on his shoulder, fixing his gaze on the road where waves of rainfall are crashing against his car.

"Hi, Dad." Genji's glum voice rings in his ears and it takes everything in Gregor not to drop everything and visit his son, maybe then he will sound a bit more joyous.

"Happy birthday Genji!" Gregor chirps, trying to soothe the tension away. "Am I late?"

"No, you called just in time," Genji mumbles, his voice still woeful, and something breaks inside Gregor's heart hearing his son's upset voice. His voice doesn't ring with glee anymore, not after the tragedy...

"How are you doing?" The question is met with a buzzing silence for a while.

"Dad..." Genji starts after a while, his voice shaky and uncertain. "Dad, I want to go to Canada."

Gregor understands the reason why and it tears his soul to shreds.

"Sure, anything you want kiddo."

The night has come and the world has been lulled to sleep by the soft moonlight that shields everything beneath.

Felix peeks his head out of his room and looks carefully around. He tiptoes outside and moves closer to his parents' room. Taking a deep breath, he steps inside where his parents are deep in slumber. He stands still for a while by the door frame, afraid to even draw a breath. He watches them sleep, the way their chests heave with each deep breath, and when he believes that they're not waking up any time soon he staggers away.

In his vision, there is a red door at the top of the stairs. The door he's forbidden to open. But the longing to know the big mystery of the room takes over his heart, and so with short steps he walks upstairs. His hand lingers on the handle for a moment, not daring to open the door. With a sharp intake of breath he counts to ten and only then decides to open the red door.

He has no time to solve the mystery before his mind is consumed by blackness.

Felix flicks his eyes open with a low grunt as he drowsily adjusts his vision to the white walls surrounding him. A soft groan leaves his lips as he stretches his sore limbs, and rubbing his eyes he blinks once or twice, fighting the sleep away. He feels a throbbing headache coming on with greater force the more he thinks, the more he tries to remember the dream. As he fully regains consciousness, the dream becomes foreign to his mind and gets lost somewhere in the depths of lost memories, leaving no trace behind and only enveloping him in an odd kind of noiselessness.

He shakes his head and swiftly hops off the bed, placing his feet on the cold floor and forcing himself to stand up straight inside his cold, lonesome house. He only realises what time it is when he checks his phone, and he sprints outside.

As Dylan slowly walks up the stairs he hears frantic footsteps echoing through the thick walls. He turns around, looking for the source of the loud noise, and at the same instant someone falls right into his arms.

Dylan takes a moment to process what has occurred—his eyes are glazed, staring blankly into space before he shakes himself out of the shock and looks down only to be met with the familiar raven hair.

"Felix?" He asks uncertainly. The person is still breathing heavily, holding tightly onto Dylan. Dylan gives Felix a few more seconds to gather himself, and as Felix appears to snap out of his trance, he jumps back awkwardly, his eyes wide in shock.

"I, I'm sorry," Felix stutters, his voice weak, unusually frail.

"Are you okay?" Dylan asks as he tilts his head to the side to observe Felix better, making Felix tense up even more.

His eyes roam helplessly around as his body twitches restlessly. It takes him time to fully gather his thoughts, and when he finally does he looks up at Dylan with his usual forced, stoic expression, but Dylan can see the mask cracking as Felix's lip wobbles with wordless worry.

"Yes." He clears his throat. "I'm fine." His voice goes back to the normal monotone.

Felix looks around, his lip caught between his teeth as his leg unconsciously taps on the floor, "I'm late for work," he blurts out before he can stop himself.

"Oh," Dylan muses, looking at his watch. "I can drop you off if you want?" he suggests timidly, rubbing the back of his head, unsure if he has the right to ask.

Inhaling a shaky breath and putting his pride to one side, Felix looks at Dylan.

"Okay," he mumbles before sprinting outside. Dylan follows behind him.

"So it's a motorcycle," Felix notes the evident, unamused as he glares at the machine glistening under the sunlight.

"Yeah? What else does it look like?" retorts Dylan. Felix scoffs nervously at the obvious truth, chewing down on his fingernails as his eyes shake at the sight of the coffin on wheels.

"When you said you could drive I had an idea of a car—you know, four wheels, roof, airbags, actually safe to drive!" His voice jumps a pitch higher on the last sentence. Embarrassed, he clears his throat and gives Dylan a dirty look.

"I'm an excellent driver, and very safe too, for your information," Dylan says sulkily, sounding childish as he hastily puts a helmet on Felix, who yelps in protest.

Felix looks ridiculous and he doesn't need a mirror to know that, his head is way too small for the headgear, and with his already bad posture, he slumps a few more inches down.

Dylan checks Felix's helmet for the last time, fastening the chin strap with a loud click, but still worried about his safety, he grabs it and shakes it lightly, just to make sure that it is sitting nicely, protecting Felix from any possible harm.

In response Felix huffs in pique, fogging the shield.

"That's it!" Dylan claps his hands, beaming at his clearly joyless friend. "We are ready to go!"

Felix grumbles something under his breath, which Dylan can't make out because Felix's voice is muffled through thick layers of the safety headwear. Then Dylan hops on the motorcycle and pats the back seat, gesturing Felix to sit down while Felix stands there for a few more seconds, regretting every life choice that has led him to this very moment. Eventually, though, he remembers the main reason why he is in that situation in the first place and he jumps on the motorcycle.

"What about you? You're not wearing a helmet." Felix practically screams, his voice not only blocked by the helmet but also by loud revving noise of the engine, buzzing against the ground and sending vibrations through his body.

"Don't worry about me, as I said I'm a great driver," Dylan assures him with a smile, clearly enjoying Felix's distress.

"Well, I will be the one to judge that!" Felix bites back, fogging his shield once again, but Dylan just rolls his eyes back, still grinning.

He guides Felix's arms to his waist, holding him close and patting his fisted hands in a comforting manner. "Hold on tight!" is the last thing he says, or rather shouts, before taking off, and he swears he hears Felix squeal as his arms hold onto him for dear life, squeezing him in a death grip and crumpling his shirt in the process. But Dylan just chuckles as he rides towards life.

Felix doesn't feel as much fear as he thought he would, safely settled as he is on the back seat. He watches the world spiral, everything blending into a blur as they drive through the streets full of busy people.

When they stop at the red light, Felix dares to look at Dylan's back and becomes lost in his many thoughts. Dylan is solid to the touch, he isn't disappearing in his bare hands—he is real and he is there, with Felix. Having somebody by his side is all too new and bizarre for Felix. He's not used to having company, he has lived alone for so long that he has forgotten how to be human. Even if his sound mind tells him that Dylan isn't a threat, that he wants to be friends, something deep down in the depths of his dark soul is telling him otherwise. He's torn apart by his heart and the mind, demanding two different things.

As the engine starts, he lets his eyes rest and lays his head on Dylan's back. He puts his thoughts to one side, deciding that the present is worth giving a try.

Felix makes a choked sound and inhales a deep breath when Dylan finally removes the heavy helmet from his head. Dylan giggles at the dishevelled appearance of his friend, his hair sticking out in different directions, his face tinted an unhealthy red, and his eyes wide, gazing blankly into space, swinging from side to side, still high on the adrenaline.

"I'm never doing this again," he mumbles, his speech slurred a bit. He still looks dazed, but his expression quickly changes into a worried one, and before Dylan knows what's going on he's already rushing inside the cafe. Dylan ponders if he should turn around and leave now but a few raindrops fall onto his skin, washing his doubts away, and so he follows him inside.

"Here's your coffee," Felix declares as he puts a drink on Dylan's table.

"Thank you," Dylan murmurs, blowing the heat from the drink.

Felix throws a nervous glance behind him before deciding to sit in front of Dylan and take a short break.

"How long have you been working here?" Dylan asks as he takes the first sip.

"Almost a year," Felix answers tiredly, remembering all the sleepless nights.

"Must be hard..." Dylan muses with his chin in his palms. "To have two jobs."

"I manage." Felix lies as he brushes away a few strands of hair.

Felix's phone rings, gaining both of their attention.

"I'm sorry." Felix holds his hand out and answers the phone.

"We found him." William sounds out of breath and the heavy sound of rain makes it impossible to hear his words.

"What?" Felix jolts, holding the phone tightly in his hand as his knuckles turn white.

"We've found Damon..." The thunder strikes, cutting William's speech short. "We've found Damon's body."

Hearing these words makes the blood freeze in his veins and shivers go down his spine, and he feels as if punched, struck by the overwhelming train of thoughts. His body starts to tremble as he gazes into nothingness with shaky eyes. The realization slowly sinks in—another attempt by the universe to tear him down. He sits dazed as William shouts from the other side, only the noise of the rain registering in his hectic mind.

"Are you okay?" Dylan asks, the familiar worried expression crawling back onto his face.

"I need to go," he mumbles and tries to stand up but falls back onto his seat as his legs give way.

"I must go," he whispers again, his eyes glossy, shaking with horror.

He removes dried branches from his way as he walks through the forest through the mud that sucks his feet beneath the wet ground as the rain pours down on him, lancing him to the bone with each drop. He hears the chaos unfolding behind the mighty trees that have held so many secrets for so long. He blinks and blinks but his vision remains hazy and blurred.

Soon his eyes catch a gathered crowd of policemen running away from the rain into the shelter of a black tent.

"What are you doing here?" someone shouts in his face, shoving him by his shoulder, but in a daze he stays wordless, just blinking the raindrops away.

"He's with me." The familiar husky voice of William dawns on his senses. "Come on." He feels an arm wrap around his trembling body and soon the rain stops streaming down on him as William unfurls an umbrella over him.

They walk through the filthy mud, and from the corner of his eye he sees a blanket placed down on the ground and spies a bone sticking out through the filth.

"Is it him?" he whispers as he gazes at the scene, surrounded by yellow signs.

"Yes," William says with a sigh, his grip around Felix's shoulders tightening.

Felix has a sudden urge to revolt, to scream till his lungs give up as he gazes at the remains of the devil of his past. He is left with more questions than ever before, and closure seems ever more distant, ever more out of his reach.

"Come on in." William guides him inside the tent where all the policemen have gathered, covered in mud from head to toe.

"How do you know it's him?" Felix asks as he sits down, accepting the hot coffee from William.

"We found his ID," William answers simply as he sits down in front of him. "We also found his phone but it's damaged beyond repair so it may take months before we'll be able to use it."

Felix scoffs at the drollery that he calls life.

"Tomorrow we'll need your testimony, is that okay with you?" William asks gently, leaning closer towards him.

Felix just nods and listens as the rain washes away his past.

Felix's vision is blurred as he gazes through the window of the car. He still hasn't recovered from the shock—his mind is still hazy. The only thing he wants to do is to go back home.

"How are you?" William asks, turning his head back, but Felix doesn't answer—an appalling feeling of hopelessness is devouring him alive.

"Felix?"

The car starts to spiral, and as a cold sweat starts to gather on his forehead, he feels sick to his stomach.

"Stop the car!" he yells, and the moment he jumps from the car he vomits all over the ground. Tears gather in his eyes, and as he gasps for air, his whole body shaking, he digs his hands deeper into the mud. trying to gain any kind of balance.

He feels William touch his back so he swiftly moves away from his reach.

"Leave me alone!" he rasps. He notices that he's already next to his dormitory so with much struggle he stands up and staggers towards the gate.

"Felix!" He hears William call out to him but promptly ignores him.

With sluggish steps, he walks up the stairs, trying as hard as he can not to fall down. He hears loud footsteps trail behind him so he swiftly turns around and shouts, "Stop following me!"

The outburst takes William aback, and he freezes in place as he watches him with wide eyes.

"Your job here is done, so move on with your life!" Felix yells, his shout echoing through the thick walls.

"Felix, listen..."

"No, I won't listen to you, you had all the time in the world to care about me, now it's too late!" he roars as he holds tightly onto the metal rails.

"Felix..."

"Just leave me alone like you always did!" His shriek awakens the night. He feels tears welling in the corners of his eyes so he quickly turns around and runs towards his door, only to find Dylan standing in front of his room, gazing at him with horror-stricken eyes.

Felix thinks he's ruined it, his last hope stripped away from him as he watches the way Dylan is gazing at him. Fumbling with his keys he curses under his breath, finally gets the door open, and closes it with a loud crash.

"When are you going to tell him?" Logan asks when William sits in the car with a gloomy shadow following him from behind.

"It's too late," William whispers as he gazes at the building where Felix remains out of his reach.

He sinks down on the floor as his world collapses—everything he has believed in, every small hope slips away from his bare hands and he can do nothing but watch as his life becomes ruins of the past.

Felix has to cry but his eyes are long dry so he glares at the floor with a shaky, deranged look. The scream inside of him builds up and demands to be freed into the wild but he decides instead to bite his tongue until he can taste blood. With a silent yowl, he ruffles his hair, pulling on the locks as if he wishes to rip his flesh open.

A light knock brings him to his senses, soothing the turmoil. He stands up like every other time and staggers towards the door only to find Dylan standing there with a worried frown on his face. He sniffs and rubs the tears away with his arm but he's not fooling anyone for his eyes stay bloodshot red.

"What do you want?" he asks, his voice raspy from the unshed tears that remain as a lump in his throat.

"Are you okay?" Dylan asks, moving closer to him, and Felix steps back, unwilling to show benevolence.

Dylan freezes in place but his solicitous expression stays.

Felix tries to stand still but his shoulder starts to tremble as fresh tears gather in his eyes, stinging and piercing through his skin. He drops his gaze down and lets the tears rain from his eyes, and for a while he stays cold and empty before he feels a warm touch encircling his body as Dylan wraps his arms around him.

Maybe Felix has let his guard down too early, maybe it's too soon to demolish the walls around him, but spending this moment alone brings more sorrow to his crestfallen soul, and so he lets Dylan in, lets him step forward onto the broken bridge as the one who has been brave enough to do so.

They both fall to the ground without ever breaking the bond between them.

Felix's world collapses but at least he doesn't feel lonely amongst the chaos. The wires around his neck loosen, no longer suffocating him, and for the first time he can breathe. He doesn't feel as if he's a hollow, a ghost in the shell—he feels whole. It feels like going back home after wandering alone for so long. He has never dwelt for long on his feelings, but this time he lets himself savour each and every one of them, and as Dylan holds him closer, gently patting him on his back, Felix completely surrenders to his feelings and lets the wall that he's built through his sorrow be destroyed.

"I'm so tired," he wails as the tears stream down on his face. "I'm so fucking tired." He punches Dylan on his chest but Dylan stays attached to him, letting Felix extrude the sheltered depths of his woe.

"It's okay," Dylan murmurs as his body sways with each hit. "I'm here."

"This is so unfair!" Felix grabs him by his collar, shaking him back and forth as the tears pain his spent soul. Suddenly out of breath, Felix finds his body starts to shake, to bounce with each intake of oxygen.

"Deep breaths," Dylan says reassuringly as he holds Felix in place. "Take a deep breath."

Hyperventilating, Felix starts to lose consciousness, Dylan's face becoming more unrecognizable with each short breath.

"Breath with me, I'm with you." This is the only thing his brain registers as everything darkens in his vision.

The red door carved from his nightmares comes to his vision once more. He's standing right in front of it this time and his hands linger on the door handle a tad too long. He blinks, second guessing himself, but curiosity for the unknown takes over his sound mind and with a deep breath he opens the door. At first glance there is nothing out of the ordinary—it's just another storeroom.

With shaky hands, Felix turns the lights on. There are two big closets filling up the space and in the corner, there is a freezer laid down on its back. He doesn't understand the deep secret of the place—it just looks like your typical room.

Looking around he notices a stack of bottles filling up the glassed closet so he walks towards it and only after counting to ten does he open it. At first, he doesn't understand what is inside the bottles. They look like chunks of skin so he looks closer, and when the realization sinks in, his breath catches in his throat.

Numberless embryos are placed in the jars, floating in the filthy waters.

Terror-stricken, Felix staggers back trying to get away from the minacious sight, but as he does he hits his back on the second closet. The glass door shakes, and in a blur the jars fall upon Felix, soaking his clothes wet as the flesh of the embryos brushes against his skin, leaving permanent stains behind that will linger on his flesh no matter how much he scrubs.

In fear and trepidation, Felix runs to the corner and wraps his arms around himself to shield himself from the horrors. He feels his heart jump from his chest with each beat, and breathing becomes tough as he's left shivering to watch the foetuses splatter on the ground.

From the corner of his eye he notices the freezer. Its buzzing rings in his ears, urging him to open it and discover something that will haunt him even in his deepest dreams. With shaky hands, he leans towards it, wrapping a tight grip around the handle he awaits his doom.

His shriek disturbs the night as the decomposing body of the new-born lies upon him, looking at him with two holes where its eyes should be, rotten flesh and bones sticking out from its sage green skin. His body set aflame, he rushes out, trying to escape the hideous truth of the room, stepping carelessly over the dead foetuses and slipping and falling onto the ground. He screeches as he feels the soft touch of the flesh on his palms, and his whole body shakes as he tries to scratch the feeling of repulsion from his skin.

His hands slip, wet from the fluids of the bottles, but somehow he stands up and sprints out the room. He runs down the stairs but loses his step, and as he tumbles down the moth-eaten staircase, he feels someone grabbing him by his legs. "Theodore!" Damon shrieks, but in sheer panic Felix wriggles away from his reach. He runs towards the door, opening it onto the ruthless rain that awaits him, but before he can move his body forward, to get away from the house of horrors, Damon grabs him by his leg once more, causing him to collapse on the ground.

"Help!" he screams as Damon drags him across the cement, his fingernails digging deep into the ground and leaving traces of blood behind.

"Someone, help!" he wails but to no avail—there is no one to save him on this serene night.

"Why did you go in there?" Damon roars as he closes the door with a loud crash, making Felix flinch in fright. Unable to muster a word, Felix shakes in fear as images of the new-born become imprinted on his mind.

Damon grabs him by his collar, shoving his face closer to his as he shouts, "I told you not to go in there!"

One moment he sees a hand in the air and the next he feels a stinging pain on his cheek. "No!" he wails as the hand once more rises up into the air. "No!"

"No!" With a shriek, Felix jumps up in the air.

He pants as the memories slowly sink in, and he feels out of breath as the sweat starts to drip from his face. He raises his hand to his mouth and makes a croaky noise as the images of that night come rushing to his senses.

"Are you okay?" He hears Dylan speaking and realises it's the first time he hasn't woken up alone.

"I need to call William." He bounces off the sofa and rushes toward his phone. His legs shake as he taps his foot on the ground, and after what feels like an eternity William answers the call.

"Hello?"

"There is another body!" Felix yells, not wasting any time.

"What?" William sounds dumbfounded.

"I saw the body of a new-born." He paces around with loud steps as he ruffles his hair in angst.

"Are you sure?"

"The night they disappeared I saw the body of a baby in the freezer."

For a heartbeat, William stays silent, leaving only a buzzing sound to fill Felix's mind.

"Okay, I'll tell the team."

Felix can only sigh in relief as he crouches down.

"Is everything okay?" He hears Dylan speak, and having completely forgotten about him, he jumps up in surprise.

"It's a long story," he answers as he falls down onto the sofa once more with his face in his palms as he gazes into nothingness.

"What are you doing here?"

"You passed out during a panic attack and I didn't want to leave you alone." Dylan rubs his nape with a shy smile. "Sorry."

Felix nods, not having the energy to speak.

"Mind if I ask what is wrong?" Dylan asks meekly, his voice unsure but inquisitive.

Felix dwells on the thought for a while, not knowing whether he can fully trust Dylan, but then he decides it's better for Dylan to hear it from himself than somebody else.

"I lied to you," he starts as he watches for Dylan's reaction, but Dylan just nods. "I'm not Canadian, heck I don't even know where I'm from."

Dylan's brows perk up.

Gently, as if not to open a wound, Felix slips his fingers through his hair, displaying the scar. "I don't remember anything from my past up until I was around seven or eight years old, I'm not sure since I don't remember my date of birth either."

Dylan visibly flinches as the worrisome expression returns to his face.

"How come?" he asks.

"Amnesia from head trauma, I don't even remember how I got it." Felix sighs as he reopens the sealed scars. "The people I was talking about were my adoptive parents but they disappeared one night, leaving me alone, so I grew up as an orphan in the orphanage."

The frown on Dylan's face deepens as he carefully listens to the boy. "Today the police found the remains of my father."

Dylan's breath catches as he leans back with his hand placed on his chest, gazes at Felix woefully.

"I'm sorry to hear that," he says.

"Well life can be unfair, can it?" Felix scoffs and leans his body against the sofa.

As he finally shares his past for the first time, it is as if a heavy weight has been lifted from his shoulders. It wasn't as scary as he thought it would be, instead it brings a sense of comfort in him.

"What are you going to do now?" Dylan emerges through his train of thoughts.

"Find my biological parents," he answers with a tired smile.

"I'm sure they are waiting for you."

And maybe it's the way Dylan says it, the certainty in his words, that gives Felix a glimmer of hope that maybe somewhere someone is waiting for him to come back.

IX

Genji and Ayumu are sitting on the wooden stairs as they munch on their onigiri, which are too big for their tiny hands. They gaze at the wildness before them, where snow has become the permanent host, covering everything with a soft, white duvet. Ayumu blinks the snowflakes away as he turns his gaze toward Genji.

"I had a strange dream," he mumbles, his voice muffled by the food.

"What dream?" Genji asks without tearing his gaze from the white nature.

"I was Yuki Warashi and I was with a family that wasn't mine..." Ayumu dangles his legs in the crisp air. "They were foreigners, the woman had beautiful blue eyes."

At that Genji finally looks at his friend, his eyes twinkling with inquisitiveness.

"I stayed with them throughout the winter but in the spring I had to go."

"Were they sad?" Genji asks, his eyes not leaving Ayumu, who hunches down with a sigh and turns his gaze towards the woods, where naked trees are peeking out through layers of the snow.

He nods and starts to play with his fingers. "They didn't want to let me go so I had to run into the forest, to hide from them..."

Genji purses his lips as he leans his weight on his arms, gazing at his friend with a serious expression.

"And then what?" he asks.

Ayumu hesitates for a moment, looking down at his legs before turning his gaze upon Genji. "You found me."

"Come on in." William guides Felix with his arm into the interrogation room.

Looking around he notices the wide mirror on the wall that reflects him under the dimmed light hanging above the table in the centre. For a while he gazes at himself—the reflection is distorted, making his face unrecognizable, and the more he stares the more he envisions Verlee standing next to him, her arm around his shoulders as she keeps him close like she always did, as if warning him. After all these years Felix is still afraid to displease her. With a sigh he sits down on the chair in front of William, who is typing something on his computer. Only the sound of the keyboard fills the room, and the angst inside of him swells, turning into nausea.

"Did you find the body?" he asks then, finally mustering the strength to voice the question that is devouring him alive.

"Yes, we found Theodore, he was buried nearby." With a sigh William leans back, his gaze heavy as he observes Felix from afar. "How did you know that there was a body?"

"I remembered the night they disappeared," he starts as he fumbles with his fingers, putting pressure on the scar on his leg. "That night I went into the room, the room they've forbidden me to see." He inhales a deep breath as he tries to maintain eye contact with William, but his eyes keep shaking from side to side. "There I saw numerous embryos placed in bottles. I think she kept all of her miscarriages..."

He remembers the terror he felt as the night came crashing at him like a storm.

"Then in the freezer, I found Theodore's body." He finally finishes his speech and drops his head low, looking at his legs that have never stopped shaking.

William just nods and leans his body closer to him, placing his chin into his hands as he watches Felix for a few moments.

"Don't get me wrong, but how do you know it's the truth?" he asks.

Felix gulps, his heart heavy in his throat. "I have dreams of my past ...," he starts, pinching his scar a tad too hard. "Most of the time I can't remember them but I remember I was forbidden to go inside that room. I just couldn't remember what I found inside."

William nods as he types everything into the computer.

"How did Damon die?" Felix asks the question that hangs so heavy on his heart.

"He committed suicide, the examination showed bullet hole in his skull," William explains nonchalantly, with no trace of angst in his voice.

An uncomfortable silence washes over the interrogation room as Felix fumbles with his fingers, scraping the skin off and marking his fingertips in red.

"Now what?" Felix croaks, his wretched soul weighing him down.

"We still need to find Verlee and unlock Damon's phone. The investigation isn't over," William says with certainty. He looks sincere and Felix wants to believe him, wants to find his past.

"Do you have any more questions?" he asks Felix, but Felix shakes his head and stands up from his seat with a struggle as his legs continue to shake vigorously.

He gives a last glance towards the glass, only to find both Verlee and Damon lurking behind him, watching his every move, reminding him that he can never leave their claws. Only when he's standing at the door does William decide to speak again.

"I wanted to adopt you."

Felix's heart stops for a second or two as shivers go down his spine. He freezes where he stands, hanging onto the door frame.

"But I couldn't because I was going through a divorce and then it was too late..." Felix's fingernails go deep into the wood, marking it in red as his heart starts to hammer in his ears. "You started to resent me."

Felix swiftly turns his head back, gazing at William with wide eyes.

"I don't blame you." William drops his gaze down, his voice dropping with it. "I let you down so many times," he says, full of woe.

Felix just blinks at him in response, his mind going haywire.

"I'm telling you this because I genuinely care about you, Felix." Finally, William looks up, gazing at him with such rueful eyes, eyes holding all the apologies he could never put into words. "Can you forgive me?"

For a moment Felix stands still, leaning against the door as he observes William's every move, trying to catch him in a lie, but William's eyes shimmer with pure honesty. Felix can feel the bridge shake beneath him as William makes a step forward, piling up the first brick onto the broken bridge. For the first time, Felix hopes that the bridge can be repaired, that he can stand with everyone else around him, that his life is worth living.

And he nods, full of faith in a brighter future.

It's winter but spring is blooming inside him as he runs over the bridge, rushing to the first person he can share his excitement with. He feels like he's in elementary school all over again, sprinting with an Aero bar in his hands, buoyant to meet his newly made friend, except that this time he's sure it will all end well.

Out of breath, he knocks on Dylan's door, his appearance dishevelled, his hair sticking out in every direction from so much running, his cheeks dusted red by the crisp winter air, and his teeth chattering from the coldness of the evening. After a moment Dylan opens the door, dressed in a cosy robe.

"Felix?" he asks dumbfoundedly, his round eyes wide with wonder.

"Want to hang out?" Felix asks without missing a beat, blinking expectedly at him.

Dylan looks around and with a shrug opens the door wide, letting Felix inside.

"I was planning on going to the museum today, we can go early if you want to?" Dylan says as he guides Felix towards the sofa, gesturing him to sit down.

"What exhibition?" Felix lands down on the sofa with a sigh, letting the leather fabric engulf him.

"Japanese art after 1392."

Felix is enchanted by the idea so he nods swiftly.

"Let me get dressed then," Dylan says as he walks inside his bedroom, leaving Felix buzzing with excitement.

They prance through the white hall with paintings hanging on display for curious eyes.

"This one is from the Muromachi period," Dylan speaks as he points at the painting.

The painting is beautiful, a winter landscape drawn in ink shows mountains and a traditional Japanese house, and in the distance a cliff where the only visitors are naked trees. Felix gazes at the drawing, his eyes soaking up the lovely images as he imagines himself standing on that very cliff. A sense of familiarity settles inside his heart as he looks at the house peeking through the mountains. He imagines the kind of life could he live in that house, the stories it would tell.

"And this one is called Kintsugi." Dylan's voice startles his thoughts away.

Felix's eyes follow where Dylan is pointing, only to find a vase placed on the stand. The vase itself is black but it has golden lines running all over it.

"It's the Japanese art of mending broken objects with gold or silver," Dylan explains as he walks closer to the artwork. "It's believed that when something has been damaged over the years and is left broken, it becomes more beautiful."

And so just like a vase, Felix will take the pieces of his broken heart and mend them with gold. He will turn his pain into something beautiful and proud to display for any eyes to see.

"There is a word for that, it's called Wabi-Sabi," Dylan rambles on as he refamiliarizes himself with his heritage and remembers all the wisdom passed down to him by Mizuki. "It means admiring imperfections."

Felix nods as he takes in the information, curious to hear more. Maybe it's not all that bad that his heart is impure, cracked into oblivion—he can always rewrite the stars and make them something beautiful. Now he knows that, the future feels a bit more serene to his soul.

His steps are engulfed by the coating of snow as he marches through the night. Snowflakes waltz through the soft, silver moonbeams, excited for the depths of winter, and fall one by one, decorating Dylan's flesh in white. His house stays standing behind him, watching him leave for the unreachable crooks of the woods.

He rubs his eyes, removing snowflakes from his vision, his only lantern the crescent moon that is doing everything in its might to light him the way. He finds the familiar tree marked with blood, the exact tree where he and Ayumu fell asleep that night, the tree that nudged them towards the catastrophe awaiting them, and he sits down, tired from his journey through the past. He lets his eyes flutter closed as he takes in the crisp air that embraces him in a tight hug.

But then he hears rustling coming from the bare trees so he flicks his eyes open, only to find a deer standing in front of him. Its brown fur is covered in a cloud of white dust and its horns, proud and mighty, are outstretched towards the navy sky. Dylan blinks at the animal, unsure what to do, but the deer doesn't wait and gracefully starts walking down the path Dylan knows by heart. For a heartbeat he considers staying still and letting himself be consumed by the winter night, but curiosity gets the better of him and he stands up from the wet ground.

He walks towards the cliff of his doom, meeting with his fate once more. He passes the trees, all vast and full of his deepest secrets. Finally he sees Genji and Ayumu playing in the field, throwing snowballs at each other, and their joyous laughter brings life to the soulless night. He smiles, full of woe, as he's taken back down the road towards the past that has never left him.

"Dylan?" Out of the blue, he hears Felix speak and in a panic he looks around, only to find Felix sitting at the edge of the cliff, dangling his legs into the snowy air. "You're back." He smiles at him and it takes everything in Dylan not to topple over. He gazes at Felix with wide, lost eyes as the atmosphere between them suffocates him.

"What are you doing here?" he finally asks as he walks closer towards him, leaving footsteps in his wake. Felix stays silent for a while, just staring at him with a sad smile.

"I was waiting for you to come back," he says.

"Why?" Dylan asks confused as he sits down next to him, keeping his knees close to his chest.

"You told me, remember? It's our forest." Felix says as he glances up towards the moon, the moonlight softly illuminating his eyes.

"I don't understand!" Dylan's voice jumps as he leans closer to Felix in search of any kind of explanation.

"Time will show anyway. Don't try to fight fate," Felix whispers and slowly turns his head toward him. "I made the right choice. The chaos will be repaired into something quiet." He smiles at him, and it holds an unspoken assurance. "You just wait, our story ends soon."

"I don't…" From the corner of his eyes, Dylan sees a white light creep upon him, embracing him as it always does. "Wait!" He screams but Felix just smiles at him as he fades through the light.

And then everything bleaches into nothingness.

With a gasp, Dylan jumps from his bed. He looks around only to find himself in his bedroom, with no forest around. Slowly the yearning to see Felix takes over his sound mind, and even though he doesn't understand the explanation for the sudden urge, it itches his skin. He is itching to see Felix's face. Ungracefully he jumps onto the floor and runs towards the balcony, hoping to meet again with his friend.

Felix is sitting on his balcony with a notebook in his hands as he lets himself bathe in the soft moonlight. Disturbed by the noise he looks up, but this time his face doesn't morph into the familiar scowl. Instead, he gazes in confusion at Dylan.

"What?" he asks.

The question doesn't quite reach Dylan's ears at first, he just watches the boy in front of him. They are both real and present at the moment. He shakes his head and slides down the wall, sitting down on the cold floor.

"I just can't sleep," he says.

Felix nods in understanding and turns his gaze back towards the book. For a while, only the rustling of the paper fills the night as Felix reads through his notebook.

"What are you reading?" Dylan asks then, desperate for the conversation.

"My philosophy notes," Felix answers with his nose still deep in the notebook.

"What do you think?" Dylan starts, now gazing at the moon. "Can the future be changed?"

He hears Felix put the notebook down and for a while, there is a comfortable silence hanging in the air between them before Felix clears his throat.

"Well, as quantum science suggests, each future is held to rest until it's provoked by choices we make in the present. So there are many possible futures at the same time as we are in the present moment," he says as he puts away the book. "As the professor explained, there are events leading towards the effect, and changing the event changes the outcome as well."

Deep in thought, Dylan gnaws on his lip. He's certain his future cannot be changed—he knows he is doomed to everlasting grief, his future lies with his present and it cannot be repaired. So Felix's words fall deaf on his ears and he sighs, looking at Felix with tired eyes.

"Would you change your future?" he asks.

For a moment or two, Felix just gazes at him with an unreadable expression but the way he watches Dylan tells him more than he needs to know. "I already did."

They both look away from each other and trace their gazes towards the sky as the night welcomes two different people, on a different path.

X

On a warm Christmas night, the families have gathered together at the table, filling the air with their joyous chirping. Ayumu gnaws on the food, dirtying his whole face as he dives into a bucket of KFC chicken, keeping the Christmas traditions close. The door creak interrupts the gleeful atmosphere, displaying Gregor with bags of gifts in his hands. "Who missed me?" he pips with an outstretched smile decorating his face.

"Dad!"

"Gregor!"

The kids jump from their seats and come rushing towards the man, crashing against his legs as they wrap their arms securely around him.

"Hey, kiddos!" he exclaims in joy and as he leans down and takes both of them in his arms, bouncing them up in the air.

"Do you have gifts from Canada?" Ayumu's question makes everyone in the room laugh as they watch the overexcited kid.

"Yes, I brought a lot of gifts!" Gregor mimics the eager tone of the kid.

They settle down in front of the table once more and the room buzzes with even more glee this time.

"Will you come on my birthday?" Ayumu asks as he sits comfortably on Gregor's lap, munching on the strawberry cake.

"Of course, I will. Do you want anything as a gift?" the man asks as he wraps his arms around the frail body of Ayumu.

Ayumu turns his head towards him, gazing at him wordlessly for a moment before a beam breaks onto his face. "A telescope!"

The answer takes Gregor aback and he opens his eyes wide in curiosity. "Why do you need a telescope?"

"I love stars," the kid answers simply, wriggling deeper into his grasp.

"Okay then, I'll buy you the coolest telescope in the world," Gregor promises as he ruffles the curly locks of the kid.

"What are you doing at Christmas?" Dylan asks, sprawled on the sofa as he gazes into the corners of the wall.

Felix perks up at the question, gazing at him with lost eyes. "Nothing...," he murmurs uncertainly.

"How come?" Dylan sits up with a groan and gazes at him expectantly.

"I've never celebrated it," Felix explains, his lip caught between his teeth.

"Why?" Dylan sounds genuinely surprised as he leans his body closer to Felix.

"An orphanage isn't the most joyous place to celebrate Christmas," Felix answers truthfully as he gazes at Dylan with a sad smile, remembering the dull nights spent in the orphanage even if caretakers tried to cheer the sorrowful kids up.

Dylan grimaces as if punched as he watches Felix with a worrisome expression, but then the light beams through his face and he grins at Felix. "Do you want to celebrate with my family?"

Felix's eyes open wide, bewildered as he stares at Dylan without mustering a word. "I don't want to trouble you," he whispers as he starts to play with his fingers, peeling the skin off his fingertips.

"It's only going to be my dad and Sophia, so don't worry." Dylan pats him on his back and stands up from his seat, leaving Felix alone with a busy mind.

Celebrating Christmas with a family... That must be nice.

Felix runs from one table to another whilst keeping an eye on the clock on the wall so as not to be late.

"Felix!" his co-worker calls out to him from the kitchen. "Bring food to table four!"

With a huff Felix fixes his apron and rushes towards the kitchen, his heart hammering with excitement. This will be the first Christmas he won't spend alone dwelling on his gloomy thoughts.

"My dad is a businessman," Dylan explains as they walk up the stairs. "He produces eco-friendly items."

Felix nods in response, gesturing that he's listening. Sophia on the other hand stays eerily silent, her chin tucked into her coat as she shields herself from the merciless winter night.

"He's friendly, you'll like him," Dylan says through a grin as he knocks on the metal door.

It takes a moment before the door opens, displaying Gregor looking cheerful. He looks at everyone in turn, but the moment his eyes lock with Felix's they open wide as if in terror. As a sense of familiarity washes over Felix, he shrinks back from Gregor's heavy gaze. Gregor stares at Felix for a long moment, gawking at him wordlessly, his eyes telling stories Felix has heard before but can't remember. "Dad?" Dylan interrupts, looking at his dad with raised brows.

Gregor clears his throat and the familiar smile comes back to his face as he opens the door wide.

"Come on in," he says.

Felix stays glued to his place as Sophia and Dylan wander into the living room. He feels out of place to be dining with a family that isn't his. No one seems to be bothered by his presence, though, so he soon relaxes.

Dylan looks around the house, noting every change since his last visit, when his eyes catch a photo on top of the chest of drawers that he didn't see last time. His heart drops when he looks at the picture and the familiar sense of dread settles in. It's a picture of him and Ayumu, taken on the last Christmas they celebrated together. He draws a deep breath before hiding the frame behind another, out of his sight.

Felix watches Dylan move the photo frame and something inside him lights up with curiosity to see the picture or to ask why he moved it, but he thinks better of it and turns his gaze away from Dylan.

"Aren't you going to introduce me to your friend?" Gregor asks as they settle down in the kitchen after taking their coats off.

"This is Felix." Dylan points at Felix. "And Felix, this is Gregor, my dad."

"Nice to meet you." Felix holds his hand out and Gregor takes it gladly, but his fingers linger a tad too long as he gazes at Felix with charmed eyes.

As they lay out the tableware and put the food on the table, Gregor suddenly clicks his tongue and puts his hands on his hips.

"I forgot to put the decorative plate I brought, Felix, since you're the tallest, can you help me?"

Felix nods eagerly as he follows Gregor, wanting to leave a good impression on man. They walk inside his bedroom and Gregor points at a large wooden closet. "Can you reach the top?"

Tiptoeing, Felix stretches his hand up and shuffles through the layers of items piled on top.

"It should be in the corner."

He feels a cold touch on his fingertips and carefully grabs the item. It's a telescope, he notes, and he tilts his head to the side in confusion as he blinks at the item.

"Do you like it?" Gregor's voice awakens him from his thoughts, making Felix flinch.

"Sorry." Felix puts the telescope back and starts searching for the plate again.

"You can keep it if you like it," Gregor speaks again, leaning against the closet.

"I can't," Felix stutters, gazing at him with wide, lost eyes.

"They left before I could give it to them so it's meaningless for me to keep it anyway." As he speaks, something morphs onto Gregor's face, a mixture of dolour and longing.

"You should keep it, think of it as a gift."

Felix takes the telescope in his grasp and gazes at the glimmering metal—it looks expensive even to untrained eyes.

"Thank you," he murmurs as he traces his finger over the cold metal, feeling more and more at home.

"So how did you guys become friends?" Gregor asks as he bites down on the chicken, keeping to Japanese traditions.

"We go to the same university and work at the same clinic," Dylan answers immediately. "He has the best GPA of all the students and he's the best at the clinic as well," he explains with a proud smile.

Felix shrinks in his seat, shying away from the attention as all eyes dart onto him.

"That's great to hear," Gregor exclaims and pats Felix on his shoulder. "Your parents must be proud."

An uneasy silence cuts through the kitchen as Dylan and Felix fall mute. Felix shuffles on his seat and taps his legs nervously on the floor.

"Dad...," Dylan whispers, and Gregor, who is oblivious to the changed atmosphere, nods in response.

"Well...," Felix starts, biting down on his lip. "I don't have parents."

This time everyone falls silent as their eyes watch Felix's every move, and avoiding their gaze, he drops his head low.

"I'm sorry." Gregor finally speaks, gazing at him with eyes full of pity, and it makes Felix's blood go cold in his veins.

He shakes his head. "No need to apologize." He wipes his lips with a napkin and stands up from his seat. "Excuse me."

Everyone watches him go. Sophia gazes for a while before standing up as well and following behind him. An uncomfortable silence settles in the room before Gregor clears his throat.

"You don't find anything weird about Felix?" he asks.

"Don't talk about my friend like that," Dylan argues with a frown growing on his face.

Gregor sighs and leans his weight against the chair. "What do you think, is it possible that Ayumu is alive?"

"I don't want to talk about it." Dylan cuts him off fast, his gaze drops down onto his shuffling fingers.

"His body wasn't found after all." Stubbornly Gregor continues.

"I said I don't want to talk about it!" Dylan pounds down on the table, his fists turning white. "And why do you keep the photo anyway?"

"Because it's dear to me!" Gregor shouts back. "Just because you can't move on it doesn't mean others can't!" His eyes are wide in horror as he says the last part and Dylan gazes at him with a rueful expression.

"Why can't anybody understand my position?" He croaks as he scrapes the skin off his fingers, painting them red. "Someone is dead because of me."

"It wasn't your fault." Gregor rubs his eyes in annoyance at having had to repeat the same conversation over and over again for years. "You were a kid."

"But it's my fault, I took him to that forest! I screamed at him and hurt his feelings, he died hating me!" Dylan drops his face into his palms as he groans and the well-known feeling of guilt greets him.

"He might be alive," Gregor repeats, gazing in the direction Felix went.

"He's dead!" Dylan jumps from his seat. "And he's dead because of me!"

Felix splashes water on his face and gazes at his own reflection for a while. The more he looks the more out of the place he feels. He doesn't belong here. Having a family around feels nice, but not as nice as it would be if it were his own. With a sigh he opens the door and finds Sophia leaning against the wall, waiting for him to come out.

"How long have you been friends with Dylan?" She asks, her voice neutral but interested.

"About a month?" Felix answers, confused by Sophia's demeanour.

"Dylan doesn't have friends, you're the first one," she says as she straightens up. "So don't hurt him." And her eyes are accusing as if she has seen through the darkness of Felix.

Felix just blinks at her, fear settling in. "I don't have any friends except him either."

Sophia nods, seemingly trusting his words. "He's had a very hard life, so it won't be easy with him."

Suddenly the room shakes with a loud crash, making both of them flinch. They share equally confused looks before rushing towards the kitchen where they find Gregor hunched down with his face in his palms. Dylan is nowhere to be seen.

"Where is Dylan?" Sophia demands and after a stretched smile Gregor just points at the door. Without a word and without much thought they both sprint outside into the cold.

"Dylan!" Sophia shouts through cupped hands as her vision blurs with white snowflakes. "Where are you?"

"Dylan!" Felix joins the screaming as his eyes desperately roam around in a search of his friend.

They rush down the road, and even when their legs slip on the frozen ground, they keep running. In the distance they see a figure walking away, disappearing through the white, so they keep up their pace, trying to reach him before he slips from their bare hands.

"Dylan!" Sophia exclaims as she tugs him by his arm but Dylan doesn't budge from his place, remaining standing with his back to them.

"What happened?" She tries again but to no avail, so Felix runs and stands in front of him, blocking his way.

"What's the matter?" he asks.

Dylan just sniffs in response and drops his head down as he rubs the tears away with his arm.

"Let's go, it's cold." Felix tugs him by his arm, where the only layer of clothing is a thin shirt.

"Leave me alone," Dylan finally whispers, his voice hoarse with unshed feelings. "I want to be alone."

"No one wants to be alone." Felix pats him on his back in a comforting manner while still keeping a distance between himself and the distressed boy. "We don't have to talk about it, just let's go inside, I'm cold."

Dylan stays still for a heartbeat, visibly deep in thought, planning his next move before finally nodding and turning around. He has no desire to ruin the night for Felix even more, he's already messed up Christmas anyway.

XI

"This is the best Italian place in town," Dylan chirps as he guides Felix inside the local restaurant.

The restaurant is homely; family pictures hang on display like trophies, and the green undertones of the walls give the space a sense of cosiness. They walk towards the empty seats but before they can sit down, suddenly there is a loud crash coming from behind them and before Felix has only a moment to turn his head back before his heart comes to a halt as the familiar husky voice rings in his ears.

"Felix?" It's the voice of Noel, he's certain, even in the depths of his dreams he can still hear him call out his name.

The terror strikes up in him and his hair stands on end as his heart tries to jump from his chest with each painful beat. The sensations are all too physical—he can feel each drop of his blood go cold, chilling him to the marrow. His teeth start to chatter as his whole body shakes with the shivers going up and down his spine and the goosebumps standing upwards.

"Are you okay?" Dylan's voice traces his befogged senses, keeping him to some sense of reality.

"I need to go," he croaks through trembling lips, and without looking back or waiting for Dylan he rushes towards the door.

He runs towards the nearest alley and lets his body collapse to the ground as he holds onto the concrete wall for balance. His breathing is short and uneven as he tries to gulp the air down into his lungs that ache with each drawn breath. His eyes start to well up with tears as the panic consumes him as a whole. He is choking for oxygen as his lungs block his airways, not letting the air inside. He doesn't know if he's crying from the shortness of his breath or from the pain of the wound being slashed open once again.

He feels a warm touch on his back and he doesn't need to look back to know the owner of the intruder into his mental collapse.

"It's okay, I'm here," Dylan assures him as he rubs comforting circles on his back, allowing his lungs to open once more and let in the intake of air.

He coughs once or twice before slanting his body towards the wall and letting his forehead rest on the gnarled concrete.

"Are you okay?" Dylan asks as he sits down next to him, no sight of pity in his round eyes, just compassion and solace.

"Yes..." Felix heaves and twists his body around, now sitting next to Dylan.

"What happened?" Dylan dares to ask but Felix just groans in response, hitting the back of his head on the wall.

"I don't want to talk about it," he croaks meekly, his voice strained.

And with that Felix lets the past consume him whole as he sets off on the journey of memories that have never vanished completely, always staying in hiding, lurking in unreachable spots.

What is the past if not unpredictable, always following from behind, waiting for a moment to strike and steal your heart away?

"Can you escape your past?" Felix asks as they twirl in the air on the swings, letting their bodies fall gently into the lavender sky.

"The past lives within you. You just learn how to live with it," Dylan explains as he drops his head back, pointing his eyes up toward the sky.

"How do you live with the past?" Felix asks with curiosity as he gazes at Dylan.

"I don't." Dylan sighs and stops the swing as his fingers clutch the metal chains. "It haunts me every waking moment."

Felix blinks as he watches Dylan from afar, and the distance between them has never seemed so great. There is something that Dylan is secreting away in the depths of his heart and Felix is determined to explore every corner of his soul to find it. Now may not be the right timing, but Felix hopes they have all the time in the world.

As they gather outside the university, they chat about the previous lecture, and Felix feels carefree talking to him about nothing—it turns out having company isn't as frightful as he thought it was. He realises it was worth giving it a try to repair the broken bridge, and he feels more connected to the world with each passing day.

Felix hears the grass rustle behind him but pays no mind to it as he continues the conversation.

"Felix."

But then, like a lulled curse, he hears Noel's voice caress his senses with its claws, ripping his mind open.

Sensing the shift in the atmosphere Dylan stands up and walks over to Felix, shielding him from Noel.

"Who are you?" he asks.

Felix doesn't hear the answer as his mind is fogged by the panic taking over his body and making him freeze in fright.

"I need to talk to Felix," Noel says with an unnaturally soft voice, his tone trembling.

Something ignites inside of him, the flames of anger set free once more as he jumps from his seat, tackling Noel to the ground, making his leg bend abnormally.

"What do you want from me?!" he howls as he throws a punch at his face, pounding his head on the rough concrete. "Why can't you leave me alone?" His fists plough into Noel's face, and before long his hands are painted in blood once again. The flames of vengeance burn him from inside with each punch. But Noel doesn't fight back, he just gazes at him with helpless eyes as Felix decorates his skin in red with hit after hit.

"Just leave me alone!" His voice breaks from the pressure as the veins arise on his neck for everyone to see, but before he can hit the devil in disguise again, Felix feels arms wrap around his body, tugging him back.

"Leave me the fuck alone!" He continues to shriek as Dylan drags him back, holding him in a death grip as Felix tries to wriggle from his grasp.

Noel sits up slowly, leaning closer towards Felix, which only serves to further intensify the terror inside him.

"No! Don't hit me!" Felix howls as he raises his arms into the air, shielding himself, and Dylan can only watch with wide, horror-stricken eyes. "Please don't hit me!" His whole body shakes in fear as he's struck by the waves of the past, drowning him in dread.

"I don't know who you are but you need to leave," Dylan rasps sternly, glaring at Noel with a hatred he has never felt before.

With a sigh Noel rubs his face, wiping away the blood, and putting weight on his palms he stands up, his leg once again bending visibly. He limps away, taking the fear with him.

"He's gone now," Dylan assures Felix, whose body is still shivering to the touch. "Everything's fine."

It takes a moment before the flames settle down, leaving only ashes, and as the fear fades away with Noel's silhouette, the heartache finds its way in, and Felix drops his head down and lets tears pour down his face as the horrors of the past, which have never left him, reveal themselves again.

"How are you feeling?" Dylan asks as he hands Felix a cup of tea. Felix is wrapped in layers of blankets but his body is still shivering in fear.

"Better...," he murmurs as he blows the heat away from the tea.

Dylan stares at him for a heartbeat before sitting next to him. "Can you tell me who it was?"

Felix grimaces, and he takes his time to answer, listening to his beating heart.

"I was bullied at school," he starts, his voice trembling with nerves. "He was one of the main bullies."

His hands roam over his body to the places where the scars of the past remain, every cigarette butt, every cut, every mark. Dylan's eyes follow his movements, wetting his dry lips before he speaks again.

"Are they from him?"

Felix nods, his head dropping low.

After a moment's silence, Dylan again puts voice to his thoughts.

"I'm sorry you had to go through that..."

Felix nods with a tired smile on his face.

"But everything is fine now."

Felix stares at this person for a moment, this person who was brave enough to step onto the bridge without fear of falling. He thinks about how much his life has changed since meeting him. Sometimes it takes just one person to make flowers bloom in the graveyard. He smiles at him gratefully before his face morphs into a scowl once more.

"Should I talk to him?"

Dylan is taken aback and he stares at Felix with wide eyes for a moment.

"Do you want to?"

"I want to be free from the past," Felix admits out loud.

He wants to be free, so completely free that he won't be afraid of falling even if he crosses the bridge. He has stayed on that forbidden bridge for too long and loneliness has finally taken over his sound mind. He doesn't want to be afraid anymore.

"I'll talk to him."

With timid steps Felix walks inside the restaurant. The atmosphere is calm, in complete contrast to his heavy heart. He looks around hesitantly, praying to catch a glimpse of the person he's looking for, and yet his heart also pleads to never see his face again. His heart rages in his chest when he notices Noel wander over to an empty seat in order to clean the table, and with shaky legs he walks towards him, his heart hammering with each step he takes.

"Noel." When he calls out his name Noel freezes on the spot, his hand lingering on the table. "You wanted to talk."

Felix inhales deeply as Noel slowly turns around, his heart ready to jump from his chest. Noel gazes at him with sorrowful eyes and for a moment there is only silence between them as Felix lets himself be drowned in the sea of the past.

"How did you find me?" Felix asks first as he watches Noel sit down with a struggle, holding onto the table as he lets his weight drop onto the seat.

"Our classmate goes to the same university as you," Noel explains, his head hung low as he fidgets with his fingers.

Felix nods with a sigh and glares at the male through a scowl, impatiently waiting for him to speak.

"Didn't you want to talk?" he asks.

"I need a moment," Noel croaks, his face still oriented downwards. Then, with a heavy breath, Noel finally looks up at him with pure sorrow-stricken eyes. "I want to apologize."

Felix's eye twitches but he doesn't let his demeanour collapse and, with his heart in his throat, he nods.

"You probably don't even want to hear it."

"No, I need to hear it," Felix interrupts, the scowl deepening on his face as he glares at the man in front of him. "Why me?" He asks the question that has been weighing him down all these years.

Why him? What did he do to deserve to go through hell on earth? It's the question he doesn't know the answer to even after so many years have passed by.

"I'm afraid you will hate my answer," Noel starts, hanging his head down once more. "I didn't have any reason, I did it…" He gulps. "Because I could."

Felix narrows his eyes as the anger flares inside him, the devil begging him to go back to his wicked ways, but now he has found a saint in his heart to settle down the fire inside him.

"I was so consumed by my own worries that I didn't understand the severity of my actions," he says as he rubs his leg, wiping the sweat away from his clammy hands. "But the day you asked me to kill you, it finally dawned on me that what I was doing was horrible."

"It took you a long time," Felix scoffs as he crosses his arms, his eyes still burning with hatred.

"It made me go down in a spiral of doing everything to avoiding feeling guilty and admitting my wrongdoings but also deep down I knew that what I did to you was unforgivable," Noel says as he wraps his fingers around his jeans, turns up the hem and displays the artificial leg, letting the metal glimmer in the light.

Felix's brows rise as he takes in the sight. He was not ready for this kind of outcome.

"The accident, which was entirely my fault, changed me, it was the last push I needed" Noel explains as he hides his leg from curious eyes once more. "I'm a changed man and I can't say that before apologizing to you."

Felix stays silent for a heartbeat, Noel's words finding their home inside his mind as he hears his explanation, which still doesn't bring ease to his scarred heart. He still can't comprehend why him, why he had to go through all that, but maybe sometimes you need to leave everything in the past without gaining the answers you need.

And even if Felix got the apology he dreamed of, now he isn't sure if it would make him feel better.

But he is grateful that he wasn't the only one who was left wounded.

He heaves a deep breath and leans his body back on the chair. "Okay," he says, "I don't forgive you."

Noel grimaces as he drops his head low, his eyes shining with sorrow. "I didn't expect you to," he replies with a sigh. "But I've really changed-"

"I don't care." Felix cuts him off. "I don't care what kind of person you're now since it doesn't affect me anymore, only Noel I know, is Noel from middle school." Felix says calmly, yet sternly.

Noel's face grimaces in heartbreak but he can only nod as he hangs his head low in forever shame.

"Even if apology doesn't fix anything," Felix continues. "Since rest of my life I will have to live with scars you left, both mentally and physically." He watches as Noel's face flash with woe and rue that will never go away, and with a sigh he stands up, holding onto the table as his heavy body drags him down. "I'm still glad I got my closure and I hope you won't make same mistakes again."

The moment he steps outside he starts sprinting, and as the flowers start to bloom on the bridge and glow brightly in the warm sunshine, Felix can feel the rope of his past loosen its suffocating grip around his neck and release its hold on his tired heart. His heart beats in relief as for the first time he has someone to share his excitement with.

The phone rings and Dylan takes it in his hands, noting that it's his mother who is calling.

"Hello," he chirps, happy to talk to her after a long time, but his mother stays silent, only the buzzing of the phone rings in his ears.

"Mom?" He tries again, sounding more worried this time.

"We think...," Moriko croaks and Dylan can hear the sniffles coming from the other side, making his heart sink and his blood go cold. "We think we've found Ayumu's body."

The world spins, taking the balance from his legs, and he falls to his knees, his phone falling out of his grasp. He can hear his mother talking from the other side but it doesn't reach his fogged ears. He blinks the tears away as he watches the life he has built collapse in front of his eyes, knowing he can do nothing but watch. His heart slows down almost to a stop, leaving him little reminder that he's alive.

And he doesn't want to be alive in this world where Ayumu doesn't belong. He can't live a life as vicious murderer, his palms tainted in blood. This time he allows himself to drown in the sea of rue, letting the waters surge inside his lungs and making breathing impossible.

This is it...

This is how the story ends.

This is the story of how his life ends.

He rushes outside, not caring even when his body shivers in the cold as he stands in front of the motorcycle in a plain shirt. He turns the engine on and hops onto the machine letting it take him where his heart leads, trying to escape from himself.

The road is blurred by the tears pouring down his face.

"Fuck!" he wails as his grip on the handlebars tightens, turning his fists white. A car honks at him from behind, but he has no intention of moving out of the way. He fixes his jaw as he tries to stop the waterfall of tears that haze his vision. He pounds at the clutch with his fist, momentarily losing control over the machine, but he swiftly regains his balance.

What is he supposed to do now? He has dreaded this day for sixteen years. His life starts and ends with Ayumu, there is no point in moving on with life, not without Ayumu. There is no reason for a murderer to be alive when the victim rests somewhere tangled in the mud.

His vision blurred with tears, he doesn't notice the stop sign placed by the roadside, and as his body leaps forward from the impact he prays for eternal slumber.

Felix knocks on Dylan's door, shaking in excitement to share the story of his bravery, but no one answers, and with a frown he knocks again, knowing that Dylan should be at home. In the midst of knocking, his phone rings so he takes it out of his pocket and sees that Sophia is calling him. Since they exchanged numbers she has never called him, and so with raised brows, he answers the call.

"Hello?"

"Dylan!" she wails in his ears, making him jolt.

"Sophia?"

"Felix!" she shouts again, sounding out of breath. "Dylan, he…" She coughs her words out, sounding almost inaudible.

"What is going on?" Felix yells as the angst settles within his heart.

"Dylan is in the hospital!" Her final answer makes his heart drop and his gut wrench painfully. He stays glued to his place, the only company to his raging mind the beeping phone.

Dylan blinks open his eyes and is instantly blinded by the unmerciful rays of light. He squeezes them shut and it takes a blink or two before he opens them again and scans his surroundings. He's in a hospital bed, he would recognise the feel of the rough sheets anywhere. Bleached walls surround him from every corner and the beeping of the heart monitor throbs in his ears.

The more he regains consciousness the more the pain becomes apparent. His whole body aches in unbearable pain, as if set on fire. He tries to sit up but his body presses him back down. He looks down at his body, only to find his hand wrapped in bandages, and when he tries to move it, an agonizing pain strikes his whole body. He falls back onto the bed, surrendering himself to fate.

His mind wanders towards Ayumu once more. Poor Ayumu, his body has been rotting beneath the earth for sixteen years while he has continued to live on. It's so unfair how he continues to stay on this earth when Ayumu is long gone. There is no valid reason for him to continue to live on, not now the story has reached its epilogue.

At that moment a dishevelled-looking Felix barges inside the room, his eyes full of tears as he gazes at Dylan with tired, bloodshot eyes.

"You idiot!" he wails as he walks toward him. "You're beyond stupid!" His arm lingers in the air, not daring to hit him. Dylan watches him awestruck, lost as to why Felix seems so distressed. Felix sniffles and rubs the tears away but they continue to fall.

"Never do something like that again!" he cries, and Dylan nods, still not understanding how someone can care so much about an evil being like him.

A moment of silence passes by with Felix gazing at him with sorrow-stricken eyes before his lips tremble in an attempt to speak.

"I have no one but you," he murmurs just above a whisper, almost inaudibly, but it reaches Dylan's ears, making his heart jump. "So don't you dare leave me."

And for a moment Dylan wonders whether maybe his life has some purpose after all.

XII

Felix and Dylan walk down the street, moving towards the clinic that stands proud at the end of the road.

"Give me your backpack," Felix says, gently removing the backpack from Dylan's shoulders while taking care not to damage his injured hand as he notices Dylan whimpering in pain from time to time.

When they arrive at their destination they see a man standing on a ladder and pinning a wide poster on the white wall.

"Welcome Miracle Children" it reads and Felix's blood goes cold as he reads the sign, questioning the meaning of it all. As the realization slowly creeps in, he opens his eyes wide and reads the sign all over again, but he has no time to dwell on his thoughts as a van comes rushing through the gate with a loud shriek.

When he turns his gaze towards the incoming noise he sees Hotaru coming down the stairs with a white cane in his hands, swinging it from side to side as he walks towards them.

"Hotaru." Felix greets him, and Hotaru seems surprised as his eyes stretch wide and brows perk up.

"Felix?" he asks uncertainly, turning his head in their direction. "What are you doing here?"

"I work at the clinic," Felix explains as he gazes into Hotaru's eyes, but this time they don't burn with hatred towards him.

"Here." Felix gently nudges him by his shoulder, offering him his arm to hold onto, and Hotaru looks lost for a heartbeat, just gazing in his direction for a while before wrapping his arm around Felix's with a sigh. And with that, they walk inside the clinic with slow, careful steps, with Felix guiding Hotaru along the way.

"Sign it here," Felix murmurs as he takes Hotaru's finger and places it on the corner of the paper. Hotaru does as he is told, quickly signing the papers and turning his head towards him.

"Why are you being so nice all of the sudden?" he asks.

"I'm tired of playing rivalry with you," Felix answers truthfully, his tone tired and frail.

Hotaru doesn't look convinced and he blinks at him as if trying to catch him in a lie, but eventually he nods.

"Will you be there at the camp?" he asks then, his tone sounding as if he is testing Felix.

Felix falls silent for a moment, the possibilities going through his head as he thinks deeply. He remembers all the bright spring days spent at the camp, showering bits of light on his weary heart, and he thinks he wants to give some happiness away if it brightens a day for even a single kid.

"Yes, I will come."

Hotaru nods and with that, he takes the cane in his hands once more and staggers away, disappearing from sight.

"Who was that?" Dylan, who has stayed silent this whole time, finally speaks, gazing at him with eyes that twinkle with curiosity.

"We were raised together in the orphanage," Felix answers rather simply, with no shame in his voice. Dylan leans his body against the wall as he watches Felix with eyes shining with interest.

"What was he doing here?"

"The annual trip planned by the orphanage." Felix sighs as he puts on his white coat. "This time they're cooperating with our clinic."

Dylan hums in response and crosses his arms. "Let's go or we'll be late."

Felix draws shapes in the dirt with a stick, listening to the joyful laughter of the kids from behind him. He has no desire to participate in the joyous atmosphere as he gazes at his reflection distorted in the mud, and the longer he gazes, the more unrecognizable his face becomes.

"What are you doing here all alone?" Xaria walks up to him, kneeling down to his level.

Felix just shrugs as he throws the stick away. He looks towards where the noises are coming from, gazing at the kids running around the field. Even though they're bonded by the same pain, he feels out of place.

"Come with me, play with other kids." Xaria offers him a helping hand and for a moment Felix just stares at her open palm before he interlaces his fingers with hers and they stand up from the ground. In the end, though, he doesn't join the game the kids are playing, he just sits down on the ground, watching them with sorrowful eyes.

"This trip is stupid." He hears Hotaru speak from the side and he gazes at the kid who just like Felix has no desire to join the game, to be a part of the jovial mood.

Felix just nods in response, longingly watching the kids having the time of their lives.

With Nathan in his lap, Felix gazes outside the window, watching nature unfold right in front of his eyes; he looks at the trees that pass by the car, blurring into one another as the green scenery strikes the onlooker's eyes. His body bounces as the bus carelessly moves over the ground, and with yet another bump he feels a light weight drop onto his shoulder. He turns his head and sees Dylan sleeping soundlessly by his side. Felix feels pleasant, light in his heart, and for the first time he is excited for the trip.

The moment the bus stops the kids barge out in the blink of an eye, stretching their frail bodies, some already rushing towards the open field and engaging in play. Felix takes the boxes in his arms as he walks down the steps, careful not to slip. He sees the second bus, the bus of the orphanage, stop next to them, and in a moment kids are running down the steps, joining the kids from the clinic with their gleeful screaming and laughter. With a sigh, Felix places the box down and twists his sore body, his muscles aching from sitting down for too long.

Amid the mighty trees, he smells spring coming home to him. He looks around the meadow, at the wildness of nature, the bracing flowers peeking up through the fresh green grass and decorating the earthy ground with their dazzling colours. Spring is bidding winter farewell with a soft kiss as the white duvet is completely melted away from the earth. He inhales the smell of the crisp grass and closes his eyes for a moment, savouring the sense of tranquillity.

But then he feels a light nudge on his arm, cutting the moment short, and he looks over at the visitor to his quietude and finds Dylan gesturing at the box.

"Everyone is going inside the cabin," he explains and points at the crowd gathered in front of the cottage. With a sigh, Felix takes the box into his arms once more and they both walk towards the building.

"Kids! It's time to eat!" Felix shouts as he makes delicious sandwiches. Hotaru is standing next to him wanting to help so Felix puts an orange in front of him. "Peel it for me."

Hotaru sways his hand into the air for a moment before he finally reaches the fruit and carefully, so as not to cut himself, he takes the knife.

A moment of silence falls between them, the only disturbance the happy laughter of the kids. Then Hotaru sighs, gaining Felix's attention.

"You've changed," Hotaru whispers as if he's embarrassed to admit to it.

Felix blinks at him before the verity behind his words reaches him, but when it does he simply smiles and looks away, fixating on the food once more, his heart full of life.

Hungry kids come rushing towards them as they dive into the food, emptying the plate in mere seconds. Felix then counts the kids one by one and to his dismay he finds Nathan missing.

"Where is Nathan?" he wonders, his question reaching Dylan's ears.

"Is he missing?" Dylan asks, and Felix nods as his eyes roam around in search of the kid.

"I'll go find him," Dylan, who is unable to help with the food because of his injuries, declares, and Felix once more just nods, although his face is painted with worry.

"Nathan!" Dylan shouts through cupped hands as he goes deep into the woods, his legs getting tangled in the crisp bushes.

"Where are you?" He curses when he stumbles upon a rock, almost falling over. The mighty trees hover over him, shielding him from the rays of warm sunshine, leaving him shadowed in the dark.

"It's dangerous Nathan, come here," he yells once more, but again with no response, only the soft breeze rustling through the grass.

He's ready to turn around when he catches a glimpse of the kid, sitting at the edge of the hill. His eyes grow wide in horror as he finds himself in the forest alone once more with no help around. His legs take over his body and he's running without even realizing it. Images of that night come rushing back to him and he wonders if he's cursed to be awakened on the same night over and over again. His heart rages inside his chest as the kid looks more out of his reach with each step. He feels the blood burning inside his veins as he desperately tries to get close to Nathan.

When he does, he grabs the kid roughly by his arm, dragging him back from the cliff and shoving him behind. The perplexed kid just gazes at him with wide eyes for a moment before his lips tremble and produce a throaty wail, shaking the trees around them.

"What are you doing?" Felix snarls as he glares at Dylan with unforgiving eyes, moving quickly towards the kid and checking for any injuries, but Dylan just dazes into nothingness as his eyes shake with fear. Felix's scowl disappears and is replaced by a worried expression when he takes in the state of his friend.

"What's wrong?" he asks, but the answer never comes as Dylan collapses to the ground, his body shaking vigorously.

"Dylan!" Felix yells as he runs towards him, holding him safe and trying to stop his body from shivering.

Dylan's teeth start to chatter as his eyes roll back and his body twists from each side.

"Stay with me," Felix croaks as he holds Dylan's face in his palms, slapping him gently, but Dylan's body never stops shaking as he rocks back and forth trying to get away from the claws of the past.

"Let's sit up," Felix speaks reassuringly, wrapping his arms around Dylan's torso and pulling him upwards. "Let's go to the cabin, shall we?"

Dylan doesn't respond. His eyes are gazing aimlessly at nothing.

With a struggle Felix lifts himself and Dylan up from the ground, still holding onto Dylan for dear life. With his free hand, he takes Nathan's hand and they walk through the unwelcoming forest.

"Open your eyes!"

Felix's ears hear the desperate voice of the kid. His whole body sways as he feels tiny fingers dive into his flesh, shaking him from both sides. He opens his eyes, only to be met with wide, round eyes staring into his soul. He recognizes Genji looking down on him, and from the corner of his eye he also sees Ayumu sitting by his leg.

"Run!" Genji yells as he shakes his body once more, urging him to stand up.

"What's wrong?" Felix asks as he sits up, rubbing the sleep away from his eyes.

"Dylan!" Genji shouts, stumbling over his words. "He's in danger!" He points at the depths of the forest, where permanent visitors have become trees encircling them threateningly, and Felix jumps up from his seat, where his body has become one with the moss, ready to run.

"Where is he?" he shouts, his eyes desperately trying to catch a glimpse of Dylan.

"At the cliff!" Genji yells back, and without thinking Felix rushes back into the cursed woods.

The spring sunshine is too weak to melt the winter snow, and his legs slip on the frosted ground as he runs. Even so, he continues to run. He removes the branches from his way as they cut deep into his skin, making the blood pour, but he's not physically aware, his mind is focused only on Dylan, and finding Dylan. He finally sees the boy sitting at the edge of the cliff, his posture hunched, shrunken down.

"Dylan!" he calls out to him, moving closer. "It's dangerous, step away from the cliff."

But Dylan doesn't respond and remains with his back turned towards Felix.

"Come on." Felix's voice trembles with fear. "Step over here."

A peal of thunder strikes in the mountains, painting the sky in lavender and shaking the ground beneath, making Felix flinch, but still Dylan doesn't budge from where he sits.

"Dylan, please," Felix pleads as he wraps his arms around himself, desperate for a sense of comfort, rumpling the fabric of his coat in the process.

After a stretch of silence Dylan stands up and Felix tries to leaps forward to catch him, but his body is frozen in place, paralysed by fear.

"I no longer can bear the pain," Dylan whispers as he opens his arms wide. "I've lived with this weight for sixteen years, I've fought enough."

"What are you talking about?" Felix wails as tears well up in his terror-stricken eyes. "Move away from the cliff, Dylan!" He is shrieking now, his voice filled with unsaid pleas as he tries to move forward.

"I'm sorry...," Dylan murmurs as he closes his eyes and leans forward, letting himself be engulfed by the air as he falls, disappearing in front of Felix's eyes.

"No!" The shriek shakes the earth beneath Felix as he rushes towards the cliff, but Dylan is long gone, vanished into thin air and only the sound of the river is there to accompany him. Without wasting even a second, he runs towards the hill that connects to the river and keeps running even when his legs become stuck in the mud, the forest doing everything in its might to stop him from finding Dylan. His heart beats erratically in his chest as the road seems to get further away with each step. He curses as branches get in his way, trying to prevent him from entering the woods, but he continues to run regardless of how painful the deep lunges of the branches are into his skin.

He doesn't know how long he runs but finally he's standing at the river bank, panting heavily. He gazes at the unmerciful waves crashing against the rocks, devouring everything in their way, and for a moment he feels afraid, ready to run away like a coward so he won't drown in the same river twice, but his heart is telling him to find a way into the river towards Dylan, and the need to save his companion is stronger than any fear. And so, taking a deep breath, he jumps into the raging waters.

He marches against the wrathful stream as the river crashes against his ribcage, stealing his last breath, like a carp weakened but full of life and determination, and with a deep intake of air he jumps down. At first, he sees nothing but darkness as the cold surrounds him entirely. He swims deeper into the water, following his heart rather than his vision. He stops and floats in the pit of darkness for a moment, but his heart is ready to burst from his chest and guide him towards Dylan.

Out of the blue, his eyes catch a glimmer of light in the dark, and when he looks down he sees his necklace glowing in soft white light, shivering to the touch. He blinks, surprised as he touches the warm pendant. Then, from the corner of his eye, he sees a faint glimmer coming from below so he swims deeper into the depths of the river.

There, finally, he notices Dylan, unconscious, drifting deeper into the waters, his ring placed neatly on his finger and shining just as brightly as Felix's pendant. Felix grabs him by his arm, tugging him upwards as he drags their bodies through the callous waves doing everything in their might to drown them once again in this ill-fated river. With a gasp, they gulp down the air as they're struck by the waves that crash against their flesh.

"You fool!" Felix yells breathlessly, punching Dylan's side as they're carried along with the current. Dylan chokes on the water and falls into a coughing fit; Felix is still glaring at him as water splashes onto his face and he slowly fills his lungs with air. Fighting fate is pointless, they won't be able to win against the heartless current, and so they let the river guide the way.

At a bend in the river they spot the Eguchis' house rising up from the ground. They exchange equally confused expressions as the river leads them back to their home, and with much struggle they swim out from the current, their clothes drenched and cold as they open the door to the house.

At first there is darkness and darkness only, but slowly some light seeps in through the window, displaying the home in all its warmth, filled with love and joy just as it used to be, the echo of the kids' laughter still ringing through the wooden walls that hold so much familiarity within them. They find Mizuki and Moriko standing in the centre of the room, as if they've been waiting a long time for them to come back.

"You're finally back," Mizuki says with a welcoming smile as she embraces Felix in a gentle hug, and Felix freezes to the spot not comprehending the situation they've found themselves in.

"What is going on?" Dylan asks as he looks at his mother who just holds his face in her palms, carefully tracing her fingers over his cheeks.

"No need to dream anymore," she says reassuringly. "You can wake up now." But Dylan is lost, not understanding the meaning of her words.

"Look." Felix nudges Dylan by his shoulder, pointing at the window, which displays the world crumbling apart.

The forest is collapsing, with earth falling into the river in big chunks that break off from the riverbank. The river is demolishing everything in its way with its unmerciful current. One by one trees fall over the cliff, their mighty roots hanging up in the air. Animals run for cover, trampling each other and trapping the luckless ones to the ground, painting the earth and the river in blood. The sky turns black, robbing nature of colour and leaving only the bloody red on display as the world of the dreamland surrenders to its fate

Because there is no need to dream no more. The story has come to an end, and they can only blink in awe and watch as the world they've built together through their blood and tears fall into ruins right in front of their eyes until there is nothing but darkness, a void from where the forest used to stand proud.

With a gasp, Felix jumps up from his place only to find himself in the same position, on his knees right next to the bed, from which Dylan is gazing at him with tired eyes.

"Are you awake?" Felix asks through a yawn, rubbing the sleep away from his eyes.

"Just woke up," Dylan answers, his voice equally faint.

For a moment Felix just watches him, waiting for the explanation, but it never comes as Dylan avoids his gaze.

"What happened back there?" He decides to ask himself.

Dylan bites his lip as he drops his face low. "I had a panic attack."

"I know that," Felix snarls, annoyance bubbling inside him. "But why?"

"You will hate me," Dylan whispers as he looks up, locking their eyes together. "And I don't want to lose you."

"There is nothing in this world that would make me hate you," Felix assures him, patting him on his fisted hand that has turned white from the tight grasp.

For a while Dylan doesn't speak. He just stares at him with rueful eyes. "I'm a bad person."

"Everyone thinks they're bad, I'm sure you're wrong…"

"I killed someone."

Felix freezes to his place, his eyes wide in horror. Unconsciously he removes his hand from Dylan's, but this makes the boy's face grimace and shrink further down into his body.

"What did you do?" Felix croaks as he watches Dylan in terror, one question after another springing up in his mind.

"Ayumu," Dylan mumbles through trembling lips. "His name was Ayumu."

Felix nods but still keeps a distance between them.

"I loved him with my whole heart," Dylan croaks, tears already gathering in the corners of his eyes. "But I fell asleep…"

A light rustling caresses Genji's senses as he flutters his eyes open. At first, his eyes register nothing but dark, and he looks up at the sky, where the crescent moon is shining down on him with its crooked smile. The night is all calm, lulling him back to sleep, and he almost shuts his eyes, only to realize that Ayumu is no longer by his side.

When he looks around he finds himself surrounded by mighty trees, shielding him from the moonlight and plunging the vast woods into darkness. Terror takes over his sound mind and his heart rages, hurting his chest with each beat and becoming an intruder into the serene night, the only sound disturbing the silence of the woods.

He jumps up from the ground and turns his head this way and that in search of the kid, his vision growing gauzy as the trees follow his every move.

"Ayumu!" he shouts as dread quickly settles inside his raging heart. "Where are you?"

The darkness consumes him. From the corner of his eyes, he sees shadows lurking towards him, ready to devour him alive, and with a shriek he runs, trying to get away from their reach.

"Ayumu! Genji!" He hears his mother call out to them but a yearning to find the kid takes over his heart, demolishing his fear of the unknown entities creeping behind the trees and what secrets the forest holds. He runs even when his legs get tangled in the mud, dragging him back, forbidding him to enter the woods.

"Ayumu!" he wails once more before coming crashing down. He groans as the ache spreads through his body and squeezes his eyes shut.

When he opens them he finds Ayumu lying beneath him with an equal grimace on his face. Tears well up in his eyes as he gazes at the kid, and irrational anger builds up inside him as he grabs him by his collar.

"Why did you go?" he shouts, spitting in his face.

Ayumu gazes at him with lost eyes as Genji shakes his body back and forth.

"You know it's dangerous! Why did you leave my side?! Do you know how scared I was?!" Genji continues to yell, shaking the earth with his roar. "I hate you so much!"

Something breaks inside Ayumu's heart, and his eyes glimmer with tears in the soft indigo moonlight. He shoves Genji to the ground and races off into the depths of the forest, leaving Genji alone to ponder his mistakes forever.

"And then he fell off the cliff…," Dylan says quietly, holding his face in his palms. "My last words to him were that I hated him."

Felix nods along as he listens. Then he leans towards Dylan with a sigh, taking his hand in his.

"You were just a kid," he says.

"Kid or not someone died because of me," Dylan bites back with anger in his voice, but whether it is aimed at Felix or himself, Felix doesn't know.

"You didn't kill him, you made a mistake and a human can't be human without mistakes," Felix assures him as he pats him on his shoulder.

"How can I live with this?" Dylan wails as he rubs the tears away, but fresh ones are ready to pour down his face.

"Do you remember what you told me? You need to learn to live with your past," Felix says with a timid smile.

"I don't want to live."

His answer hangs in the room for a heartbeat, leaving Felix speechless, gazing at him before shaking his head with a sigh.

"If you can't live for yourself, live for me," he says, and Dylan looks at him with confusion written all over his face. "Maybe it's selfish but I have no one but you and I wish you could see how important you are."

Dylan just gazes at him wordlessly, unable to find the right words to speak.

"I need you with me, Dylan. Learn to accept your past, you've fought enough."

Dylan wonders what he has done to earn this much respect, and the unavoidable thought of letting Felix down weighs heavy on his heart. At the same time, though, his heart isn't sure if it's possible for him to continue to live on without Ayumu by his side.

The realization slowly creeps up on him that there is a new person whose life depends on the choices he makes. He doesn't know if it's worth it to try to be a better person for someone else, but maybe along the way he will learn to live for himself too. He knows there is only a one path that will lead him to the answers he wants, and so before he can stop himself he speaks.

"Do you want to come to Japan with me?"

Felix looks taken aback as he gazes at him with wide, perplexed eyes before his face morphs into a warm smile that outshines the sun.

"I will come with you to Japan."

XIII

The night is all calm; the quiet susurration of the trees takes over the blood-hot air that burns everything to the ground. Leaning over on the crutches, Genji carefully staggers down the stairs with short steps so as not to slip and fall. He pours water into a cup and lets the water stream into his throat, cooling him off from the hell-like night. He hears the wooden floor creak from behind and he looks back into the darkness, where the only source of light is the dim glimmer of the lamp placed on the desk. At first, his eyes catch nothing as he gazes at the timbered walls of his house, but then he notices a light glow waltzing in the air, morphing into a varied shape, and before he can blink he sees Ayumu standing in front of him, radiant in the dark.

"Ayumu?" Genji calls out to him as he freezes to his place, the cup still tightly held in his hands. "What are you doing here?"

But Ayumu doesn't speak, he just watches him fervidly, his eyes flashing with vengeance.

"What's wrong?" Genji asks meekly as he tries to get close to him, but in the midst of the bizarreness of the situation he forgets to take his crutches, and so he falls with a loud crash, shaking the walls around him. He squeezes his eyes, where tears from the ache in his wounded body have already gathered. Then he hears an upstairs door open with a loud thud, and after a moment his mum comes sprinting down the stairs.

"What happened?" she asks as she falls on her knees, roaming her hands around his frail body, checking for any new injuries, but Genji doesn't answer; he just gazes at the place where Ayumu was standing moments ago, before he vanished into thin air.

"Ayumu was here..." he murmurs and something changes in Moriko's expression, sadness washing over her delicate face as she holds Genji close to her chest. "Go to sleep, we need to wake up early tomorrow."

Genji nods as he stretches his hand out towards the crutches, taking them into his grasp as he tries to stand up with his mother's help. They stagger away with Genji's eyes darting back to the corner where Ayumu was before, the line between reality and delusion slowly fading.

As they walk through the police station they're surrounded by chaos. Genji is careful with each step to avoid bumping into the legs of the policemen that rush from one corner to another, towering over him and making him feel oh, so small and fragile. His eyes linger on the poster of Ayumu, smiling brightly in the photo with the words Missing Child written above it.

Moriko knocks on the door and they both wait for a moment before the door flies open and crashes against the wall, revealing Kuragari with a cigarette in his lips. Genji grimaces at the foul smell of the smoke and waves his hand in front of his face, trying to block the smell from entering his body.

"You came," Kuragari says, and his voice sounds so worn, almost inaudible.

They walk inside the dull room, the walls painted in bland grey, papers splattered everywhere in every corner, and a dusty flashlight lying on the desk. The place is rotten with despair. They sit in front of Kuragari, who takes a paper and the pen in his hands, ready to write.

"Where is Ayumu?" Genji asks, full of innocence, and Kuragari's face wrinkles with sorrow as he closes his eyes.

"We haven't found him yet," he says in a tired tone as his fingers start to fidget in angst.

"But I saw him yesterday..." But before he can finish his sentence Moriko nudges him by his shoulder, urging him to stop.

Kuragari's eyes are wide in hope but before he can speak Moriko shakes her head and his face falls.

"Tell me Genji, what happened that night?" he starts as he takes the stack of papers in his hand.

"We were playing hide and seek," Genji mumbles as he plays with his fingers, ready to tear the flesh open.

"I know that. What happened after?"

Genji bites down on his lip as his gaze drops to the floor. "I took him to the forest."

Kuragari nods, writing everything on the paper.

"Then we fell asleep." Genji's voice is tight with fear as he shuffles on his seat, unable to find a sense of peace within his body.

"And then?" Kuragari looks down at him with accusing eyes and it's all too much for Genji as his body starts to shake.

"Kawa Akago took him," Genji mumbles, and his reply makes Kuragari 's face pinch in irritation as he rubs his eyes, trying to sooth the tension away.

"Forget Mizuki's stories, tell him what happened." Moriko scolds him and it makes Genji shrink back into his seat, trying to get away from the unwanted attention.

Suddenly it's hard to breathe, the room is humid with tension.

"I didn't do anything!" Genji yells, even though he doesn't believe in his own guiltlessness.

"What happened after, Genji." Kuragari rasps sternly, making shivers go down his spine.

"I told him to move from the cliff but he didn't listen!" Genji tries to prove his innocence as he leaps forward, his body shaking with dread.

"Did you push him?"

The question is like a claw that leaves a mark on his mind.

Did I push him?

Suddenly the lines between the truth and the lie get tangled with one another, leaving no clear answers. The more he dwells on the thought the more he believes in his own wickedness Images of that night blur into obscurity as in one moment he sees Ayumu falling over the cliff and the next he witnesses himself pushing the kid.

"I don't know...," Genji murmurs through trembling lips as the memories of that night leave another permanent scar on his psyche.

The moment Genji walks inside the classroom he feels all eyes fall on him like daggers, going deep into his skin. He grimaces as he looks around, seeing the kids he used to call his friends avoid looking at him as if afraid, or glaring at him with hatred burning in their eyes. He drops his head down and staggers to his seat only to find his desk decorated with words in ink.

Killer

Murderer

Bring back Ayumu

Go to hell

Die

Genji yelps with heartache as the words like sharp knives leave permanent wounds on his mind. The more he looks at the words, the more he believes them, and at that moment he wishes to die, to completely vanish without leaving any trace behind. In an attempt to shield his mind from the threat he closes his eyes, but the words linger like uttered curses, finding their forever home in his brain.

He sits on the swing as he gazes at the kids playing around him. He used to think of those kids as friends but they seem distant now, unreachably far. He sighs as he drops his head low, swaying back and forth before something touches his feet. When he looks around he finds a ball near his leg so he takes it in his hands.

"Throw the ball!" one of the kids yells as they come rushing towards him. Genji gazes at the ball for a brief moment before looking at his friends.

"Can I play with you?" His voice is full of hope as he gazes at them with expectant eyes. Grimaces washes over their faces as they fall mute for a heartbeat before contorting their faces into forced smiles.

"You know what? My mom asked me to come home early," one of them says as he turns around and sprints away, leaving the two of them alone. For a moment the other kid seems hesitant, looking back and forth at Genji and the ball.

"I need to go too," he says and rushes away as well, leaving Genji alone in the vast field, making him feel small and vulnerable. With a sigh, he drops the ball that bounces up in the air, and he wonders if he will have to get used to this isolation from his peers and everyone else around him.

Everyone despises murderers.

An unknown voice chortles in his ears, making him flinch, and at that moment he sincerely believes the voice.

A light susurration caresses his senses as he hears trees whistle in the night. Flicking his eyes open he finds himself one with the ground, moss spreading over his body like a blanket. He rubs his eyes as if to make the world disappear, but when he opens them he finds himself back in the same doomed forest.

Genji stands up and dusts the earth from his clothes and his eyes roam around, taking in his sights. He sees familiar trees hovering over him, sheltering him from the silver moonbeams that caress the world with their soft touch. He sets off walking, the crooked shadows of the trees following him from behind, and everything seems all too real to his touch as his hand lingers on the dried-up branches of the trees that block his way as if forbidding him to enter the mighty woods. Soon he finds himself at the edge of the forest, at the cliff of doom, and as he looks around he notices a silhouette hunched over the edge, gazing at the darkness beneath.

"Ayumu?" Genji wonders as he moves closer to the petite figure, but Ayumu doesn't budge, his body leaning into the depths below.

"What are you doing here?" he asks as he touches Ayumu on his shoulder, but the body shrinks and melts through his touch.

Ayumu turns his head back, and Genji's breath is stopped in his lungs as he takes in the sight of the kid. Blood is pouring down on Ayumu's face, and his face is mutilated beyond recognition as he glares at Genji with fires of hatred in his eyes.

"Why did you kill me?" he whispers as he stands up, making Genji stumble and fall to the ground.

"I'm sorry!" Genji cries as he crawls back, trying to get away from the dreadful sight.

"I was your friend!" Ayumu roars as he throws his fist into the air and ploughs it deep into Genji's body, bruising him in purple. "And you killed me!"

Ayumu sprints towards him with unstoppable speed and wraps his hands around Genji's neck, shoving him to the ground and making him one with the earth.

"I'm sorry," Genji coughs as the air is blocked from entering his lungs. His skin flushes pink and tears well up in his eyes as breathing becomes impossible.

"I trusted you!" Ayumu wails as he pushes Genji deeper into the mud, painting him in earthy colours.

The ground shakes and breaks as thorns barge through the earth, spreading over Genji's body. Genji tries to get away from their painful grasp, but as the thorns embrace him in a breath-taking hug, the forest claims him as its own. As the thorns claw their way into his heart, Genji can only open his eyes wide in terror. Everything morphs into pitch black, the shriek of the kid awakening the night.

Genji lies in the coffin that his bed has become, ready to be buried six feet under. He gazes aimlessly through the darkness at the beam of the moonlight that has fallen through his window. He hears a light knock on the door but pays no attention as his body rots, melting into the bed.

"Are you asleep?" Moriko peeks her head inside the dim room, and not having the strength to speak, Genji just shakes his head.

Moriko walks towards him with short steps, her legs trembling like a leaf about to fall from a tree. She kneels in front of him, gently tracing her fingers through his hair and letting her touch linger on his cheek. They stay in silence for a heartbeat before Moriko leans in and leaves a soft kiss on his forehead.

"You know I will always love you, right?" she asks in a trembling voice as she gazes into eyes that refuse to meet hers. Genji stays silent, gazing into nothingness as his mother's words makes his heart wrench in pain.

"But..." Her voice drops to just above a whisper, almost inaudible. "But I think it will be better if you stay with your dad for a while," she murmurs as she removes a few strands of hair that have fallen onto his eyes. Gaining no response she sighs, and wrapping her arms around the stiff body she hugs him close, afraid of losing the second kid dear to her heart.

The taxi driver puts the suitcase in the trunk and closes it with a loud thud, making Genji flinch. As the car moves off, he watches the house he used to call home fade into the past. He shuffles on his seat and fidgets with his fingers, scraping his skin, and only then does he feel the empty touch on his middle finger, bringing tears to his eyes.

"What's wrong?" Moriko asks worriedly as she traces her hand over his cheek, wiping the tears away. "You can always visit whenever you want to."

But Genji stays silent as the cold tears drop from his round eyes, dripping onto his hands where the empty feeling lingers.

"I forgot the ring...," he murmurs as he is taken towards his future, leaving the past behind.

May 5th, 2016

William sits in front of the computer, trying to concentrate as the chaotic sounds of the working policemen fill his ears. As he types he hears the clock ticking, reminding him of the passing time.

"We unlocked the phone." He hears a policeman shout from behind and jumps up from his seat, letting the chair fall with a loud crash as he rushes towards him.

He grabs the phone and switches it back on. First, he checks the messages but finds nothing in particular, just ordinary conversations between Verlee and his colleagues. Then he goes to the photos, hoping to find anything that would help the case, but all he finds are photos taken in nature. With a sigh, he drops his hand down as the annoyance burns inside him, making it hard to breathe. He checks the phone once last time and sees the notes app flashing in front of his eyes. With a final glimmer of hope he opens the app.

I didn't mean to push Verlee, I loved her with all my heart even though she was evil, I found peace in her cruelty. If her body is never found, she fell off the cliff near the new road with the stop sign in front of the old oak tree.

"Get the guys!" William shrieks as he puts his jacket on, ready to blast off, while his shaky eyes continue to read through the note.

I hope Theodore rests in peace, I shouldn't have taken his body, I shouldn't have listened to Verlee when she begged me to but I'm a weak man by heart.

And to Ayumu, I'm sorry, we shouldn't have ripped you away from your family but Verlee just wanted a kid and you happened to be in the wrong place at the wrong time.

I don't know how long the secret will last if the hospital ever tells the family the truth, even though we paid them enough for their silence. But it's the truth that keeps me awake at night. I hope he will forgive me one day.

"Ayumu?" William wonders out loud as he sits in the car, reading the letter over and over again until the realization comes crashing against his heart and causing his eyes to widen in terror. Immediately, with shaky fingers, he dials Felix's number.

"The number you are trying to reach has been disconnected or no longer in service."

Felix sits next to the window as he watches the soft clouds waltz through the blue sky, and he wonders if he can touch them. They bring a sense of familiarity to his heart, as if he has seen these same clouds some time ago, even though it's his first time flying in an airplane. In search of comfort, he looks around to find Dylan sleeping soundly with his head securely placed on Felix's shoulder as they fly to Japan.

"There's no service," Felix says as they jump from the taxi, standing in front of Dylan's house.

"We have a phone in the house if it's an emergency," Dylan answers as he lifts his bag onto his shoulder.

Felix shakes his head and takes his own bag in his hands. Meanwhile, Dylan puts a hat on, shrinking in his posture as he walks by, and with a sigh, Felix removes the cap from his head, saying "You don't have anything to hide from."

Lost in his thoughts Felix comes crashing into Dylan's back, and for a moment he scowls at his friend, but his scowl soon disappears when he catches Dylan gazing longingly at the house next door.

"What's wrong?" Felix asks as he also turns his gaze towards the house. It looks similar to Dylan's house, both built from wood with two steps up to the door. It's a small house but it looks welcoming and cosy.

"Ayumu lived there..." is the only thing Dylan says as he shakes his head and walks towards his house, avoiding looking at the Eguchis' home.

Felix gazes at the home glistening in the crescent moonlight for a long time, something tugging him by his heartstrings, but he can't pinpoint what it is and so, not to dwell on the thought, he shakes his head and follows behind Dylan.

Dylan knocks on the door and after a moment it opens, revealing a dishevelled-looking Moriko as she gazes at her son with teary eyes, her body trembling. She jumps on him, wrapping her arms tightly around his shoulders and nuzzling her face into the crook of his neck as her shoulders shake violently. Dylan wraps his arms around her torso, holding her close, and they stay like this for a while, satisfying the hunger of their longing.

"This is Felix." Dylan says, and Felix holds his hand out and shakes Moriko's. She gazes at him for a moment, her eyes sparkling with nostalgia, before she smiles at him and opens the door wide, saying "Come on in."

They walk inside the home and Felix looks around, enchanted by the new environment. He sees papers with doodles plastered to the wooden walls and he smiles to himself at the childlike drawings. He looks closer at one of them and sees two figures standing in a field. A feeling that is new to him settles inside his heart, weighing him down, and he leans back with a scowl, as if trying to get away from the feeling.

"Let's sit in the kitchen," Moriko chirps as she walks by, and Felix's eyes linger on the drawing as he moves away.

"So Felix, tell me about yourself," she says as she pours tea into his cup, after which Felix thanks her in a whisper.

"I was raised in Canada," he starts, raising the cup to his lips.

"Then where you were born?" she asks innocently, oblivious to the change in Felix's demeanour as his face falls.

In a panic, Dylan jumps up from his seat. "We're out of juice," he says stupidly as Felix and Moriko watch him in confusion. "I'll go and buy some." And with that he sprints outside, leaving the two of them dumbfounded.

After a silence, Moriko puts on her familiar warm smile again as she gazes at Felix.

"Do you want to see childhood photos of Dylan?" she asks.

They sit in Dylan's old bedroom amid stacks of photo albums scattered around a worn-out old box.

"That's when I took him to the waterpark," says Moriko, pointing at a photo on which Dylan's face is all scrunched in fear as he sits in the boat. "He's never been photogenic," she cackles, making Felix chuckle.

"This photo we took at Disneyland, when we went to Tokyo." In the photo, Moriko and Dylan are beaming with wide smiles, and next to them stands a woman with a baby in her arms. Felix narrows his eyes—the woman seems weirdly familiar but he can't figure out from where.

To his surprise the next picture has been slit, with the faces of the kids cut out, and in search of answers he looks at Moriko, who just gazes at the picture with sorrowful eyes.

"Ayumu cut the faces out so they could put them inside the necklace and the ring."

Unconsciously Felix touches his pendant that is placed securely around his neck.

"It was a memorial of their friendship. Ayumu had Dylan's photo and Dylan Ayumu's," she says through a sad smile as her eyes fill with tears.

His chin starts to tremble as the world starts to spin into obscurity, as questions to which he doesn't yet have the answers appear in his mind.

With a shaky voice, he asks, "Can I see the ring?"

Moriko looks at him with wet eyes that shine with confusion, but she nods regardless and walks towards the box, shuffling through it. After what feels like an eternity, while Felix shakes with angst, Moriko finally finds the ring and hands it to him. His heart momentarily comes to a halt when he looks at a picture of himself placed neatly in the ring, and his whole body shakes with unshed tears as the ring trembles in his hold.

And then he remembers.

The memories of the night they spent cutting the faces out the picture, and of how long it took them to put them inside the ring and the necklace, come rushing back to him like a storm in a calm sea.

He also remembers him. He remembers Genji.

He jumps from the bed, his head spinning as his body urges him to run but without telling him where.

"I need to go," he says.

"Where, my dear?" Moriko asks, not understanding the sudden change in Felix's mood.

"The forest...," Felix says as he rubs the necklace in between his fingertips, and when her eyes land on the jewellery they grow wide with terror. "I remember the forest."

Before she can speak, Felix is already rushing out of the house with his heart leading the way.

"Thank you," Dylan murmurs as he pays for the food.

He looks down at the bag of products, and when he looks up his heart comes to a halt as he sees Mizuki gazing at him with eyes that shine with nostalgia.

"You're back," she says, awestruck as she watches him with sorrow-stricken eyes. This time, however, her eyes don't burn with vengeance but with a deep sense of longing.

Dylan's body starts to shake as he begs her wordlessly to despise him for his unforgivable sin, but the hatred never comes as she leans closer to him, trying to reach him, and something in Dylan's heart breaks, knowing that she still loves him even after what he did. And so he runs away like a coward, running away from the past once more, unable to face the woman he took everything from.

He runs towards the forest he used to call home. She shouldn't have forgiven him, he shouldn't be here when Ayumu isn't. No matter how much he has tried to hide from the past, its claws have always found their way back into his heart. He comes to a stop when he sees a stone hidden beneath the fresh grass, glistening in the moonlight.

Eguchi Ayumu
05.05.94-05.05.00
Gone but not forgotten.

He reads it and his heart shatters into a million pieces.

He shouldn't be here.

He shouldn't be alive.

He doesn't know if it's his tears dropping onto the stone or the rain that has started to fall to earth, but without a second thought, he enters the forest once more, for the final time, to bring to everything to an end in the place where it started.

Felix runs through the forest, his heart aching with each clumsy step he takes. His feet get stuck in the mud as the rain pours down onto the earth, flooding the ground that embraces him, holding him back as if in a warning.

"Felix!" He can hear Moriko call out to him, making him feel a dreadful sense of déjà vu.

"Dylan!" shouts Mizuki from afar.

Everything's the same as it was that night, he has lived his whole life in a never-ending cycle and tonight he is determined to break the curse.

The susurrations of the mighty trees fill his ears, telling him to go, to leave the forbidden forest. With each step he remembers, he remembers a hand holding his, entering the terrible woods. He remembers as the bushes cut through his skin, letting the memories flow with the blood. A bleak sense of déjà vu consumes his heart as the memories pour down in merciless waves, crashing against his mind, making his head throb. The towering trees spin as he twists around, trying to find the way, but he is surrounded by darkness, the dim moonbeams of the crescent moon unable to penetrate the thick canopy.

He groans in irritation as the path blurs into obscurity, one road leading to another, leading to nothing. His heart races, hammering in his ears as tears of annoyance gather in the corners of his eyes. And the whispering of the trees never stops, threatening to take his soul once more as it did the first time.

Shaking his head and letting the raindrops drip from his face he runs to where his heart is guiding him. Pushing the dried branches out of his way he sees Dylan standing at the edge of the familiar cliff, gazing into the void beneath. He sighs in relief and slows his pace, walking steadily toward the boy.

"Dylan!" he shouts through the rain in a muffled voice.

Dylan turns his head back to him, his eyes full of sorrowful stories that Felix is yet to hear, and Felix realizes he has been living in a bad dream, bringing nothing but despair. He hopes it's not too late to fix the chaos they've created.

"Move away from the cliff, Dylan," he yells once more, his eyes half-closed from the stream of rain falling mercilessly to the earth.

"I can't...," Dylan murmurs, turning his head towards the precipice once more. "I can't live with this pain, Felix."

"Move away, Dylan, we can fix that!" Felix says as he moves closer, his whole body shivering with both fear and the cold.

"I'm sorry...," Dylan whispers, and with his eyes closed he staggers forward, letting himself become one with the air.

"I won't let you go so easily!" Felix screams as he catches Dylan by his arm as his body dangles in the air.

"Let me go!" Dylan cries, trying to get away from Felix's grip, but Felix's fingers just dig deeper into his skin, leaving red claw marks.

"I won't let you go, not now, not ever!" he yells back as he tries to lift Dylan's heavy body in the air.

Through gritted teeth he catches Dylan's arm with both of his hands, dragging him upwards.

"Just let a lowlife die!" Dylan howls as he grabs Felix by his hands, trying to slip away from his reach, but Felix fights back, his blood pumping with adrenaline, and eventually he manages to hoist

Dylan's body up one more time, this time successfully shoving him to the side, far away from the cliff.

Felix pants as he watches Dylan drop his head low, his shoulders shaking as the tears stream down his face, mixing with the cold rain. A thunderbolt strikes through the sky, painting the sky in lavender as the ground beneath shakes.

Felix gazes at him for a moment before he screams, "You know it's dangerous! Why did you leave my side?! Do you know how scared I was?! I hate you so much!" He shrieks in Japanese through the callous night, Dylan just watches him with lost eyes.

Felix continues to scream, tearing his lungs apart. "I don't want you to get hurt and I'm sorry that I shouted at you." He pounds his fist against his chest "I promise I will never shout at you. So please let's go back, okay? I will give you all of my toys! Just please let's go, I'm very scared."

Dylan gazes at him with eyes full of wonder and confusion before realization settles in between his round eyes. "How...," he croaks. "How do you know that?"

Felix lets out a heavy breath before tearing the necklace from his skin and throwing it toward Dylan. His fingers shuffling through the mud, Dylan takes the pendant in his hands and when his eyes land on the picture of him, the picture Ayumu himself cut out, his eyes go wide in horror as he swiftly looks upon Felix.

"Where did you get it?" he asks, but he receives no answer in return as Felix collapses in his arms, wrapping his arms around him and holding onto him for dear life.

"Genji," he whispers into the cold air, and Genji's eyes look ready to pop out of their sockets. He stays frozen in place as Ayumu's body warms him up and his eyes shake with angst.

Soon tears are welling up in his eyes as the realization sinks in, and he wraps his arms around Ayumu and wails, "I'm so fucking sorry!"

He can finally open the wound and spill all the apologies he has held on to for so long.

"I'm so sorry," he cries as he tugs Ayumu closer to him, and Ayumu falls as easily into his arms as a leaf on an autumnal night.

"Stop apologizing," Ayumu murmurs as he holds Genji's face in his palms, tracing his fingers over his cheek as he wipes the tears away. "You've found me."

Genji's chin wobbles as more tears stream down from his pure eyes.

"I'm sorry it took me so long," he says, and Ayumu nods with eyes also full of tears of delight, wrapping his arms around Genji as he hugs him once more, finally feeling at home after wandering alone for so long.

Moriko and Mizuki stand there in the rain watching the two souls return to one another, interlacing the red strings once more as their two worlds collide, finally finding peace through the hell of life they lived without each other. Moriko looks at Mizuki first, letting the tears glimmer under the moonbeams, and as slowly she takes her hand in hers, Mizuki's shoulders shake, tears pouring from her eyes as she watches her son come back to life.

And as the story comes to an end, a new one begins.

"For as long as I could remember I was consumed by utter rage. My tarnished sight viewed life in black and white but there was no kindness that I could see, I was blind to the affections surrounding me.

Our dreamlike expectations of love ruin love. We search for it and search for it with no end, when all the time it's right in front of our eyes.

My wretched heart couldn't see the bright future ahead of me as it slumbered in the past, tainted in black, but it's still a color nonetheless, doesn't matter if it's a dazzling, bright one or a dull one; life is still full of colors and there is nothing bad at being colourful, mixing them up, they all tell a story, same beautiful story of your life.

The story of my life is forever tainted with blood and tears, and no matter how much I scrub it, it remains as a stain on my soul. And so, slowly but surely, I've learned to accept it and claim it as my own.

As Carl Jung once said, "No tree", it is said, "can grow to heaven unless its roots reach down to hell."

Now I stand proud, and my branches of hope, once withered and frail, stretch out towards the sunshine. I've learned that there is no past and no future, just a present moment to cherish, and this knowledge has made my heavy heart lighter as I move through life.

The bridge that connects us to the world can be broken, but it also can be repaired; nothing disappears without a trace.

Suffering changes you completely, inside and out, but it's up to you who you're going to be reborn as. It's easy to turn into a monster, but being a saint with a heavy heart, that's what a lot of people cannot do. To stay kind in the midst of despair, that's what makes life hard, but it's never too late to be reborn.

And I have finally accepted joy as my own, making it easier to go through the storms.

In the end you're the god of your life. It's up to you to rewrite the stars above, and once you hold on to this faith nothing can stop you.

I've made mistakes along the way, no one is perfect, even the saints keep unshed truths deep within their hearts. But I have also had to learn from them. I learned to accept the deepest shadows of my conscience, because even in the brightest sunshine, the shadow remains by your side. And as I claimed the darkest depths of my soul, not fearing them anymore, life got easier.

I want a quiet life – even if I know the storm is unavoidable, I still long for the rainbow afterwards, filling my soul with its many colours.

One thing I want you to remember is to never give up, not even when you're drowning, because you don't know how far the seashore remains, it could be within reach. Stay kind and warm in the coldness of the world and see the light even in the darkest hours.

A letter to myself.

May 5th, 2016

www.ingramcontent.com/pod-product-compliance
Lightning Source LLC
Chambersburg PA
CBHW070632310726
48982CB00001B/265

* 9 7 8 1 7 7 2 3 1 2 4 2 3 *